TREMORS OF THE PAST

THE OMNI TOWERS SERIES BOOK 3

JAMIE A. WATERS

Tremors of the Past © 2018 by Jamie A. Waters

Cover Art by Deranged Doctor Designs
Editor: Beyond DEF Lit

ISBN: 978-0-9996647-2-8 (Paperback Edition)
ISBN: 978-0-9996647-6-6 (eBook Edition)

Library of Congress Control Number: 2018907713
First Edition *September 2018

THE OMNI TOWERS SERIES

Tremors of the Past

CHAPTER ONE

KAYLA SHIMMIED across a beam spanning the length of the storage room ceiling, pausing about halfway to peer over the side. Three OmniLab security officers searched behind a wide assortment of crates and equipment, and she raised an eyebrow. Did they really think she was a beginner when it came to evading authority figures?

"I know you're in here," a voice called out.

Kayla narrowed her eyes as Brant Mason, the dark-haired security officer from the special sect known as the Inner Circle Shadows, scanned the room below her. He'd been hounding her ever since Alec assigned him to watch over her. He was taking these babysitting duties a little too seriously for her taste. Sure, someone might try to hurt her again, but Lars and the Coalition were on the surface and not in the towers. It was far more likely she'd accidentally cause another earthquake. As long as she didn't actively use her energy abilities, and no one pissed her off, they'd all be just fine. She hoped.

Kayla rested her head against the tie beam for a moment. Okay, so maybe it was a good idea to stick close to the man in

2 · JAMIE A. WATERS

case the ground started shaking, but she couldn't bring herself to do it. The nonstop scrutiny was grating on her nerves, and she needed a break. Every instinct screamed out for her to flee. When they'd followed her to the bathroom again just a few minutes ago, she'd thought she might lose her mind.

Hence her decision to climb into the rafters of one of OmniLab's basement storerooms to escape from security's watchful eyes. It might not have been the smartest decision, but even a short break was a welcome relief.

One of the officers muttered his frustration and made a disparaging remark about Inner Circle members, but Brant silenced him with a sharp look. "Watch your mouth. And no, I can sense her. Keep looking."

Kayla wrinkled her nose. *How does he do that?* She didn't even realize she was using her energy most of the time and tried to concentrate, clamping down on her energy usage. Brant had explained she had a tendency to leak energy when she wasn't concentrating on it. It was an exercise in constant frustration to keep it suppressed.

Brant's gaze darted around the room as though he sensed her trying to control the energy. He snapped his fingers at the guards, ordering them to look faster. Kayla draped herself over the beam to get into a more comfortable position, prepared to wait them out. The minute they moved on in their search, she'd backtrack and hide out in the Research and Development Lab, where an irate scientist had chased her out of earlier. Apparently, he didn't appreciate her taking one of their latest prototypes apart, which was a shame because she would have drastically improved his design after a few tweaks.

Her commlink vibrated in her pocket. Shifting her body enough to pull it out, she disabled video and audio. No need to advertise her whereabouts to either the caller or searchers.

A message from Carl displayed on the screen when she pressed a button.

Where are you?

She hesitated before answering. Carl would curse up a storm when he found out what she was doing. They'd only released her from the medical ward yesterday, and her injuries hadn't fully healed. Apparently, crashing a speeder, dislocating her shoulder, being shot with a stun gun and then stabbed wasn't the healthiest of lifestyle choices. Go figure. She considered her options in replying and then tapped out a brief response.

Playing hide-and-seek with Brant in the basement. I can meet you back in Seara's quarters in an hour.

When he didn't respond, Kayla slid her commlink back into her pocket. Brant and his team had finally given up on their current location and were moving toward the next room. Kayla waited, poised to make her escape once they crossed the threshold. If she hopped on the next beam, she could then slide down to reach the other side of the room. They'd never have a clue.

A tingling in the air was the first sign something wasn't right. She reached out with her energy senses, trying to decide what was different. Before she could figure it out, a sharp wind kicked up, upsetting her balance and causing her foot to slip. Her instincts took hold, and she hooked an arm over the beam to prevent falling. She gasped in pain as the sharp movement pulled at the injury in her side. She couldn't do anything except hang on.

Shouts echoed from below, followed by the pounding of approaching footsteps. There was a loud, metal clang and then more footsteps running in the opposite direction.

"Don't move!" Brant shouted below her.

Seriously, that's all the advice he has?

She blew her dark hair out of her face and tried to figure

out how to get out of this predicament. In her current position, she couldn't tell if there was a nearby ledge or crate to use as a springboard. The pain in her side was excruciating, and she was almost positive she'd torn open her injury again.

Forcing herself to focus beyond the pain, Kayla tried to maneuver one of her legs back over the side of the beam. Suddenly, a powerful wind gave her a small boost and lifted her enough to secure herself. The warm embrace of Alec's energy surrounded her, and she glanced down to find Alec and Carl standing below.

Kayla grimaced, squeezed her eyes shut, and thumped her head against the beam. Great. She was in for it now. She opened her eyes again to take another peek, hoping she'd been wrong, but no such luck. They were still there, and neither one looked happy. Both men were standing side by side with mirrored expressions of disapproval on their faces, but that's where the similarities ended. Carl and Alec were as different as night and day.

Carl's dark hair was tied at the nape of his neck, exposing his powerful jawline. He had a more athletic build, with broader shoulders and a chiseled physique. The man's body was mouth-watering, and she still got butterflies in her stomach whenever she looked at him. He was devious, resourceful, and more than a little cocky and self-assured—all traits she deeply admired. It was his understanding and compassionate nature, though, that had overcome all her resistances and made her fall in love with him. Although, right now, it was clear his thoughts weren't warm and fuzzy. He crossed his arms over his chest as he gazed up at her with his penetrating brown eyes. Yep. She was definitely screwed.

Kayla glanced over at Alec and blew out a breath when she realized he was equally perturbed. Where Carl was more rugged and could pass for a ruin rat, there was no mistaking Alec's position within the towers. There was something almost regal in his bearing. He wore the mantle of High Council leader as though born to it, which wasn't far from the truth. From the elaborate clothing to the expensive jewelry he wore, Alec carried an air of unmistakable privilege. With his piercing blue eyes and blond hair falling neatly to his shoulders, he was every bit the golden boy of the towers. Kayla couldn't deny he was attractive, but there was more to it. He was unlike anyone she'd ever known, and it was those differences that made him intriguing. Like a moth to a flame, he captivated her. And like the proverbial moth, Kayla suspected she was about to find herself in a very uncomfortable situation.

At her scrutiny, Alec arched one of his eyebrows, and she blew out a breath. Oh well. She'd had a good run. Time to face the music.

"Brant tattled on me, didn't he?" she accused from her perch.

Alec clasped his hands behind his back. He didn't answer her. Instead, he turned to Carl. "I don't know how you managed to catch her on the surface. She's been out of the medical ward for less than a day and my security team has already lost her twice."

Kayla lifted her shoulder in a half-shrug and then shimmied back across the beam. Carl was pretty good at staying one step ahead of her. Apparently, Alec was taking notes. That didn't bode well for her.

As she reached the end of the beam, she hooked her abdomen over the bar and swung her lower body upward to dismount in an underswing that would make any gymnast proud. The landing jarred her, and she winced as the movement pulled at the injury even more.

Cursing under her breath, she gingerly touched her side. When she removed her hand, it came away wet with blood. *Crap.* She glanced up to see if they'd noticed.

They had. She groaned as Carl crossed the room in a handful of steps.

"Dammit, Kayla. You just got released from medical." He yanked up the bottom of her shirt to inspect the injury and let out a low hiss at the sight. "Shit. You pulled it open again."

"Hey!" she protested at his abrupt handling but glanced down to see the damage. *Ouch.* He was right. Her careless acrobatics had reopened the wound. She wrinkled her nose as she examined her side. It wasn't any prettier the second time around either.

Carl lifted his head, and his worried gaze met hers. The depth of love, concern, and raw emotion in his eyes was staggering, and her objections melted away. With a sigh, he trailed his fingers across her cheek and then tucked a loose tendril of hair behind her ear.

"You've got to be more careful, sweetheart. If you had received an injury like that when you were on the surface, it would have laid you up for weeks. You're lucky to be out of medical so soon. The doctors can only speed up your healing so much. You still need to give your body time to recuperate the rest of the way. I don't want to lose you," he said in a low voice.

Carl cupped her cheek in his hand, and she leaned into him, relishing the contact. It was hard to argue with him when he was right, especially considering she'd almost lost him a short time ago. The thought of losing the man she loved had been more than she'd been able to handle. In her grief, she'd nearly pulled a building down on top of them.

Fortunately, Carl had only been stunned. The experience, however, had only reinforced what she knew from the past. Each moment they had together needed to be treasured because there was no way to know how long it would last. She'd been in the medical wing for nearly a week recovering from her injuries. The medics had made it clear she might not have survived if Alec hadn't gotten her back to OmniLab so quickly for treatment. For that, she'd always be grateful to the High Council leader.

She glanced up at Alec to find several emotions tracing over his features. He'd been keeping a tighter clamp on their energy bond ever since she'd admitted how she felt about him, and it made it more difficult to read his feelings. It was a little easier to relax around Alec without the fear of being inundated with the allure of his energy, but she'd be lying if she said she didn't miss the closeness of their shared connection.

Alec took a deep breath and called to Brant over his shoulder. The security officer jogged over, bent down, and assessed Kayla's injury with a critical eye. He spoke into his wrist unit, ordering a medic to their location.

Kayla wrinkled her nose at their overprotective hovering. "Come on, guys. It's not that bad. If we slap a bandage on it, it'll be fine."

Carl frowned and lowered her shirt. His fingers brushed against her skin and, despite her injury, she shivered. She turned into putty every time the man put his hands on her. He pressed a kiss against her forehead and shook his head in exasperation.

"Do you want to explain why you were hanging from the ceiling?"

Not really. She shifted her weight and tried to decide on a plausible explanation. Since she still planned to escape the guards at the earliest opportunity, she didn't want to volunteer her future plans. Luckily, she didn't have to get inventive because one of the security officers came rushing over. After expressing an out-of-breath apology, the officer announced, "I couldn't catch them. They had too much of a head start. I think they slipped down one of the side halls."

Alec's eyes narrowed on Brant. "What happened?"

"We were attempting to locate Kayla when I sensed someone channeling energy. Next thing I knew, she was about to fall. One of my men attempted to track down the suspect when they fled. We've sealed the floor and are bringing in another team to search. If they backtracked to the service side of the floor, they may have already escaped. This area isn't secure."

Kayla bunched up her shirt, pushing it against the wound to wipe up the blood. Damn. Maybe she did need more than just a bandage. Her side was throbbing.

"I didn't fall. I felt a tingle and then a gust of wind tried to knock me off the beam."

Carl and Alec exchanged a look but didn't reply. They'd been doing that a lot over the past two days, and it was getting annoying.

Brant frowned. "I'll have someone review the surveillance system footage right away."

Kayla shifted from foot to foot and bit her lip. "Um, about that..."

Carl groaned. "Please tell me you didn't disable the surveillance."

She released her shirt and threw up her hands. "I didn't know someone planned to tornado me off the ceiling. You guys have people watching me every second. Between Brant and his band of merry men following me and the cameras tracking my every move, I don't get a break." She slapped her hands on Carl's chest, grabbed his shirt, and stared him down. "It's making me crazy. I can't handle it."

Carl's mouth twitched. He lifted his hands, wrapping them around her wrists, and kissed the tip of her nose. "We'll figure something out."

Kayla let out a breath and relaxed against him. He draped an arm around her shoulders, tucking her into his side.

Alec turned to Brant. "Check the outlying cameras and

see who was in the general vicinity when the incident occurred. Were you able to pick up a signature from the energy channeling?"

Brant shook his head. "They were too far away. As soon as I approached, they stopped and ran. The only thing we have to go on is their ability to channel air energy."

Footsteps interrupted the conversation. Carl's arm fell away, and Kayla looked up, her shoulders stiffening at the sight of the approaching medic. She glanced toward the exit, calculating her chances of successfully escaping before they started poking at her.

As though sensing her intention, Carl moved to block her exit. She scowled at him, but he merely shook his head. In a low voice, he whispered, "Behave."

The medic, accustomed to dealing with difficult patients, appeared unfazed by her reluctance. He pulled an imaging wand out of his bag, ran it over her abdomen, and studied the display.

"The surface mending is torn. The deeper reconstruction still appears to be intact though." He glanced up at her, disapproval etched in the lines of his stern expression. "You're fortunate this wasn't more serious. The original wound was deep, and even though it's patched on the surface, it needs more time to heal internally. We should admit you to the medical ward for observation."

Kayla's eyes widened as she took a step backward. *No way. Not going to happen.*

Alec put his hand behind her back, halting her retreat. "That's not feasible. What are the other alternatives?"

The medic pursed his lips but didn't argue. He studied her side again, prodding the injury. "I suppose we can reseal the wound and give her another metabolic booster to speed up the healing. It's sooner than I'd recommend, so there may be a few side effects."

"Sure. Sounds great. Let's go with that option," she readily agreed, eager to get this done. After spending days being poked and prodded by the doctors in the medical ward, she'd had enough of Omni medicine to last a lifetime.

Carl frowned in concern and took a step closer. "Wait. What side effects?"

"A racing heartbeat and insomnia are most common. Nothing too serious, but the side effects may last a few days. I'll give her a lower dosage, but if the side effects are trouble-some, we can give her something to help her sleep."

At Alec's nod, the medic cleaned the wound. When he brought out a compact device and pressed it against her side, Kayla flinched at the sensation of her skin being pulled together. It didn't hurt, but it was far from pleasant. The smell was worse. Her stomach lurched at the acrid odor of the resealing device fusing her skin back together. When he finished, he gave her the injection and dropped his tools back into the kit.

She touched her fingers against the barely noticeable line marking her injury. It would fade within weeks, leaving no trace at all. OmniLab had some amazing tech. She wondered if she could get a couple devices shipped to her former ruin rat camp. It might come in handy next time someone got hurt.

Before she could inquire about the possibility, the medic asked, "Do you need anything for the pain?"

Kayla grimaced and shook her head. If both Carl and Alec were giving her the stink-eye, she needed to keep her wits about her.

"All right. Try to avoid doing anything that will further aggravate the injury. If it gets any worse or you open it again, we won't have a choice about admitting you to the medical ward."

Carl gave her a pointed look. "She'll be careful."

Kayla grumbled under her breath but nodded. The medic didn't hide his skepticism, but he remained silent. Instead, with a brief bow to her and Alec, he picked up his bag and left the room. Once he left, Carl took her hand and interlaced his fingers with hers, pressing a kiss against the back of her palm. Touched by the intimate gesture, she gave him a small smile. Carl was still being cautious about displays of affection when anyone else was around. Except for a select few, most of the tower occupants still believed she was engaged to marry Alec. Until the political situation in the towers stabilized, Kayla had agreed to continue with the ruse.

Brant cleared his throat. "If Kayla would like to return to her family's quarters to rest, I'll have the rest of my men finish canvassing the area."

Kayla turned to the security officer with a frown. She wasn't a fragile artifact that needed to be coddled.

As though sensing her impending objections, Alec interrupted. "Actually, I was planning on having two of our designers meet with you to discuss your idea about building a home for the surface dwellers. If you'd like to return with me to my office, I can ask them to meet us there. We'll have someone run over to your quarters to pick up a change of clothes."

Kayla glanced down at her bloodstained shirt. She'd probably throw some delicate Omni sensibilities into a tailspin if she walked around like this. Besides, Alec's suggestion had merit. Ever since her mother had planted the idea about building another tower for the ruin rats, Kayla had been considering the possibilities.

Life on the surface was harsh and a sharp contrast to the posh lifestyle in the towers. Some of her former ruin rat campmates would reject OmniLab's offer of a permanent residence simply upon principle. There wasn't much she could do about their preconceived prejudices, but there were others who would jump at the opportunity for safety and security. Leo and his camp had not only saved her life as a child and given her a home, but they'd given her the tools she needed to survive. It was now her turn to repay the debt and offer them the same. Whether they accepted it was up to them.

"Okay. I'll go with you, but I want to look at the outlying video footage first. I want to find the asshole who tried to knock me off the beam."

Alec hesitated and then glanced up at the beam. He was either trying to figure out how she got up there, or how to prevent it from happening again. "That might be wise. You may have witnessed something from your unique perspective. Maybe you'll recognize someone from the feeds."

Kayla thought back to the tingle she'd felt. She might have glimpsed someone in her peripheral vision, but she couldn't be sure. Everything happened too fast. Her only focus was on not becoming an ugly smear on the ground.

Brant pulled off his jacket and handed it to her, nodding toward her injured side. She looked up at him, surprised by the gesture. The security officer was standoffish, but he'd warmed up slightly ever since Lars and the Coalition had abducted her. Kayla suspected he didn't care much for Inner Circle members, but she didn't know the reasons.

"You're not still pissed off that I dodged your minions?"

Brant shook his head and curved his lips in the slightest hint of a smile. "No. If anything, they'll learn to be more cognizant of their assignment." His expression became more serious as he added, "I understand not wanting to have someone watch your every move. But Kayla, please remember I'm only here for your safety. As evidenced by what happened a few minutes ago, there may be people within the towers who wish you harm. I hope you'll give me the opportunity to prevent that from happening."

She hesitated and then pulled on the jacket, accepting the

peace offering. It was still warm and smelled nice. *Huh*. She brushed her nose against the collar, trying to figure out the scent. It reminded her a little of Alec but with more earthy undertones. It was probably an Omni thing.

"I'm not sure that's necessary. Now that I'm out of medical, we need to get started on mapping the underground river. We can be back on the surface by tomorrow," she replied.

Carl and Alec exchanged another look. Kayla narrowed her eyes and tried to put her hands on her hips. The sleeves of the jacket were too big and got in the way. She huffed and then wiggled her hands in the air to push up the sleeves. So much for her badass image. She felt like an overdressed doll.

"Okay. What's up with that? Why do you keep looking at each other like there's some big secret?"

Carl's lips twitched in a smile at her antics. He took her hand and folded up the sleeve of the jacket. "I know you're eager to start on the river analysis, but it's not safe for you to return to the surface right now. We don't know what Lars and the Coalition are planning, but we're trying not to take any chances with your safety." He frowned at Alec before focusing again on her. "Although, I'm not sure how safe you are in the towers after what just happened. I know you don't like the security detail, but we're hoping you'll at least try it until things settle down. If you can tolerate it a bit longer, we should have a better handle on things soon. It'll also give you a chance to finish healing."

"Lars wasn't trying to kill me," she pointed out, watching as Carl switched to the other sleeve. "He was just trying to escape. I mean, he apologized before stabbing me. Sure, it hurt like a bitch and I owe him some serious payback, but he made sure not to hit anything too vital. It affected me worse because I'd already been knocked around so much. Besides, if Lars or Sergei contacts me again, I can try to talk to them. I think they'll listen. Although, Lars is due for a swift kick in the balls first."

Carl dropped her sleeve, grabbed her shoulders, and shook his head. "No, Kayla, you need to stay away from them and not get involved. Let Alec handle it." She opened her mouth to object, but he pressed a finger against her lips. "How would you feel if someone meddled in your personal business?"

Kayla's mouth clamped shut and her eyes narrowed. Her gaze darted to Alec, who was watching them with a puzzled expression.

As much as she might want to shove Lars's stunner up his ass and pull the trigger, Alec should have the first shot. Lars was Alec's cousin, and she had no business interfering in his family business. Besides, their conflict predated to her even finding out about her family origins. It had only been a month since she'd learned she was born in the towers. She hung her head and nodded. "Dammit, you're right. Okay. I'll stay out of it for now."

Carl's shoulders relaxed, and he pulled her back into his embrace. "Do you want to meet with the designers now? I have a meeting with Director Borshin, but I can meet you there when I'm finished."

Kayla glanced at Alec and then up at Carl. It looked like they were going to insist on babysitting her a while longer. She sighed but nodded in agreement. If they wanted to keep her out of the situation with Lars, fine. But someone here in the towers was targeting her. That made it her business, and neither one of them could stop her from finding the person responsible.

CHAPTER TWO

ALEC SHOOK his head in bewilderment. Watching Carl and Kayla interact in the storage area fascinated and baffled him at the same time. He'd wanted to curse the surrounding ineptitude when he'd received the message that Kayla had disappeared from her security detail again. How could three trained guards manage to lose a slip of a girl in an enclosed building? There were only so many places she could have gone.

Carl had jumped in and handled her with a deft hand, even going so far as to get her to agree to backing off the situation with Lars. Alec still didn't fully understand how the trader had managed to convince her. Kayla's emotions had been riled up and she'd been ready to argue, but Carl's words caused her to immediately backpedal. She almost seemed contrite.

When Alec had felt her reach out for him along their bond, it had taken an immeasurable amount of self-control not to give in to her. She was reaching for him more and more, trying to gauge his thoughts and feelings. He wasn't sure if it was conscious or not, but he couldn't afford to take any chances. Not now. Not when she'd finally given him hope by acknowledging her feelings for him.

In so many ways, Kayla was naïve to the mechanics of their world. Alec had already made too many mistakes with her by moving too quickly from an energy standpoint. The consequences of scaring her off had become dire. It went against all his instincts, but he needed to suppress their shared energy bond and allow her to get to know him on a level she felt comfortable exploring.

It wasn't just the energy, either, although that was part of his attraction to her. When Leah, Carl's reporter friend, had questioned him about his feelings, he hadn't lied. Those green eyes of hers had captivated him since the first moment he'd seen her in Carl's camp. Then, once he had a chance to get to know her... he was lost. He'd never met anyone so wonderfully complex and unpredictable. She was a fascinating combination of contradictions. Alec couldn't help but admire the way she continuously met every obstacle head-on with fierce determination and perseverance.

The Inner Circle had become complacent over the years, including himself. He wasn't sure if any of them would have been able to thrive on the surface the same way Kayla had. It was a testament to her strength of character, and he admired her all the more for it. Each day he spent with her forced him to see the world in a new light, and he fell a little more in love with the woman who continued to challenge his perspectives.

Alec recalled his promise to Carl about not interfering in their relationship and sighed. It might pain him to do it, but he'd stand by his word. Kayla's ability to channel energy with such natural grace and talent might take his breath away, but he'd keep his distance. For now. Kayla had no idea of the draw she had to their kind. She was like a drug he couldn't seem to get enough of. Even Lars had been taken in by her. Alec clenched his fists, remembering the covetous look he'd seen in his cousin's eyes and the way he'd touched her.

To make matters worse, no one had heard anything from Lars or the Coalition since OmniLab raided their camp to rescue Kayla and Carl. The silence concerned him almost as much as the growing tensions within the towers.

He glanced at the screen in front of him and skimmed over the latest security report. As he suspected, there was nothing new about the Coalition. However, they'd picked up more chatter from members of the Inner Circle who were growing increasingly disgruntled. The combination of the recent regime change and the threat of the Coalition hovered like a guillotine about to drop. The latest attack on Kayla in the basement was just one more indicator that things were escalating.

Alec drummed his fingers on his armrest, trying to figure out a motive as to why someone within the towers would target Kayla. He could understand why someone would attempt to use her against him, but harming her didn't make sense. Kayla had nothing to do with council politics.

If this were some sort of political power play, it would make much more sense to target him or Kayla's mother, Seara. They were both co-leaders of the High Council. However, even if both he and Seara were removed from power, the High Council would remain in control of the governance of the towers.

Frustrated, he pushed away from the desk and began to pace the length of his office. From all reports, most of the population within the towers was thrilled to have Kayla back. Her father, the former High Council leader, had been beloved by the masses, and their adoration had passed along to his daughter. To them, she represented hope and a return to the old ways before Alec's father had taken over.

He rubbed the back of his neck and frowned. Regardless

of how he looked at it, an attack against her just didn't make sense.

Unfortunately, Brant and his security team hadn't been able to discover anything from the surrounding video footage. The only thing they knew for sure was that whoever was responsible for Kayla's near fall was an air channeler and had access to the service area in the basement. That didn't mean much since members of the Inner Circle typically didn't advertise their elemental alignment. Unlike other civilians, Inner Circle members also had access to the majority of the towers. There were plenty of clues but no solid leads.

Alec paused at the one-way conference room window where Kayla was working with the building designers. He absently brushed his hand against the glass, outlining her image. His desire to protect and be close to her was becoming a near obsession. When he'd agreed to wear the mantle of co-leader after his father's death, he believed it was in the best interest of the towers. Now, he was no longer sure. Although Seara continued to claim it was the right move, Alec couldn't help his doubts. Ever since the showdown with Lars, he'd begun to question his loyalty to the towers. He would have given anything in that moment to keep Kayla from harm, and his failure in protecting her still weighed heavily upon him.

At a time when OmniLab could least afford any liabilities, his feelings for Kayla had become his greatest weakness. Alec pinched the bridge of his nose, squeezing his eyes shut. There was nothing to be done about it until Kayla was ready to embrace her heritage. Unfortunately, even if she were willing, that time wasn't now. He couldn't afford to create a rift between her and Carl. Until the threats against OmniLab and Kayla were resolved, Alec needed the trader's help. Once again, this morning's attack proved that decision to be the correct one.

Alec sighed and lifted his head. He studied Kayla through the one-way mirror and the corners of his lips curved upward. Now that he'd found her, it was impossible to imagine a life without her in it. She was exquisite and unlike any other Inner Circle member he'd ever met.

Unmindful of the dress she now wore, Kayla was sprawled out on the floor with the female designer. Her shoes had disappeared again to whereabouts unknown, and she'd apparently convinced the normally straight-laced designer to remove hers too.

Notes and designs were scattered around, and even though they'd just met, the scene had the appearance of a meeting with an old friend. Kayla suddenly threw her head back and laughed at something the other woman said. The life and sensuality in that small movement captivated him.

Apparently, he wasn't alone. The other designer was sitting in a chair at the conference table and eyeing Kayla's legs with far more interest than he should. Brant stood against the wall in the room and glared at the oblivious man. When Kayla shifted, causing her dress to slip even further up her thigh, the male designer leaned forward expectantly. Alec could almost see him drooling.

Without pausing to consider his actions, Alec crossed the room and flung open the door. The conversation in the room halted. Kayla glanced up and gave him a brilliant smile while the other woman scrambled to a standing position. The female designer quickly smoothed down her chestnut hair and tried to make herself presentable. The male designer also hastily stood.

"Alec!" Kayla rose to her feet. Her obvious pleasure at seeing him flowed through their bond and staggered him. How did this woman get him so twisted up? She grabbed his hands and pulled him over to where she'd been sitting. Her touch was like a soothing balm on his soul.

She leaned against him, pressing her hand against his chest. He looked down into her guileless green eyes and wondered if she even realized she'd been seeking his touch more often.

"Wait until you see the ideas Marline has come up with. She's fantastic," she said.

A flustered Marline seemed to collect herself enough to pick up one of the tablets off the floor. She offered Alec a nervous smile as she handed it to him.

He glanced down at the design, immediately impressed at the extensive workup. "It looks like you've made quite a bit of progress."

Kayla beamed up at him. He faltered for a moment. If he could keep this look in her eyes all the time, he'd consider threatening or cajoling every single council member into agreeing to this ruin rat tower idea. Unable to resist, he raised his hand and brushed his thumb across her cheek. Her eyes widened, and her lips parted slightly. His gaze lowered to her mouth, and he swallowed. He was never going to survive this. She was an impossible temptation.

Alec took a deep breath and forced himself to turn back to the efficient Marline. "Have you been able to determine what building materials you'll need?"

Marline pressed a button on the tablet and a list populated the screen. "We're still working out the details. Kay— Er, Mistress Rath'Varein has some interesting ideas about features that would cater specifically to the needs of the new tenants. We'll need to do some additional research since we currently don't have anything like that here. I think we can get the information from our pre-war archives."

Alec arched an eyebrow. "Oh?"

Kayla didn't answer right away. He looked down to find her still looking up at him with a pensive expression. He could sense her trying to explore their bond, but her thoughts were a confusing jumble of conflicted emotions. Without opening their bond more, Alec wasn't able to get a clear view, and he wasn't willing to risk it. After a moment, she averted her gaze and offered a small shrug.

"Um, yeah. It's great as a base of operations, but the ruin rats aren't going to want to give up their lifestyle. It'll need to be easy for them to come and go, and they'll need a place to store their speeders. The goal of this building shouldn't be to keep the occupants inside, but instead offer a haven from the outside world. Besides, you're going to need people to work the surface and hunt for resources. Why can't the ruin rats do that and earn their keep?"

Alec paused. He hadn't considered using them in that capacity in exchange for housing. It was similar to what they were doing now with trading for supplies, except on a larger scale. Her idea had merit.

"You're right." He turned to the male designer who'd remained silent through the conversation. Alec narrowed his eyes at the man whose gaze now seemed glued to Kayla's chest. Alec barely resisted the urge to pummel him. "What are your thoughts, John?"

The man's eyes flew up to meet his, suddenly aware he'd been caught ogling the High Council leader's fiancée. It didn't take a telepathic connection to know exactly what the man's thoughts were. The designer cleared his throat and stammered, "I-I'm sure it's an excellent idea. We should investigate it."

"Why don't you do that back in your office?" Alec bit out.

The man paled and quickly gathered up his belongings. Marline frowned, darting her gaze between the other designer and Alec. She was clearly worried her partner had jeopardized working on such an illustrious project.

Alec turned back to Marline and gestured to the designs scattered on the floor. He had to remind himself it wasn't necessarily her fault if her partner was an idiot. Besides, Kayla had obviously taken a liking to the woman.

"You've done excellent work so far, Marline. Perhaps you and Mistress Rath'Varein can resume your discussions and plans tomorrow. Around this same time?"

Marline's eyes widened, and she nodded. "Of course. It'll be my pleasure." She gave Kayla a warm smile and began collecting her things.

Alec caught Brant's attention and gestured toward the other designer. In a low voice, he said, "I want him banned from this tower. Marline may return, but John's services are no longer needed."

Brant nodded and immediately followed the designer out of the room. Alec had no doubt his instructions would be carried out, and the man wouldn't be permitted near Kayla in the future. He glanced down to find Kayla's arms folded across her chest and her green eyes lit up with humor. She'd obviously overheard him.

"Do you disagree with my decision?" he asked her telepathically.

She cocked her head to study him. *"Nope. Although I'm surprised Marline hasn't ditched him before now. The guy's an idiot."*

He didn't answer right away and instead waited until Marline left the room. In truth, he needed some time to decide how to respond. Alec wasn't sure Kayla would take too kindly to his initial reaction of wanting to tear the man apart for daring to look at the woman who belonged to him. Kayla hadn't yet realized most of their kind were fiercely possessive. He'd noticed her instincts kick in several times, but she had the remarkable and infuriating ability to suppress and even reject them.

"I didn't care for the way that insufferable man was watching you."

Kayla blinked. "I thought you were annoyed with him

because he wasn't contributing. He just sat there and let Marline do all the work."

Alec paused. Was she truly unaware of her allure? He opened their bond slightly and was taken aback by her genuine surprise. He chuckled and shook his head. This woman was going to drive him insane.

"He wasn't working because he was too busy undressing you with his eyes."

She frowned and shrugged. "Well, either way, he's a dumb-ass. I think he's been taking advantage of Marline for a while now. She didn't say anything, but I got the impression he's been using some of her ideas and passing them off as his own."

Alec watched as she turned away and bent down under the table to locate her shoes. The hem of her dress slid upward as she stretched, revealing a creamy expanse of her thighs. He swallowed. No wonder the designer was practically drooling while she crawled around on the floor. Any warm-blooded male would do the same.

Kayla turned halfway and held up her shoes in victory. As she slipped them back on her feet, her dress hiked up even further to reveal a hint of black lace covering her most inti-mate parts.

"I like her though. She's smart and knows how to cut through the bullshit. I had more fun today than I thought I would."

"Kayla," he croaked, "please. Stand up."

She paused and leaned forward to look up at him, a ques-tion in her eyes. He made the mistake of glancing down again and the soft curves of her cleavage beckoned him. More black lace. What the hell had Seara been thinking to buy her this dress? He couldn't take it anymore. Alec reached down and pulled her to her feet. Without saying another word, he drew her into his arms and held her tightly. He knew he shouldn't, but he just needed to hold her for a moment until he managed to get himself under control.

Kayla stiffened against him and reached out across their bond. Some of his emotions filtered through, and whatever she sensed caused her to relax in his arms. Inch by inch, her body began to mold against his. Sliding his hand around to rest against the small of her back, he pressed his face against her hair. He'd needed to touch her like this for days, ever since Lars had hurt her and she'd collapsed in his arms. His fingers tightened reflexively, remembering the fear of almost losing her.

"Just one more minute," he whispered and inhaled deeply, wanting to breathe her in forever. She smelled like wild abandon and every promise he'd ever beheld. Alec closed his eyes and wished he could stay in this moment forever. Even without the energy, this woman captivated him completely.

He forced himself to pull back and clamp down on their bond. Keeping it open and letting her invade all his senses was too dangerous. His self-control around her was tenuous at best. The confused expression in her eyes wounded him, but the alternative would be far worse. Alec couldn't risk alienating the trader. Not now. "I shouldn't have done that. I... I need to get you back to Carl."

"That's not necessary. I'm here."

CHAPTER THREE

KAYLA PULLED AWAY to see Carl standing in the doorway with his jaw clenched and his fingers curled tightly into fists.

Crap. He does not look happy.

Both men stared at each other for a handful of heartbeats. Kayla's body tensed, as they seemed to engage in a primitive and wordless communication. A moment later, Alec gave Carl a curt nod and took a step away from her.

Without taking his eyes off Alec, Carl moved to stand beside her and slipped his arm around her waist. Kayla raised an eyebrow, wondering if they were going to start beating on their chests next, or if she was going to need to air out the room from the testosterone overload. Before she could comment, she noticed the three other men who had accompanied Carl into the room wearing similar grim expressions.

Brant was back, along with Commander Thomas, the head of OmniLab security, and Director Borshin, who oversaw the traders and their sectors on the surface. Something was definitely going on for them all to be on edge.

She glanced up at Alec who had noticed the newcomers as well, but his face was carefully blank. He'd shifted into High

Council mode. Whatever thoughts had been plaguing him a few moments ago were now buried too deeply for her to reach through their bond.

"I apologize for the interruption," Thomas addressed Alec. "We need to speak with you about some new developments. Perhaps in your office?"

Alec inclined his head and led them out of the conference room. As they headed into the office, Kayla leaned into Carl and whispered, "What's going on?"

Carl shook his head and murmured, "Trouble."

At her frown, he bent down and brushed a kiss against her temple. If the gesture was meant to reassure her, it didn't work. The tension in the men's body language was screaming that disaster was imminent.

Alec walked over to stand beside his desk and turned around to assess the group in front of him. "What's happened?"

Commander Thomas, a short, stocky man with sharp eyes and a commanding presence, clasped his hands behind his back and began to report. "We've intercepted communications that were meant for some of the High Council. The contents of the transmissions may have been a warning of some sort or possibly a test to see if the councilors' interests aligned with their own. The transmissions suggested a regime change within the towers might be imminent. To what end, we aren't sure. We're in the process of attempting to trace these messages back to the source but have not yet had any luck."

Alec's eyes narrowed. "I want to see copies of these messages. Which councilors are being targeted?"

"The two we've been able to confirm are Lenora Ballentor and William Gavron, but there may be others," Commander Thomas informed him. "We've wired both their quarters and have surveillance teams tracking them. It's too soon to determine whether they are targets or possible conspirators. With your permission, we can arrange to allow these transmissions to be delivered and then monitor their reactions. They may lead us back to the targets or, at the very least, let us know where their allegiance lies. As a precautionary measure, and since no specifics were mentioned in the transmissions, we'd also like to increase security for Mistress Seara Rath'Varein."

Kayla frowned, worried that her mother might be at risk. They'd only recently begun getting to know each other after spending the past sixteen years thinking the other had perished, but Kayla was already extremely fond of her. The only thing that eased her mind was knowing Alec would make every effort to keep Seara safe. They'd developed a close relationship over the years, and her mother had admitted that she considered Alec like a son.

Alec crossed his arms and nodded. "Make sure it's done immediately. What else?"

Commander Thomas gestured for Director Borshin to speak. The director stepped forward. "We've verified which records the Coalition extracted from Trader Carl's camp during the attack. Their primary interest, as you suspected, was Mistress Kayla Rath'Varein. However, they also accessed the personnel files on all individuals working within the trader camps. It appears they were also able to extract some information on the newly discovered underground river. Although Mistress Kayla Rath'Varein attempted to destroy this information, we believe they may have been able to salvage some river data before they abandoned the location we raided."

Kayla straightened at the mention of the water source she'd found. That was *her* river. If the Coalition knew they'd found a viable water source, they'd be all over it. There was no way she was going to let the Coalition have a chance to get to it before she did. Inwardly, she cursed at all the time she'd wasted in medical. That was time that should have been spent working on the excavations. She needed to get back to the surface immediately.

As though sensing the direction of her thoughts, Carl squeezed her hand before addressing Alec. "I've contacted my camp and left Cruncher temporarily in charge until I return to the surface. The stability scans of the ruins are complete, and they're finalizing the cavern imaging from the data Kayla collected. There have been a few delays due to the attack, but they should have it completed within the next seventy-two hours. Once it's finished, they'll be ready to begin the exploration. If the cavern is a potential target for the Coalition, we may need an additional team or two to help secure the location."

Kayla pulled away from Carl and scowled. "Seriously? You didn't think to share this with me? I should have been involved in this process."

Carl stiffened slightly and frowned. He glanced at Alec before focusing again on her. "I agree, but that wasn't an option at the time. We couldn't wait. Most of the prep work was done while you were still unconscious. Right now, we're just trying to stay ahead of the Coalition as much as possible by working with the information we have. We don't know what they're planning or even how much they know, but we want to be prepared in case the river becomes a target. Rand sent over a new tech and scavenger to help expedite the process. Now that you're feeling better, I told Cruncher to send over the mockups of the cavern imaging to you. As soon as that's finalized and we get the go ahead, we can launch a full-scale excavation."

Alec shook his head. "No. I understand our water consumption is reaching critical levels and this is a priority, but I won't be clearing any exploration until we get more information about the Coalition. I have no intention of sending dozens of people underground and putting them in unnecessary danger."

Kayla opened her mouth to argue but fell silent as a sharp pang of regret and sadness echoed along their shared bond. Although Alec was keeping a tighter clamp on their connection, a few thoughts and emotions filtered through. He was recalling what happened the last time there was political turmoil in the towers and they sent a team down into the ruins. The entire group, including Alec's mother and her father, had been killed. She'd been the only survivor.

Dammit.

Her shoulders slumped in resignation and she lowered her head, barely resisting the urge to kick his desk. Alec might have a point, but she didn't like it. She took a steadying breath and lifted her head, determined to stay involved. The minute they were ready to start exploring, she was going to be down there. In the meantime, her focus turned to the two unknowns working on her project.

"Fine. I'll get started on the mockups and manually fill in any gaps between the images. Who did Rand send over to work on my maps? So help me... if he sent over some half-brained morons who screwed up my images, I'm going to dropkick him and dance on his innards."

Carl chuckled. "I wouldn't worry. Rand had a feeling you'd be furious if he sent over anyone but the best. I believe their names are Minko and Felix. Minko's a longtime tech, and Felix is one of his newer scavengers, but I've been assured he's also an extremely skilled tech."

Kayla jerked back as though struck. She'd heard of Minko, but it was the other name that caught her attention. She squeezed her eyes shut as painful memories washed over her. Carl rubbed her shoulder, and she opened her eyes to find his filled with concern.

"What's wrong? Do you know them?"

"I didn't know Felix was working in Rand's camp. He's a good guy. I just haven't seen him since..." Kayla rubbed her arms to ward off the sudden chill. Between Alec alluding to the cave-in that had nearly killed her as a child, and now Felix's name coming up in conversation, the room was becoming thick with ghosts from the past. "Felix is Pretz's brother. I haven't seen him since Pretz was killed."

Carl frowned and searched her expression. "I didn't realize they were related. Are you going to be okay with him working on this project? We can request a replacement."

"No," she said in a rush, pushing her emotions aside. "It's fine. He's good. Very good. I've worked with him before. It's... just been a while. I didn't expect to hear his name."

Carl exchanged a concerned look with the High Council leader. Alec shook his head and turned back to Thomas. "Is there anything else?"

"Nothing solid at this point, just supposition. Call it an old man's hunch, but I suspect much of our internal unrest may be tied to Lars Cerulis and the Coalition. Until we find out differently, I agree with your decision to hold off on the exploration of the ruins. If you begin launching an undertaking of that magnitude, there will be numerous people and departments involved. We won't be able to keep the information contained. If I'm correct, and some of our residents *are* working with the Coalition, our people on the surface could be vulnerable."

Kayla bit her lip. She didn't know much about politics, but she was beginning to believe there were no such things as coincidences. "I think you're right about a link between them. The first time I saw Lars, he recognized me. He knew exactly who I was but pretended like he didn't."

Alec raised an eyebrow. "You're not easy to forget, my dear. Lars hasn't seen you since we were children, but it's possible he remembered you. Not only that, but the Coalition worked with Ramiro. He could have easily shown them your image or described you."

She shook her head and frowned. It was more than that. "No. I thought I'd seen him too, but I wasn't able to place him. At first, I wrote it off because he reminded me of you."

Kayla rubbed the back of her neck and began to pace, trying to replay her first impressions of Lars. It was his eyes that had first reminded her of Alec. They were almost the exact striking shade of blue, except Lars's eyes had been colder. She'd never seen eyes like that until she'd come to the towers.

The memory suddenly hit her, and she whirled around. "The shopping area. On my second trip to OmniLab." At Alec's questioning look, she explained, "When we went to that restaurant with the fish tanks, I saw him when I was sitting outside with Seara. It was the eyes. I remember because the color was so distinctive."

Ignoring the stunned faces surrounding her, she continued with her train of thought. "It makes sense. I mean, the Coalition was working with Ramiro for a while. The asshole probably gave Lars the inside scoop on how to access the towers. Getting him into OmniLab was probably as simple as smuggling him in on one of the trading camp caravans. From there, it probably wouldn't be too hard to either ride back out with the next shipment or bribe someone to look the other way."

Everyone in the room froze at her words as the implication set in.

Carl broke the silence with a loud curse. Alec, however, was more cautious. He turned to the head of security. "Is this a possibility, Thomas? Could Lars or members of the Coalition have infiltrated the towers?"

Commander Thomas rubbed his forehead. "Anything's possible. Commerce reported some discrepancies with shipment numbers. Equipment has also disappeared from the roster for several weeks. It's not a substantial amount, but it's enough that it flagged our system. I assigned two men to try to trace down the shipments, but they haven't reported back yet." He frowned and seemed to consider the possibilities. "If the Coalition has a contact working in distribution, items could have been smuggled out and diverted to their camps. People are another issue though. Our facial and bio-signature recognition system should flag anyone not part of OmniLab. I'll run scans on our software immediately to check for tampering, but no one from the Coalition would be able to move throughout the towers without alerting security."

Alec's eyes narrowed as he moved to stand behind his desk. After keying in a few commands, an image of Lars appeared on the screen. "Except Lars Cerulis was born into OmniLab. Like Kayla, he remained in the system. We don't purge names. He could have easily moved through the towers without being flagged, unless he attempted to access a secure area or his accounts. He would have known this."

"I'm going to strangle the idiots who didn't catch this," Thomas growled, jumping into action and yanking out his commlink. A moment later, he was barking instructions into the unit.

"Seal off all exits to the towers. I want a complete list of every employee who has access to the doors, both primary and auxiliary. We have a leak and I want to flush it out." He lifted his head and pointed to Director Borshin. "Get your traders on call. Cancel all deliveries and receivables until further notice. We're suspending all trading until we get this situation locked down."

Director Borshin opened his commlink and headed out of the room, speaking into the unit along the way. Kayla's mouth dropped open as panic flooded through her. What had she done? Her thoughts flew to the people living in Leo's camp on the surface. She reached over to grip Alec's arm and shook her head.

"You can't do that. The ruin rat camps need those supplies. I don't even know for sure if I saw Lars in the towers. It could have been someone else."

Carl frowned and looked at Alec. "She's right. The trader camps would be okay for a while, but I don't think the surface camps can survive very long without supplies. We've created a dependency. If you take away their supplies, you could be killing them."

Alec didn't have a chance to reply. The commander snapped his commlink shut, his jaw clenching as he stared at the screen. "We'll start running the names of all family members who were... exiled from the towers. If any of them returned to the towers, we may be able to determine who they met with and their activities."

Kayla shook her head. This was fine and great, but it didn't solve the problem with the ruin rats. "Okay. Do that. There's no need to cancel the supplies to the ruin rat camps though."

Alec looked down at her, his eyes filled with regret. "I'm sorry, love. A lot of this is speculation, but I agree with Commander Thomas. We need to err on the side of caution. We'll try to figure it out as quickly as possible. I need you to trust me."

Panic rushing through her, she shook her head adamantly and pointed toward the window. "Trust? This isn't a matter of trust, Alec. Those are my friends on the surface. My family. The people who raised me. Stopping those supplies could kill them. You don't know what it's like out there!"

Alec grabbed her arms and pinned them to her side. His eyes hardened, but there was an almost desperate plea under the surface. "And the alternative could kill *you*. If you're right and the Coalition has been sneaking people into the towers, what's to stop them from targeting you? Or your mother? What if one was responsible for you nearly falling off that beam earlier today? There are too many unknowns, Kayla. I told Lars the truth that night. I would do anything to protect you. I'll be damned if I'm going to just sit by and let you get hurt again."

Kayla gaped at him, shocked by his visceral reaction. The raw emotion that was leaking through their bond was staggering.

Carl stepped forward to intervene. "Let her go, Alec."

Alec turned his thunderous expression toward Carl, but instead of tearing into him, the High Council leader took a shaky breath and released her. Through their bond, she could feel his internal battle as he struggled to get his emotions under control.

After a long moment, he said, "You have my word that we'll try to get the supplies back on schedule as soon as possible."

Kayla swallowed and took a step back, rubbing her arms as she tried to get her feelings under control. "How long?"

Commander Thomas cleared his throat, ignoring the intimacy of the scene that had just played out in front of him. He tapped his fingers against his tablet, scrolling through the information on his display.

"We'll need to screen all personnel before opening the trading routes again. Unfortunately, we can't rely on our usual methods. Everyone with access to the chain of distribution and points of egress will need to submit testimony under a truth barrier. We'll need to find an Inner Circle member beyond reproach to monitor it. It could take a few weeks."

A knot formed in the pit of her stomach. Carl was right. She didn't think the ruin rats could handle weeks without supplies. Leo usually received at least one shipment a week from whatever trader he was working with. They might be able to stretch out their supplies a bit longer, but not if the demand from the outlying family camps was critical. This time of year was always brutal in terms of supplies. With the heat of summer in full force, the sun was breaking down the equipment faster and people were using more hydrating packs.

Although hesitant to stir the hornet's nest again, she needed facts—and fast. She wouldn't let anything happen to her former ruin rat family. Kayla turned back to Alec. "What's a truth barrier? Is that the thing we stood in when we appeared before the High Council?"

"Yes. It's an energy field monitored by an Inner Circle member. It's far more effective than any computerized lie-detector test. Unfortunately, it requires a significant amount of control to erect and maintain the field. It can only be held in place for an hour or two at most."

"Can I help hold the field? We can try to speed up the process."

Alec sighed and leaned forward, pressing his palms against the top of the desk. "No, Kayla. It takes years to master the ability. I know you don't want to hear this, but the best way you can help is to stay safe and begin training again. Given the circumstances, you need to learn some basic defensive techniques before moving on to more specialized abilities. If there's a chance the Coalition has infiltrated the towers, we need to resume your training immediately."

Kayla blew out a breath. Training was definitely a necessity, but she couldn't just sit here on the sidelines in the comforts of the towers while her family on the surface suffered or died.

As though picking up on her agitation, Carl pressed his hand against the small of her back. He bent down and whispered close to her ear, "It'll be okay, sweetheart. Let them figure it out from their end. I promise we won't let anything happen to your camp."

Kayla nodded and leaned against him, curling her fingers into his shirt. Never before had she been more grateful for his support. She'd already made the decision to do whatever was necessary to protect the ruin rats, but it was nice to know she had an ally too.

CHAPTER FOUR

CARL WAITED until Kayla was asleep before climbing out of bed and pulling on the pants he'd worn earlier. It worried him that Kayla hadn't said much after the scene in Alec's office. Instead, she'd turned to him in an almost frenzied passion, channeling her frustrations in a form that was easier for her to express. Kayla's seeming acquiescence of the situation wouldn't last. If Carl had learned anything over the past year, it was Kayla was too headstrong to sit on the sidelines for long. With a heavy sigh, he pulled his shirt over his head and looked down at her.

Kayla lay on her stomach with the blanket down around her hips, revealing the graceful slope of her naked back. Her dark hair tumbled in careless waves over the pillow, the color contrasting dramatically with her fair skin. Even while sleeping, she took his breath away. There was little he wouldn't do for her, including allying with the one person determined to take her away. Giving her one last lingering look, he brushed a light kiss against her temple and pulled the blankets over her. She murmured something unintelligible and burrowed deeper into the blankets.

Satisfied she'd sleep a while longer, he quickly pulled on his boots and made his way out of the Rath'Varein quarters, nodding a greeting to the two security officers stationed outside the door. They gave him a cursory glance as he left but didn't acknowledge him any further. It was just as well. He had business with Alec. The sooner it was finished, the quicker he could get back to Kayla.

The two founding families' quarters were situated across the hall from one another and separated by a decorative fountain. Like the door to Kayla's family quarters, Alec's door also had an elaborately detailed carving. Instead of a tree with winged creatures, though, this door was a more abstract representation of the elements. It all somehow tied into the whole Drac'Kin thing and the unusual abilities the Inner Circle members possessed.

Ignoring his misgivings, Carl pressed his palm against the panel next to the door. An automated voice indicated the residents would be alerted to his arrival and to please wait. After a long interval, the door finally slid open. Carl did a double-take at the extremely attractive woman wearing a nearly translucent robe over a black negligee. At first glance, she reminded him of Kayla, but it took less than a second for him to begin noting the differences.

She was a few inches taller than Kayla, and the barely-there attire showcased her artificially enhanced assets to perfect advantage. Her hazel eyes scanned him up and down before full lips settled in a coy smile. Dark hair fell past her shoulders, and he realized it was her hair that first reminded him of Kayla. Most of the women in the towers tended to embrace more elaborate fashions. However, this woman wore her hair in the exact same style and length as Kayla.

Even so, the similarities were disturbing. He'd normally feel some pity that the woman was being used as a poor substitute, but from the calculating gleam in her eyes, Carl suspected she was aware of the resemblance and taking full advantage of it.

"Well, hello. Can I help you with something?"

The corner of Carl's mouth twisted in a barely suppressed grin. He was fairly confident Alec hadn't intended him to meet the woman standing in the doorway. Things just got interesting.

"I'm looking for Alec."

The woman crooked her finger and beckoned him inside. He followed, watching her saunter over to the bar area. She poured herself a drink and glanced over at him. "Do you want something? Alec's in the shower, but I'm sure he'll be out in a minute."

"No, I'm good," Carl replied, looking around Alec's home. The rich opulence was impressive, and the cool colors seemed to reflect Alec's reserved nature. Carl couldn't help but wonder what Kayla would think of this place. It was a far cry from their living conditions on the surface.

But even more intriguing was Alec's female friend. The woman had the same air of sophistication and polish most Inner Circle members possessed. She moved about the room with an intimate familiarity as though she were perfectly at home. Carl couldn't help but wonder how long she and Alec had been involved. Since Alec was otherwise occupied, Carl decided to take the opportunity to get to know the mystery woman.

"I'm sorry, but I don't believe we've met. I'm Carl Grayson."

She turned and took a sip of her drink, studying him over the rim of her glass. "Mmm. I know exactly who you are, Trader Carl." She approached him slowly, as though giving him ample opportunity to admire her, and then held out a perfectly manicured hand. "I'm Brianna Kisbell. I've heard a great deal about you."

Carl raised an eyebrow and took her hand. "It's nice to meet you. I apologize for the intrusion. I wasn't aware Alec was entertaining company."

She lifted a shoulder in a deliberate movement, causing the robe to slip and reveal a bare shoulder. "Oh, I wouldn't exactly consider myself company. Especially considering how much time Alec and I spend together. Besides, I'm sure Alec will want to know all about how our little Kayla is getting along. It was so fortunate you were able to help locate her for us."

There was no doubt about it... Alec had a viper in his nest. Whereas Kayla possessed an innate grace and sensuality, this woman was acutely aware of every move she made and how best to play it to her advantage. The entire scene seemed contrived, and he wondered if Alec knew what sort of woman he'd invited into his lair.

Alec took that moment to emerge from one of the back rooms. His hair was still damp from his recent shower, and he wore a loose pair of lounging pants which hung low on his waist. Other than a gold chain around his neck, his normal accessories were gone. His eyes swept the room and he froze, his gaze suddenly cold when it landed on Carl.

"Where's Kayla?"

Carl crossed his arms over his chest, pausing to enjoy Alec's momentary discomfort. It might be petty, but given their history, it was difficult to feel much remorse. Their roles had been reversed just a few short days ago when Carl's former ex-girlfriend, now turned reporter, had cornered him and insisted they have breakfast together. "She's sleeping. I needed a private word with you."

Alec's shoulders relaxed slightly, and he nodded. He strolled over to the bar, poured himself a drink, then waved his hand in a dismissive gesture. "Brianna, collect your things and go."

Her mouth turned downward into a small pout. She crossed over to Alec, put her hand on his arm, and tossed her hair back. There was no mistaking the invitation in her eyes. "I thought you might want me to stay tonight. I came by just to see you." She stood on her toes and whispered something in his ear.

Alec looked down at her with disinterest. "No. I told you to be gone by the time I finished showering. I suggest you remove yourself now or I'll arrange to have you removed."

Brianna took a step back, her mouth dropping open. She obviously hadn't been expecting him to rebuff her advances. Her eyes flashed with anger before turning away and stomping toward the back room.

Carl raised an eyebrow. "Interesting. I didn't know you were seeing anyone."

Alec tossed back his drink. "I'm not."

Carl glanced back toward the door where the young woman had disappeared. Alec might not call it that, but she obviously had very different ideas. Carl shrugged. He had other priorities. As long as Alec held up his end of the deal and didn't interfere with his relationship with Kayla, Carl didn't care who the High Council leader was screwing.

"We've got a problem," Carl began. "You're walking a dangerous line with Kayla and stopping those shipments. If she thinks Veridian and the other people on the surface are in danger, she'll be inclined to do something reckless."

Alec refilled his drink and sat down in one of the over-stuffed chairs. "The trading camps have already been suspended. Director Borshin issued the order to recall all members of the trader camps an hour ago. They should be here by tomorrow afternoon. We're setting up temporary accommodations for each camp in one of the lower levels of the main tower. Since they're under contract, all members of the trader camps will remain under our protection until the suspension is lifted."

"That's a start." Carl sat across from Alec and leaned forward, resting his elbows on his knees. "It takes care of Veridian, but it's not going to help anyone in her former scavenging camp. Kayla considers them her family, and quite frankly, she's not wrong. When she went running back to the surface, they took her in without blinking an eye."

Alec sighed and drummed his fingers on the armrest. "What do you suggest?"

"I don't know. You could arrange to give her former camp a large supply shipment to hold them over until trading resumes, but she also has contacts in other camps. I suspect she'll be worried about them too. I just wanted to warn you that she'll snap if you push too hard on this. This is one of those hard lines for her."

Alec opened his mouth to reply but stopped. He cocked his head for a moment, and then a strange expression crossed his face. He paled and whispered Kayla's name before running for the door.

Fully alarmed, Carl ran after him as Alec barreled his way past the two guards. He shouted at them to find Brant before bursting into her bedroom.

———

THE RUINS WERE COLLAPSING. Kayla could hear the screams and voices crying, but she couldn't help them. She could see Carl trying to reach her through the dust, but Edwin had them trapped. Ramiro's voice laughed in the background, and Pretz yelled for her to run. She cried out for Alec, reaching for him across their bond, but Lars's voice whispered in her ear that she couldn't trust him. She just wanted it all to stop. Tears streamed down her face. They were all going to die, and she couldn't save any of them. Veridian, Xantham, Cruncher, Leo, Mack, Marie... she couldn't help them.

"It's not real, Kayla," a voice urged.

The bond between her and Alec flared to life, and Kayla gasped at the sensation of powerful energy that flowed through her. It surrounded her, filling her and enveloping her in its warmth. She blinked open her eyes to stare into Alec's worried blue ones.

Carl crouched down beside her and Alec. He brushed her hair away from her face and frowned. "What's wrong, sweetheart?"

"C-C-Co-l-d," she managed. Her teeth were chattering so violently she could barely form the word.

Carl's head shot up to look at Alec. "What the hell is going on? What's wrong with her?"

Alec pulled her into his lap and tightened his arms around her. Kayla choked on a sob and buried her face against his chest. She couldn't stop shaking. The images from the vision still lingered, and she couldn't get them out of her head. They were all so real.

"It was an energy attack. We need to get her warm. Quickly, turn on the shower and bypass the gradual heat increase. We need it hot but not scalding," Alec instructed.

Carl ran for the bathroom, and a second later, she heard the rush of water.

"Shh, it's all right, love. It wasn't real," Alec promised and lifted her up.

Whatever it was, it wasn't a dream. She hadn't been able to escape the vision. It had pinned her down and forced the images and memories through her. The dark claws of all her fears continued to loom over her, threatening to push her back into that frozen black abyss. She whimpered and clung to Alec like he was a beacon in the storm.

"The water's heated," Carl called out as Alec carried her

into the bathroom. "No one was in here, and we had guards posted at the door. How could this have happened?"

Alec didn't answer Carl immediately. Instead, he continued to weave complex energy threads around Kayla. She eagerly consumed everything he offered as though she'd been starving. The more energy he sent to her, the more the surrounding shadows dimmed. It wasn't enough. The hollowness inside her was consuming.

"Shh," he murmured and brushed his lips against her ear. "I've got you, love. Just take what you need."

Kayla couldn't do anything else. She inhaled and tried to breathe in the very air that seemed charged with energy. Her tears had stopped, but she still couldn't stop trembling. She leaned in closer, needing Alec's warmth as much as the energy he offered. She'd never been so cold.

Alec shifted her and stepped into the shower with her still in his arms. Hot water pelted against them, but Alec didn't release his hold on her. With the heated water on her skin and his energy warming her from within, the shadows feeding upon her slowly began to disperse.

Alec slid down against the wall until they reached the floor. He continued to cradle her in his lap while the water rained overhead. She buried her head against his chest. Footsteps approached from the bedroom, but she didn't bother looking up. She heard Brant's voice asking something, but it was too low to make out the words. Carl replied in low, strained tones, and then Brant's voice grew louder.

"We're conducting a search right now. Even if they used one of her belongings as a focus for the attack, they would have needed to be relatively close for it to work. If she's that cold, it may be the work of someone channeling water."

Alec lifted his head. "No. Someone attacked her using shadow energy. I don't know how it's possible, but this is unlike anything I've ever felt. I can push the shadows out the rest of the way, but I need to see if you can pick up on the energy signature first. I've gotten it under control enough so it's not progressing, but she's walking a thin line in this state."

Was that what happened? She rubbed her cheek against Alec's chest. He was right. The heat from the water and the warmth of his energy were beginning to take effect. She was still cold, but it was no longer numbing. Her fingers flexed, and she realized she was touching Alec's bare skin. On some level, she was sure this would be a problem for Carl, but she couldn't bring herself to pull away. Not yet. She was still so cold.

As though sensing her thoughts, Alec began rubbing her back in a soothing caress. "Don't worry about that right now. Everything will be fine. Just breathe."

Suddenly, a cool chill settled over her again. It penetrated her skin and into her bones. This one was slightly different, but the result was the same. Her breath caught in her throat as it drew her energy away. Kayla tried to shove away the darkness, but instead of retreating, it eagerly absorbed everything she had to offer and demanded more. It felt as though her very soul was being siphoned away. She began to shake as the cold darkness crept back in.

Alec shouted at Brant to stop, tilted her head back, and kissed her.

She gasped as his tongue swept inside her mouth, claiming her. It wasn't one of the tender kisses they'd shared before, but one full of desperate passion. It felt as though Alec was breathing her soul back into her. Curling her fingers around his arm, she whimpered into his mouth. Energy flooded her senses, and the cold melted away from the heat of his kiss. He took his time exploring her mouth and tasting her. All the while, his energy poured into her, chasing away the shadows. His hands cupped her face and held her in place, obliterating every one of her senses with his touch.

When he finally pulled away and the flow of energy tapered off, Kayla was nearly drunk from the power he'd shared. Her body felt boneless, and her emotions were completely raw. She blinked up at him. Passion-filled blue eyes were gazing at her with unreserved adoration and love. The memory of their kiss now replaced any of the earlier haunting images she'd witnessed.

He brushed her wet hair away from her face and searched her expression. "I'm sorry, love. I didn't know how else to stop it. Are you all right now?"

Kayla swallowed, feeling dazed. She wasn't sure she'd ever be all right ever again, but she managed to nod. The water continued to beat down upon them, and Alec motioned for someone to shut it off. It cut off suddenly and the room fell silent, except for the sound of dripping water.

She noted with some surprise that her hands were pressed up against his well-defined, bare chest. Several droplets of water trailed downward, and she followed the riveting movement with her eyes. Although they'd shared a few intimate moments, she'd never seen him without a shirt. She bit down on her lower lip, unable to tear her eyes away from him but knowing she should.

Alec suddenly seemed to become aware of her undressed state as well. His gaze drifted downward, and he inhaled sharply. Starting to slide his hand up her thigh, he caught himself and stopped. He cursed under his breath and squeezed his eyes shut.

"Carl, you need to take her. Now."

A moment later, strong arms wrapped a soft towel around Kayla and lifted her up and away from Alec. She looked up into Carl's worried face, hating the fact she kept putting that look in his eyes. She wrapped her arms around him and buried her head against his chest, murmuring his name. He tightened his arms around her, clutching her even closer.

"Get her dry as quickly as possible. She needs to stay warm," Alec instructed and pointed to the drying tube on the wall. "Don't leave her again while she's asleep. She'll be fine if she's awake, but without training, her natural defenses fall apart when she's sleeping."

Carl immediately carried her into the frosted-glass tube, not bothering to remove his clothes. He continued to hold her, his touch more gentle than usual, while the heated air caressed her skin. Once it was finished, he bundled her again in the towel and lifted her back in his arms. She didn't object. He carried her over to the built-in bench and pulled her onto his lap. Kayla leaned into him and curled her fingers into his shirt. Carl brushed a kiss against her hair and looked up at Alec.

"Do you know what happened?"

Alec didn't bother with the air dryer. Instead, he scrubbed himself with a towel and threw it across the room. It hit the wall with a loud *thwap*. He whirled around on Brant.

"You tell me. What the hell happened? I told you to check the energy signature and you start *stealing* her energy? Give me one good reason I shouldn't have you taken into custody and your rank stripped right now."

Brant lowered his head. "I'll accept whatever action or punishment you see fit, Master Tal'Vayr." He lifted his eyes to look at Kayla as though she were a puzzle he couldn't solve. "I attempted to separate her from the energy threads to read the echo from her attacker. Instead of cutting off her connection using our normal techniques, I somehow absorbed her energy. It's... I didn't think it was possible. Nothing like this has ever happened before. Shadows normally negate energy, but she's too closely entwined with it. It's as though the energy is part of her. Instead of channeling it like other people, she's an actual conduit."

Alec frowned and glanced at her. "Are you suggesting Shadows can manipulate stolen spirit energy from Kayla?"

Brant hesitated and then nodded. "I believe so. Even now, I can still sense her energy within me. I don't know if I have the ability to use it though. I suspect the attacker wasn't anticipating this result either. I don't know his or her intentions, but if the person was using shadow energy, I doubt they would have expected what occurred."

Alec fell silent for a moment and then approached Kayla. He knelt in front of her, his eyes full of concern. "Is that what it felt like to you? Can you tell us what happened?"

She sat up a little straighter, but Carl didn't relinquish his hold on her. "I don't know. I was sleeping, and the next thing I knew, I was trapped in this horrible dream. I knew I was asleep, but I couldn't make myself wake up. It was almost like I was underwater. I could see the surface of the water, but I couldn't break through. It kept pulling me down. The images got darker, and I kept getting colder." She shivered at the memory.

Alec put his hand over hers and sent another slight pulse of warming energy through her. He glanced over at Brant. "You might be right. I sensed shadow energy, but it's possible a water channeler was working in conjunction with a Shadow. The water channeler could have been feeding her images to distract her while the Shadow tried to disconnect her energy flow."

Brant frowned. "So you're thinking it was two separate individuals? Someone from the Inner Circle is working with a Shadow?"

Alec nodded. "I don't see an alternative. As far as I know, no one from the Inner Circle could have stolen her energy. But a Shadow doesn't have the capability to influence dreams. That's a water talent."

Carl pressed a kiss against her temple. "Brant mentioned something about a focusing object."

"That's a likely scenario," Alec admitted and looked over at Brant. "They could have used an object with some sort of connection to Kayla as a marker to target their energy attack. Depending on the strength of their abilities and skill level, the focusing object could have been something as trivial as the clothing Kayla wore yesterday or a napkin she used at dinner. Anything with Kayla's trace energy would have sufficed. In the meantime, get someone in here to search her room. It might be too late to try to pick up trace residue, but we need to figure out what was used to target her. It might give us another lead. Since she was asleep in her quarters, they wouldn't have been able to get close enough to attack her without a focus." He turned back to Kayla with a frown and ran his thumb over the top of her hand. Almost to himself, he mused, "They had to know I'd sense your distress and come for you."

Brant nodded. "Yes. Unless their intention was to test the strength of your bond and your response time."

A knock at the door interrupted them. Brant opened it a fraction. Kayla could only make out the barest hint of the OmniLab security uniform through the cracked door.

"I apologize for the interruption, but the only people we found in the corridor were Mistress Seara and another young woman. The young woman claims to have seen someone running from the hall. We have her in the next room, if you'd like to speak with her."

"Yes." Alec squeezed Kayla's hand and stood. Addressing Carl, he added, "I'll be back in a moment. Stay with her and keep her warm." Without another word, he motioned for Brant to accompany him and they followed the guard out of the room.

Kayla shook her head. *Nope. Not gonna happen.* Although

she was still a little shaky, she wanted some answers. Now that the chill was starting to wear off, a mantle of fury was beginning to set in. How dare those bastards use her memories against her? If someone was attacking her, it was time to go on the offensive. Whoever had decided to fuck with her had made a serious mistake. With the towel still wrapped around her, she tried to stand.

Her knees wobbled, and Carl stood, wrapping his arm around her waist to keep her from falling. He frowned, not bothering to hide his concerned expression.

"Sweetheart, maybe you should sit back down."

Kayla shook her head, drawing on her anger to give her strength. With a deep breath to steady herself, she managed to pull herself up straight. "I can't. I need to find out who's responsible for this. I'm not just going to sit here and wait for them to attack me again. What happens if Alec isn't around next time? I won't let some zap-happy circle freaks use my memories against me. Those bastards are going down."

He lifted her chin and tilted her head back. From the hard look in his eyes, she realized Carl's anger was simmering just below the surface and ready to bubble over.

"I don't blame you for being angry. I want to find those bastards just as much as you do, but you can't do everything on your own. Dammit, Kayla, you could have died tonight. Again."

He turned away and slammed his fist into the wall. She jumped involuntarily and gaped at the sizeable hole. Carl started to pace the bathroom, his radiating anger making the room seem much smaller.

"For fuck's sake, Kayla. What the hell are you going to do? Go into the other room and interrogate some random stranger? You can barely stand on your own two feet."

"If that's what it takes," she snapped. "I'll do what needs to be done."

He spun around to face her. "Why does it have to be you? Why can't you trust someone else to handle things for once? You don't trust Alec. You sure as hell don't trust me. When does it end, Kayla?"

She pressed a hand against the wall to steady herself. If her legs gave out now, her argument would collapse too. "You're one to talk, Carl. When we were in the Coalition camp, your first instinct was to tell me to run. You wanted to sacrifice yourself for me."

"Because I love you, dammit!" he shouted.

"And you don't think I feel the same way, you idiot? Have you thought that maybe this isn't about trust, but instead I'm trying to protect the people I care about?"

"By dying?" Carl demanded, exasperation and frustration taking their toll on him. He shook his head and sighed. "If that's the result, I'd rather you stop trying to protect everyone. Don't you understand how much you mean to me? I can't bear the thought of losing you."

When she didn't reply, he took a step toward her. Kayla instinctively started to pull back in reflex, but Carl refused to let her. Instead, he wrapped his hand around the back of her neck and drew her even closer. His touch was firm but gentle. It was the naked fear in his eyes, though, that stopped her resistance.

"Kayla, sweetheart, I've never seen you like that. I won't pretend to understand what happened with this energy attack. But the fact Alec and Brant don't seem to understand what happened either scares the hell out of me. I'm terrified of you going off half-cocked and ending up hurt even worse. There's too much we don't know. I promised I would never force you to do anything against your will, and I'll stand by you if that's what you want, but I wish with everything in me that you'd give yourself a break. Leaning on someone else and trusting them to help doesn't mean giving up control. You don't have to do everything yourself. You have options."

Options. Her entire body tensed at the memory of the last words Lars had uttered before he stabbed her. Kayla frowned and looked away, but her fingers curled around Carl's wrist, holding him to her.

Did she really have options? Sometimes it felt as though she was just along for the ride. Even though she'd repeatedly convinced herself she was going to stay on the surface and not return to the towers, something kept happening to drive her back here.

Kayla had learned from an early age that every choice had consequences, both good and bad. What was happening now wasn't a direct result of her choices; it was the ripple effect from those choices that seemed to be spiraling out of control. From the moment she'd stolen the Aurelia Data Cube to everything happening now, all the events surrounding her seemed to be interconnected.

Veridian used to talk about Fate guiding things. She'd always preferred to believe she was the one directing her own circumstances. But given everything that had happened, maybe Veridian had a point. Carl, on the other hand, was claiming she had options and the power to make her own choices. She bit her lip, wondering if both of them could be right.

If so, when it came down to it, which one was more powerful—Fate or free will? How much control did Kayla really have over her own destiny?

The puzzle pieces were all around her—she just needed to understand how they all fit together. One thing was clear though: she wouldn't figure out anything by lying around. She looked up into Carl's brown eyes, her heart clenching at the frustration and worry in his expression. They might not share an energy bond, but the tension in his body language made it clear he was agonizing over the attack. Sometimes, she was amazed he had the patience to keep putting up with her. What she felt for this trader was deeper and more consuming than anything she'd ever known.

Fate had guided them toward each other for a reason. In so many ways, Carl was her balancing point. He'd been her unfailing support and guide as she traversed this strange new world around her. Alec was right when he admitted she needed Carl. Without him, Kayla wasn't sure if she'd be as adept at bridging the chasm between the world on the surface and the strangeness of life within the towers.

A wave of love and gratitude rushed through her. With everything that had happened since they first met, Carl had always been there for her. He challenged her and protected her, but he also gave her the freedom and strength to stand on her own feet. Even now, she knew he wouldn't stop her if she insisted on diving headfirst into an investigation. He might not be happy about it, but he'd continue to stand beside her in case she should fall.

Standing on her toes, Kayla brushed a soft kiss against Carl's lips. When she pulled away, she let him see everything she was feeling. All her hope, passion, and adoration for this trader who had stolen her heart reflected in her eyes. His gaze softened as he looked down at her, understanding her wordless communication. She pressed her hands against his chest, feeling the warmth of his skin beneath his shirt and relishing the contact.

His concern and unwavering support touched her, but there was only one choice of action. If anything, Kayla was a woman of action—she could never pretend to be anything else.

"I'll be careful, but I need to do this. I won't allow them or anyone else to turn me into a victim. I need to take a stand." She hesitated for a minute, considering his previous words. She used to believe she needed to do everything on her own. Now she was starting to realize that wasn't true. People who loved her surrounded her. The logical side of her understood they would help and support her if she asked. It was a strange shift from always believing she needed to remain independent. Kayla bit her lip and looked up at him, feeling uncertain for the first time in a long time.

"You're right though. I'm not very good at relying on anyone else or asking for help. I've never trusted anyone like that before. Not completely. I don't think it's in my nature to relinquish control and rely on someone else, but..." She paused for a moment and looked away. Why was this so hard, and why did it make her feel so vulnerable? "I do need you, Carl. More than I've ever needed anyone. I know I don't always show it, but I do trust you. I believe in you, but it scares me to put so much faith in one person."

"Kayla," he whispered, his voice heavy with emotion. He cupped her face, brushing his thumb across her cheek. "You undo me completely. All you ever have to do is ask. I'll always be here for you, sweetheart."

She lowered her head against his chest, letting the intensity of her emotions warm her from within. He wrapped his arms around her and held her, simply stroking her hair. After a long moment, she looked back up at him and gave him a small smile.

"Maybe... for starters, you could help me out to the living area? I'm not sure I can make it without falling on my ass. Then we can find out what's going on... together?"

As though sensing her need to lighten the mood, the corner of his lips curved upward.

"It's a deal," he agreed, helping her pull on a light robe. Leaning heavily on Carl, they headed out into the crowded common room. Together.

CHAPTER FIVE

THE FIRST THING Kayla noticed was a team of security personnel searching the front room of her family's quarters. Most of them were using some sort of scanning device, running it over each piece of furniture before moving on to the next. Seara was standing in the center of the chaos helping to direct the search. Although she still carried an air of elegance and refinement, the older woman's cheeks were hollowed and pale. Brant and two other guards hovered nearby while a gorgeous, dark-haired woman stood next to Alec. He was engaged in an argument with Brant and didn't notice her and Carl right away.

At the sight of them, Seara rushed over and enveloped her in a hug. "Oh, sweetheart, please tell me you're all right. Security's doing a scan to find any trace energy so we can find whoever was responsible."

Kayla managed a smile for her mother and nodded, silently reassuring her she was fine. Once Seara appeared mollified, Kayla directed her attention back to the other woman. Hopefully, this stranger had some answers.

The unfamiliar woman wore a form-fitting black dress

which barely reached mid-thigh. Her eyes focused on Kayla, taking in her damp appearance, and then her eyes narrowed slightly. Kayla cocked her head, surprised at the animosity in that brief look.

Who the hell is she?

Still holding Kayla's gaze, the woman leaned close to Alec and put her arms around his neck. Her body pressed against him, the slit in the side of her dress exposed even more of her long legs. Even from across the room, Kayla could sense the ripple of intimate energy between them. The echo of it coursed along the bond she shared with Alec.

Kayla froze in shock. A sudden, almost violent wave of nausea hit her as the woman's energy filtered through their bond and crawled over her like a vicious parasite. It was too much. She was suffocating from the toxicity. Desperate to be free, she grabbed hold of her bond with Alec and tore apart the energy threads connecting them, nearly doubling over from the combined sense of loss and relief. Carl caught her before she collapsed and managed to keep her upright while she tried to calm her racing heart and breathe normally.

Alec brushed the woman off of him and spun around, his face paling at the sight of Kayla. Although they were still connected on some level, the surrounding energy was strangely silent. Kayla still didn't feel firmly encased within her own skin, but that could be attributed to the borrowed energy she'd taken from Alec. She'd much rather deal with that than the prickling sense of wrongness from the woman contaminating their bond.

Alec started to move toward her, but Kayla quickly stepped backward into Carl's arms. Her knuckles whitened as she clenched the robe around her in a death grip. No way. She didn't want to get anywhere near him and that woman right now.

Alec stopped in his tracks. Without taking his eyes off

Kayla, he said in a low voice, "Brant, get Brianna out of here. Immediately. Find out what she knows and have her removed from this floor."

The woman didn't appear happy with this announcement. She tossed back her dark hair and tried approaching him again. "But Alec, I'm frightened. All these guards and people are running through the halls. I don't know whom to trust. Don't leave me with one of the Shadows. I overheard the guards talking about a shadow energy attack. We should warn the rest of the Inner Circle. What if they come after someone else next?"

Indecision warred on his face, and after the slightest hesitation, Alec's eyes narrowed on the woman. Grabbing her arm, he led her toward the door and motioned for Brant to follow him outside. Kayla felt him weave energy around Brianna, but it was the heavy thread of influence she was beginning to recognize. Even so, the thought of Alec using energy on the woman sickened her. It was too reminiscent of the intimate combination of their energies she'd felt through the connection she shared with Alec.

"I felt her in our bond," Kayla whispered, trying to explain her reaction. Carl tightened his arms around her but remained silent. She buried her head against his chest and inhaled deeply. She loved Carl and couldn't deny the sense of rightness at being in his arms, but she couldn't deny the strong feelings she had for Alec. Her visceral reaction just now was proof of that. Wasn't it? Was it truly possibly to love two men?

Either way, she hadn't been expecting to witness that scene. She knew Alec wasn't celibate. He'd admitted he had his own "distractions," as he called them. She just never expected to feel the shared intimacy between him and his unknown lovers. Even now, the thought made her stomach pitch. In some ways, it was worse than the jealousy she'd experienced when the reporter had been flirting with Carl. At least then she hadn't had to suffer through the echo of their passion. What she just experienced made her want to gag.

Seara's voice interrupted her thoughts. "Kayla, I'm so sorry. I had no idea that woman... I mean, I... She looks... I'm sure it's just a misunderstanding."

Kayla looked up. Her mother was frowning at the door where Alec had disappeared, disapproval etched on her face. "I'm sure what happened just now wasn't as bad as it looked. Alec cares a great deal for you. I hope you'll give him a chance to explain."

Carl tucked Kayla into his side, running his hand down her back. She leaned against him for support and said, "There's nothing to explain, Seara. I felt her and the intimacy between them. Alec is free to be with whomever he wants. It's none of my business."

The devastation on Seara's face was heart-wrenching. The older woman let out a small cry of denial as her hand flew to cover her mouth. "No. I just can't believe... Why would he...?" She lowered her hand and shook her head sadly. "I'm sorry. I... need some air. Excuse me." Without saying another word, she turned away and headed down the hall.

Kayla swallowed. Her mother seemed to be taking the whole thing worse than she was. Carl frowned and then looked down at her. "Are you okay?"

She straightened her shoulders. How could she be? Someone had tried to kill her, not once but twice in one day. Her yearly tally of close calls was approaching the double digits. She'd made Carl suffer through witnessing another intimate moment with Alec, who was apparently getting it on with a brunette when he wasn't reducing Kayla to a pile of brainless mush. Her mother was having a nervous breakdown on her behalf. Emotions were a bitch and a half.

She. Was. Done.

"No, but I will be. I'm getting dressed. I want access to OmniLab's security system, and I want to know *exactly* whom I'm dealing with. Once I get ahold of them, they're going to wish they'd never fucked with me."

Carl's raised his eyebrows and his mouth lifted in a half smile. He gave her an approving nod before leading her back down the hall.

———

"ENOUGH WITH THE GAMES, BRIANNA," Alec bit out. "What did you see?"

She blinked up at him. He'd had to use quite a bit of influence to discourage her from sharing information about the attack with the rest of the Inner Circle. Although Brianna could be quite alluring at times, he was at the end of his patience with her. For the past several days, ever since Kayla had returned to the towers, Brianna had been pushing for something more than just the casual affair they'd begun.

Even though he'd been clear about his intentions from the beginning, Brianna hadn't taken the hint. The small energy pulse she'd sent to him while Kayla was in the room had been artfully executed to achieve the desired effect. It didn't help that Kayla was extraordinarily sensitive to energy manipulation. The pain he'd felt from her was excruciating. He'd wanted to strangle Brianna right then and there for causing Kayla a moment of hurt. Kayla didn't understand the petty energy games some men and women played in relationships and was ill-equipped to deal with them. Another woman might have lashed back at Brianna and staked her claim, but Kayla had no such inclination.

Instead, she'd gone the opposite direction and denied her bond with Alec. Given her history and lack of understanding of their ways, he couldn't blame her for terminating their mental connection. It was imperative he remedy the situation as soon as possible in case there was another attack. He couldn't afford to allow Kayla the distance she wanted. But right now, he had to get Brianna under control and make sure the towers were protected. At least Alec knew Carl would watch over Kayla until he could try to straighten things out.

Brianna glanced over at Brant and frowned. Some of the Inner Circle were apprehensive about the Shadows, and Brianna was no exception. At the very least, Brant's presence would emphasize the severity of the situation.

She bit her lip. "You told me to leave. I was on my way out when I saw someone running down the hall. They nearly knocked me down. Then one of your security officers found me and brought me to you."

Alec nodded impatiently. "Who did you see?"

Brianna lowered her head and peeked up at him through darkened lashes. "I'm so sorry, Alec. I don't have any idea. I was just so frightened. They could have killed me."

She pressed her hand against his chest, and he resisted the urge to push it away. He knew exactly what she was attempting to do, and while he might normally indulge her little games, she'd made a grievous error in interfering with the bond he shared with Kayla.

"Was it a man or woman?"

"I don't know," she admitted with the slightest of tremors in her voice. "It happened so fast. I was too afraid to pay much attention."

She leaned against him and he felt the press of her breasts against his chest. Annoyed, he grabbed her shoulders and forced her to step back.

"Drop the act," he said, weaving a thread of influence into his words. "You're an expert energy channeler, Brianna. You wouldn't have been fazed unless someone was standing in your closet and threatening to destroy your wardrobe."

Like a curtain suddenly falling away, Brianna's entire demeanor changed. Her eyes narrowed at him. "Fine. You want the truth? I didn't *care* enough to pay attention. People come down this hall all the time hoping to get a glimpse of your precious Kayla. You keep her to yourself and everyone's wondering about her. We all want to know why. What's so special about her?"

Alec frowned. He knew the Inner Circle was curious about her, but he hadn't realized the extent. He'd need to heighten security on this floor. "What are they saying?"

She pulled back out of his grasp and crossed her arms. "We know she's powerful. After all, she broke the bracelets with your help. But why does she keep going to the surface when you've announced your intention to marry? She was gone for weeks. Some of us have our doubts and think the whole thing is a lie. *I* was the one in your bed, not her. She was off on the surface doing who knows what." Her lips curled into a knowing smirk. "Although, I have a pretty good idea now. I saw the way she looked at that trader. He couldn't keep his hands off her either."

Alec cursed under his breath. This was worse than he thought. "What the hell have you been telling people, Brianna?"

She tossed her hair back and glared at him defiantly. "I haven't needed to tell them anything. People have seen me coming to your quarters, Alec. They talk, and I let them. I won't be your dirty little secret."

Alec glanced over at Brant's impassive face. "Were you aware of this?"

Brant inclined his head. "There's been some talk and curiosity, but it was expected. Kayla's return and continued presence in the towers has helped quell some speculation. Although, Mistress Kisbell is correct. The Inner Circle is anxious to meet your fiancée. It may help stop some rumors if you make more appearances together."

Alec took a deep breath and flexed his fingers. The thought of sharing Kayla with the rest of the Inner Circle wasn't appealing. Their bond was still too new and vulnerable. With the continued threats looming over them and Brianna's little energy stunt, he'd lost any progress he'd made with her. Until Kayla fully embraced their bond, he didn't want to risk sharing her with anyone else. It was bad enough watching her with Carl, but the thought of another energy user trying to coax her away from him was intolerable.

He scrubbed his hands over his face, feeling as though he'd aged a dozen years in the past several months. With a sigh, he lifted his head to look once more at Brianna. He couldn't deny she was a beautiful woman. At first, he'd found it amusing she'd attempted to emulate Kayla in an effort to seduce him. Once she'd managed to work her way into his bed, though, she'd begun dropping hints she was open to a more permanent arrangement.

There was never any possible chance of that happening though. Other than Kayla, he'd only ever seriously considered bonding with one other woman. Brianna hadn't even appeared on his radar. Unfortunately, she refused to accept that. When Kayla last returned to the tower and confessed her feelings for him, he'd reached a tipping point with Brianna.

Alec recalled the way Kayla felt pressed up against him in the shower. The softness of her naked body in his arms and the intoxicating taste of her on his lips was forever etched in his mind. When she'd looked at him with passion-filled eyes and he felt her desire through their bond, his control had nearly snapped. After experiencing a glimpse of what he could have with Kayla, the thought of touching Brianna now left him feeling flat. Even her energy repulsed him.

Brianna would remain persistent though. Her little stunt with sneaking into his room this evening to seduce him was just one more example of how far she was willing to go. After a council meeting had gone overly long, he'd provided her with a set of customized access codes so she could wait in his quarters for him. She must have used those same codes to get in tonight. He'd never bothered to rescind her access, a mistake he intended to correct immediately. That was only part of the problem though.

He needed to make things clear to her and outline the consequences if she continued to push. He wouldn't risk Kayla getting hurt again. One more incident could be the final drive to send Kayla away from him and the towers permanently.

Brianna watched him with guarded eyes. He'd pushed her with his influence tonight, but he had no regrets. As much as she might want to try to take Kayla's place, it would never happen. He once more wove the strong bands of influence around his words, reinforcing them with his emotions.

"We're finished, Brianna. You're no longer welcome in my quarters. Kayla Rath'Varein is my bonded mate. If you ever interact with her again, I trust you'll remain civil and give her the respect afforded by her position. If I hear otherwise, we'll have words again and it won't end pleasantly. You will also keep your observations and opinions regarding the trader to yourself. If I hear anything, I'll know exactly who was responsible for instigating the rumors." He gave her a chilling look. "I promise, you *will* regret it."

Brianna's mouth dropped open as uncertainty flickered in her eyes. "What? You can't do that. I thought—"

"I just did. You may go."

As he withdrew his energy from her, Brianna's eyes flashed in anger, but it was gone almost immediately. She sniffed and took a small step toward him. "Alec, please. I'm sorry, darling. After everything we've shared, I thought I meant something to you."

Alec raised an eyebrow. Oh, she was very good. If he didn't know her as well as he did, he might be taken in by it. As it was, he pitied whichever unfortunate fool she set her sights on next. "No, Brianna. You'd do well to drop the act entirely. I might actually have a smidgen of respect for you then. You know as well as I do that neither one of us cared a whit about the other. We both enjoyed ourselves. Nothing more. Now it's done."

Her eyes lit with a strange fire, and she snarled at him. "You self-righteous prick. No wonder your precious Kayla's screwing some trader who digs around in the dirt. You may be good in bed, but beyond that, there's nothing there. You're as heartless and as big of a bastard as your father."

Alec forced himself to keep his expression blank. "Then I suggest you remember how ruthless he could be when challenged. Ask yourself if you want to find out if I'm capable of the same."

A flash of fear crossed her face but was quickly gone. It was enough. Even if he hadn't bound her with his influence, she'd think twice before spreading more rumors. As soon as Brianna rushed out of the room, Alec instructed Brant to follow her and then to check on Kayla. Brant merely nodded once and disappeared. Once Alec was alone, he slumped down in a chair and dropped his head in his hands. He'd screwed up on an epic scale.

―――――

KAYLA STARED at the video feed. There was nothing. Absolutely nothing. It was almost as though the persons responsible were either invisible or had managed to erase any trace of themselves. She had to be missing something.

She slid closer to Brant to get a better look at the screen. He'd come back an hour ago and offered to help her review the files. Alec hadn't returned with him, but it was probably for the best. Her emotions were jumbled, and she didn't know what to say to him. Even worse, though, was knowing Alec was probably with that other woman right now. The loss from their suppressed connection was a dull ache in the pit of her stomach.

Kayla turned her attention back to the screen, determined to get the image of them together out of her head. Drumming her fingers on the desk, she froze as the realization hit her. That was it! That was what was missing. Brant had mentioned the dark-haired woman supposedly saw the attacker, but Brianna wasn't on the video either.

She grabbed Brant's arm. "Stop. Pull up the metadata on the video."

Brant inhaled sharply dropped his gaze to where her hand rested on his forearm. She felt a slight tingle under her fingertips and slowly drew her hand away.

Okay. That was freaky. She'd only felt that when she'd touched other Inner Circle members.

"Sorry. Did I zap you?"

She caught a flicker of disappointment on his face, but it was quickly gone. "No. You're just siphoning off more energy. It's fine." He turned back to the computer and entered in a few commands. "So you believe someone may have edited the date and time tags?"

Kayla nodded and leaned forward to look at the screen, careful not to put her hands on him again. Touching him felt far different than what she'd experienced during the attack. It wasn't painful, and there wasn't a cold chill. There was definitely transference though. At the earliest opportunity, she was going to investigate the whole "stolen shadow energy" thing. But first, she needed to find the person responsible.

All videos and images contained metadata, which was essentially hardcoded information embedded into the file. It detailed basic information about the type of equipment used, the date and time the image was taken, and even the location coordinates where the file originated. If someone had manipulated the video footage, they should be able to tell right away. Granted, they could have scrubbed the metadata, but it was likely they would not have had enough time.

After a brief moment, information flashed upon the screen. Kayla frowned as she read through the data. As she suspected, the timestamp associated with the file was from several days earlier. Someone had replaced the footage.

Brant scowled and muttered a rather colorful oath under his breath.

Despite herself, she grinned. It was somewhat entertaining to watch a straight-laced Omni lose his cool. "At least now we know why it didn't pick up anything. They replaced the video."

Brant stood and yanked out his commlink. "That's only *one* issue. Whoever is responsible for this has access to the security feeds. We already suspected Shadow involvement, but this confirms whoever else is responsible for this attack is highly placed within the Circle."

Brant called the head of security on his commlink and began detailing the discovery. As he paced the small room, Kayla stood and yawned. She raised her arms over her head and stretched her tired limbs. Brant paused, fixing his gaze on her for a long moment with a thoughtful expression on his face. He then turned away, continuing his conversation with Commander Thomas.

Brant was an enigma. He reminded her of the ruin rats with how closed-lipped he could be about everything. But Alec seemed to trust him, and he'd proven himself back at Carl's camp when he tried to save her. In some ways, Brant seemed uneasy around her. Kayla wasn't sure if that was because she was technically an Inner Circle member, or some other reason. Part of her wondered what the security officer would be like if he ever let his hair down.

When he finished his conversation, Kayla asked, "So... what did he say?"

Brant glanced at her briefly before turning to the screen and entering a few commands. "I'm sending him the video files. He's contacting Alec and then compiling a list of everyone who has access to the security feeds. We need to cross-reference that list with people who could have accessed this level. I should hear back from him in a few minutes." He frowned and added, "We're going to have to make some adjustments to your security detail and limit access to this area even more. Unfortunately, it appears the corruption goes even deeper than we suspected. From the looks of things, some Shadows and Inner Circle members are working together."

Kayla cocked her head. "You say that like it's unusual for them to work together."

Brant hesitated for a moment. "In this context, yes, it's very unusual."

Kayla frowned, puzzled by the strange dynamic between Inner Circle members and Shadows. There was a link between the two, but the relationship was something she didn't quite understand.

"You don't like the Inner Circle, do you?"

His eyes flickered to hers and then back to the screen. "I don't have any issues with the Inner Circle."

"Bullshit," she retorted and sat next to him, determined to elicit more of a response. Leaning back, she began ticking off the points on her fingers. "You seem to find Alec somewhat tolerable, but you're clearly uncomfortable around me. You hide it well, but I'd say you feel little more than contempt for the rest of the Inner Circle. I overheard what some of your Shadow buddies said about Inner Circle members earlier when I was hanging in the rafters. So what's the deal?"

Brant's shoulders tensed, and she knew she'd struck a nerve. "The officer who spoke out of turn has been reprimanded. It won't happen again. As far as the rest, Master Tal'Vayr specifically requested me to be assigned to your security detail. However, if you have issues with my performance, I'm sure he will discuss my reassignment with you."

"Fuck that," she retorted and crossed her arms, growing annoyed by the entire conversation. She wanted to yank the stick from his ass and beat him over the head with it. "Just play human for a minute, Brant. If there's corruption that involves Shadows and the Inner Circle, I need to know why. I'm not trying to get all up in your business. You can hate me for all I care. I don't give a rat's ass what your buddies think of the Inner Circle either. Hell, I probably feel the same way. I just want to know why someone is targeting me."

Brant lowered his head, rubbed his temples, and sighed. "I don't dislike you, Kayla. I don't necessarily agree with your choices, but it's not my place to criticize. My role is to act as your protector within the parameters Master Tal'Vayr has set. To be honest, I don't know why someone would target you. Other than being a pain in the ass, you have little bearing on what happens within the towers."

Kayla gave out an unladylike snort. At least he was honest. "Okay. So it's not me personally, but I know I'm not imagining the bad juju between the Shadows and Inner Circle."

Brant paused long enough that she wasn't sure he was even going to respond. Finally, he admitted, "You're not wrong, but I'm not certain I'm the best person to answer your questions."

Her eyes narrowed. "Why not?"

He frowned, rubbing the back of his of his neck as though

debating his next words. "The Shadows and Inner Circle have a long and somewhat adversarial history. It's to be expected when our abilities are in direct opposition with each other. My perspective is going to be vastly different than someone from the Inner Circle."

Finally. She was actually getting somewhere. She leaned forward, eager to learn more. "Right. That's why I want to know your opinion. I can always get Alec's thoughts later, but it's better to know both sides, so tell me from your point of view. What's the deal?"

Brant gave her a sharp look, as though surprised by her words. Finally, he shook his head. "Your willingness to consider other perspectives is admirable, but you'll need to speak with Master Tal'Vayr on such matters. At the core of it, I am a member of a completely different sect. Inner Circle members and Shadows are vastly different. Differences can sometimes cause distrust. Shadows, in particular, have to be prudent about respecting certain boundaries, more so than many others."

Kayla fell silent. His words carried the resonance of a warning. She suspected she was putting him in a difficult position by asking such questions. *Dammit.* She needed information and didn't have time to play these stupid games. At the same time, she was in a whole new arena and still learning the rules.

Kayla scowled. "I really hate the stupid politics in the tower. You know, if people actually put aside all the double-talk and innuendos, we might actually get shit done."

Brant's lips twitched in a smile.

Encouraged, she leaned back in her chair, crossed her arms. "Let's try this another way. I was told the Shadows help protect Inner Circle members. Carl said there's a whole special-elite security division created for you guys." She raised one hand, waving it in a grandiose motion. "You're supposed to be a big deal. The big men on campus."

When he arched an eyebrow, she grinned and continued, "The fact you can shut down my energy is why I don't mind keeping you around. You know I don't like having someone all over my ass, but since we don't want the towers to crumble from an earthquake, you get to stay. But why would you bother sticking around babysitting me if you don't like Inner Circle members?"

"When you're given certain talents or abilities, isn't it your duty to use them?"

She shrugged a shoulder. "Not necessarily. Just because someone *knows* how to make a bomb doesn't mean they *should.*"

"True," he admitted, "but this goes back to the original purpose of the ICS. Our unit was created and given special status within the towers because of our ability to handle adversaries both physically and psychically. My purpose at this moment is to protect you from both yourself and outside sources. However, we were not always utilized as bodyguards."

Kayla's eyebrows arched at this information. "What else did you do?"

Brant lowered his hand, and she noticed his fingers curl into a fist. His eyes hardened ever so slightly. "We were considered 'jailors' by some. When Edwin Tal'Vayr controlled the towers, he used us in that manner. Many Inner Circle members resent our ability to negate energy. That's caused contention between us. How would you feel knowing a Shadow could interrupt your abilities?"

She smirked. "If I remember correctly, I asked you to shut down my energy already. *You* were the one who refused."

His lips curved in a small smile. Wow, maybe he was human after all. "That's only part of the reason you're different, Kayla. You don't rely on your energy to the same degree as other Inner Circle members. They're dependent upon it."

Brant's commlink beeped. He glanced at it and then answered, speaking in short, clipped sentences. He watched her as he spoke, presumably to the head of security. She returned his gaze, only partially listening to his end of the conversation as he outlined the current security surveilling this level. Her thoughts, however, were on their conversation. What Brant had said about the Shadows made sense, but she had the feeling there was more to it. She needed to find out the whole story, but Brant wasn't exactly forthcoming with information.

As he turned back to the computer and continued his conversation, Kayla stood. Her movement caught his attention, and he looked at her expectantly. She resisted the urge to roll her eyes. He was taking this babysitting gig very seriously. She motioned that she was going to get a drink. He gave her a curt nod before focusing again on the terminal in front of him.

She slipped out of the room and headed down the hall, considering her options. The relationship between the Shadows and Inner Circle was somehow significant. She was sure of it.

Sadly, her best and fastest source of information was probably Alec, but she wasn't ready to face him yet. Carl didn't seem to know much about the Shadows, which wasn't entirely unusual. He was just as new to this whole energy thing as she was. He may have grown up in the towers, but the Inner Circle was largely segregated from the general population. In short, they were snobs.

The whole thing with secrets, conspiracies, politics, weird powers... It all just made her want to kick something. They were just more reminders she didn't fit in here. In addition to the emotional turmoil from the earlier scene, exhaustion was creeping in. Unfortunately, the thought of going to sleep wasn't appealing. The attack was still too fresh in her mind. She didn't want to risk something else happening while her guard was down. If they'd come at her head-on with a physical assault she could combat or at least understand, it would be different. But this version of energy-based warfare was beyond her.

Kayla slowed her footsteps as a thought struck her. There might be more information about the Shadows in OmniLab's archives. Brant had mentioned Alec's father earlier, so she had a timeline to use in her search. With a renewed focus, she headed toward her room to set up her equipment. As she turned the corner, Carl's angry voice sounded from their bedroom.

"—find out who's responsible for the attack on Kayla. This entire thing is unacceptable. Someone's gone after her twice today. I find the timing rather suspicious."

There was a pause. Kayla hovered just outside the door and watched his darkened silhouette pace back and forth. He was listening to someone over his commlink. As though sensing her presence, Carl stopped and looked up, the light from the hallway illuminating his features. His frustrated gaze met hers and he sighed.

"Yes. She actually just walked in." He listened for a moment and then snapped the commlink shut. "Is everything okay?"

Kayla cocked her head and walked into the room, closing the door behind her. "Yeah. Someone replaced the video feed, so we don't have anything. Brant's looking into it." She gestured to his commlink. "What was that about? Why do you think the timing is suspicious?"

Carl slid his commlink into his pocket. "Two attacks in one day is a pretty bold move. Based on what I've gathered from Alec, you have three different assailants at work here.

Supposedly, people who can channel multiple types of energy aren't common. So it's likely whoever attacked you tonight wasn't the same person who tried to push you off the beam earlier."

Kayla nodded. She'd already considered the same thing. "Right. We have an Air channeler from earlier, then a Water and Shadow tonight. When I asked Brant about it, he seemed surprised a Shadow would work together with someone from the Inner Circle. He wouldn't say much more than that, so I think it's time to hack into OmniLab's files to get the lowdown on the situation with the Shadows."

He arched an eyebrow. "I'm assuming that means you're avoiding Alec? You could always just ask him for the codes."

She made a face. "Don't give me shit about it. I've had just about all I can handle with this energy crap. I need a break."

He chuckled and took a step toward her, reaching up to tuck her hair behind her ear. His hand slid down and curved around the back of her neck, drawing her closer. A small shiver ran through her at his touch. "I think we can both use a break."

Grateful for the distraction and a chance to firmly cement herself in the physical world, Kayla curled her fingers in Carl's shirt and pulled him down toward her. She closed her eyes at the gentle pressure of Carl's lips on hers but sensed the storm brewing just underneath the surface. Winding her arms around his neck, she gave herself over to the kiss. Even though she no longer felt chilled from the earlier attack, the heat radiating from his body was intoxicating.

There was a hardened edge to his kiss, as though his carefully maintained control was quickly unraveling. Her heart thudded in excitement. She pressed herself against him, wanting to feel him let go completely. The promise and threat of the impending eruption hovered between them.

His hands slid downward, their progress marking her like

a brand searing across her body. He lifted her up, sliding her against his hardening length. In response to his silent demand, she wrapped her legs around his waist. With both hands on her backside, Carl carried her over to the bed and laid her down.

Her mouth went dry at the sight of him yanking his shirt over his head. The man was a gorgeous specimen. She lifted her hands, wanting to feel every spectacular inch of him. He threw his shirt on the floor and captured her wrists with his hand.

Her eyes widened at the intense, heated look on his face. Pinning her hands over her head with one hand, he covered her with his body. One of his legs slid between hers as his free hand moved up her thigh. It slipped under her dress, pushing it upward. She was beginning to understand why Omni women wore them. The access thing was more than convenient.

She hooked her leg over his, wanting to draw him closer. The evidence of his arousal pressed against her, and her head fell back as he began kissing her neck. She let out a soft moan and squeezed her eyes shut at the sensations he evoked. The man seemed to know her body better than she did. His fingers brushed over the silk of her panties and she trembled, craving even more of his touch. She was already damp with arousal.

Kayla arched her back as he dipped his hand inside her panties. His fingers slid through her wetness, teasing her with the promise of everything he offered. She whimpered and rocked against him as he stroked her, begging him to grant the release building within her. When it finally reached a crescendo, she cried out his name and shattered beneath him.

She was still trembling from the intensity of her climax when Carl released her wrists, gathered her in his arms, and murmured her name in her ear. The vibration of his lips against her skin sent little shockwaves through her. He shifted her, hooking his thumb in the waistband of her panties. Anxious to feel him inside her, she lifted her hips to help him slide them downward.

Someone cleared his throat and tapped loudly against the wall. Carl froze. He lifted his head, glaring daggers at the intruder. "You've got to be fucking kidding me."

Kayla twisted so she could see who was standing in the doorway. Brant coughed and averted his gaze to stare at something over their heads. His discomfort was palpable. "Excuse the interruption. The locks were temporarily disengaged as a precaution after what happened earlier. Master Tal'Vayr is in the common room and would like a word with Mistress Rath'Varein."

A laugh bubbled out of Kayla before she could stop it, and she clamped a hand over her mouth. Two minutes later and Brant would have gotten more than an eyeful. Carl swore and readjusted her panties and dress before he stood. She rolled over onto her side, unable to quell another burst of hysterical laughter. The entire situation was so outrageous she couldn't do anything except laugh.

Carl wasn't as amused, but then again, he hadn't grown up in a ruin rat camp where privacy was an unaccustomed luxury. He also hadn't just experienced an earth-shattering orgasm, which had left her pretty damn relaxed.

Carl glared at Brant. "I bet he does, but that's just too damn bad. It's late, and we're entitled to some privacy. He can speak with her tomorrow. And I suggest that next time, you don't just walk in here unless there's an emergency."

Brant winced. It was clear he'd rather be anywhere but there at that moment. "I understand your concerns and will do my best to accommodate them. However, I must insist Mistress Rath'Varein join me in the common room. Master

Tal'Vayr needs to discuss their bond. He's concerned about the possibility of not being able to sense another attack."

The laughter died in her throat. She couldn't catch a break, could she? Kayla threw her arm over her eyes. If she didn't reestablish their communication bond, Alec wouldn't know if someone tried to go after her again. She bit her lip and tried to decide which was worse: the cold chill, or feeling Alec's lover through their bond. It was close, but the cold chill won. She rolled over to stand but paused at the unmasked fury in Carl's expression.

His jaw clenched as he shook his head. "Fuck it. I'm not playing these games. I've had it with this whole damn bond thing. He obviously can't keep her safe."

Carl turned and stormed out into the hallway. Kayla's eyes widened, and she catapulted off the bed to follow him. Carl's temper was like a slow burn. He put up with a lot, but once it ignited, it was time to look out.

Brant was already going after him. Before Carl could reach Alec, Brant tackled him and pushed him against the wall.

"Stand down, Trader. I understand where you're coming from, but don't make me do this."

Carl's eyes narrowed as he shoved Brant back, seeming to welcome the chance to release his anger through physical contact. Brant grabbed him, and the two grappled together. Kayla rushed forward trying to decide if she should intervene or let them duke it out, but a strong pair of arms wrapped around her and pulled her back. She glanced up at Alec's angry expression, but he was focused on the two men fighting.

"Enough!" he ordered in a loud voice. Both men ignored him, slamming into the wall again. Alec issued the command once more, but this time with a sharp sting of air emphasizing his point.

Carl shoved Brant away from him. Both men were

breathing heavily. Carl turned his head, and his eyes narrowed on Alec's arms around Kayla. His voice was cold and contrasted sharply with the fury in his eyes. "I think you need to let her go, don't you?"

Alec immediately released her. Kayla frowned and stepped away, wondering what was going on. Something had changed in the dynamic of the relationship between the two men, and she didn't understand it. She looked back and forth between Carl and Alec.

"What's going on?"

Carl glared at Alec, his fists clenched at his sides. "I'd like to know that too. I agreed to help keep Kayla here to protect her. That's obviously not working. Until you plug some of these leaks and get the situation in the towers straightened out, she's not going to be safe. I'm beginning to think it might be best if we went underground for a while."

Kayla blinked and tried to figure out if she'd just heard him right. She held up her hand. "Whoa. Wait a fucking minute. You agreed to help *keep* me here?"

Carl paused. His jaw worked, and a flicker of some emotion flashed in his eyes. He didn't answer.

Her gaze whipped back and forth between the two men. It all made sense now. The conspiratorial looks, Alec's suppression of their bond, Carl sneaking out of bed to speak with Alec...

"You bastards," she whispered, taking a step backward. The betrayal cut deep, especially after everything Carl had said about supporting her decisions. "You two just decided what's best for me and were working together to manipulate me into doing whatever the hell you wanted? Instead of talking to me and letting me make my own decisions, you're once again trying to control me?"

Carl cursed under his breath and ran a hand through his unbound hair in agitation. "No, it wasn't like that." He took a step toward her, exhaustion etched on his face. "Sweetheart, we almost lost you. I can't stand by and go through that again. Both of us want to protect you, and we agreed to work together to make that happen. You have my word that I'm not trying to control you. Yes, we thought it would be safer if you were here in the towers, but neither of us ever intended to force you into anything. Alec and I don't always agree, and sometimes it's a fine line to walk, but both of us know how much your independence means to you. You'll always have the final say in every decision."

Kayla looked over at Alec. His expression was pained, but he nodded in agreement. She turned back to Carl and bit her lip. Their alliance was doing weird things to her system, and she didn't quite know what to think about it. She'd considered going back to the surface after being released from the medical ward, but she'd been so distracted with everything else going on. It was obvious now that the distractions had been intentional.

Sheesh. Was she *that* predictable? All they had to do was dangle some prototypes from Research and Development in front of her nose and she'd follow them around anywhere. Or better yet, let's allow Kayla to build a home for the ruin rats and she'll stay safe and secure in the towers. She shook her head, disgusted with herself.

Even so, she wasn't sure it was a good idea to leave just yet. There were too many strange things happening within the towers, and she needed to find out who was targeting her and Alec. The sooner they cleared up the mysteries, the quicker things could get back to normal. After her last falling out with Carl, though, she needed to make sure they were on the same page. "Are you serious about wanting to go back to the surface?"

Carl hesitated and glanced at Alec before shaking his head. "No, not yet. It's a tempting thought to take you away from everything, but there are more risks out there. Until we get a handle on everything with Lars and the Coalition, you're safest here. I don't like it much, but it's probably for the best. Besides, Alec recalled the trader camps earlier tonight. Veridian and everyone else are heading here in the morning. If anyone can help find out who's trying to hurt you, it's those guys."

"That should make things interesting," she murmured, considering the implications. Having a bunch of semi-reformed ruin rats running around the towers would definitely stir up more trouble than OmniLab realized. But it would make it easier to turn the advantage in her direction. With everyone's combined skillsets, they could help solve the puzzle of the attacks within the towers.

Kayla rubbed her temples, warning off the beginning of a headache. "Look, I get it. I do. You're both feeling protective, but you need to back off and stop trying to make decisions for me." She lifted her head to meet their gazes. "I'll stay in the towers for now, but I won't tolerate you two conspiring against me. No more secrets. If you don't trust me enough to make my own decisions, we have a bigger problem than Lars and the Coalition."

Carl relented first and nodded. He crossed over to her and brushed a kiss against her hair. When she leaned against him, he put his arm around her. "Fair enough. I won't ever force you into anything, Kayla. You may drive me crazy sometimes, but I won't ever try to take away your free will."

Kayla turned her head to meet Alec's gaze. His eyes were guarded, but she could see the sadness and longing in them. She reached for him with her energy threads and felt his eager acceptance when they brushed against him. A rush of relief and love flooded through their bond at the contact. She closed her eyes at the onslaught of emotions before he tapered them back.

"He's right, love. Carl's shown me how much you need your freedom. I'll do my best to honor that, but I can't make any promises. Perhaps I'm a lesser man, but I'd rather have you hate me for trying to protect you than to risk losing you."

Kayla swallowed and leaned her head against Carl's chest, not believing either one of them to be lesser in any way. There was no doubt in her mind they would do anything to protect her. They might have different ideas about the best way to do that, but their intentions came from their hearts.

Kayla pulled away from Carl and walked over to Alec, reaching up to put her arms around him. He swallowed and jerked his head up to look at Carl. The stunned look on Alec's face was almost comical. She ignored his surprise, leaning against him in a long-overdue embrace while Alec's arms wrapped around her as though she were a fragile piece of glass. She stood on her toes and brushed a light kiss against his lips.

"You'll never be a lesser man in my mind, Alec. Just keep your 'distractions' away from our bond. It's icky."

His lips twitched in a smile, and his eyes shone with emotion. He gave her a small nod of understanding. With a smile, she stepped back and reached for Carl's hand. Without another word, she turned away and led Carl back to the bedroom. It was only after she'd left the room that she realized it was the first time she'd ever reached out to Alec without him using energy to entice her.

CHAPTER SIX

A LIGHT TAPPING on the door woke Kayla the next morning. She cursed the person and their mother in the most colorful language she could manage before burying her head back under the blankets. A swirl of cold air hit her as Carl's weight shifted off the bed. She grumbled and scooted over to suck up the warmth from his abandoned spot.

Muffled voices reached her through the blanketed cocoon, and she squeezed her eyes shut, trying to burrow into the bed even deeper. It was too early to wake up. Everyone needed to go away. Between the metabolic booster that was messing with her system and the entire ordeal from earlier, sleep hadn't come easily. She'd spent the majority of the night trying to hack into OmniLab's sealed records. Sure, it would have been easier to pester Alec for the access codes so she could read up about the Shadows, but where was the fun in that? Unfortunately, with the heightened security, they'd put safeguards on top of the safeguards. Carl had finally managed to lure her away from the computer sometime just before dawn.

On the plus side, she'd managed to finish looking at the

Research and Development files. It wasn't as much fun as hanging from the rafters, but she was still able to improve some of the prototype designs. Her lips twitched in a smile. That scientist wouldn't know what hit him.

Uh oh. Maybe he's already seen the schematics and that's why they're knocking.

"—appointment with a water channeler this morning to begin training. If a Water was responsible for the attack, this may help circumvent any future attacks while she's sleeping," Brant said.

She lowered the blanket enough to peek over the top. Carl's back was facing her, and he'd only bothered to throw on a pair of pants before answering the door. Damn. The man had a great ass. She wanted to run her hands down his back and tug those pants—

Carl turned around. When he saw her watching him, he raised an eyebrow. "What do you think?"

Kayla blinked. Yep. She'd definitely missed something. She frowned, trying to clear her head of the sleep and lust-induced fog. She had all sorts of thoughts, but most of them gravitated toward him climbing back in bed with her. Her gaze roamed over his body as she bit her lip. How the hell did the man get to be so yummy?

"Uh, sorry. I was distracted and didn't catch that."

His eyes warmed, his mouth twitching slightly. He knew exactly what she'd been thinking. Turning back to Brant at the door, he said, "Give us a few minutes."

The door slid shut, and Carl turned around to face her. With a determined look, he stalked toward her. Her eyes widened as he crawled up the bed and caged her in his arms, his loose hair brushing against her cheek as he bent down to kiss her.

"Brant and Alec want to start your training this morning. What do you think?"

Kayla pushed away the blanket to reach for him. His gaze drifted downward, following the line of the blanket to her exposed skin. The heat in his eyes was instantaneous. She loved the effect she had on him.

"I think it would be more fun to stay in bed with you all morning."

He wrapped his arms around her and rolled over so she was sprawled on top of him. She laughed as their limbs tangled in the blankets.

"We can do whatever you want, sweetheart," he said, tucking her hair behind her ear.

Kayla propped herself up on an elbow to look down at him and trailed her hand along the contours of his muscular chest to his abdomen. It was moments like these that were the most precious. The love and desire in his eyes was the motivation she needed to keep fighting. In all honesty, the depth of her feelings for him frightened her. She'd been schooled not to open herself to such deep emotions, but she hadn't been able to resist him. Carl touched a part of her no one else had ever come close to reaching. It made her even more determined to find the unknown zap-happy freaks threatening them and fry their databanks. She wouldn't lose Carl or what they shared together.

"I'm going to go train. I want to learn how to kick some energy ass. Then, I want to come back here and celebrate by spending several hours getting naked with you."

He laughed. It was such a great sound— husky and warm at the same time. His eyes danced with amusement. "I fully support that idea." He reached up to cup her face and pressed a kiss against her lips. "I'm going to head down to see Director Borshin and get a status update. Veridian and the rest of the crew should be here by the time you're finished." His expression turned more serious. "Will you be okay training with Brant and Alec? If you want me to go with you, I can."

Kayla shook her head. Even with everything they shared, she still felt uncomfortable using her energy around him. It was a part of herself that was still too new. Until she understood more of that aspect of herself and had it under control, she was determined to protect him from it.

"No, it's fine. I'll catch up with you later."

———

KAYLA LOOKED down at the diaphanous coral-colored cover-up dress and frowned. When Seara had insisted she wear it over what looked like undergarments, she'd laughed. It didn't cover up anything. Half the time these Omnis were so prudish that she was amazed they still procreated naturally. The rest of the time they wore things that made her wonder why they bothered wearing anything at all. She wasn't sure she'd ever understand the logic.

Seara adjusted the strap and took a step back to survey her work. "Once you get to the pool area, you can remove the dress. You don't swim in it. You can slip it back on when you're finished."

Kayla's head jerked up. "What? Swim?"

Seara's hand fluttered to her mouth, her eyes widening. "Oh my. You've never been swimming, have you?"

Kayla shook her head, feeling more than a little anxiety about submerging herself in water. They didn't really want her to do that, did they? Until they'd discovered the river, she'd never even seen a large body of water except on a vidviewer.

Seara brushed off the concerns. "I wouldn't worry about it. You only need to touch the water, and Alec won't let anything happen to you. Not only that, but Ariana Alivette will be the one working with you on water energy. I was surprised Alec asked her after..." Seara glanced away, a small frown on her lips. "Well, let's just say I was surprised. It was a good decision though. I think you'll like Ariana. Not only is she a remarkable young woman, she's a highly skilled water channeler too."

"Yeah, that's what Brant told me earlier," Kayla said and stepped away from the mirrored glass. It was strange having Seara dress her like some sort of doll. "He said she's beyond reproach and couldn't be the Water channeler responsible for what happened last night."

Seara picked up a pair of sandals and handed them to Kayla. "He's right. It's not in Ariana's nature. You'll be safe with her, especially with Alec there." As Kayla slipped on the shoes, Seara started to turn away but paused. "You're all right after what happened last night, aren't you? You weren't hurt?"

Kayla frowned. She'd forgotten about Seara's strong reaction to the energy attack and the woman hanging on Alec. "I'm fine. It wasn't pleasant, but Alec was able to stop it. I don't want to go through it again, but it's done."

Seara opened her mouth to say something but stopped and nodded instead. "I'm glad Alec was close enough to sense your distress through your bond and was able to help you." She lowered her gaze and murmured, "Sometimes, I wonder if this bond between you two is truly a blessing. I don't understand why Fate would put you two together unless you were meant to be. I have to believe there's some grand purpose in all of it."

Kayla lifted her head at her mother's words. There was the whole Fate thing again. Before she could consider it further, there was a knock on the door.

Seara appeared to shake off whatever thoughts had been plaguing her and pressed the button to open the door. Alec stepped inside and froze at the sight of Kayla. His eyes flared with heat as he slowly scanned her up and down. When he finished, he met her gaze and swallowed. She felt her skin flush from the rush of desire that escaped through their bond.

He embraced her energy and their bond in the gentlest of caresses, but she felt him struggling to hold back. A pained look crossed his features as he took a deep breath. Kayla hesitated, frustrated that she couldn't read him completely. She took a step toward him, putting her hand on his arm. Contact seemed to strengthen their bond and made it a little easier to read him. She understood the desire, but there was something else troubling him.

"Alec, what's wrong?"

He put his hand over hers and glanced at Seara with a frown. "Apparently, your mother has made it her mission to test the limits of my willpower by dressing you in such a manner." He sighed and gazed once more into her eyes. The deep-blue was hypnotizing, and she wondered what it would be like to get lost in their depths. "You're irresistible, love."

Seara sniffed, dabbed at her eyes with a handkerchief, and waved them off. "Go. Ignore me. I'm just feeling sentimental. I'll see you two later."

Alec raised an eyebrow but followed her instructions and led Kayla out of her family's quarters. When they exited, Brant fell into step behind them and followed them down the corridor. It gave a whole new meaning to the word "shadow."

Kayla looked over at Alec. "Is something going on with Seara? She's been acting different."

Alec sighed. "She's been like that ever since the Coalition abducted you. I've tried to talk to her about it without much success. The latest attacks on you haven't helped matters. She's worried about you and angry with me."

Kayla's brow furrowed. "Angry with you? Why?"

Alec's mouth formed a thin line. "I'm not performing my

duty as your bonded mate. Our relationship is highly unconventional, and it worries her."

She halted in her tracks, putting her hands on her hips. "Excuse me? What *duties* are we talking about here?"

Alec glanced around. The corridor was currently empty, but she could tell he didn't want anyone to overhear the conversation. She took his arm again, and he led her further down the hall, switching to their silent form of communication.

"When two Drac'Kin bond, both mates are usually committed to each other and stay close to one another. In addition to sharing energy between them, they protect each other from harm. I haven't protected you as well as I should have."

Kayla shook her head. It wasn't Alec's job to protect her. Besides, their bond was an accident. Even though she cared deeply for Alec, Carl was the one who owned her heart completely.

"Maybe I should talk to her."

Alec gave her hand a reassuring squeeze. *"That's not necessary. I spoke with her earlier this morning. She was angry about the situation with Brianna and worried you'd leave the towers again."* He paused for a moment, and she felt his uncertainty like a prickle against her skin. *"She's right to be angry with me. I need to apologize for what happened yesterday. I believe Brianna was hoping to make you jealous. She—"*

Kayla held up her hand, cutting him off. She didn't want to think about him with another woman. She knew it was wrong to feel possessive, especially given the situation with Carl, but there were limits. In this instance, ignorance really was bliss. *"I don't want to know. What you do in your spare time is your business."*

Alec stopped walking and turned to look at her. He searched her expression, and the love that shone in his eyes staggered her. *"She never should have touched our bond. I* don't want to be responsible for you even feeling a moment of discomfort. You're precious to me, Kayla."

Her heart fluttered at his words, and she cursed herself for it. She might not want to know about his affairs, but she didn't know what to do with his declaration of feelings either. She loved him—there was no doubt in her mind—but she loved Carl too.

He pressed a finger to her lips to prevent her from saying anything. *"I care about you more than you'll ever know, Kayla Rath'Varein. But I have no expectations. I want you in my life, but right now, I know you need to be with Carl."*

She paused, wondering if she'd heard him right. Was this why he'd been tamping down on their bond and not pushing her with energy? Was he was trying to give her what she wanted?

He gave her a sad smile and nodded. *"You're lost and trying to figure out how to fit into this new world. Carl gives you strength. I'll always be here for you, but I haven't earned the right to be your support. One day, that may change, but for now, I know you need him. I told him, just as I'm telling you, that I won't attempt to interfere in your relationship. But I won't give up hope that one day you'll accept our bond and me."*

"Alec," she whispered, and her eyes welled with tears, overcome by the strong emotions flooding through their bond. She blinked, trying to hold back her tears as she threw herself into his arms. A wave of gratitude and relief rushed through her. The fact Alec understood and was willing to accept her decision to stay with Carl lifted a weight off her shoulders.

She loved him. Despite her reservations, it *was* possible to love two men at once. It wasn't the same as the love she felt for Carl, but her feelings for Alec were undeniable. She'd somehow managed to fall in love with both of them. Yes, she'd chosen to remain with Carl, but it didn't change the intense feelings she had for Alec. They were both so different and represented two vastly different worlds. There was always a balance in life. Was it possible she was close to finding hers? She couldn't imagine her life without both of them in it, just like it was impossible for her to imagine not living on the surface or being part of OmniLab. Both aspects were now an integral part of her identity.

Alec was wrong about Carl being the one who gave her strength though. They both did. They both challenged her in different ways. The realization caused something inside her to ease. She needed both men in her life.

"You have both of us, love. We'll both do what we can to help you find the balance you need. No one understands the need for balance more than a Drac'Kin. That's why we're drawn to our counter elements."

Kayla lifted her head to look up at him, captivated by the sincerity in his eyes. She'd never been good with words; it was only with actions that she felt comfortable sharing her feelings. Kayla stood on her toes and pressed a small kiss against his lips. It wasn't a goodbye kiss or even the promise of something more. It was a kiss between two people forced together by Fate who had found strength in their freedom to choose. As she melted against him and he wrapped his arms around her to draw her closer, a voice interrupted them.

"Well, well. If you're trying to stir up more gossip, this is definitely a good start."

Alec tightened his arms around her and lifted his head. Kayla turned to see a tall, dark-haired man and woman with similar features standing a few feet away.

"Jason," Alec said in lieu of a greeting, although the cadence of his voice lent the impression he wasn't happy to see the man.

The corner of Jason's mouth twisted upward in a small smirk. "It's good to see you too, Alec. Some of the Circle members were wondering where you've been hiding. After seeing that little scene, though, I'd say the mystery is solved."

His eyes fixed on Kayla, and she was taken aback by their color. They were the palest of silvery-gray. His hair was cut short, but it was long enough it had started to curl slightly and gave him a boyish appeal. The darkness of his hair only served to accentuate the mirrored luminosity of his eyes. He was probably one of the most beautiful men she'd ever seen, although in her mind, Carl still won out in that department.

As though aware of the effect he usually generated, he gave her a sly grin and lifted her hand. Holding her gaze, he brushed a kiss on the back of her palm. A teasing trace of cool energy caressed her almost intimately, and she shivered at the sensation, her lips parting on a gasp.

Alec gripped her midsection possessively and pulled her away. Kayla glanced up at Alec's furious expression. "You're crossing a line, Jason. She's still being trained."

Jason's eyes shone with amusement as he laughed. "You're one to talk, Alec. You decided to stake your claim within days of meeting her." His eyes roamed over her again, this time with undeniable interest. "I can't say I blame you if she responds to that small of an energy pulse. I can only imagine how she must be in the throes of passion."

Kayla's eyes narrowed. Without stopping to consider what she was doing, she hurled a large pulse of energy at him. Pretty boy or not, she'd dealt with egotistical assholes her entire life. It was best to smack them down immediately and establish firm lines before they got out of hand.

Jason stumbled back and landed on his ass, his expression a mixture of shock and disbelief. The woman behind him gasped and took an uncertain step backward. Alec swore and pulled Kayla behind him, weaving a band of protective energy around her. Brant stepped forward to intervene, but Alec shook his head.

"I've got her."

Like hell he did. Kayla jerked away from Alec and put her hands on her hips, still feeling his tightly-woven energy around her. He was either trying to prevent her from launching another attack or trying to protect her from potential retaliation. She probed at Alec's shield, searching for weak spots. She didn't like being imprisoned in any capacity.

Jason threw his head back and laughed, drawing her attention back to him. He looked up at her from where he was sitting on the floor and grinned. "I'll be damned. I saw that little display at the council meeting, but I thought it might have been a fluke." He glanced at Alec and gave him an approving nod. "I like her. She won't put up with any of the bullshit the Inner Circle hands out."

Alec glanced at Kayla again, the corners of his lips twitching. "No, she won't."

Jason stood, brushed off his pants, and walked over to Kayla. "Let's try this again. This time, I'll behave." He held out his hand in greeting. "I'm Jason Alivette. It's nice to meet you."

Kayla cocked her head and felt Alec's protective energy shield fall away. With a quick glance at Alec to find him giving her an encouraging nod, she took Jason's offered hand. He gave it a small squeeze before releasing it and gesturing to the woman standing behind him.

"This is my sister, Ariana."

Kayla looked at the gorgeous woman who had remained silent until now. She was a feminine version of her brother with silvery eyes and long, dark hair wound into elaborate braids, but there was a quiet serenity surrounding her. She was tall and slender, with a delicate, ethereal beauty. She still seemed apprehensive about approaching, but the smile she gave Kayla contained genuine warmth.

Kayla was momentarily taken aback because Ariana was

so far removed from most of the other Inner Circle members she'd met. Intricate waves of calming energy seemed to emanate from her, deceptively subtle in their power. It was tantalizing, alluring, and unlike any other form of energy Kayla had seen in the towers.

Not only that, but Alec seemed just as drawn to the strange energy coming from the woman. Although she couldn't pick up much from him through their bond, Kayla sensed a lingering regret and sense of protectiveness for the dark-haired woman. Despite herself, it made Kayla even more curious about her.

"Ariana," Alec murmured, his eyes softening as he gazed at her. "It's wonderful to see you again." He stepped forward, taking both her hands in his, and kissed her cheek. Kayla sensed their energy touch in a familiar greeting, but there wasn't the intrusiveness she'd experience with Brianna. Instead, there was only the sensation of a cool energy wave floating just out of reach of their bond as though acknowledging and respecting the boundary. Ariana beamed up at him and then directed her smile at Kayla.

Alec turned back to Kayla. "Ariana is a skilled water channeler. She's agreed to display some of the intricacies of channeling water energy."

Jason cleared his throat. "Alec, if you're interested in a display, I have some time this morning. I can show her a few things."

Alec stiffened. "That won't be necessary."

"Afraid of a little competition?" Jason wiggled his eyebrows and gave Alec a teasing smirk. He turned to Kayla and added, "My sister is quite talented, but if you want to experience the full potential of our abilities, I'm your man."

The double meaning in his words didn't escape her, and she crossed her arms. It was tempting to drop him back on his ass. Alec, on the other hand, was regarding the other man thoughtfully. After a long moment, the High Council leader inclined his head.

"Very well. Your assistance would be welcome, provided you give your word that anything discussed today will remain between us."

Jason paused for a moment, as though surprised by Alec's acquiescence. "You have me intrigued. Of course, you have my word."

Alec looked over at Ariana and she nodded. Her voice, when she finally spoke, had a soft, musical tone. "You have mine too, Alec. I would never betray your trust."

Alec nodded, giving Ariana a warm smile. "Thank you. Kayla will need more than a demonstration. You're two of the most skilled water channelers within the towers. Jason, you in particular can help with a problem. Kayla needs to learn how to manipulate water energy enough to defend herself against potential attacks."

Jason's brow furrowed. The teasing smirk that seemed to be one of his trademarks fell away, and he frowned. "She's not a water channeler. I sensed fire energy when she blasted me."

Alec shook his head. "That's only because it's your counter element." He glanced down at Kayla. "Go ahead and make a small connection with him. Send a small pulse of energy so he can see what I'm talking about. He won't believe it otherwise."

She hesitated. Ever since Lars had forced a connection, the thought of forging more connections made her uneasy. Alec gave her a reassuring squeeze and said, *"I won't allow anyone to hurt you. Trust me."*

Right. Trust him. This relying-on-other-people crap wasn't easy. Taking a deep breath, Kayla reached out with her energy threads and felt Jason eagerly accept the contact. Goose bumps broke out over her skin as the coolness of the connection settled over her. It wasn't an unpleasant sensation, just different. At his expectant look, she steeled herself and sent him a long, steady pulse of energy.

She could not only feel his response but could see his reaction as her energy hit him. He inhaled sharply and took a few steps toward her. Disconcerted by his response, Kayla immediately ceased the flow. He stared at her with a look of awe and longing, lifting his hand as though to touch her.

"Jason," Alec said, warning in his voice.

A wide smile crossed Jason's face as his gaze darted back and forth between them. "She's exquisite, Alec. Other than with Ari, I've never felt anything quite like that before. How is this possible?"

"She's a spirit channeler."

Ariana gasped, staring at Kayla with a look of wonder and hope. "I thought I sensed something similar to my own energy signature, but I wasn't sure what it was. May I form a connection with you, Kayla?"

Kayla stiffened. She was curious about Ariana's words, but there was no way in hell she was going to become some little toy they passed around like a novelty.

Alec, sensing her irritation, hesitated and then shook his head. "I believe you're right, Ari. That's part of the reason I asked you to come. However, it would be best to limit Kayla's number of connections until she learns more about our ways. She's had some bad experiences."

Ariana studied Kayla, obviously troubled by Alec's words, but nodded in agreement. "Of course. Please let me know if there's any way I can help."

"Thank you, but I think Kayla just needs time." Alec then took Kayla's hand and threaded their fingers together before turning back to Jason. "Now you understand why I want to keep this information contained. Only a few people know of Kayla's talent. You both can relate to these special circumstances better than most. It'll eventually come out, but I'd like to make sure she has more training before it becomes public knowledge."

Jason and Ariana exchanged looks and nodded. Jason turned back to Kayla, sweeping his gaze over her again. She shivered as he explored their forged connection with the slightest pulse of energy. His touch was light and playful but not threatening. "Well, Alec, several of us wondered whether or not you two really intended to bond. Brianna was telling people it was all for show at that council meeting. That's not the case, though, is it?"

Alec's hand tightened around hers, his eyes narrowing. The bond between them flared to life as he severed the lingering connection between her and Jason with a quick shove.

Kayla gasped. She had no idea he could do that.

"Make no mistake," Alec warned, taking a threatening step toward the other man, "Kayla Rath'Varein is my bonded mate. I will not tolerate any disrespect to her or any attempts to manipulate our bond."

Jason raised his hands and chuckled. "Understood. My apologies." With another long look at Kayla, he muttered, "You're a lucky bastard, Alec."

Ariana gave her brother a disapproving look. "I apologize for my brother, Kayla. You'd think he'd know better by now, but it appears he's decided to give our family a bad name with his poor behavior." When Jason merely shrugged, Ariana turned to Alec. "It might be best to go into the pool room and begin the lesson. I think Jason could use a little cooling off, and I'm sure Kayla would actually like to learn something about our ways."

Alec nodded. "Let's begin."

———

CARL STUDIED his commlink while he waited in line for the replicator to finish restructuring molecules to manufacture a cup of coffee. A woman placed the beverage in front of him, and he murmured his thanks. Taking the drink, he turned away and continued reading the message from Jinx. She'd detailed a list of canceled supply deliveries and the camps associated with them. As he'd suspected, Kayla's former camp was on the list of those not receiving their needed supplies. He needed to speak with Alec again or Kayla might be inclined to do something hot-headed and dangerous.

An incoming message caught his attention. He pressed the earbud into his ear and accepted the call.

"Carl? This is Elyot. We just arrived in the towers, and we're getting set up. I know you're busy, but I was hoping to have a chance to speak with you privately about Lisia. Do you think I could get in to see her?"

Carl hesitated before answering the man's request. Lisia was still being held in the prison ward within the towers. OmniLab hadn't yet issued sentencing for her involvement in Kayla's abduction. Based on the daily reports from his camp and Cruncher's comments, Elyot had been having a difficult time coping with his sister's betrayal and imprisonment. Despite himself, Carl felt a wave of pity for the man. Lisia was his only family, and even though her actions were misguided, ruin rat loyalties ran deep.

OmniLab would never allow Elyot access to the prison without Carl accompanying him. The thought of seeing the woman who'd betrayed him wasn't appealing, but he couldn't hold that against Elyot. He needed to remember the former ruin rat hadn't been responsible for his sister's actions.

"I'll see what I can do, but I can't make any promises. I have some time before my next appointment. Where can I meet you?"

"I'm in the basement area outside the main hall. All the

trading camps are arriving so it's a little crazy down here. I can meet you in one of the empty conference rooms on this level. Can you come to..." There was a muffled pause as Elyot spoke with someone else. "Room C-12? Do you know where that is?"

Carl agreed and disconnected the call. He slipped his commlink back into his pocket before heading downstairs.

The basement area was more than packed by the time he arrived, heavily congested with the influx of new arrivals from the trading camps. Carl navigated through the crowded corridor, nodding greetings to people he recognized, and then headed down one of the lesser used hallways. He located the conference room and stepped inside to find Elyot sitting on the far side of the room. The defeated look on the ruin rat's face tugged at Carl's sympathies.

"Elyot? Sorry it took me a while. It looks like all the camps arrived at the same time. I didn't see Cruncher and everyone else yet. Do you know where our camp is setting up?"

At the sound of Carl's voice, the scavenger lifted his head. He grimaced and quickly looked away. Carl frowned at the strange behavior and took another step into the room.

"What's going on?"

When Elyot didn't reply and merely shook his head, Carl's apprehension grew. Something wasn't right.

"I apologize for the subterfuge, Carl. We didn't know how else to get you alone. I needed to have a private word with you," a woman's voice sounded from behind him.

He spun around to find Miranda and Lars were both in the room, moving to block the exit. Carl took a step backward and pulled out his commlink to warn Alec, but he never got the chance.

Lars lifted his hand, and with a flick of his wrist, a swift wind knocked the device from Carl's grasp. Fuck that. He wasn't going to play with these assholes. Carl threw his drink in Lars's direction and rushed him. Before he could make contact, the liquid froze, suspended in midair.

The sight of the frozen droplets and Miranda's raised hands caused Carl to hesitate for a fraction of a second. Unfortunately, that was all the time Lars needed. With another wave of his hand, a strong gust of wind shoved Carl across the room and slammed him into the wall with a *thud*.

Carl grunted at the impact but pushed away from the wall, ready for round two. Miranda shook her head. "Please, Carl, we don't wish to harm you. We only want to speak with you."

Miranda lowered her hand and the contents of his drink fell to the ground in a harmless puddle. Carl eyed the two renegade Omnis warily, not trusting them for a second. He glanced at Elyot and wondered what they'd promised him in exchange for this deception.

As though sensing the direction of Carl's thoughts, Elyot shook his head. "I'm sorry for tricking you, Carl. You know OmniLab won't ever release Lisia. I can't just leave her here. I know she's troubled, but the Coalition has offered to give her a place with them. Lars and Miranda just wanted to meet and talk to you. I think if Lisia just gets away and has a chance to start over, things will be better."

"He's right," Miranda agreed, taking a step closer. "We know about your relationship with Kayla and the forced bond with Alec. We have a way of removing their bond, but we need your help to do it."

Carl's eyes narrowed, amazed they had the audacity to ask him for help when Lars had nearly killed Kayla a few days ago. "I have no reason to believe or trust you. Your buddy here shoved a knife into Kayla. You can both go to hell."

Lars arched an eyebrow. "Yet you would trust Alec? From my understanding, her injury wasn't serious. Alec had a medic to her in minutes. She's already up, running around the towers and... I suppose you could say, 'hanging from the rafters.'"

Carl clenched his fists and took a threatening step forward. "If you had anything to do with her almost falling..."

"On the contrary," Lars admitted and held up a hand, interrupting Carl's threat. "I need both you and Kayla. We were not responsible for her... sudden fall from grace. Although, we may be able to point you in the right direction if you wish to find the culprit."

A chill filled Carl at the realization that someone else in the towers had been responsible. He glanced over at his abandoned commlink on the ground. Lars, observing his focus, shook his head and reached down to pick up the device.

"You won't be needing this. You'll have a chance to contact Kayla, but not quite yet." He studied the device for a moment before slipping it into his pocket. When he lifted his head to look at Carl again, his eyes were filled with purposeful intent. "Tell me, Trader, where is your precious Kayla right now? Do you really think Alec is sitting back and not taking advantage of every moment alone with her? All he has to do is send a small pulse of energy in her direction and she won't be able to resist him."

When Carl's entire body went rigid, Miranda touched Lars's arm and shook her head in warning. In a softer tone, she said, "He's right, Carl. Nothing is permanent, not even their so-called permanent bond. Alec is using Kayla and their bond to enhance his own abilities. He wants the power, both from her energy and her social position as Andrei Rath'Varein's daughter." She took a small step forward and clasped her hands together, her eyes pleading with him to listen. "It was obvious to all of us how deeply Kayla cares for you. I've never witnessed such raw pain as when she thought you'd been killed. If we don't remove the bond between them, you're going to lose her to Alec. It's just a matter of time."

Carl flexed his fingers, forcing them to relax. He needed to keep his cool and remember they were trying to manipulate his emotions. While the logical side of him knew this, he couldn't help but wonder at Miranda's words. He'd never agree to help them, but the thought that there might be a way to sever the bond gave him hope of a life with Kayla without Alec's influence. "What do you mean?"

"Every day that passes, she'll want him more and more. You may have already seen it for yourself in the small touches and looks between them." When Carl didn't respond, Miranda nodded in understanding. "So it's already begun. You have to understand, Carl, the energy is addicting and intoxicating. It'll only worsen with time. If we're going to remove the bond, we need to do it soon. The longer they're together and the closer they become, the more difficult it will be to eliminate."

Carl's jaw clenched. On some level, he knew she was right. Something had already changed between Kayla and Alec. He'd seen the way she'd begun looking at the High Council leader. He'd been concerned at first, except Kayla hadn't changed the way she behaved toward him. If anything, she'd given Carl the impression her feelings for him had deepened too. Just recalling her response to him that morning quelled any concerns he had about losing her to the charismatic council leader.

He'd be lying if he said that part of him wasn't tempted by what Miranda offered, but it was more than simply not trusting the renegades. If Kayla truly wanted to be with Alec, Carl wouldn't stand in her way. It would devastate him to lose her, and he might seriously consider hurting Alec, but loving someone meant putting their wants and needs above your own. He'd promised to never take away Kayla's free will, and he wouldn't start now. He loved her too much to ever clip her wings.

Carl shook his head. "If you came to me with hopes I would force Kayla into something, you have the wrong man. If what you're saying is true, this has to be Kayla's choice. She might be open to severing their bond, but I won't push her into anything. If she decides to be with Alec, I'll accept it."

Miranda lowered her head in disappointment and sighed. "Then if you won't help us, I'm afraid we can't help you."

Before Carl could respond, Lars flicked his wrist and sent a small device flying. Carl flinched at the sharp prick against his neck. His hand flew up, clamping around the small cylindrical object and yanking it out, but it was too late. Numbness was already beginning to spread through his body. He stumbled against the conference table as his legs stopped supporting his weight. His arms were clumsy in their movements and refused to cooperate.

Elyot jumped up and rushed over to help him. His furious gaze darted back and forth between Lars and Miranda. "What are you doing? You said he wouldn't be hurt."

Lars stepped forward and motioned Elyot aside. "There's been a change in plans. If you want our help in freeing your sister, you'll keep your mouth shut and do as you're told. We can't have him reporting us to security. As it is, we're nearly out of time. Our contact said they could only circumvent the scanners in this area for thirty minutes."

When Elyot backed away, Lars checked Carl's responsiveness and turned back to his female companion. "Are you satisfied, Miranda? You saw Kayla's reaction when he was threatened. What made you think he was any less devoted?"

Miranda refused to meet his gaze and adjusted her jacket. "I had to try. Kayla was right. Too many people have been hurt already."

Lars's blue eyes were almost eerily cold. "Focus, Miranda.

Lay the blame where it's deserved. Once Alec is dealt with, we can put an end to all of this. All we need to do is lure Kayla to the surface. Carl can help with that, willing or not."

Miranda gave Carl a pitying look and turned away. "Fine. Let's get out of here."

Carl's eyes widened, and he struggled to call out or get someone's attention. Whatever drug they had injected worked fast. He was fully aware but unable to move or do anything more than blink. Lars motioned for Elyot to help him drag Carl over to a conveyor cart. As they lifted him inside and covered it, Carl squeezed his eyes shut. The moment Kayla found out he was missing, she'd go rushing into danger to try to save him. He needed to warn her. Somehow.

CHAPTER SEVEN

"YOU HAVE to bring her to the party later, Alec. You can't keep this gorgeous creature locked up. Although, I can't say I blame you for it," Jason teased.

Kayla laughed and swatted him with her towel. Now that she'd gotten to know him better, she actually liked him. With his flirting and teasing, Jason reminded her of some ruin rats. He didn't mean anything by it, but she suspected he wouldn't be opposed if she expressed an interest in something more. He was relatively harmless though. She'd learned quite a bit from him and Ariana about channeling energy. She had no idea their talents were so diverse.

They'd spent the past couple of hours in the pool. After getting over her initial shock at submerging herself in such a large amount of water, they'd taught her the basics of manipulating water energy. She still needed a lot of practice, but she was beginning to get the hang of differentiating between the different types of energy.

Jason was a wizard at offensive and defensive strategies, but it was clear Ariana excelled at the more nuanced water channeling abilities. Together, they were a formidable team.

They were also as different as night and day. Kayla now understood Seara's comments about Ariana and had to admit her mother was right. Ariana was one of the few Omnis she'd met who wasn't pompous and egotistical. She couldn't help but like the young woman. In fact, Ariana's nature and temperament reminded her quite a bit of Seara. There was a soothing serenity about her that drew Kayla in. Ariana's energy was still markedly different from anything she'd experienced so far. It was almost as though Ariana's energy had an additional component her brother's lacked.

Ariana stepped out of the pool, looking like a dark-haired water goddess emerging from the sea. She took the towel her brother held out and wrapped it around herself. "That's a wonderful idea. Oh, Alec, please bring her. It won't be a large gathering, so it would be a great opportunity for Kayla to get to know just a few of us without being overwhelmed." She smiled at Kayla and added, "I don't know how much Alec told you, but I can somewhat relate to your experiences. Until recently, I hadn't had much interaction with anyone outside the Inner Circle. Sometimes, when I meet new people, it's hard to remember not to introduce myself with energy like I would with others of our kind."

Jason grinned. "She's right. It's led to some rather humorous moments when she sits there waiting for someone to respond to her energy greeting. We tend to use energy to express emotions even in casual conversation. It's second nature to us."

Intrigued by Ariana's words and Jason's description, Kayla turned back to the dark-haired woman. "What do you mean? You don't usually leave this tower?"

Ariana hesitated and then shook her head. "No, not until recently. Some of our kind have difficulty being around non-sensitives. It's only been in the past few months that I've started learning how to interact with other people."

Kayla felt a surge of frustration and something akin to regret pulse through the bond she shared with Alec. She glanced over to see him rubbing the back of his neck with a haunted look in his eyes. He finally let out a heavy sigh. "It's all right, Ari. I appreciate you trying to soften the truth, but what was done to you was wrong. That's time you'll never get back."

Ariana opened her mouth to object, but Alec shook his head. "No. I won't have you, of all people, defend him for anything he did." When Ariana lowered her head in acknowledgement, Alec turned back to Kayla. "My father was the main reason Ariana was kept in seclusion. Her parents wanted to keep her outside of my father's awareness as long as possible. Her talents in energy manipulation are rather unique and rare. Wearing one of the bracelets would have been dangerous for her, so once her abilities manifested, they made the decision to keep her mostly isolated."

Ariana bit her lip and looked up at the High Council leader. His shoulders tensed, and it was clear he felt the weight of the guilt as though he had been responsible. Before Kayla could say anything, the slightest hint of calming and soothing energy filled the room. It was so subtle she barely noticed it, but she watched as Alec's shoulders relaxed. Kayla arched a brow and wondered if Ariana was responsible for it. If so, she'd have to learn more about how this water channeling stuff worked. That was cool. She was like a human mood adjuster.

Ariana's luminescent eyes were focused on Alec and filled with understanding and sorrow. "Alec, what happened wasn't your fault. It wasn't as bad as you're making it sound. I was simply encouraged not to leave the Inner Sanctum and to avoid doing anything that would draw attention to myself." Ariana gave a careless shrug and smiled. "Now I get to enjoy all of these new experiences. It's been an adjustment, but I've met so many interesting people. I imagine you must feel the same way, Kayla."

Kayla frowned. "I guess. I'm not real fond of people throwing energy all over me though. It's kind of creepy."

Ariana nodded and gave her brother a pointed look. "I can see why you would feel that way if you're not used to it, especially when you have people like Jason causing trouble."

Jason harrumphed, winked at the two women, and crossed his arms over his chest, pretending to be affronted. Ariana merely shook her head and cast her gaze toward the heavens, as though seeking divine assistance.

"My brother may be a troublemaker, but he truly doesn't mean any harm. Unfortunately, there may be people in the towers who will try to take advantage of your inexperience." Ariana waved her hand, and water droplets from the pool spouted upward in a complex design and froze in midair. She held it for a moment before allowing them to fall back down. "The water shield we showed you can help buffer some of the ill effects. You can also try to pull the water out of the air, depending on the humidity levels, but that tends to be more difficult. Drinking a glass of water or even adding a little water to your wine can help you focus on the energy threads and give you a chance to reinforce your shields. No one will even know what you're doing."

Alec looked at Ariana for a long moment, and Kayla caught a trace of some softer emotion through their bond. "I'd forgotten how you used to do that."

Ariana laughed, a musical sound. "I still do it, Alec. You just haven't been around as often lately. I have an easier time being around people now, but it can be a little overwhelming if there are too many. Having a glass of watered wine helps keep up the illusion that I'm a formidable energy channeler." Her eyes sparkled with humor. "But Alec, if you go telling everyone my secrets and ruin my reputation, you'll find your plumbing suddenly having problems at the most inopportune time. Just a fair warning."

Alec's mouth curved upward in a smile, and he chuckled. Kayla cocked her head, looking up at him, surprised by the lightness in his expression. These were his friends, she realized. She'd met his business associates and some OmniLab personnel working for him, but this was the first time she'd seen him engage with his peers and people he respected and even liked. It had obviously been a while since they'd socialized, and Kayla couldn't help but wonder how much he'd sacrificed in the past few months with all the responsibilities he'd taken on.

As though aware of her scrutiny, Alec looked down at her. He gave her a small smile and wrapped his arm around her waist. As he drew her close, she shivered at the feeling of his touch along her bare skin.

With his other hand, he reached up to catch a rivulet of water that had beaded at the end of her hair. "What do you think of their suggestion? Would you like to meet some other Inner Circle members?"

Kayla looked up into his hypnotizing eyes. It might be sort of fun. At the very least, it would give her a better list of suspects who might be trying to target all of them. Alec's smile slipped, and she realized he'd sensed the direction of her thoughts. Before he could object, she pressed her palm against his chest. "Yes. I'll go."

Alec's brow furrowed, but he didn't dispute her words. Brant took a step toward them, interrupting their conversation. "Excuse me, Master Tal'Vayr. The trading camps have arrived and are gathering in the lower levels. Director Borshin and Commander Thomas would like to speak with you."

Alec nodded and instructed Brant to let them know he'd be with them shortly.

"Ah. Duty calls," Jason murmured. With a playful smile, he

grabbed Kayla's hand and pulled her away from Alec and into a warm hug. In a voice loud enough for Alec to hear, he said, "If you get bored with the High Council leader and want a distraction, I'm always available for you."

Alec scowled. Jason chuckled at his reaction and released her. His smile quickly dimmed as he added, "Just a warning, my friend. Your father wasn't the only reason we've kept quiet about Ariana's talents. When word gets out about your bondmate's abilities, you won't need to concern yourself with her safety. It'll be yours that will become an issue."

The men stared at one another for several heartbeats, communicating wordlessly. The undercurrent of tension grew, and Kayla anxiously looked back and forth between them. "What do you mean?"

Neither one responded. Ariana gave them both a reproving look before turning to answer Kayla's question. "There's a reason we're instinctually drawn to men of power, Kayla. Those of us who are powerful in our own right or possess more desirable abilities tend to act as a beacon to others of our kind. A strong bondmate protects you from potentially unwanted advances." She gave her brother a pointed look and added, "There are few among us who can compete with Alec's level of power. A bond challenge is usually only issued if the challenger is confident he can win."

Kayla's eyes widened. Was this what Miranda had been trying to tell her and why Lars asked about bonding with her? "Wait a minute. So a bond isn't really permanent? It *can* be removed?"

Ariana hesitated and then shot a concerned look at Alec before shaking her head. "No, Kayla. You misunderstand. The only way a bond is transferred is when the challenger *kills* the bondholder. In that moment, the bond becomes vulnerable and can be stolen by a powerful energy channeler."

Kayla felt all the blood rush out of her head. She took a

step back, and Alec quickly moved to stand beside her. He wrapped his arms around her, pulling her close. She pressed her forehead against his bare chest. This was a medieval cluster fuck of the highest order.

"I'm sorry, love. I didn't want to tell you yet. I knew it would upset you."

Kayla looked up into his concerned eyes and swallowed. If there was one thing she knew, it was mankind's greed and obsession when it came to power. "If spirit channelers are rare, someone's going to challenge you. Even if they can't win, someone will be stupid enough to test the limits, won't they?"

Alec's jaw clenched, and he gave a curt nod. "It's not common, but it happens. Most of the time, challenges are issued *before* a bond is formed. That way, no one dies and the stronger energy wielder wins. My parents' bond was the result of such a challenge."

Jason cleared his throat. "For what it's worth, Ariana's correct. There are only a handful of people who come close to Alec's level of power. There are only five or six potential challengers I can name off the top of my head."

"Who?"

Alec pinned Jason with a harsh look and shook his head in warning. "It doesn't matter, Kayla. Even if someone is within my level of power, it doesn't mean they would automatically have an interest in challenging me for your bond. Strong feelings for your bondmate strengthens the bond and makes it more difficult for a challenger to break."

He gave Jason a pointed look and bent down to brush a kiss against her lips, emphasizing his point.

When he pulled back, Kayla pressed the palms of her hands against his chest. She couldn't help the sense of foreboding that came over her.

"What about Lars? Does he have your same level of power?"

Alec took a deep breath and nodded. *"He's one of the few who does."*

———

KAYLA LOOKED AROUND in surprise at the mixture of ruin rats, traders, and security officers. She hadn't realized OmniLab had so many people working on the surface. She knew Carl's camp was the smallest, but there were at least six-dozen people in the meeting hall. The combined voices were growing louder and more agitated. Alec gripped her hand tightly and led her toward the front of the room where the head of security and Director Borshin waited.

Even though they'd entered from an obscure doorway away from the loud group, Brant and four security officers positioned themselves in a protective formation around them. Their appearance and heavy escort were already generating some attention. She'd changed out of the clothing she'd worn to the pool to better blend in, but the finer cut of the material on her outfit stood out among the more ragged and well-worn clothing surrounding them. She was still too conspicuous. Kayla sighed as she realized it was only a matter of time before the ruin rats knew her identity too.

As they made their way through the room, she tried to locate Carl. She thought he would have been with Director Borshin, but she didn't see him in the front of the room. Suddenly, Kayla heard someone call out her name. A face she hadn't seen in more than a year stepped out of the crowd. She stopped short, causing Alec to miss a step. He paused to look back at her, but she couldn't tear her eyes away from the man in front of her.

Felix looked so much like his brother, it was like a punch in the stomach. His dark hair was longer than the last time she'd seen him and nearly reached his shoulders. He had a slightly more muscular build than Pretz had, but their eyes were the exact same shade of burnt umber. Except for the small scar next to his right eye from a scavenging accident several years ago, the two of them could have been twins. His eyes lit up with warmth at seeing her, but it was impossible to miss the hint of sadness within them too.

"Felix," she whispered. Without saying another word, she dropped Alec's hand and ran over to him. She flung her arms around his neck and he grabbed hold of her, lifting her off the ground. Burying her face against his neck, his masculine scent enveloped her and reminded her of everything she'd lost. Brant's clipped voice in the background ordered the other security officers to stand down.

Felix's voice was a low whisper in her ear, but she could still make out the raw emotion in his voice. "Fuck, Kayla. I've missed you, crazy girl." He leaned back to look at her, his eyes scanning over her features and drinking in her image. "Do you have any idea what trouble I had to go through to find you? I even joined a trader crew to track your ass down."

Her eyes widened, and she started to pull back in surprise. He grinned at her but didn't release his hold. Kayla reached up to cup his face and tried to decide if she should kiss him or smack him upside the head. "You moron, you hate traders. Why would you do a thing like that? If it's because I took off, I just—" Her voice broke off, and she looked away. She couldn't talk about Pretz here—not with all these people around.

Felix shook his head, lowering her to the ground. He pressed his finger against her lips and spoke in a hushed voice. "Don't. I know what my brother meant to you, and I know why you disappeared. You can't hide shit like that. What the hell were you thinking stealing that data cube from Ramiro? You should have come to me." His eyes hardened, and his grip on her arm tightened. "If you ever pull a stunt like that again, I'll take a strap to your ass. Pretz made me swear to watch out for you if anything ever happened to him. Do you have any idea how pissed he'd be if he knew what you'd done?"

Kayla jerked away and shoved Felix. "I did what I *had* to do, you cocky ass. I *couldn't* go to you. If you knew what happened, you would have gone after Ramiro yourself. I couldn't lose both of you."

Felix grabbed her arms again, pinning them to her side to prevent her from smacking him. He obviously remembered her temper well. "You did anyway. You ran away from me. It took me almost a year to track Mack down after you guys moved. He wouldn't tell me much except you'd joined up with a trader's crew. Dammit, Kayla. Do you have any idea what it was like not knowing what happened to you?"

Her shoulders slumped. Kayla knew exactly what it was like. She'd constantly wondered about him, too, but hadn't been able to bring herself to see him again. The guilt she'd harbored over Pretz's death still hung like a heavy cloud over her head. In a twisted way, losing Felix had been a suitable punishment. She hadn't meant to punish him too.

She'd missed him terribly though. Memories of her first meeting with Felix's younger brother rushed through her, and she smiled sadly. She'd refused to give Pretz the time of day. He'd been part of Ramiro's crew and she didn't want to have anything to do with anyone from a trader's crew, even if he was a former ruin rat. He'd brought Felix around to try to convince her he wasn't half bad. Both brothers ended up charming her.

Felix sighed, pulled her back into his arms, and gave her a long hug. "You're still a pain in the ass, aren't you?"

She smiled against his chest.

"You must be Felix. Trader Rand's spoken highly of you."

Kayla glanced up at the sound of Alec's voice. Felix's body

tensed, but he kept his arms around her in a protective gesture. He scanned Alec and his rich clothing with thinly-veiled disdain. "I am. Who the hell are you?"

Kayla winced. This was about to get awkward. She took a step back from Felix and opened her mouth to introduce them, but Rand approached. The newest trader bowed low to both her and Alec, beating her to the punch. "Hello, Master Tal'Vayr and Mistress Rath'Varein. It's good to see you again. I apologize for interrupting, but we're trying to locate Trader Carl. Cruncher received a message he would be here, but we haven't seen him. Have you heard from him?"

Kayla shook her head. "He said he was meeting Director Borshin earlier and then coming here." She glanced up at Alec in concern.

He frowned and motioned to Brant. He whispered something into the man's ear. Brant immediately pulled out his commlink and began speaking into it as he walked away.

Alec stepped closer, slipping his hand behind the small of her back. "I'm sure he's just been delayed."

Kayla caught the shocked look on Felix's face at Alec's possessive gesture. The ruin rat's jaw clenched as he glared at the High Council leader. Crap. This whole situation was a sticky mess.

Kayla caught his eye and shook her head. In a low voice, she said, "He's a good guy, Felix. Give him a chance. I wouldn't be here if it weren't for him and Carl."

Conflicted emotions crossed his face. He eyed Alec again and frowned. Even though he'd joined a trader's crew, his disdain of OmniLab was still apparent. "We'll see."

Brant ended his commlink call, and Alec took a step away to speak with him privately. Her scavenging partner, Veridian, took that opportunity to approach them. She grabbed him, hugging him tightly, thankful he had arrived safely.

Veridian grinned, scanning her up and down. "Man, it's

good to see you up and running around. How about you try to stay out of the medical wing from now on? That place smells weird."

Kayla laughed and nodded in agreement. When Veridian had heard about Lars stabbing her, he'd rushed to the towers. Both he and Carl had taken turns at her bedside until she was out of danger. Once she'd been released, Veridian had returned to Carl's camp. She didn't blame him. He'd missed Jinx, the sassy redhead who had captured his interest.

"Hey, man," Veridian said, bumping fists with Felix. "You're one of the last people I expected to find here. It's great to see you again."

"Maybe not under these circumstances though," Felix said with a shrug.

Veridian's smile faded, and his eyes darted around the room worriedly before resting on Kayla again. "Yeah. Things are getting pretty tense around here. More security keeps showing up, and no one seems to know what's happening. Do you know anything about this trading hold? They're saying no supplies are going out."

Rand nodded. He leaned in closer, keeping his voice low so only they could hear. "Director Borshin's going to make an announcement in a few minutes. For the time being, all deliveries are suspended. They're hoping to have it lifted soon, but it may take a few weeks. Things are going to get ugly in here when it becomes public knowledge."

Veridian's eyes widened, and he turned to Kayla. "They can't do that. Leo contacted me a few hours ago to find out what's going on. They missed their last delivery because of the attack on the trading camp. They were scheduled for a double delivery today, and it's been canceled. They can't make it a few weeks, Kayla. Their supply levels are critical."

She frowned. Leo was too independent to ask for help. He

wouldn't have reached out to Veridian unless things were dire. "Do you have a list of the supplies they need?"

Jinx had approached and stood beside Veridian while Rand was delivering his news. At his words, the tall redhead pulled out her commlink unit. "I do. I prepared the request earlier. Carl knew you'd want to know. I'm sending both of them to you now." Jinx lifted her head when she finished. "There are three other camps we had to cancel on too. I'm sure the other traders have their own lists. It's bad though. There are a lot of camps waiting on supplies without any idea when OmniLab is going to resume delivery. We had to bring a lot of our supplies with us and lock down what we couldn't. Cruncher's worried about the camp being raided if people get desperate."

Kayla felt a pang in her chest as she considered the magnitude of the effects from the trading suspension. Almost everyone in this room was originally from a ruin rat camp. Many of them agreed to work with traders to earn some additional credits for their home camps. Unlike some of the others, though, every credit Kayla made working in Carl's camp went directly to Leo. Given her ties to OmniLab, she no longer needed to save her earnings. Although, with the suspension of the supply deliveries, credits were essentially worthless. Only tangible items had any real value now.

"We'll figure something out, V."

His shoulders relaxed, and he nodded. Before she could broach the subject with Alec, another security officer approached. Alec ended his conversation with Brant and addressed the newcomer. "What is it?"

"Pardon the interruption. We'd like to escort both you and Mistress Rath'Varein to the annex. Director Borshin is about to begin, and the security director would prefer it if you were off the floor."

Alec nodded and started to lead her away, but she hesitated. She couldn't leave things the way they were. Kayla grabbed Felix's hand and pulled him aside. He frowned, eyeing the security officer with suspicion. "What the fuck is going on, Kayla? Is it true? Are you really one of them?"

This was what she'd been dreading. Letting out a long exhale, she wrinkled her nose and gave a small shrug. "They think I was born here in the towers. I don't have any memory of it though."

Felix studied the security officers and Alec before turning back to her. "So... what then? You live here now?"

Kayla lifted her head to meet his gaze and raised an eyebrow. Their mutual dislike for the towers was one common theme they used to share. Her feelings toward OmniLab had changed dramatically in the past several months, but she was still the same person underneath. She might be a temporary resident, but that's all it was—temporary. There was a whole world out there to explore.

"Do you really think I could handle staying in one place for long?"

His mouth twitched in a grin. His shoulders relaxed, and that familiar teasing light lit his eyes. "Glad to hear it. I'll see you soon, crazy girl." He bent down to give her another hug. Keeping his voice low, he whispered next to her ear, "When you're ready to ditch these guys, say the word. Those guards look like they'll be fun to play with."

She squeezed his arm and laughed. "You have no idea."

———

KAYLA PACED BACK and forth in the common room of her family's quarters. The room had quickly become filled with OmniLab security personnel. No one had heard anything from Carl. To make matters worse, they'd received an alert that Elyot was missing and Lisia had escaped from the detention hall. One of the guards had been killed during the escape and the other was still unconscious, so they hadn't been able to question him.

Kayla clenched her fists and flexed her fingers in frustration. She was going out of her mind with the waiting. When she tried to go back to the meeting hall to talk to Cruncher, Alec and the other security officers refused to allow it. With these latest developments, they had her on lockdown in her family's quarters. That alone was bad enough, but her worry for Carl was increasing by the second. She felt like she was about to come out of her skin. She needed to get out of there and find Carl.

He didn't show up to the meeting with Director Borshin and wasn't answering any calls. His commlink was offline, and they couldn't even track it. Contrary to initial speculation by the head of security, who was now on her shit list, she refused to believe Carl had been a willing participant in helping Lisia escape. The whole idea was absurd. Carl had too much integrity, and he was still furious about how Lisia had betrayed all of them.

Although, she could understand why Elyot would have rescued his sister. If it had been Veridian, she would have done the same thing and damn the consequences. Family was family. Desperation drove people to do bold things.

Her own desperation was reaching a crescendo. She knew something had happened to Carl. He wouldn't have left her unless he had no choice.

Alec looked over the technician's shoulder to the screen in front of him. "Pull Carl's account history records and find out where we are on reviewing the security feed. I want to know every movement he made from the time he left here this morning."

The technician nodded and entered a few commands into the computer.

Having had enough, Kayla stalked over to Alec. "I want a computer terminal set up. I'll double-check the security feeds myself. Can we get into his commlink records to check his messages? Maybe it'll give us a clue."

Alec hesitated and then nodded. He waved at Brant. "Set her up with something."

While Brant called someone on his commlink, Kayla went back to pacing. There had to be something more she could do. She wished she could just reach across her bond like she did with Alec and—

"Alec," she whispered and spun around to face him. He lifted his head from where he'd been watching the screen, a question in his eyes. She ran over to him and grabbed his arm. "The energy! You told me one of my abilities is finding lost or hidden objects. Carl's not exactly an object, but he's missing. Can't I find him?"

Alec's brow furrowed as he considered her words. "I don't think so. For the most part, we use objects as focal points. People, or rather their life forces, are made up of energy. Since it's a fluid thing, it's extremely difficult to latch onto without a bond to lead you there. That's why we form connections with each other. It's not impossible, but it usually requires some form of touch."

Kayla nodded, remembering how he'd touched Director Borshin to communicate wordlessly with him. In fact, he'd even touched her in the beginning to show her how to create energy connections. "How does the focal point thing work?"

Alec paused for a moment as though trying to decide out how to explain. "Do you remember when you located the glass globe in my quarters?"

When she nodded, he continued, "You were able to find it because you channeled energy into the object itself. When our energy touches an inanimate object, it responds differently. I believe that's one of the reasons you're able to locate missing objects so easily. Your energy focuses on life or spirit, but by definition, an inanimate object is the *absence* of life. You're able to find these items because it conflicts with your own ability."

She frowned. "Could I latch onto an object Carl has with him?"

"It's a possibility, but the distance may be a factor. Is there an object he usually carries with him?"

His commlink.

But if he had that, she would have heard from him by now. She couldn't think of anything else he routinely carried with him. Looking down at her hands, she wondered about the point in having this ability if it couldn't help when she needed it most.

Alec sighed and took her hands in his. He wove a subtle thread of soothing energy over her. "We'll find him, Kayla. They're doing everything possible."

Commander Thomas snapped his commlink shut and gestured to the monitor on the desk. "We've traced him to the basement area. He bypassed the meeting room and went to one of the conference rooms. That's the last sighting. Three other individuals exited from that room several minutes later. Trader Carl Grayson wasn't with them."

He motioned for the technician to pull up the video feed on the screen. A moment later, the image displayed three familiar individuals. Two of them were pushing a conveyor cart down the hall while the other followed. Based on their body language, it was apparent the cart was unnaturally heavy. Kayla's heart thudded as she looked at the images of Lars, Miranda, and Elyot. Panic gripped her.

Alec's eyes hardened. "Which way did they go?"

Thomas frowned. "They went directly to the detention room, where they met up with two other individuals who were also previously exiled from the towers. During their efforts to free Lisia Carpan, one of our security officers was killed. They then proceeded to one of the sub-basement levels. We believe they managed to escape the towers during the chaos of the trading camp arrival."

Fury and wild fear ripped through Kayla. They'd taken Carl from the towers, and she had no way to know if he was alive and unharmed. Energy swirled around her, growing in intensity as her emotions became more turbulent. She was going to kill all of them if they hurt Carl.

Alec's arms immediately encircled her, and he whispered into her ear, "Breathe, love. You need to calm yourself before you do something you'll regret. Close your eyes and release the energy."

Kayla didn't want to calm down. She wanted to go after them. Alec quickly began weaving a stronger blanket of soothing energy around her. She was tempted to smack aside his efforts to temper her anger, but he was right. If she didn't get herself under control, she might cause another earthquake or worse. Kayla took a deep breath and tried to slowly release the energy, struggling under the weight of it. Alec quickly threaded his energy with hers and helped her release it.

Once it was gone, she turned her face into his chest and clutched his shirt. "We need to get him back, Alec. I can't lose him."

Alec tightened his arms around her and began issuing instructions to the men in the room. "I want surveillance drones dispatched. Find out what direction they headed and start tracking them. They couldn't have gotten inside the towers again and released the woman in detention without assistance. Find out who's been helping them."

Kayla shook her head. "It's not enough. I have contacts on the surface. If we go down there, I can reach out to some of the people—"

"Absolutely not," Alec interrupted, grabbing her arms and holding on to her. "I will *not* risk anything happening to you."

"I can't just sit by and let something happen to Carl," she argued, pulling away from him. "We're not doing everything possible if there are untapped resources still on the surface. I know people in dozens of different camps. If I reach out to them, they can help us look for him. We can even offer a reward."

"No," Alec declared, his tone firm and unyielding. "If those people are willing to be bought, there's no way to know whether they've already been compromised. We don't know who the Coalition has working for them."

Kayla's eyes narrowed. "*Those people*, as you call them, are my friends, Alec. They're some of the same people I grew up with and who raised me. I spent my life around them, and I trust them. Be very careful what you say about them."

"I'm not debating this with you. The answer is no. One of those former friends of yours just helped kill one of my security officers. We'll find another way."

Kayla's jaw clenched as she glared at him. Their mutual frustration coursed along their shared bond as they stared at each other. Their differences and similarities had never been more apparent than that moment. She might care for Alec, but she wouldn't allow him or anyone else to force her into abandoning her past or being someone she wasn't. Alec's protective instincts were roaring to the surface, but so were hers. What Alec didn't understand, though, was that she didn't want or need protection. She needed a partner.

Kayla knew she didn't always have the right answers, and she frequently made mistakes, but she knew the surface and the people on it better than he ever could.

Alec's commlink buzzed. He reached down and pulled it out of his pocket. "Yes, Sheila? What is it?"

"I apologize for the interruption, Master Tal'Vayr. The

High Council has requested your presence in the council chambers, along with Mistress Seara Rath'Varein. They've received notification about the breach in the detention area and the possible involvement of the Coalition. They're requesting an update on our alert status."

Alec hesitated and looked down at Kayla. It was obvious by his conflicted expression that he didn't want to leave her, especially after their heated words. He reached up to brush his thumb across her cheek. She squeezed her eyes shut and allowed the contact, not wanting to leave things unsettled between them. Wrapping her hand around his wrist, she nodded at him, letting him know she'd be fine.

He sighed. "Very well. I'll be there in ten minutes."

He closed the commlink and looked over at Brant. "Stay with her. I'll be back as soon as possible." He gazed at her again, worry etched along his face. "If you need me, just use our bond. I'll come to you immediately."

She shook her head and waved him off. "I'll be fine. Brant can always zap me if the energy gets crazy again."

Her words didn't appear to reassure him. He gave Brant a few last-minute instructions before he left. Kayla sighed and turned back to the screen to watch the launch preparations for the surveillance drones. Unfortunately, even if they found the direction they'd taken Carl, the drones were limited in how far they could track him.

Kayla leaned forward, resting her hands on the desk, and contemplated her options. The only reason Lars would have taken Carl was because of her. If he was trying to draw her out of the towers, it was an effective tactic. But no matter what, she couldn't let anything happen to Carl. A plan began to form in her mind, but it was risky enough that she didn't dare mention it to Alec, especially given their last words to each other.

The likelihood of the drones finding Carl was slim, but no

one outside the towers knew the surface like her former ruin rat camp. Even if Alec didn't trust them, she knew them as well as she knew herself. If they were desperate for supplies, Kayla would make sure they got them. In return, she'd insist they pass along any information they had on the whereabouts of Lars and the Coalition. After all, ruin rats were born to barter... and she'd learned from the best.

CHAPTER EIGHT

KAYLA GLANCED OVER AT BRANT, who was watching her and Veridian from across the room. Although he had stubbornly refused to let her leave her family's quarters, he'd finally relented and allowed Veridian to visit. In light of Elyot's betrayal, Brant was reticent to allow anyone else near her without Alec's permission. The restrictions grated on Kayla's nerves, but given her new plan... it was better to pick her battles.

"You sure about this?" Veridian whispered, running a hand nervously through his frizzy, brown hair. "Leo's desperate for the supplies, but I'm worried about Alec's reaction when you leave the towers."

She turned back to Veridian, careful to keep her voice low enough so only he could hear her. "Yeah, I'm sure. I don't see another option. I cross-checked the manifest with Jinx's list of supplies. The shipment for Leo's camp was already prepared for delivery. It's sitting on a pallet down in the sublevel basement."

Veridian nodded. "All right. What's the plan?"

Kayla looked over in Brant's direction again. He crossed

his arms over his chest and continued to watch them, suspicion clearly etched on his face. Unable to resist, she gave the security officer a brilliant smile. At his scowl, she turned away, angling her body so he couldn't read her lips. They probably only had a few more minutes before Brant came over to see what mischief they were brewing. "Have Xantham hack into the transport system to transfer the shipment to the docking area. Just make sure he wipes his computer clean afterward so they won't know he initiated the transfer. I'd do it myself, but I won't have a chance with Brant breathing down my neck."

Veridian's eyes flickered to the security officer. "How are you going to get out of here?"

Kayla gave him a half-hearted shrug, hoping her cavalier attitude reassured him. "I'm going to take him with me. He just doesn't know it yet."

Veridian raised an eyebrow but didn't dispute her words. Instead, he reached over and gave her a hug. "Give us thirty minutes to set up. I'll send a message to your commlink when we're ready."

Kayla nodded and watched him head out. There was too much room for error in her plan, but she didn't have many options. She'd likely only have one opportunity to do this, and the window was rapidly closing. Once Veridian was gone, she turned back to Brant. "We need to talk."

He arched a brow. "What would you like to discuss?"

"A couple of things," she admitted, motioning for him to join her. Without stopping to see if he was following, she walked into her bedroom. Her emergency bag was still stashed in the corner within easy reach if she ever needed a quick escape. Kayla tossed it on the bed and began rummaging through it, glancing up briefly as he entered.

"At some point, we need to talk about the whole shadow energy thing. I want to do some tests to figure out if you can use my energy. We can start with me trying to channel energy to you and see what happens from there."

Brant froze next to the door. An indiscernible emotion flickered across his face but was quickly gone. "I'm not sure that's a good idea. Your— Alec may have an issue with that."

She dismissed his objections with a wave of her hand. "Later. I don't want to try it right now. I need to focus on finding Carl first." She located her UV-protective gear and pulled it out of the bag.

Brant's eyes narrowed on the clothing. "What are you doing with that?"

She didn't bother to answer. Instead, Kayla pulled off her shirt and let it fall to the floor. Brant inhaled sharply, cursed, and spun around. She rolled her eyes at his modesty and kicked off her pants. There was no difference in what she was wearing now and what she wore to the pool. She'd never understand the way these Omnis worked.

Kayla pulled on her UV pants and fastened the belt, tapping the buckle of the hidden blade for luck. "I'm going to the surface. I figured I'd give you a chance to go with me this time. You know, just in case I start another earthquake."

"Out of the question," Brant declared and turned back around. His eyes lowered to her bra, lingering on her cleavage for a moment. He squeezed his eyes shut and muttered something under his breath about hazard pay before meeting her gaze again.

"The Coalition is using Carl as bait to get you back onto the surface. It's too dangerous. We have over a dozen people working on locating Carl right now. Once he's found, OmniLab will send in a team to extract him."

Kayla pulled a tank top out of the bag and shook her head. "I can't just sit here and not do anything. The Coalition's cloaking technology is really advanced. The only reason OmniLab found us when we were captured was because I created that earthquake. They're not going to find Carl without help."

Pity crossed his face, but he remained firm. "I'm sorry, Kayla. I can't allow you to go."

Kayla huffed, resisting the urge to roll her eyes. If she accepted it when people told her no, she wouldn't have gotten anywhere in life. She pulled the tank top over her head and grabbed her boots.

"You don't have a choice. I'm going. You know I'll get out of here one way or another. The only option on the table is whether or not you come with me to keep me from blowing anyone up."

At his scowl, she added, "Look, Leo's camp worked with the Coalition before. I think I can barter with them for help in finding out their location. Believe it or not, I'm not going into this without a plan." At least not without a partial plan, but she didn't need to share that tidbit. Improvisation was a ruin rat's way of life. "Once I get the location, I can give it to Alec. I'm not planning on rushing into a dangerous situation unless there's no other option."

Giving him a moment for that to sink in, she finished tying her boots. She didn't want to have to resort to threats, but desperate times called for desperate measures. Reaching into her bag, she pulled out the weapon she'd borrowed when she was last in the towers. It was a little big for her hand, but its sleek design made the size irrelevant. The only important thing was the trigger, and her finger fit easily over that. Holding the weapon in one hand and casually waving it in his direction, Kayla put her other hand on her hip.

"So what's it going to be? Are you going to come with me, or do I need to put you down again, Fluffy?"

Brant looked upward as though seeking divine intervention. Finally, he let out a long sigh. "Fine. I'll help you. You have to promise me you won't put yourself in unnecessary danger though. We'll contact OmniLab the moment your friends give us a possible location."

With a huge smile, Kayla walked over and gave him a hug. He stiffened at the sudden energy transference that shot through them at the contact. They both jumped away from each other. She couldn't help but laugh at his wary expression.

"Yeah. We're definitely going to need to talk about that."

————

KAYLA PEEKED around the corner in the sublevel basement. According to the security feeds, three guards were stationed in the room. Once Xantham transferred the shipment into the docking area, they needed to find a way to get the doors open. A distraction was going to be necessary. She eyed the beams spanning the length of the warehouse area and grinned at the sight of the mounted equipment.

"Crap, I know that look," Veridian muttered.

She pulled back from the doorway and motioned for Veridian and Brant to follow her into a nearby storage room. Once they were inside, Veridian dropped the bags he'd been carrying and began checking the shelves for any other useful equipment.

Kayla propped her terminal on a shelf and used Brant's access codes to patch into the security feeds. Unfortunately, his codes didn't provide them access to everything they needed.

Glancing over at Veridian, she asked, "Where's Xantham? I'm going to need him to hack into the system controls for me."

Brant frowned, peering over her shoulder. "You can't do it? I thought you were an expert."

She zoomed in to study the rotation of the guards in the basement. They were more alert than she would have liked, but it made sense with the heightened security in the towers. "I'm good, but I can't dodge the guards, climb the walls, and hack the controls at the same time. It's all about delegation."

His eyes widened, and she chuckled.

Veridian picked up a retractable rope and stuffed it in a bag. He gave Brant a pitying look and muttered, "Hope you packed something for an ulcer. If you keep hanging around Kayla, you'll probably need it."

When Kayla elbowed him in the ribs, Veridian grunted and then winked at her. "Fine. Xantham's on his way. He wanted to confirm the order to make sure they had the right pallet. These Omnis have been moving stuff around all day to accommodate the trading camps moving in."

Kayla nodded and focused again on the guard's movements. At first glance, there wasn't any recognizable pattern. But the longer she watched, the more she began to see a bit of routine. Two of the guards appeared to have a patrol system, but it was the third that was the wildcard. She suspected this wasn't his usual assignment.

Brant cleared his throat. "I'm not sure it's wise to bring anyone else. We can't be assured your former camp members aren't working with the Coalition."

"We can trust Xantham," Kayla replied. "But you're right about keeping the number of people involved to a minimum. Alec's going to be pissed when he finds out. I don't want him taking it out on them."

A patterned knock at the door interrupted them. Veridian opened it, allowing Xantham and Felix to slip inside. At the sight of Felix, Kayla inwardly cursed.

So much for keeping involvement to a minimum. "What are you doing here?"

Felix swaggered over to her. With the same cocky smirk she remembered, he put his hand around the back of her neck, pulled her close, and pressed a kiss against the top of her head.

Brant grabbed his wrist. "Release her. Now."

"Fuck you, man," Felix snarled and tried to shove the security officer away. Brant sidestepped, twisting the ruin rat's wrist. Felix swore and released Kayla, trying to take a swing at Brant, and the two men jostled into a nearby crate, causing it to topple over with a loud crash.

"Knock it off! You're going to get us caught," Kayla snapped, grabbing Brant's arm.

The energy transference was enough to get his attention. He jerked away, continuing to eye Felix with a thunderous expression. Felix glowered in return and looked ready to go another round.

Dammit. This was the last thing she needed. Kayla turned to Xantham. "Why did you bring him?"

Xantham snorted. "Fuck it all to hell, Kayla. I didn't have a choice. The guy was all over our system like a bad rash. He figured out you were going to try something. He's got almost the same hacking signature you do."

Felix raised an eyebrow at Xantham, not bothering to hide his smug expression. "Of course the signatures are similar. Who the fuck do you think taught her?" Without waiting for an answer, he narrowed his eyes on Kayla. "You think I'm letting you pull something like this again without me? It's not going to happen, crazy girl."

Kayla sighed. Xantham was right. She was already a decent hacker when she met Felix, but he had stepped things up to make her even better. His talents would definitely come in handy. As though sensing her resignation, Felix draped his arm over her shoulder. She didn't miss the challenging look he gave Brant. The security officer's jaw clenched as he slapped his hand to the butt of his weapon.

Kayla scowled at them. Now wasn't the time to figure out

whose dick was bigger. She pulled away from Felix and started outlining her plan. "Okay. Xantham, I need you to hack into the environmental system on this level. With the increased security, I'm going to need to manually set off the alarm as a distraction. Your job is to make sure the doors are triggered to open so we can escape."

Xantham gave her a mock salute. "No problem. The pallet's already been transferred to the docking area."

She turned back to Felix. "I'd have you access the environmental system, but I need you and Brant to connect the supply load to the transport while the guards are distracted by the alarms." At Felix's wicked grin, she added, "*No* fighting. I'll meet up with you as soon as I can, but I'm probably going to need a pick up. We're only going to have a few minutes to get the transport out of the towers after the alarms shut off."

Brant frowned and eyed Felix with skepticism. "Does he even know how to drive a transport?"

She shrugged. "Felix can drive anything with wheels. He'll figure it out."

Veridian looked back and forth between them. "What do you want me to do?"

Kayla bit her lip. This was the hard part. Even though she knew Veridian was willing to go with them, she needed him in the towers. He wasn't going to be happy about it though. "I need you to run interference with Alec." He started to object, but she grabbed his arm. "Please, V. He's not going to listen to anyone except you. Alec knows how important you are to me. I just want you to try to keep him from chasing me down as long as you can. See if Seara can help you calm him down. As soon as I figure out where they're keeping Carl, I'll let OmniLab know."

She sighed and lowered her hand. "Lars wants to kill Alec. He wants to challenge him over this stupid bond. He's trying to lure me out of the towers because he knows Alec will follow. I need to keep Alec here, but I have to get Carl out of there too."

Veridian frowned but nodded in agreement. "Fine. I'll try, but he's not going to listen. The minute he finds out you're gone, he's going to go after you."

Kayla turned away, knowing he was right, but she was out of options and out of time. Alec wouldn't be in that council meeting forever. They needed to be out of the towers before he discovered she was missing. She gestured to the terminal Xantham had set up. "How long do you need to access the controls?"

Xantham tapped in a few commands. "Alec gave us his codes when we worked on the program to mask the energy fluctuations on those bracelets. If his codes still work, I'll need less than ten minutes. If not," Xantham shrugged, " we're pretty much fucked. Either way, he's gonna be pissed about this."

"Then let's hope they still work." After inserting her earpiece, Kayla grabbed a few pieces of equipment from the shelves and shoved the items into her pockets. "I'm going to get into position. Felix, while Xantham's doing that, I need you to monitor the security feeds and guide me. Two of the guards are on a rotating pattern, but the third is a random."

Felix stepped over to her abandoned terminal and glanced over at Brant. "Hey, Fuckwad, do we have ears on your security friends' comms or just visual?"

If looks could kill, Brant would have roasted Felix alive by now. He grudgingly entered his access codes to connect Felix with the audio frequency. When he finished, Brant turned back to Kayla. "I'm going with you."

She shook her head. "It's too risky. Besides, wouldn't you rather stay here to keep an eye on everyone? You know, to make sure they're not Coalition spies?"

He turned, narrowing his eyes on Felix. Kayla bit her lip

to keep from smiling. That little seed sown, she cracked open the door to peer outside. The coast was clear. Without waiting for Brant to raise any further objections, she headed toward the docking area.

Felix's voice came over her earpiece. "Okay, crazy girl, let's get this done so your pet Omni will quit giving me the evil eye."

She grinned. "It might help if you stopped provoking him. I'm almost at the docking area now."

"Where's the fun in that?" Felix retorted. "Okay, I've got eyes on all three Omnis. Two of them are currently on the west end. The third is about to pass by the door. On my count, move in and hug the left wall."

She waited, poised in position, and replayed the guard's patrol routes in her head. The adrenaline was starting to kick in, sharpening her senses and urging her to move. Timing was going to be everything.

"Now," he ordered.

Keeping her footsteps as silent as possible, Kayla moved along the wall. The room was filled with shelves of crates and pallets on the floor with various supplies, their purposes mostly unknown. Over a dozen vehicular transports were housed within the basement, and Kayla recognized them as the ones used to deliver supplies to the trading camps. She'd need to create a distraction so Felix and Brant could attach the supply load without detection.

Kayla scanned the aisles, trying to determine the best place to start climbing. Unfortunately, most of the crates were stacked evenly and didn't come close enough to reach the beam.

"Dammit. One of the bastards just turned around. Hide fast," Felix instructed.

Kayla swore inwardly and ducked behind a large crate, using the shadows to mask her movements. She was still too exposed. If the guard spotted her, there wasn't much room to hide. Footsteps approached rapidly, halting almost directly in front of the crate where she was hiding. She froze, able to make out the edge of the man's gray security uniform from her position.

"I'm not sure. I thought I saw something," the guard told someone over his comm unit.

Kayla swallowed, her throat suddenly dry. She reached down, her fingers wrapping around the stunner. *Dammit*. If she took him down, it would only alert the other guards.

"I've got you," Felix said through her earpiece.

A moment later, screeching feedback blared from the guard's comm unit. The guard swore loudly, bumping into a nearby crate and causing it to fall. The noise spurred her into action.

Diving backward, Kayla dodged out of the guard's line of sight. She scrambled upright, pressing herself between crates and trying to put as much distance between herself and the wildcard guard. She followed the aisle down to the far side of the room, giving a silent thanks to Felix's quick thinking.

Kayla squeezed behind another large set of containers, navigating forward until she was directly below the beam she wanted. Her heart pounded, reminding her that precious seconds were being wasted.

The towering stack of crates in front of her would have to do. The guards would be circling around any second. She gripped the edge of the metal lip of the nearest container and used her arms to pull herself on top of it. Leaning forward, she made a small jump to the next set of containers.

"Thirty seconds until they're around the corner," Felix warned.

Balancing precariously on a metal crate, Kayla reached upward for the next container. The injury at her side protested the stretching, but there was no time for alternatives. She continued scrambling up the crates, using the slight gaps between the stacked containers as hand and footholds. Higher and higher, she continued climbing until she was within touching distance of the beam.

With one last burst of speed, Kayla pushed herself off the top crate. Airborne, she hooked her arm over the beam and slammed into the side, her injury screaming in agony. She lifted her leg, scissoring it over the beam, and pulled herself upright. From her position, she could see the two guards beginning to approach.

"Hold that position."

Only too happy to comply, Kayla pressed her forehead against the cool metal of the beam. She forced herself to take some deep, calming breaths. *Nothing like close calls to get the blood pumping.* She looked over the side, watching the two guards talking to one another.

"Nah. It was probably just interference on the comms. Just put it in the report so maintenance can take a look."

The other guy muttered something, too low for Kayla to hear. As they continued their patrol, their stances became a bit more relaxed.

Crisis averted, she touched her side to see if she'd torn open the fusing again. At least there wasn't any blood. Somewhat reassured, she began inching along the beam that crossed the length of the warehouse. The panel box for the fire suppression equipment was located on the far side of the room. Other than pausing periodically to monitor the guards, she continued making steady progress. It was almost strange how people never seemed to look up.

Once she was within arm's length of the equipment, Kayla pulled out some packing material and the miniature hand torch she'd swiped from the storage room. She twisted the material enough so it would hold its form and then tapped her earpiece.

Xantham's voice came over her earpiece. "Veridian's taking over watching the guards. Felix and Brant are moving into position to start the transfer. On my mark, let's light it up and get these doors open. Ready... Go!"

Pressing the button on the hand torch, Kayla lit the packing material on fire. A small blaze began to glow, and she held it toward the box. Nothing happened. She needed more smoke. Leaning closer to the flame, she carefully blew on it. Within seconds, the fire had fully engulfed the packing material and was emitting a healthy dose of smoke. A few seconds later, a siren pierced the air. Fire suppression foam began pouring from vents in the ceiling. She tossed the burnt packing material over the side of the beam. It was submerged seconds later.

Shouts of alarm came from somewhere below, but she disregarded them. Her job was done. Now it was up to the rest of the team.

A moment later, Xantham's voice came back over the earpiece. "Fuck, fuckity fuck. Alec's codes were changed. I can't get in to open the damn doors. Hang on, let me try something else."

"Move it, Xantham. We're almost out of time," Felix warned.

"Shit, I know!" Xantham muttered several more colorful oaths under his breath.

The large bay door closest to her began to slide open, and Kayla winced at the bright light. *Dammit.* They'd opened the wrong door. She needed to get the rest of her UV gear before she damaged her eyes or was burned to a crisp. Kayla tried to turn around on the beam to start her descent, but her fingers slipped, unable to find purchase in the greasy foam. It kept pouring out, trailing over the beam to the top of the containers and onto the floor.

"Shut off the fucking foam!" Kayla shouted into her

earpiece. It didn't matter who heard her at this point. She was about to be nothing more than an ugly smear on the basement floor. At least the foam covering her was offering some slight protection from the sun.

It was still pouring out for a good minute until it finally shut off. The alarm, however, was still blaring. She wrapped her arms and legs around the beam, using her weight to keep her balanced. There was no way she was climbing out of here with the greasy substance coating everything. Unfortunately, the longer she stayed in place, the more likely she'd end up causing irreversible damage from the elements.

The loud sound of a transport engine starting up cut through the sound of the siren, and as the engine roared, growing louder, she heard another voice in her earpiece.

"Drop down, crazy girl!"

Some of the foam trailed down her forehead and into her eyes. She brushed it away, squinting over the side of the beam. The transport was almost directly below her. And Felix thought *she* was crazy?

With no other option—unless she wanted Alec to come down and clean up her mess—she took a deep breath and released her grip on the beam. She landed on the top of the transport with a loud *thump*.

"Fuck, that hurt," Kayla muttered, wincing as she rubbed her abused side. Carl was going to give her so much shit when he found out what she'd done.

Before she could even move, Brant's hands wrapped around her and pulled her off the top of the vehicle. He helped her into the transport and said, "You really are crazy, you know that?"

"So I've been told," she agreed and tried to wipe off some of the greasy foam. It was everywhere. Until she got a shower and managed to wash off the rest of it, there wasn't much she could do about it. Brant slammed the transport door shut, sandwiching her between himself and Felix. At least the transport offered protection from the sun.

"Drive like hell," she said to Felix.

With a responding grin, he revved the engine and pulled the heavy transport out into the sunlight. She reached over to grab one of the bags from the floorboard and pulled out a multi-purpose tool. Twisting her body, she crouched down to access the area under the dashboard and used the tool to remove the cover panel.

"What are you doing?" Brant demanded, grabbing her arm to stop her.

Kayla shrugged him off. "Reprogramming the control board. OmniLab isn't going to crash our little party until we're good and ready."

Brant gaped at her, but she ignored him and focused on her task.

"Xantham didn't open that door," Felix informed her.

Kayla glanced up at him, frowned, and focused again on the control board. She didn't think it was Xantham either. He was too meticulous to make such a careless mistake.

"Of course he did," Brant argued. "How else did the bay doors open?"

Felix shrugged. "No idea, but whoever did it opened the wrong fucking door. Kayla could have died."

Brant frowned, his forehead creasing as he considered Felix's words. "Are you suggesting someone tried to kill Kayla again?"

Felix glanced over at her and arched a brow. "*Again?* You getting into more trouble without me?"

Kayla grinned. "Always, but I'm glad to have you along to bail me out this time. I think Brant's getting tired of it." She stripped another wire from the control board and routed the power to a different part of the board. "I'm not going to complain though. I don't know what they were hoping to accomplish by opening that door, but it got us out of there."

"True enough," Felix agreed and glanced over at Brant. "But I'd rather not take any chances. You'd better hand over your commlink and any other toys, Omniboy."

Brant scowled at him. "Out of the question. I'm not giving you my commlink."

Kayla ignored his protests, sat up, and held out her hand. She wouldn't be surprised if Brant was actively transmitting their location to Alec right now. If she had any hope of staying a step ahead of OmniLab, she needed him temporarily cut off from the towers. "Felix is right. If you want to stick around, you'll hand it over. Otherwise, we'll stop the transport right now and you can get out. I'm sure OmniLab will pick you up sooner or later. Hell, we're still close enough you could even walk back."

When Brant continued to hesitate, Kayla narrowed her eyes. She might want him to stay from an energy standpoint, but she wasn't planning on staying on the surface long enough for it to be much of a problem. "Time's up, Brant. I'm not fucking around. Carl is out here somewhere, and I'm going to find him. Either play along or get the fuck off my ride."

Brant's jaw clenched, but he pulled out his commlink and gave it to Kayla. She scanned him up and down and pointed to the band around his wrist. He'd used it on his last visit to the towers to communicate with other Inner Circle Shadows.

"Seriously?"

When she merely arched an eyebrow, he slipped off his secondary communication device and handed it to her. She looked down, admiring the sleek design for a long moment, and reached over and tossed both devices out the window. Brant's mouth dropped open, his stunned expression almost comical.

She sighed, hating the need to destroy such cool technology. "The wrist unit was nice, but I don't have time to reprogram it."

Felix chuckled, and she winked at him before ducking back down to finish reconfiguring the transport's control system. If Brant thought tossing his toys was bad, he was in for a rude awakening. He'd just fallen headfirst into her world... and everything he knew about life just flew out the window with the rest of his equipment.

CHAPTER NINE

ALEC LEANED BACK in his chair and listened to the argument between Marcus Staghorn and Lenora Ballentor. Lenora had been complaining more frequently, and the latest incident with the Coalition had given her more fuel for her arguments. Contrary to everything in the reports, she maintained that the entire situation with the Coalition had been handled badly. In her opinion, trading should continue and someone else should attempt to handle negotiations with the foreigners.

"Woman, you are grating on my last nerve," Marcus announced, slapping his hands on the table and standing up. "If any one of us had been in Alec's shoes, we would have done the exact same thing. The Coalition has proven to be dishonorable with their actions."

Lenora stood, her blond hair elaborately coiffed on top of her head. She shook her finger at Marcus, the movement causing the heavy fabric of her elongated sleeve to brush against the top of the table. "Don't take that tone with me, Marcus Staghorn. We need someone with more experience. Between this latest threat, the Shadows running amok, and the overall temperament in the towers, something needs to be done."

One of the other councilors leaned forward. "What are you proposing?"

Lenora made a sweeping gesture to encompass everyone sitting at the table. "It's up to us as the High Council to install someone who can handle the magnitude of these issues. Alec has done well, but what training has he had? For heaven's sake, he learned about leadership from his father. We all know how Edwin Tal'Vayr's reign ended."

Alec's jaw clenched, but he remained silent. If there was one thing he'd learned by sitting in on these council meetings, it was that sometimes they needed to simply air their grievances. He'd give her some latitude, but she was quickly approaching the line. Lenora had been one of his father's biggest supporters when he was alive. Now that he was gone, it was rather impressive how quickly she'd renounced her former loyalty.

Devan Alivette frowned, leaned back in his chair, and clasped his hands over his midsection. "I suppose you think you're the best suited for the job, Lenora?"

Alec resisted the urge to smirk. Devan Alivette was Jason and Ariana's father. Although he'd had some differences with Devan in the past, the powerful water channeler was deeply respected and even feared by some of the Inner Circle. He collected alliances and favors like rare artifacts, hoarding them until they could be used to maximize his effectiveness in swaying decisions in his favor. The fact he was speaking up now was somewhat reassuring. At the very least, those who owed him favors would hesitate before throwing in their lot with Lenora. There was no love lost between Devan or Lenora, and everyone at the table knew it.

Lenora gave him a sickly-sweet smile. "Not necessarily, but even you can't argue about my wealth of experience sitting on this council. But if not me, there are plenty of other qualified options to choose from. I simply think this situation requires someone with more leadership experience."

She leaned forward, resting her hands on the table. "For example, I was aghast to learn a Shadow had attacked Seara's daughter last night. Instead of having all the Shadows detained, they're still running around the towers. They're a threat to all of us, and something must be done. Alec even still has one of them guarding Kayla. After everything that poor girl has been through, she needs protection *from* their kind, not hand-delivered into their clutches."

Alec resisted the urge to call her out on her bullshit. Lenora didn't give a damn about Kayla. In fact, Lenora had supported his father during the council meeting when they'd broken the bracelets. If it weren't for Lenora's efforts in providing Edwin with additional energy, things might have turned out differently. He suspected this was just another attempt of Lenora's to disparage the Shadows.

Another council member inclined his head. "You're quite right as always, Lenora. At the very least, the Shadows should be exiled from our tower and sent to live with the commoners. They have no place in the Inner Sanctum."

Lenora's eyes lit up in approval. "Astute as always, William. I suggest we put it to a vote."

William Gavron stood and nodded, the light from the ceiling reflecting off his balding head. "I agree. We should also discuss someone acting as regent for Alec. I would personally be willing to take on that duty until it's determined Alec has obtained the necessary experience. We don't need a repeat of what happened with his father."

Marcus pounded his fist against the table. "This is outrageous! I will not sit here and be a party to your power play. Your family will never hold such a position as long as mine still exists."

Several other council members stood and began arguing. Alec rose, prepared to intervene, but Seara placed her hand on his arm and shook her head. Instead, she stood and raised her hands for silence. A thunderous explosion of energy slammed the room, causing the walls to tremble. Several people gasped, and the collective room fell silent, each of them turning their attention toward the petite, dark-haired woman.

Seara didn't often use her abilities in that manner, but the effortless show of force was a blatant reminder she wasn't merely a figurehead. Her family had been one of the oldest and most powerful in the towers, even before she'd married Kayla's father. That same power shone brightly as she swept her fierce gaze over each of the councilors. They all sat back down, an uneasy silence descending upon the room.

"That's quite enough," she declared. "I was under the impression this meeting was called to discuss our future plans and how they relate to the Coalition and outside trading. While the events in the past are regrettable, we all have the best interest of OmniLab at heart. We've made an effort to reach out to Lars and the others who were banished from the towers. Whether we can repair the rift between us remains to be seen. Regardless of what happens, however, Alec is *not* on trial for any wrongdoing. I suggest we focus on the facts at hand rather than idle gossip and speculation." She directed the last comment to Lenora. The woman huffed in her seat but remained silent.

Marcus nodded in approval. "I agree. While the trading suspension will affect our economy slightly, the alternative is far too dangerous. I'm happy to provide my services to establish the truth barrier to assist in discovering the possible traitors."

Devan leaned back in his chair. "I'll assist in holding the barrier as well."

Alec inclined his head, accepting both offers. "Your assistance would be appreciated. I'll have my assistant contact yours to determine a convenient time to begin the process."

His commlink buzzed in his pocket. He glanced down at the incoming urgent message and resisted the urge to swear. Instead, he kept his face carefully blank as he stood. Seara looked over at him, and he held up his commlink and motioned toward the door. She nodded at him and said, "I'll handle the rest of the meeting."

With a brief nod toward the other councilors, he made his apologies and exited the room. The moment he was outside, he met up with Commander Thomas who had been waiting for him.

"How the hell did this happen?" Alec snapped, storming toward the priority elevators.

Thomas hastened to match his pace. "She set a fire as a distraction in the sublevel basement and set off the alarms. The environmental system initiated emergency protocol procedures. We're running a damage report now."

"How the hell did she get the doors open?" Alec demanded. "I warned you she would try something like this."

"Someone attempted to access the bay doors using your previous codes from a terminal near the basement, but we had all requests blocked from that tower, as you suggested. A few minutes later, someone used security access codes from *this* tower to get the doors open."

Alec's eyes narrowed, but he didn't slacken his pace. Only Inner Circle members, authorized personnel, and security officers had access to this tower. Kayla's friends were being housed in the other tower, so it couldn't have been one of them. Someone else had to be involved. "Who opened them?"

"We don't know yet. We're tracing it now. When they left,

Kayla took a convoy of supplies. We're assuming she's headed to one of the surface camps."

Alec pressed his palm on the elevator control pad. "I'm sure she did. I want surveillance in the air in the next five minutes. Who's with her?"

Thomas began entering commands into his tablet. "Brant Mason and one of the surface dwellers named Felix Roads. It appears Brant aided her in the escape. He'll be taken into custody as soon as he's apprehended."

Alec shook his head and relaxed a fraction. The fact Brant had managed to accompany her was one of the few positives about the situation. "No. I authorized Brant to do whatever was necessary to remain by her side. I was expecting something like this. I want you to find out whose access codes were used to open the doors. If they were opened using a terminal in this tower, Brant couldn't have been responsible."

Thomas frowned but didn't argue. As furious as he was, Alec couldn't help but admire Kayla's ingenuity and determination. There had been no doubt the willful woman would attempt to escape the towers. He'd only hoped to eliminate the threat against her first. The thought of Lars luring her out of the towers sent a chill through him. While he trusted Brant to protect her, he was just one man. The former ruin rat accompanying her was another concern. He didn't know anything about the man except from the brief report he'd skimmed through after Kayla mentioned knowing him.

"I want a copy of Felix's personnel files sent to me immediately. She has a history with him. I want to know the details. Interview his camp companions and find out what Trader Rand knows about him." He paused, considering everything he knew about Kayla's friends. "Did Veridian Levanthe accompany her?"

Thomas made a note on his tablet and shook his head. "No. He contacted one of the security stations on the sub-basement level shortly after the incident and requested to speak with you. They're holding him there for you."

Alec nodded. "Have him brought up. I'll speak with him now. I also want the rest of her camp companions interviewed. Find out what they know." Stepping out when the elevator doors opened, he headed toward his family's quarters. "Brant embedded a tracking device into one of Kayla's boots. I believe you're correct, and she's most likely heading to her former camp with the supplies. Monitor her and keep an extraction team close, but do not interfere unless she's in immediate danger or leaves that camp."

Thomas frowned. "You don't want them to return her to the towers immediately?"

Pressing the button to open the door, he entered his quarters. Of course he wanted her back. He wanted to tie the infernal woman to his bed and not let her go until she agreed to stop acting recklessly. Unfortunately, he needed to move cautiously. If he showed his hand too soon, she'd just figure out another way to circumvent him. Alec activated the terminal in his common area and pulled up the surveillance feed from the sub-basement area.

"I want you to get your men into position, but do not engage until I give the order. If there's any sign of activity from Lars or the Coalition, suspend the order and bring her in immediately. I believe I may be able to convince her to return."

"Understood," Thomas agreed.

"In the meantime, you need to continue expanding the search for Trader Carl. Kayla is the priority, but it'll be much easier to convince her to return if he's back in the towers." Alec glanced toward the window overlooking the barren landscape. "Once you've made the arrangements, contact Seara. I'll need to break the news her daughter has disappeared... again."

———

KAYLA WIPED the sweat out of her eyes. The ride to Leo's camp on the slow-moving transport was hot, miserable, and had taken way too long. She'd seen the drones overhead and knew it was only a matter of time before Alec swooped in. Regardless of her precautions, OmniLab had managed to track them. They only had a brief window before they'd either need to find another camp where they could crash or go underground.

Leo's eyes narrowed on her, and he pointed to the exit. "Oh, hell no. Not again. Get out of my camp, girl. You're nothing but trouble."

Kayla put her hands on her hips and returned his glare. "Trouble? What kind of ass-monkey turns away the person who brought your missing supplies? Tell your one brain cell to stop fighting for dominance and try looking at the big picture instead."

Leo snorted and crossed his arms over his chest, eyeing Brant with distaste. "Fine. You and the shipment can stay, but I don't want an Omni in my camp. Get him out of here." He looked over her shoulder as though expecting someone else. "Where's your trader? Is he going to be beating down my door next?"

"It's just us, and Brant's with me. If you have a problem with that, I'll take that convoy outside to the next camp. Make your choice, Leo. Do you want your supplies or not?"

Leo scowled and turned to Mack. "We should have packed up and left by now. This crap is starting to become a habit. Omnis and traders in my camp. It's one big clusterfuck. Figure out a new location so we can get out of this shithole. Everyone has our damn address now."

Kayla threw her helmet down. She'd known it was going to be an uphill battle with Leo, but she didn't have time for this. "Yeah. You're a habit I'd like to kick too. With both feet." She gestured to the transport out front. "Those are the damn supplies you needed. V gave me your message. So quit bitching and have your boys bring them in. All trading is shut down between camps, so that's the last shipment you're going to get for a while, unless you pull your head out of your ass and help me."

Mack frowned. "What's going on, darlin'? We heard the shipments were canceled, but is there something more happening?"

Kayla sighed. At least Mack would be a voice of reason. She nodded and quickly explained the situation. She told them about the Coalition's attack and Carl being abducted.

Leo shrugged, but she saw the slight crease of worry on his forehead. "What the hell do I care if Sergei and Lars go after OmniLab? The Coalition will trade with us just as easily as the towers. OmniLab's never done shit for any of us. I'm not getting involved in their pissing contest. If you knew what was good for you, you'd do the same."

She hesitated. This is where everything could fall apart. Her former camp might treat her differently once they learned about her past, but she needed to convince them OmniLab wasn't their enemy. It was only a matter of time before they found out about her heritage anyway. "That's not exactly true. I—"

Brant interrupted her. "OmniLab has tentative plans to build another tower for the ruin rats. Kayla has been assisting them with design concepts. She wants to offer all of you the opportunity for a permanent home. If you choose to accept it, you would still have the flexibility to work on the surface. This would give you access to the same quality medical care, food, and supplies available within the towers."

Leo's head jerked toward Kayla. She caught a brief glint of

hope in his eyes before they narrowed in suspicion. "Is this true, girl?"

Kayla gaped at Brant. He gave her a warning look and the briefest shake of his head. That one movement made it clear he didn't want her to reveal her identity. She turned back to Leo and nodded.

"Yeah. It's still in the preliminary stages. I met with a few designers to go over some ideas. It's not definite yet, but they're exploring the possibilities. They'll need everyone's help with construction and acquiring the resources though."

Leo crossed his arms and snorted. "I'm not one for Omni fairy tales. Until I see it with my own eyes, I'll deal in cold, hard facts. The only fact I see here is you bringing trouble, along with a pallet of supplies, into my camp."

Mack blew out a breath and ran a hand over his shaved head. "I hate to say it, but Leo's right, darlin'. We can't get involved if OmniLab and the Coalition are going up against each another. It's not our fight. If OmniLab's shutting off trade between camps, we can't afford to piss off Lars."

"I'm not asking you to get involved. I'm only looking for information. I need to know where the Coalition is holding Carl. Once I find out, OmniLab can send in a team to rescue him. Someone has to know something about these guys and where to find them."

Leo rubbed his chin thoughtfully but didn't reply. This was going to be harder than she thought. Leo was notorious for being stubborn. The man had his head so far up his ass he could chew his food twice.

Mack glanced over at Felix. "I'm surprised you're going along with this. You okay with her trying to save this trader?"

Felix shrugged and leaned against the wall, looking bored. "Fuck the trader. I'm only here for Kayla."

Mack chuckled and bumped fists with Felix. Kayla scowled at them.

Idiots.

Felix grinned and draped his arm around her shoulders. "Don't be like that, crazy girl. We'll find your trader if it's that important to you. Although why you'd want to bother is beyond me."

Kayla blew out a breath and elbowed him in the gut. He grunted and dropped his hand, rubbing his abdomen. She looked up at Mack. There was no love lost between him and Carl, especially after she'd last returned to the camp. She just hoped Mack's affection for her was strong enough to outweigh his dislike for Carl.

"Mack?" Kayla began, taking a step toward him. "Have you guys even heard from Lars or Sergei? Do you have any idea where their camp is located?"

Mack shrugged. "Sergei stopped by a few days ago. He wanted to check out the scanning equipment you modified. He said he'd have more work for us soon."

Leo swore loudly and pointed at Mack. "I'm not listening to this. If you get involved, you better make damn sure there's no blowback on our camp. If OmniLab is cutting off our supplies, the Coalition is our only option. Don't fuck it up."

With a sharp look at Kayla, Leo stormed off down the hall toward his office. She watched him go and focused again on the burly scavenger. "I can't promise the new tower's going to be built, but I can promise I'll do everything within my power to make sure you guys keep receiving the supplies you need. I'll be damned if I'm going to let anything happen to anyone in this camp."

Mack's mouth curved upward. "No worries, darlin'. We'll make do, just like we always do. But judging by the company you're keeping, I'd say you need to start worrying about yourself."

Kayla glanced again at Brant, who was eyeing Mack and Felix with suspicion. His hand hadn't left the hilt of his weapon the entire time. She sighed. Yeah. That was probably good advice.

————

CARL FLEXED his wrists and pulled against the restraints behind his back. The small cell where he was being kept was nearly identical to the one from a week ago. The only difference was the faint metallic smell of recirculated air and that Kayla hadn't been captured this time. Although, if he didn't get out of here soon, that might change. Knowing Kayla, she was already plotting a rescue attempt and running headfirst into trouble.

He studied the design of the small locking panel next to the door. Unfortunately, even if he had Kayla's knack for electronics, it wouldn't do much good without the use of his hands. His captors weren't leaving anything to chance this time.

Almost as though he'd willed it, the panel beeped. The door slid open and Lisia stepped inside, followed by Lars. It had only been a week since he'd seen her, but the once-pretty, young blonde was almost unrecognizable. Her borrowed clothing hung on her frame, giving her an almost waiflike appearance. The shadows under her eyes made the harsh angles of her cheekbones even more pronounced. Even her hair hung limp around her shoulders, as though it had given up, along with its owner.

Carl's jaw clenched, trying to reconcile his pity for this pathetic creature with the memory of her betrayal. Lisia had been in his camp for a year, working and living with his crew. He'd known she was unhappy and jealous, but that was no excuse for her actions. Her duplicity had nearly killed Kayla, not once, but twice. Even so, it was impossible to look upon his former camp member and not be completely unmoved.

How could she have changed so dramatically in such a short period?

He tore his gaze away from Lisia and met the cold, blue eyes of the former Omni. It was easy to see the similarities between Lars and Alec now that he knew about their familial relationship. Even the past several years on the surface couldn't erase the aristocratic bearing Lars possessed.

"They asked me to come talk to you."

Lisia's voice was coarser than he remembered, as though it hadn't been used in days. Carl glanced over at her again but didn't reply. He had no interest in playing whatever game Lars had concocted. Judging by Lisia's hunched shoulders and the trace of fear in her eyes, he suspected life within the Coalition wasn't all they'd expected. More than likely, her position within the renegade organization was tenuous at best.

"OmniLab has placed a block on Kayla's commlink. We can't get any messages through to her. If you provide us with the access codes you used to configure her commlink, they've promised not to hurt either one of you."

Carl let out a harsh laugh. Did she really believe he'd just roll over and sacrifice Kayla? "That's the difference between us, Lisia. I won't betray the people I love. I'm not going to put Kayla in harm's way just to save my own ass."

Lisia's shoulders straightened a fraction, causing her ill-fitted shirt to slip and expose a bony shoulder. "Then you're a fool. You can sit in here and rot for all I care."

Carl shook his head in bewilderment. "What the hell happened to you? This can't all be because we didn't work out. You're not this person."

Lisia's expression turned bitter. "You betrayed me and my brother. I saw the order releasing us from our contract. You were going to kick us out and force us to go back to the life we escaped. I couldn't do it. Not again."

Carl sighed and shook his head, inwardly kicking himself

for not explaining this to her. Hindsight was a bitch. It wouldn't have done any good for her hand in selling information on Kayla to Ramiro, but maybe everything else could have been avoided. "You're wrong, Lisia. Jinx prepared the release order so I could sign off on a transfer. You and your brother were going to be sent to Rand's camp. In exchange, he was trading Minko and Felix to our camp."

Lisia hesitated. It was clear she didn't want to believe him. She glanced back at Lars, who was impassively observing the entire exchange. When she turned back to Carl, there was true fear in her eyes. She knelt beside him, her voice softer this time. "Please do what he says, Carl. Give Lars the codes so he can meet with Kayla. He's not interested in you. It's OmniLab he wants."

Carl ignored Lisia and lifted his head to meet Lars's gaze. "Forget it. I told you before and I'll tell you again. I don't give a damn what you do to me. I'm not helping you get to Kayla."

Lars regarded Carl for a long moment and jerked his head toward the door. "Leave us."

Lisia swallowed and nearly scrambled backward to get to the door. Once she'd fled, Lars moved to stand in front of Carl and clasped his hands behind his back. "I'm afraid you don't fully grasp the situation. You're in a somewhat precarious position, Carl. Other than your connection to Kayla, I have very little use for you. Unfortunately for you, resources that aren't useful to us tend to be disposed."

When Carl didn't respond, Lars continued, "I have given you ample opportunity to cooperate. Since you've chosen not to help us, I'm afraid you're going to force my hand. You see, I've spent the past week learning quite a bit about Kayla. Your former camp members and records also provided me with some interesting insight."

Carl clenched his jaw and remained silent.

Lars cocked his head, studying him. "Kayla doesn't strike

me as the type to wait around. I believe she'll come to the surface looking for you. However, with the trading camps disbanded—I'll need to thank Alec for that, by the way—she has very few allies still on the surface. As it happens, one of those allies is her former camp, and they're now feeling the pressure from the lack of supplies. Since they were most recently in my employ, it's only natural they'll turn to me again, especially since OmniLab has cut them off."

Carl forced himself to remain impassive, but his heart was pounding. *Dammit.* Lars was right. Kayla would go directly to her former camp since they had ties to Lars. He'd like to think they would protect her, but if it came down to survival, they'd likely offer information in exchange for supplies. His only option was to bluff. "If you really believed that, you wouldn't be asking for her access codes. I think we both know Kayla has far more friends on the surface than either of us realize."

"Perhaps," Lars agreed. "However, a little insurance won't hurt either. I'll give you an hour to reconsider. If you still haven't provided us with her access codes, a video of you being tortured will be sent to every single surface camp we've worked with over the past few years. Either with your cooperation or without, Kayla *will* get the message."

Carl squeezed his eyes shut. There was no doubt in his mind Kayla would respond.

CHAPTER TEN

KAYLA BENT DOWN and disconnected the last of the terminals in the workroom. Sweat dripped down her brow, and she absently brushed it away with the back of her hand.

One of the temperature controls must be on the fritz again.

She glanced over at Brant who was stacking supply crates. She had to give him credit. Despite the grueling heat, he hadn't complained when she insisted they help break down the camp.

True to Leo's word, the ruin rat camp was packing up and getting the hell out of the area. Kayla needed to do the same and head out with Brant and Felix, but she was stalling for time.

Mack had agreed to reach out to some of his contacts and try to pinpoint the location of the Coalition camp. Unfortunately, after she'd told one particularly stubborn camp leader he was living proof family members shouldn't procreate, Mack had kicked her out of the room. The last thing she heard was the sound of the camp leader shouting obscenities and threatening to hunt her down.

Felix, meanwhile, was trying to hack into some other

systems for clues on the Coalition's location and agenda. She'd tried to get involved there too, but he'd snapped at her and threatened to tie her up if she didn't get lost. Felix had always been overly sensitive when he was working. It rankled to admit, but Felix was far more skilled when it came to hacking. Especially right now when her emotions were running high. She couldn't risk making sloppy mistakes when Carl's life was on the line.

Since all she was doing was pissing everyone off, she was packing up supply crates with Brant while waiting for some word that Mack or Felix had discovered something. Every moment that crept by increased her anxiety. OmniLab knew they were here, and it was only a matter of time before Alec grew impatient and swept in. She was somewhat surprised he hadn't sent his minions to try to retrieve her yet. Maybe he was learning.

Sitting down on the edge of a crate, she reached over and grabbed a couple of hydrating packs.

"Heads-up," she called and tossed one of the packs in his direction. Brant spun, catching the hydrating pack with one hand. Kayla grinned, impressed with his sharp reflexes.

"So," she began, opening her own hydrating pack and taking a long drink, "I think we need to talk about how OmniLab's tracking me."

Brant frowned. He moved to sit on a neighboring crate, his expression guarded. "What do you mean?"

Kayla leaned forward, resting her elbows on her knees. "You're shit at lying, Brant. I disabled the tracking system on the convoy. The communication devices were also disabled, but those drones were in the air and on our trail within minutes. Alec has another way of finding me, doesn't he?"

"One of you picked up a tracker," Felix observed casually as he entered the room. Kayla's head jerked up to meet his gaze. *Dammit*. It didn't take much deduction to figure out who was responsible. She was going to kill Brant.

Felix dropped a bag at her feet and swiped the hydrating pack from her hands. "There's a low-level signal emitting from this room. OmniLab's signature is attached. They didn't tag the supplies, so it's on one of you. Ditch everything. There are clothes in the bag for both of you. We don't have time to figure out which one of you was tagged."

Brant didn't reply, but Kayla didn't miss the look of irritation on his face. Her eyes narrowed, and she reached down to grab some clothes from the bag. They looked like Kristin's clothes, which made sense because they were about the same size. Tugging her shirt over her head, she dropped it on the floor and pulled on the new one.

"You're starting to get on my last nerve, Brant. It's not a good place to be."

She kicked off her boots and began unbuttoning her pants, but Brant held up a hand to stop her.

"It was a precaution only," he admitted, averting his eyes. "I was ordered to install a tracking device in your boots. Alec suspected you might attempt to leave the towers again, and he was concerned Lars would come after you."

Kayla bent down and picked up one of her boots off the floor. She traced the outline of the sole for signs of tampering, kicking herself for being so stupid. She should have realized Alec would have done something like this. He was getting sneakier by the day. It was definitely a mistake to let him and Carl work together.

Felix leaned against the wall, finished off the hydrating pack, and tossed it in the recycler. "Fucking OmniLab. Kayla, you need to ditch this asshole. I don't know why you wanted to bring him along in the first place. I'm still running diagnostics on the rest of Leo's security. Since you left, it's gone to shit. They've got holes on top of holes. It's going to take hours to finish scanning, and we don't have that kind of time. Why not just get rid of this fucker and take off?"

"Trust me, it's tempting," she admitted, tossing her boots on the floor in disgust. Unfortunately, she needed to keep Brant around temporarily to make sure she didn't blow anyone up. Felix was right though. They couldn't stick around here any longer. Bending down, she grabbed some pants out of the bag and finished changing. She wasn't taking any chances with another tracker. When she finished, she tossed the bag at Brant and snapped her fingers. "Change. Now."

His jaw clenched, but he slowly pulled his shirt over his head. Kayla raised an eyebrow at the sight of his well-defined muscular body and shook her head to clear it.

Bad, Kayla. Very bad.

She turned back to Felix. "Can you talk to Kristin and see if she'll trade UV gear with us? If OmniLab is surveilling the camp from the air, we need to be able to lose them."

Felix nodded, catching her drift. "I'll work something out with Mack. We can send out a team with the tracker to serve as a distraction. I can intercept their visuals and detection equipment long enough for us to get out of here. I'm assuming you have an idea where we can hole up temporarily?"

Kayla sat on the crate again, considering the options. She wasn't willing to drag another ruin rat camp into this mess, and the trading camps were off limits. Her thoughts went back to the underground river. The stability scans had come back as normal, so the area was relatively safe provided Brant could keep her energy levels in check. OmniLab wouldn't be able to trace them if they were deep underground. The only problem was the lack of a quick exit. She didn't want to risk getting trapped underground.

Frustrated, she stood back up and started to pace. Her eyes fell on her discarded boots, and she froze. That was it.

The conversation with Alec about locating missing objects came rushing back to her. She'd been wrong. There *was* something Carl would have on him. She'd just found her focusing object. Now all she needed was to get a general idea of the Coalition's camp from Mack. With that and a little help from Brant, she could try tracing Carl.

A brilliant smile crossed her face. "Oh, yeah. I've definitely got an idea."

———

CARL LEANED BACK on the cot, resting his head against the wall. Time was ticking down. If he had to guess, there were only a handful of minutes remaining on his hour deadline. It didn't matter. No matter what they did or threatened, he wouldn't agree to their demands. Turning over Kayla's access codes would only guarantee her capture. As long as she was running free on the surface, there was a chance she could get out of this unscathed.

The sound of the lock beeping heralded the arrival of one of his captors. Lisia entered again, carrying a blanket in her arms. He caught a brief glimpse of an armed man guarding the door before it closed behind her.

"If you're here to ask for Kayla's codes again, don't bother. It's not going to happen."

Lisia paused for a moment and then tossed the blanket on the cot. "When I was being held in the towers, the officers told me you arranged to have a blanket and pillow sent to me. I figured I'd try to return the favor."

Carl arched a brow and nodded toward the gray blanket. "You think this makes us even?"

Lisia shook her head, glancing up in the corner where a small light shone. The camera had been recording since he'd been brought to the cell. "No, but it's a start."

Carl ignored the blanket, studying Lisia instead. From the slight tremor of her hands, it was obvious she was up to something. Whether her machinations would benefit him or not was another story. Bringing a blanket to him was hardly helpful, especially since he was only moments away from being tortured. Conversation wasn't high on his priority list, either, but she didn't seem inclined to leave.

She hesitated for a moment. "Were you telling the truth earlier? Did you really plan on having us transferred?"

Carl leaned forward, the movement pulling at his restraints. "Yes, but it hardly matters at this point. Why are you here, Lisia?"

"Just answer the question. No games. I need to know the truth."

"I told you the truth," Carl said with a sigh. "I've seen the conditions in the ruin rat camps. I never would have sent anyone back there to suffer. When you made it clear how unhappy you were in my camp, I came to an agreement with Rand about transferring you and your brother. I thought you'd be happier in his camp."

"Then why didn't you tell us?"

"I should have," he admitted, darting his gaze back to the glowing light in the corner. He needed to be careful not to give the Coalition any sensitive information. They'd extracted some information on the underground river, but there was no way to know how much they knew about it. "Nothing was definite until Kayla and I left for the towers. While I was there, I negotiated with Rand for a personnel trade. I had planned to speak with you and your brother once we returned. Unfortunately, things didn't work out quite the way I expected."

"I wish I had known," Lisia whispered, almost to herself. She fell silent for a long moment and glanced over at the corner before focusing on him again. "I've made a lot of mistakes, but the worst is that I've dragged Elyot down with me. He never should have rescued me. We're both blacklisted from OmniLab now. No ruin rat camp will take us in. The Coalition doesn't trust us either. I don't know how long we'll be useful to them."

"I'm sorry, Lisia. Your brother is a good man, but his actions were misguided. I can't help either of you anymore."

She knelt in front of him and pulled something out of her pocket. "I know. You've helped us far more than we deserved. It's time for us to return the favor."

Before he could reply, she reached behind him, and he heard the audible beep of his wrist restraints releasing. "What are you doing?"

"Helping you," she replied, jerking her head toward the camera in the corner. The light was gone. "We only have a few minutes before they realize the camera is offline."

He rubbed his wrists and stood. "What's your plan?"

Lisia pulled out a knife and drew it across her forearm. Blood welled to the surface. Carl reached for her arm to stop her. "What the fuck do you think you're doing?"

"Saving your ass," she snapped and batted him away. He watched as she ripped the edge of her sleeve all the way up to the shoulder. She shoved the knife back in her pocket, smeared a streak of blood on her cheek and then pounded on the door.

The moment it slid open, she practically fell into the guard's arms. With a wailing sob, she mumbled a few words and pointed at Carl. The guard's eyes narrowed on him. He took a step toward Carl, trying to disentangle himself from the hysterical woman feverishly clutching at him. Lisia, however, wasn't having it. Carl watched almost in disbelief as she tripped the guard and grabbed his weapon in one smooth motion.

The moment he was on the ground, Lisia pressed the

weapon against him and fired. His body jerked and then lay still. She bent down and started removing the guard's clothes. "Get undressed. You won't fool anyone up close, but we just need to get to Elyot. He'll meet up with us once he secures some UV gear and speeder codes."

Carl pulled off his shirt and tossed it on the bed. This was a side of Lisia he hadn't seen. He probably shouldn't be surprised. Ruin rats could be chameleons in their ability to show the world what they wanted you to see. Lisia cut a strip off his discarded shirt and began binding her arm. She gripped the edge with her teeth and pulled it taut.

He finished dressing and pulled on the guard's boots. Thankfully, they were about the same size. He glanced up at the camera, but the light hadn't come back on yet. Carl bent down to drag the man's body onto the cot and then draped the blanket over him. Once the camera came back on, it might buy them a few minutes.

Lisia was already scoping out the hallway. She glanced back at him and motioned for him to follow her. "It's clear. Let's go."

Carl abandoned the guard's body and trailed Lisia down the hall. Although she moved with confidence, the direction she was taking was opposite from the exit. His entire body tensed as they moved deeper into the heart of the Coalition's lair. The lack of guards only heightened his suspicion something wasn't quite right.

"I don't like this. Where is everyone?"

She shushed him and motioned for him to stay back. They were approaching an intersection, and the low sound of voices echoed through the hall. Carl pressed his back against the wall while Lisia peeked around the corner.

"Dammit," she muttered. "I thought they'd be finished by now, but they don't look like they're moving anytime soon. We'll have to try cutting through one of the labs instead, but we need to move fast. Those cameras are on a different circuit. We couldn't cut them without triggering the alarms."

Carl straightened, curiosity getting the better of him. Keeping his voice in a low whisper, he asked, "What do you mean? What's going on?"

Lisia looked around as though trying to decide which direction they should go. "I don't know. After Lars took me to see you, he got into a big argument with Sergei. I couldn't understand what they were saying, but Lars was pissed. He took off with some of the Coalition's men, and Sergei disappeared into one of the conference rooms. I asked one of the guards what was going on, but he wouldn't tell me."

"Wait," Carl interrupted. "Lars left? Do you know where he went? Did he find Kayla?"

Lisia shook her head and motioned him back down the hallway in the direction they'd come from. "I don't know. He just took off. Something's going on though. After he left, a large squad of armed men rolled out of here like their asses were on fire. That's why we were able to cut the camera feeds. We wanted to get you out of here before everyone returns. Elyot might know something else."

Carl fell silent and continued to follow her, pausing at various intersections while she surveilled their escape path. They finally stopped at a nondescript door, and Lisia slid a keycard over the panel. The light on the panel turned green, and the door slid open.

The room was small, but the wide variety of equipment and beeping machines was indicative it was some sort of monitoring room. Carl scanned the space, his gaze falling on a large map displayed on the far wall. It depicted the entire area surrounding OmniLab, with shaded areas representing all four trading districts. Peppered throughout the map were markings that appeared to identify ruin rat camps. He took a step closer, noting they'd also marked areas of potential resources. The entrance to the underground river was clearly identified.

A moment later, a loud alarm echoed throughout the camp. Lisia grabbed his arm, pulling him forward. "Come on, we're out of time."

Before they could make it to the door, it slid open. Elyot rushed in and dropped the bag he was carrying on the floor, jostling a nearby box of electronic devices with his elbow. It fell to the floor with a resounding *crash*.

"Hurry," Elyot urged, kicking fallen equipment out of the way and opening his bag. He pulled out some UV gear and tossed it to each of them. "The cameras are back up and they know you've escaped."

"What's going on?"

"Sergei just got out of a meeting with some of the higher ups in the Coalition. He ordered the remainder of the guards to get ready to leave. They've got a shitload of weapons. Something's going down. It's not just this camp either. They've got at least four other locations, and they're mobilizing everyone. We've got to get out of here now."

Carl pulled on a jacket with the Coalition emblem and tucked the helmet under his arm. "Where's Lars?"

"I think he's got a lead on Kayla."

Alarm coursed through him. "Do you know where he's headed?"

"You should be more concerned about yourself," a woman's voice spoke from the doorway. Carl spun around to see Miranda pointing a weapon at them. Her eyes narrowed on Lisia and Elyot. "Do you have any idea what we risked to help you? And this is how you repay us? Lars offered you both freedom from OmniLab, and you've done nothing but spit in our faces."

Lisia stepped forward, her blue eyes flashing with fury. "You self-righteous bitch. You and Lars lied to us. You promised me no one in Carl's camp would be hurt, but you killed Zane. You tricked my brother into helping me escape and threatened to torture Carl. You've taken everything from us. Everything!"

Miranda hesitated for a moment and then shook her head. "Zane was an accident. He wouldn't have gotten hurt if he had listened. Carl wouldn't have been hurt either. We just wanted information."

Carl took a step forward but froze when Miranda turned the weapon in his direction. "Is that really what you think, Miranda? Look at all the harm Lars and the Coalition have already caused. You have an entire camp arming themselves. For what? To attack OmniLab? How many more lives are going to be destroyed? There will be casualties on both sides."

"You have no idea what you're talking about," she snapped. "We're doing what needs to be done."

Carl lifted his hands in a passive gesture and took another small step toward her. "Lars isn't trying to do what's best for your people. He's only out for revenge. Think about your people, Miranda. Is killing us going to help them?"

"Don't come any closer," Miranda ordered, gripping the weapon even tighter. "Lars is doing *everything* for our people. He's willing to make the ultimate sacrifice and sever the bond between Alec and Kayla. Once Alec is out of the way and the other councilors are punished, our people will finally be able to go home."

Carl fell silent. From the almost feverish look in her eyes, it was apparent there would be no getting through to her. For whatever reason, Miranda needed to believe what she was saying was true. Unfortunately, that also meant Elyot and Lisia were now liabilities. Miranda and Lars might still view him as having some use as a way to manipulate Kayla, but not for his companions.

Lisia seemed to come to the same conclusion and reached for the weapon in her pocket. Miranda spun toward her, firing the weapon before Lisia could raise hers. Carl shouted out a warning, but it was too late. Lisia's body jerked. She staggered, clutching her chest and gasping for breath. Miranda stumbled backward, her back hitting the wall behind her, but she didn't release the weapon. Instead, she turned a shaking hand toward Carl and Elyot, as though warning them away.

Elyot ignored her and dropped beside his sister. "Don't move, Lisia. Just stay with me." He lifted his head to meet Miranda's gaze. "We need a medic. You can't let her die. Please, I'll do anything."

Lisia coughed, struggling for air and shook her head. Her eyes met Carl's, and he saw the plea in them. "Elyot... You have to..."

Carl swallowed, unable to deny her unspoken request. "I'll take care of him. I promise."

"No!" Elyot screamed and gripped his sister's shoulders. "Dammit, Lisia. You can't die. Breathe. Just breathe. Please... I can't lose you..."

She gripped Elyot's hand tightly, unable to speak or even take a full breath. The raspy wheezing echoed throughout the room, barely heard over the din of the humming machines. When her hand went limp and the light extinguished from her eyes, a sob escaped Elyot. He gathered his sister in his arms, rocking her back and forth. Tears streamed down his face as he wept.

"I'm sorry," Miranda whispered and aimed the weapon at Elyot.

"No!" Carl shouted, leaping forward to knock the weapon out of her hand. Before he could reach her, Miranda's body jerked. The weapon fell from her fingertips, clattering to the floor. Miranda collapsed in a heap. Carl spun around to find

Sergei in the doorway, along with another soldier. The tall Russian lowered the weapon and placed it back in his side sheath. Several guards entered the room behind him, weapons drawn and trained on Carl and Elyot.

Carl glanced down at Miranda's limp body. "You killed her?"

"She lives. For now," he replied, motioning for some of his men to remove Miranda from the room. "Never trust emotional women with weapon. Foolish mistake."

Elyot looked up at Sergei, anger and hatred etched on his face. "That bitch killed my sister."

Sergei shrugged. "Your sister paid the price for her disloyalty. Nothing more. Your price has yet to be paid."

Carl moved to stand in front of Elyot, shielding him from the armed men. "I won't allow you to hurt him."

A small smile traced Sergei's lips as though he were amused by Carl's declaration. "I see. Perhaps you wish to negotiate for his life?"

Carl's eyes narrowed. "I won't betray Kayla."

Sergei *tsked* at him. "I would not ask such a thing. No. I have something else in mind. You see, I believe we share same goals."

"What goals?"

"Desire to protect our people," Sergei replied, moving forward and gesturing to Elyot. "You say you want to protect this man... this... traitor. I want to protect my own men... loyal men. You can help me with this."

Suspicion filled Carl, but he was at a profound disadvantage. "How?"

"With Kayla's help, of course."

CHAPTER ELEVEN

AFTER FELIX LEFT to speak with Mack about arranging their escape, Kayla spent the next hour unsuccessfully trying to locate Carl. The idea of using his boots as a focal point was sound, but she couldn't figure out how the energy threads were supposed to work. The more she tried to force it, the harder it was to make sense of the energy. Alec had made it seem so easy when he'd shown her how to locate the glass globe. Now she had the suspicion he'd guided the energy without her realizing it.

Frustrated, she slid down to the floor and closed her eyes, resting her head against the wall. She was exhausted. The effects from the metabolic booster and lack of sleep were beginning to cloud her judgment. For a ruin rat, this could be dangerous. She needed to keep it together a little longer until she located Carl. At the same time, the clock was ticking, and they needed to leave the ruin rat camp. The longer they stayed, the more likely Alec would become impatient and raid the camp. Unfortunately, they were still waiting on the diversionary team to finish packing.

The sound of footsteps approached, but she didn't need

to open her eyes to know it was Brant. The absence of energy threads around him was a potent indicator.

"Are you all right?"

Kayla opened her eyes to study Brant in the dim lighting. With the change of clothes and five o'clock shadow on his face, he was appearing more like a ruin rat every day. It actually made him much more appealing and approachable.

"Yeah. It's just been a long day, and I can't seem to get the energy to work right. Pull up some floor, Fluffy. We need to talk." She scooted over and motioned for him to have a seat.

Brant arched an eyebrow, eyeing the ground with trepidation. Whether it was the fact he would be sitting on the floor or in close proximity to her, she wasn't sure. Kayla couldn't help but find it amusing that he continued to keep a marked physical distance between them. It made her want to push the limits even more and invade his space. She was a perverse woman, but she really enjoyed poking at him.

He sat on the floor, and she nearly snorted at the look of discomfort on his face. He was trying so hard to retain some semblance of professionalism. It was sorely out of place here.

"You need to learn how to relax a little, Brant. Life's too short."

He frowned but tried to emulate the way she was sitting. From the stiff rigidity of his posture, he was clearly out of his element. She had to give him points for trying though.

"I suspect my lifespan has already been significantly shortened simply due to our acquaintance," Brant observed.

Kayla laughed and bumped her shoulder against his. A slight tingle went through her at the brief contact. Brant stiffened for a moment and then relaxed. It wasn't as strong as it had been earlier, but there was still a distinctive spark.

"Yeah, we should probably talk about that. Back when we first met, we grappled when I tried to leave the towers. I didn't notice any energy transference then. Why is it happening now every time I touch you?"

Brant fell silent for a long moment. Finally, he admitted, "I suspect it has to do with the energy I took from you. I've never used my skills against you until Alec ordered me to do so. The reaction began after I absorbed some of your energy."

Kayla bit her lip and studied him, trying to resist the urge to touch him again to see what would happen. He was watching her with equal intensity, and she wished she could read him better. "So you're still holding on to the energy? Do you think the person who attacked me is doing the same?"

His brow furrowed as though he were considering the possibility. "Perhaps. It seems to be dissipating though. While I still feel your energy within me, it's not as strong as it was."

Kayla cocked her head, an idea taking shape in her mind. "Do you think you can use the energy? If I were to give you more, could you use it?"

Brant's entire body went still. "What are you thinking?"

She scooted over to kneel in front of him, just a hair's breadth away. Brant eyed her approach warily but didn't move away. "Come on, Brant. You've studied energy channeling for years. You know far more about it than I do. If I can give you my energy, you can try to use Carl's boots as a focal object to find him."

He shook his head, denying her claim. "Kayla, my studies were theoretical. I've learned techniques to negate and subdue energy. Your— Alec is the one you should be discussing this with. He can help you to direct your energy."

"You and I both know if I go back to the towers, Alec's going to try to find a way to lock me up."

The corners of Brant's mouth curved in a hint of a smile. "You have a point, but I can't say I disagree with him. I've never met anyone so inclined to find trouble."

She huffed. "Look, let's just try it. You have far more

control than I do. Besides, Alec told me my ability to find missing objects was dependent upon the distance. As long as I'm on the surface, I'm much closer to wherever they're holding Carl." She lifted her hand, hovering over his bare arm. "So... are you ready to try this or not? It may not work until we get an idea of the location of the Coalition camp, but who knows? Maybe we'll get lucky."

Brant swallowed, emotions warring across his face. He watched her hand with a combination of longing and unease. "I'm still not sure this is a good idea. We don't know how something like this will affect you. We should probably wait until Alec is with you. I don't want you to get hurt."

Kayla snorted. Life was all about taking chances. Where would she be if she always played it safe? Besides, she doubted Alec would approve of any experiments like this.

She lowered her hand, pressing it against Brant's arm. There was a sudden flicker of energy, but like Brant had described, it was more muted than it had been in the towers. Even so, Brant's eyes widened, and his gaze darted from her hand up to her face and then back again.

Kayla concentrated, trying to determine if she could create a link with Brant. There had to be a way she could send him energy without him stealing it from her. If he could take it, she should theoretically also be able to share it. Unfortunately, the individual energy threads seemed to disappear around him, making it impossible to hold a normal connection.

From what she'd learned, the Drac'Kin and energy manipulation all seemed to focus on balance. Alec had mentioned counterpoints on several occasions. If Brant naturally negated all energy, what would happen if she did the opposite and combined all four different types of energy?

She bit her lip, considering the possibilities. It was a little unusual, but it just might work. The only other option was to ask him to steal her energy again. A quick glance at Brant's expression let her know that was probably out of the question. He'd been reluctant enough about even trying this experiment, although if it came down to it, she'd figure out a way to convince him.

The thought of having her energy stolen again made her feel sick to her stomach, but she'd willingly suffer through it to save Carl. The entire experiment felt far less threatening when she remembered what was at stake. With a sense of renewed determination, Kayla concentrated on gathering some of the energy threads around her. Thanks to Alec's tutelage, she was now able to decipher the different types of energy.

She closed her eyes, fusing together a small mixture of air, earth, water, and fire. The threads sparked and almost seemed to glow in her mind's eye. Reaching out with her woven strands of energy, she tried again to create a connection with Brant.

They both gasped as the link between them settled into place. Her eyes flew open to meet Brant's shocked expression. Kayla reached out to him along the braided energy threads, noting the differences between the bond she shared with Alec and this strange new connection. She had the feeling if she stopped touching him, the temporary tie she'd forged with Brant would also break apart. It felt incredibly fragile.

He stared at her hand on his arm and then jerked his head up to meet her gaze. "What the hell did you do?"

"I can't believe it actually worked." Kayla laughed, unable to stop the grin from spreading across her face. "I just plugged you in, Fluffy. Now it's time to kick up the power and see what happens."

Before he could object, she sent a small stream of energy in his direction.

Brant inhaled sharply. His arm trembled under her hand,

and she started to pull back, worried that she was hurting him. Leaning forward, he grabbed her hand and held it against his arm. He must have also realized that touch was required to maintain this strange type of connection. "No," he urged. "Don't stop. I've just never felt anything like this before."

Kayla glanced down at his hand over hers. Reassured by his words, she increased the amount of energy flowing into him. She could almost visualize him as an empty vessel. As she poured her energy into him, she had the impression what he was experiencing was like a soothing balm that eased something within him. Something within her relaxed as well, and she was comforted by the thought she was giving him some vital element he needed. She'd gladly give everything she had to find Carl, if that's what was necessary.

Kayla looked up into Brant's hazel eyes. He was gazing at her with a look of wonder and almost reverence. As though unable to help himself, he reached up and brushed his fingers against her cheek. The contact caused a surge of power to flow between them and she leaned into his touch, enjoying the sensation. Sharing energy was almost intoxicating, and it would be easy to lose herself in the rush of power.

When he ran his thumb over her lower lip, though, Kayla shook her head and pulled back slightly. The intimacy of the moment was quickly moving into uncomfortable territory, and she needed to rein it in. The look of desire and yearning in his eyes gave her a moment of pause. It wasn't real. Brant didn't feel that way about her, and she didn't feel that way about him, but damn if the energy wasn't nice. Even so, the realization *she'd* put that look in his eyes was troubling.

The sensation of sharing a connection with Brant was different from anything she'd experienced with any Inner Circle member. Instead of losing herself in the rush of power, Kayla felt decidedly in control. She was the one steering the speeder, dictating the amount she would share and direction they would travel. It was possible Brant could steal energy from her like he had before, but he seemed content to accept whatever she was willing to offer. Like forming a bond with another Drac'Kin, this was also an act of trust. It was strange to have that level of intimacy with someone she wasn't sure she trusted.

She thought back to when she'd first met Alec. He was the one who'd dictated the terms of their energy bond. In a way, she realized her inexperience had plagued their relationship. They could never be on equal footing because, quite simply, his knowledge of the arcane dwarfed hers. Although his intentions were honorable, she would always straddle that line between the surface and the towers. That was one of her strengths and also one of her shortcomings.

When Kayla disconnected the energy flow and tried to pull away again, he reluctantly let her go. Everyone else she'd met in the towers had tried to take advantage of her for their own purposes. In a way, it was a marvel Brant so easily relinquished their temporary connection. A strange sense of understanding filled her, and it made her even more intent to explore the possibilities of sharing with him. Even though she didn't know him well, he was potentially safe. If he was letting her go so easily, his intention toward her couldn't be nefarious. He was one of the last people she'd ever believed she could trust, but he was proving himself with actions instead of empty promises.

The moment they broke contact, the threads connecting them began to fray and deteriorate. He stared at her longingly for a moment and then curled his hands into fists as though trying to prevent himself from reaching out to touch her again. "Kayla, I— You—" His voice broke off. "Is that what sharing energy normally feels like?"

Kayla frowned. She wasn't sure if their experiences were

the same. There was a sense of rightness in sharing energy with him, but it was so different from what she felt with Alec. "I don't know. It was similar, but not quite the same. Energy seems to disappear around you, but I can connect with you if I use all the different types of energy. For some reason, though, I can only channel it directly to you if I'm touching you."

"That's because you're a conduit," a voice interrupted.

Kayla's head jerked up, and she met Lars's blue-eyed gaze. At the sight of him, she jumped up, but the recent energy transference left her a little lightheaded. Brant stood and pulled her back, placing himself protectively in front of her, and drew his weapon.

Lars shook his head at the futile gesture. Several armed men wearing Coalition uniforms entered the room and trained their weapons on Brant.

"Put the weapon away, Brant. I have no intention of harming Kayla."

She snorted and rubbed her injured side, remembering their last meeting. Lars could make all the claims he wanted, but actions spoke louder than words. Brant obviously agreed and didn't lower his weapon. "Not a fucking chance. You're not touching her."

Lars raised an eyebrow. "Me? I wonder what your dear brother would say if he knew what liberties you were taking with his fiancée. Or do you not plan on telling him you were sharing energy with his bondmate?"

Brant's shoulders went rigid, and his jaw clenched.

Kayla looked back and forth between the two men. "Brother? What are you talking about?"

Lars *tsked* at Brant. "So many secrets. The towers are full of them, aren't they? I suppose I shouldn't be surprised neither one of you told her."

Kayla turned to study Brant, noting his appearance. Was it possible? There wasn't much of a resemblance, but...

"Is it true? You're Alec's brother?"

When Brant didn't respond, Lars chuckled. "Half-brother, actually. Didn't anyone tell you how Shadows came to be? They're the bastard children of an Inner Circle member and a non-sensitive. My dear Uncle Edwin was his father. Brant here is Alec's half-brother and their family's dirty little secret."

Kayla gaped at Brant, who looked like he'd be more than happy to blast a hole in Lars right now. She cocked her head, seeing Brant in a new light, and couldn't help but wonder about his relationship with Alec. He must have sought out Brant after his father's death. She'd never seen him during her first visit to the towers.

Edwin had been a pretentious and power-hungry bastard who had managed to lay waste to everything in his path. It didn't matter that Alec's hand had been the one to deal the killing blow. Alec was still trying to make reparations for his father's mistakes and greed.

Lars smirked and gestured to Brant. "I'm surprised you didn't know, Kayla. The towers view Shadows as little more than parasites, sucking out the energy threads the rest of us can use. In a sardonic twist of Fate, many of the Shadows become security officers to guard the same individuals who demean them."

Kayla blinked and shook her head, rubbing her temples and trying to ward off the beginnings of a headache. She'd already begun to realize OmniLab had some screwed-up hierarchal tendencies. As interesting as the family history lesson might be, it wasn't the most important issue.

"I don't understand. So what if he's Alec's half-brother? Who gives a fuck?" She shook her head to clear it. "Where the hell is Carl?"

Brant glanced at her in surprise. Lars studied her thoughtfully and chuckled. Giving her an easy smile, he held out his hands in a passive gesture.

"It's so easy to forget you don't have the usual prejudices of our kind. Don't worry, little one. Your trader is quite well. I have no intention of harming either one of you. I wanted the opportunity to speak with you again, and this seemed like the best way of getting your attention. Unsurprisingly enough, Alec is quite protective of you and has made every effort to prevent us from contacting you."

When Lars took a step toward her, Brant moved between them and aimed his weapon directly at him. Lars halted at the protective gesture, narrowing his eyes on the armed security officer as though he were a specimen on a microscope. "You must be enjoying this assignment. After so long without experiencing it, the ability to taste and hold energy must be intoxicating. I wonder how long this current assignment will last. Alec must have no idea Kayla can willingly share energy with you or he would never have left you alone with her."

Brant's expression hardened, but he didn't respond. Lars wasn't finished though. He gave the security officer a pitying look, adding, "I wonder what lengths Alec will go to in order to protect Kayla from the rest of the Shadows? Won't she become more of a target if word gets out that her energy can be stolen? I'm not sure how loyal your halfbrother will be to you when it comes to protecting his bondmate. Alec may very well consider you and the rest of the Shadows to be a liability. Are you willing to take that chance?"

Brant's fingers tightened on his weapon, but otherwise, he didn't move. Kayla took a step to the side so she could see around him. Time to end this nonsense. "What are you doing here, Lars?"

"Offering both of you a choice," Lars said, clasping his

hands behind his back. The gesture reminded her of Alec, and the similarity annoyed her.

Kayla scowled. "I already told you what I think of your choices. I just want Carl back."

Lars arched a brow. "And then what? You'll still be bonded to Alec. As long as you two are connected, you'll never be able to live your life independently or truly be with your trader. I can give you options, Kayla. I can help you remove the bond in exchange for your help."

"By killing Alec? He's not at fault for what happened to you, Lars. That was Edwin's doing, and he's gone."

Lars's shoulders tensed at the reminder. "I'm surprised Alec told you how a bond can be transferred. Or did he tell you in the hopes it would keep you in the towers and under his control?"

Kayla didn't respond and curled her hands into fists. Alec hadn't told her shit. It was Ariana who had let it slip, but she didn't intend to advertise the fact. Even though she still believed Alec's intentions were honorable, she was walking a very tight line with her dealings with Lars.

At her silence, Lars pinned his gaze on Brant. "What about you? You don't have to be tied to the life you were handed. You have options as well."

The security officer sneered. "I'm not interested in anything you have to offer."

"You should be. Many of your fellow Shadows have agreed to the Coalition's terms. We can give you what you've been wanting: acceptance. Your abilities could prove to be invaluable, especially considering Kayla's talents."

Kayla took a half-step backward, apprehension filling her. She didn't like the way this sounded. "What are you talking about?"

Lars turned back to her. "I need to apologize to you, Kayla. We weren't aware of the ability until Miranda's test in the towers went wrong. Harming you was not the intent. Miranda was supposed to determine the strength of your bond with Alec, but the Shadow agent we'd enlisted for help ended up stealing your energy. It's rather remarkable, really. I suspect Spirit energy may be the counterpoint to shadow energy. It's such a rare talent, we haven't done any studies."

Kayla swallowed, remembering the cold chill she'd experienced in the towers.

Miranda must be the water channeler behind that attack.

It made sense, but that meant there were Shadows within the towers who were actively working against OmniLab. She glanced at Brant, wondering if he could have known about the deception. He seemed to want to protect her, but everyone had their own agenda. Either way, she needed to warn Alec that his suspicions were correct, and the Coalition had allies within the towers.

Lars gestured to Brant again, drawing her attention back to the conversation. "You saw how you're able to feed energy to Brant. Do you think it's a coincidence you're able to channel massive amounts of energy and he has the ability to negate it? I believe that's part of your ability as a spirit channeler. You can connect with any Shadow. With your talent to transfer energy to others, you can essentially turn any Shadow into an Inner Circle member."

Brant lowered his weapon a fraction. "You're wrong. The energy dissipates. It doesn't last more than a few hours."

Lars nodded. "Of course. But think of what you could accomplish in that period of time if you learned how to control that stored energy."

Kayla held up her hands to halt the conversation. "Whoa, wait a fucking minute. I'm not a damn battery you can pass around while everyone recharges their energy supply."

The edge of Lar's mouth lifted in a hint of a smile. "Of course not. You're so much more, Kayla. There's no limit to your potential. With your abilities, you could give new purpose to the Shadows. You could give new purpose to all of us. If you work with me, we could accomplish a great deal."

Kayla's eyes narrowed. She didn't trust Lars any further than she could throw him. But at the very least, she no longer needed to try to hunt him down. It was time to steer this conversation back to where it belonged. "Where's Carl?"

"I'm more than happy to take you to him," he offered and gestured for the guards to move forward.

Brant spun, shoving Kayla down behind a crate, and leaned over to fire a shot at one of the approaching guards. The guards scattered, each taking cover behind some packed boxes.

"You're outnumbered, Brant!" Lars shouted. "Put down the weapon. No one needs to get hurt."

Kayla crouched down and looked over at Brant whose body was coiled and alert. He kept his weapon raised, ready to fire at anyone else who approached. She swallowed. This could get bad fast. There were too many innocents in the camp.

In a low voice, she whispered, "I thought the plan was to find Carl. Lars is our best chance and you're shooting at him?"

Brant scoffed. "You think Lars is just going to let you walk into the Coalition's camp and hand Carl over to you? You take one step into their camp and you won't be walking back out. He just wants to use you to kill Alec. You can't trust him."

Kayla harrumphed. He had a point. "Fine. Any brilliant ideas on how we're going to get out of here then?"

"I'd suggest you call Alec, but you decided to destroy the commlinks," he retorted and fired again at another approaching guard. The guard dove back behind some crates.

She gaped at him. "Really? You want to blame me for this? Now?"

He spared her the briefest glance. "If the shoe fits..."

She fisted her hands, resisting the urge to smack him.

"Enough!" a voice shouted from outside the room. Kayla peeked over the boxes and spotted Leo. The aging camp leader strode into the room, gazing in irritation at the mess they'd made, and glared at the armed men.

"Kayla, get your ass out here now. These fuckers are destroying my camp."

Kayla's squeezed her eyes shut and pressed her forehead against the side of the crate. She didn't want to believe it, but the evidence was pretty damning. How else could Lars have found them so quickly? "Leo, please tell me you didn't sell me out to these assholes."

Leo snorted. She lifted her head to peer over the crate at the camp leader. His arms were crossed over his chest, and he was staring in her direction. "You've gotten soft, girl. I warned you about getting involved with traders and outsiders. They're nothing but trouble, always sniffing around where they don't belong. I have an entire camp to think about. Lars contacted me an hour ago and offered a generous finder's fee if we helped keep you here. With OmniLab trading shut down, we didn't have much of an option, did we?"

Shit.

Kayla forced herself to keep her expression calm despite the hammering of her heart. Even though she'd pushed the boundaries often enough, part of her never thought Leo would actually turn on her.

Stupid. So stupid. What the hell had she been thinking by staying here? She should have dropped off the supplies and left immediately. Now Leo's entire camp was in danger, and their only play was to offer her up as a sacrifice.

As much as it rankled, it made sense Leo would side with the Coalition. The shipment she brought from OmniLab was the last one they'd see for a while, unless she got the ban lifted. At least she had an idea who was responsible for the corruption within the towers though.

Fuck.

———

CARL CROSSED his arms over his chest, watching as two guards carried Lisia's body out of the room while Elyot followed behind them. Provided Carl agreed to Sergei's request, Elyot would accompany Lisia's body back to her former camp. He wouldn't forget his promise to Lisia, but his focus needed to be on Kayla for the moment.

"What do you want with Kayla?"

Sergei casually leaned against the wall as though he couldn't care less whether Carl agreed to his terms. "Our Coalition is terminating agreement with Lars. Your capture was not part of plan."

Carl froze, turning back to study the blond man. Steely-gray eyes met his, but they told him nothing. It was impossible to discern his motivations based on Sergei's demeanor. "What do you mean?"

"Vengeance is not our concern. Our first loyalty is to our people. Your Kayla understood this. Lars does not."

"I'm not arguing that, but Miranda seems to disagree," Carl pointed out. "She talked about how Lars has done a lot for his people."

"I would not know," Sergei said with a shrug. "Love can blind some people."

Carl paused. "Are you saying Miranda's in love with Lars?"

Sergei cocked his head. "It matters?"

"No. Although, I'm a little surprised she was willing to go along with Lars's plan to try to bond with Kayla." Carl's hands clenched at the reminder. He needed to find her soon. The longer he spent chatting with Sergei, the more potential danger she was in.

Sergei pushed away from the wall and walked over to the map displayed on the wall. With the press of a button, the marked locations of potential resources lit up. "Why does OmniLab not harvest resources? You traders have not tapped into these areas. Your crews are limited. Why?"

Carl studied the map more carefully and was surprised by the extensive mapping of their territory. They must have been gathering data for years. "Until recently, the towers were self-sustaining. They're just now beginning to supplement their existing resources with outside sources."

"They use their 'energy' for this. Do you know how?"

Carl hesitated and turned back to Sergei who was watching him. "I can't say. Until I met Kayla, I'd only heard rumors of their abilities. Even now, I don't know much. They don't discuss things with outsiders."

Sergei gave a small smile. "My superiors believe OmniLab is regular facility. They do not believe these claims of energy."

Carl raised his eyebrows. "How can they not? Haven't they met Lars and Miranda?"

"A trick or superstition," Sergei replied dismissively. "Many explanations are possible. They will not believe until too late."

Understanding dawned. Their fears had been correct. The weapons Elyot had mentioned, plus the armed men, could only equate to one thing. "You're attacking the towers. That's why you've only got a skeleton crew still here."

Sergei inclined his head but didn't respond.

Carl ran a shaky hand over his face. *I need to get out of here now.* "The loss of life will be enormous if you treat the towers as any other facility. OmniLab won't just lay down."

"Agreed. An arrangement for cooperation would benefit both sides. That is why we are speaking now."

Carl started to pace. He didn't know what sort of fire-power the Coalition had at their disposal, but based on the technology he'd seen, it wasn't trivial. Otherwise, they wouldn't have been able to operate unnoticed for so long.

"I need to find Kayla. If something happens to her, there's no way in hell OmniLab will consider negotiating with you. Do you know where she is?"

Sergei pulled a small tablet from his pocket, glanced at it, and then handed it to him. "This will help track Miranda. She is awake now. My men were instructed to allow her to leave. Follow her and she will lead you to Lars. When you find him, you will also find Kayla."

Carl studied the map with a frown. The marker indicated Miranda was already on the move. He lifted his gaze again to focus on the Coalition leader. "What do you want in exchange?"

Sergei leaned forward and tapped the screen. A communication display populated the screen. "Give tablet to Kayla. She has one hour to agree to terms and negotiate with OmniLab on our behalf. I will arrange transportation for you."

Carl frowned. "I can't make any promises, but if anyone can get through to Alec and Seara, it'll be Kayla. Can you delay your attack?"

"No. My men are already in place. I have negotiated small delay with my superiors, but no more."

"Shit," Carl muttered, sliding the tablet in his pocket. The clock was ticking. "Show me to the transport."

CHAPTER TWELVE

THE ATMOSPHERE in the workroom was nearly stifling from the tension. Kayla stood behind Brant, who was currently facing off with Lars. The guards had temporarily stepped back, waiting for Lars's command. Leo caught Kayla's eye, and it was clear he wanted her to do something—and fast.

"Well, fucks to you, Leo," Kayla snapped at her former camp leader. "Why don't you go lick the Coalition's boots for a while and let the adults talk? I wonder how long it'll take the Coalition to realize their new asset is off by a couple of letters?"

"Mouthy shrew," Leo retorted angrily, jerking his head upward in approval at her show of anger.

She blinked at him, wondering if her initial assessment was wrong.

There was something about his gesture that made her take notice, and his earlier words filled her mind. *"They're nothing but trouble, always sniffing around where they don't belong."* It was the way he'd emphasized "sniffing." Maybe Leo had been trying to tell her Lars had the camp under surveillance.

Why else would they have asked Leo to *keep* her there? Felix was right when he said the camp's security had gone to shit.

Leo narrowed his eyes and pointed his finger at her. "We're done, girl. You're no longer welcome here. You've destroyed my trading relationships, cost me countless credits, and endangered the lives of all the people in this camp. I'll be damned if I know why Felix hunted you down after you got his brother killed. You two can go find a new camp for all I care."

Even though she knew it was for show, his words cut deep. Everything he said was true, and Kayla couldn't help but struggle to take a breath under the weight of the tight band of guilt constricting her chest. Despite her recklessness, Leo had supported her through everything. He was the closest thing to a father she'd ever known.

If she read between the lines, though, Leo didn't say she wasn't welcome in their camp. She was simply not welcome *here*, which didn't matter because the camp was relocating. The mention of Felix was also telling. Leo must have given Felix the coordinates to their future camp. A wave of affection and gratitude washed over her, but she pushed it aside. She clenched her fists as she tried to rein in her emotions and keep up the act.

With one more hard look, Leo added, "Do what you want, Lars. I'll be damned if I know why you want to bother though. I'm taking my people out of here." With that final parting shot, he turned and stormed out of the room.

Kayla swallowed. Good. He'd get the rest of the ruin rats to safety. Dealing with Lars and the Coalition would be up to her. She turned back to Lars.

"That was rather unfortunate," Lars acknowledged, rubbed his chin and studying her thoughtfully. "I'd heard there was some tension between you and your former camp leader. Now I see what they meant."

"Yeah, well, Leo's a bit like a hemorrhoid. Uncomfortable and always on your ass about something." Kayla shrugged and crossed her arms, trying to appear casual.

She just needed a bit more time to make sure Leo got everyone out safely. Knowing her former camp leader, he had plans to come back and pick up the rest of the equipment after this situation was resolved. She just hoped it didn't end with her being an ugly stain on the ground. Blood was a bitch to get out of electronics.

"I want to know more about this whole thing with the Shadows."

Brant frowned and raised an eyebrow at her.

Lars seemed surprised as well. The renegade Omni eyed her with suspicion. "You would be willing to aid them? Why the change of heart?"

"I didn't say I had a change of heart," she pointed out. "I just want to know more about it. What can I say? I'm a girl who likes to know all her options."

Lars clasped his hands behind his back, but the suspicion in his eyes remained. "I see. What do you want to know?"

"Well, let's say you're right and I *can* channel energy into any Shadow, which would turn them into kickass Inner Circle members. I mean, that's kind of badass, right? Except, I would be able to choose who to bestow this power on unless they decided to steal my energy."

"In theory, yes," Lars agreed hesitantly, obviously wondering where she was going with this. "I believe it's most likely possible to block Shadows from stealing your energy without your consent. There may also be easier ways to transfer energy than what you just experienced with Brant. We may even be able to find a way to circumvent the issue with Shadows being unable to sustain the energy you've channeled to them. But even if that's not possible and we work cooperatively together, we could accomplish a great deal in that short period of time."

She nodded. "Right. Except I'm still in training."

"I would be more than happy to complete your training," Lars offered.

Brant scowled at him. "I bet."

Lars narrowed his eyes on the security officer, and Kayla bit the inside of her cheek to keep from smiling. The inside of the camp was much quieter, and she had the distinct impression it was mostly empty. If she was going to make her move, it needed to be now.

"If you will agree to allow me to claim you," Lars began again, "I can assist you with exploring your talents and helping the Shadows, if that's your wish. I can assure you Alec will not make such an offer."

"See, I don't know about all that," she said, angling her body close to Brant and gesturing to him. "What's cool about Brant is he already knows how to use the energy. At least, theoretically. As for me, I fully admit I don't have a clue as to what I'm doing, but all I have to do is slap my hand on him," Kayla made a show of dropping her hand on Brant's arm, "then just funnel a shitload of energy at him, and he can blow your asses totally out of the room."

Realization dawned, and Lars's eyes widened at her words.

"Get ready to blow, Fluffy," she whispered. Taking a deep breath, she grabbed an enormous amount of energy and flooded it directly into Brant. His body arched from the sudden rush of power, and his weapon clattered to the ground.

Lars shouted out orders for the guards to rush them, but it was too late. Brant lifted his hands, expelling the huge force outward from his palms and pushing everything back in its path. Lars, the guards, and the crates were blown backward into the wall and tumbled to the ground in a messy heap.

Kayla dropped her hand and staggered from the sudden loss of energy. "Oh, shit. It worked."

Brant's hands trembled, and he reached down to grab his weapon. Tucking it into his side, he grabbed Kayla's arm. A jolt of energy surged through them at the contact. She jerked, but Brant didn't lessen his grip on her arm as he dragged her half-stumbling from the room. "We have to get out of here."

Felix came rushing around the corner, wide-eyed and looking back and forth between them. "Fuck me. I saw the whole thing on camera. You've got some serious explaining to do, girl. But we've got to go right now. Leo's got the crew evacuated, and they've officially abandoned this location. Mack's running a distraction to buy us a little time, so let's move."

Kayla nodded and took a step forward, nearly collapsing from the effort. Impatient, Felix leaned down and hefted her over his shoulder. She'd normally object, but that last little maneuver had totally fried her. She watched the ground bob absently as they hurried to the exit. Darkness was starting to creep into her vision, but she tried to stave it off.

"Felix," she whispered, trying to keep her voice low so Lars's surveillance wouldn't pick up her words, "head to the underground river. I need more time. If Alec finds out where I am, he'll drag me back to the towers. This is the best chance I have to find Carl. We need to find a way to get OmniLab and Lars off our tail—"

Felix nodded. "No worries, crazy girl. I've got you covered."

At least someone did—because she was all out of steam.

———

ALEC SLAMMED his fist on the table, not bothering to mask

his fury at the incompetence in front of him. "What do you mean you lost her?"

Thomas straightened his shoulders. "Brant's communication device was destroyed almost as soon as they left the towers. We eventually tracked them to a surface camp using the tracking device installed on Mistress Rath'Varein's person. However, they must have discovered it."

Seara frowned. "Why do you think that?"

"We believe the surface dwellers aided in the subterfuge and used the tracking device to lay a false trail," Thomas explained. "They were gone by the time we realized what happened and raided the camp. The entire camp's been abandoned. What's more is we believe Lars and the Coalition may have had some involvement. They were somehow able to mask their identities from our security team."

Alec's jaw clenched, and he glared at his security commander. The implications were clear. "You suspect OmniLab involvement."

Commander Thomas gave him a curt nod. "Yes. More than suspect at this point, but we're still investigating. We believe there might be a connection to whoever opened the bay doors during the initial escape. Based on Kayla's known associations, we suspected some of the surface dwellers staying within the towers as possible conspirators."

Veridian shook his head. "Wait a minute. We weren't able to open the doors. The codes had been changed. Kayla almost died because someone opened the wrong door. It wasn't us."

"You're correct," Commander Thomas agreed. "We traced the terminal used to open the doors and determined it originated from this tower, and not the one where the bay doors were housed. No surface dwellers were present within this tower at that time."

Commander Thomas pressed a button on his commlink. "Bring her in, Director."

A moment later, the door slid open and Director Borshin entered, followed by Brianna Kisbell and an escort of two Inner Circle Shadows. The tall brunette tossed her hair back, glaring at Alec in defiance.

Alec leaned forward, pressing his palms against the table. "What's the meaning of this?"

"Mistress Kisbell has been acting as your representative using your credentials," Commander Thomas explained. "She issued instructions to some security staff members that Mistress Kayla Rath'Varein was to be kept under active surveillance, at your orders. They complied with her request, reporting directly to her as indicated, and allowed her unrestricted access to security feeds using biometric mapping to determine Mistress Rath'Varein's location. She then used your credentials to open the bay doors, which endangered Mistress Rath'Varein's life."

Seara rose from her seat, her eyes flashing with barely suppressed anger. The similarity between mother and daughter was never more apparent until this moment. Seara crossed the room to stand before Brianna and regarded the young woman for a long moment. Without a word, Seara drew back and slapped Brianna across the face.

Brianna's head jerked back in shock, her hand flying to her cheek. Alec rushed over to intervene, pulling Seara away from the young woman.

"How dare you," Seara hissed, not tearing her eyes away from Brianna. "There is no excuse for your actions. You've violated one of our oldest laws."

Brianna took a step backward, bumping into one of the Shadows. She gasped and pulled away, almost shrinking down upon herself. "There's been a misunderstanding, Seara. I believed Kayla wanted to find the trader. I only wanted to help."

Alec's eyes narrowed in suspicion. He'd been witness to Brianna's subterfuge and ruses more times than he cared to admit. He released Seara and stepped toward Brianna, taking her arm and weaving a thread of influence around her. "Did you try to kill Kayla Rath'Varein?"

Brianna opened her mouth and then clamped it shut. She opened it again, fighting against his influence. In a voice barely above a whisper, she said, "Yes."

Alec thrust more energy toward her. "How?"

"I tried... I tried to knock her off the beam in the basement," she said on a gasp.

Seara made a choked cry, her hand flying to her mouth. She turned away as though unable to listen anymore. Alec's hand tightened reflexively around Brianna's arm. "Did you try to kill Kayla by opening the doors?"

"Yes. I just wanted her to be gone," she croaked, her eyes now wide with panic while tears streamed down her face. "I didn't care how. If she stayed, I wouldn't have had a chance with you. She doesn't deserve to be bonded to the council leader."

Alec released her. Brianna collapsed to the floor, shaking and sobbing. Her testimony had doomed her. He felt a smidgen of pity for the pathetic creature in front of him, but not enough to intervene on her behalf. This was his fault as much as it was hers. He should have known Brianna was unbalanced. He certainly knew her penchant for manipulation, but attempting to kill Kayla was an entirely different matter.

Alec waved his hand toward Director Borshin. "Have her imprisoned while we determine a suitable punishment."

Brianna sobbed even louder, pleading in high-pitched wails that she was sorry. Alec ignored her, going over to

Kayla's mother instead. "I'm sorry, Seara. This was my fault. I never should have—"

Seara held up her hand to stop him. "No, Alec. You've spent your whole life taking the blame for your father's poor decisions. You will not take the blame for that woman now."

He took a deep breath and turned back to Commander Thomas. "I assume you have more to report? Brianna couldn't have been responsible for anything that happened on the surface. She's manipulative and deceitful, but she's not a mastermind to coordinate something like this."

"I agree," Commander Thomas said. "We have not found any ties between Brianna Kisbell and the Coalition. I believe this incident to be... of a personal nature." He cleared his throat and added, "There is a leak within OmniLab, and I believe some of our security and infrastructure have been compromised. We're doing our best to isolate the leak, but it appears it's more extensive than we first thought."

"And what about Kayla? Where is she now?" Seara asked, beginning to regain her composure.

"We aren't sure yet," Commander Thomas replied. "We're retracing her last known steps. We don't know if the surface dwellers abandoned their camp before or after the Coalition arrived. Our team is investigating and regrouping now."

Alec's eyes narrowed. "Do you have the camp's new coordinates?"

Veridian interrupted and shook his head. "You're not going to find her like that. Leo probably bailed when he found out about the conflict between OmniLab and the Coalition. He won't let his people get caught in the middle. Kayla won't stay with them either. She'll find out where they're heading but stay as far away from them as possible to protect them."

Seara sat down in her chair. "He's right, Alec. Kayla will want to protect her former campmates. Now that she's delivered their supplies, I'm sure she's trying to locate Carl. That's where you need to focus your efforts. If Lars finds her..." Her voice trailed off.

Alec frowned. He turned away from the table and looked out the window across the desolate landscape, trying to get control of his emotions. "Thomas, I want you to activate the tracker in her bloodstream. It'll take about thirty minutes to start getting a reading, but the entire duration will only last a few short hours. I want to be informed as soon as you have her coordinates. I'll accompany your team to retrieve her."

Seara's eyes widened in shock. "You had a tracker *injected* into her?"

Alec's jaw clenched, and he gave her a curt nod. "The deception was necessary, Seara. If I have to clip your daughter's wings, so be it, but I'll be damned if I'm going to let anything happen to her."

"I cannot fault you for this, Alec," she murmured. "Not if it will save her life."

Veridian pushed away from the table and stood. "With all due respect, I'm asking you to reconsider. Kayla asked me to stay and try to convince you not to go to the surface. I don't understand everything between you two, but she was convinced Lars is going to try to kill you. She said something about him challenging you for her bond."

Seara paled, her knuckles turning white as they gripped her armrest. "Alec, is this true? Is that Lars's intention?"

Alec clenched his fists. "That's irrelevant. It will not happen."

Seara stared at him. "You can't be serious, Alec. This must be a trap. He's trying to lure you out of the towers to challenge your bond. How could he even be considering such a thing? What is Kayla to him?"

"Nothing more than vengeance," he replied in a cold

voice. "Lars still blames me for my father's actions. As he should."

Seara stood, fury causing her to shake. "That's absurd. You were a child. No child is *ever* responsible for their parents' actions. I don't know if we can reason with Lars, but Trenon Noltreck is a good and honorable man. He stood by my husband's side as one of his most valued advisors. Kayla said she met him while she was on the surface in the Coalition camp. We just need to find a way to contact him. I can't imagine he would allow something like this to happen."

Veridian rubbed his chin. "I might have a way. If I can get a message to my former camp, they may be able to let the Coalition know you're trying to contact him."

Seara nodded. "Do what you can, Veridian. We need to explore every avenue to avoid more bloodshed."

Alec turned back to Thomas. "In the meantime, I want to be on the surface in the next thirty minutes. We have a limited amount of time to locate Kayla once you've activated the tracker. I won't risk your men losing her again."

"Alec, don't make any rash decisions," Seara urged. "Give us time to talk to Trenon."

Alec took a deep, steadying breath. Time was exactly what they didn't have. "I don't have a choice in this, Seara. If Lars is already on Kayla's trail, there's a chance he could find her before we can get to her. I won't risk him harming her. If he wants a challenge, by the gods, he'll get a challenge."

Seara squeezed her eyes shut and lowered her head. "That's your right as Kayla's bondmate, Alec." She took a deep breath and lifted her gaze to meet his. "I won't allow you to go alone though. Thomas, make the arrangements and notify the High Council that leadership of the towers is temporarily in their control. Marcus Staghorn and Devan Alivette shall act as High Council liaisons in our absence. I'll accompany the retrieval team."

Thomas bowed. "Of course, Mistress Rath'Varein. I'll make the arrangements immediately."

As the security commander left the room, Alec took a step toward the woman who had acted as a surrogate mother to him for more than a decade. "Seara, don't do this. It would be safer for you to stay in the towers."

Seara gave Alec a sad smile and shook her head. "No, Alec. If history is about to repeat itself, I refuse to stay behind in the towers this time. I won't lose my family again." She moved to stand next to him and put her hand on his arm. "And you, Alec, are my family just as much as Kayla. I won't stand by and lose either of you."

———

KAYLA WRAPPED her arm around Felix's waist and held on while they sped across the arid landscape. They passed ruined and collapsed buildings, heading deeper into Carl's district. She didn't need to look back to know Brant was right on their tail; the energy sparked and crackled around him. She nearly snorted at the thought of all the times he'd given her a hard time about leaking energy. The man was a freaking geyser and struggled to control it.

Although she normally hated being a passenger, she was thankful Felix had insisted on driving. The energy transference still had her feeling shaky. Brant, on the other hand, was wired like he'd stuck his finger into a live electrical socket.

"Not sure it's a good idea to be heading underground," Felix told her over the headset.

"It's not ideal, but we don't have many options. After the earthquake hit, Carl ordered a secondary exit route installed. We shouldn't get trapped underground if someone shows up," Kayla advised.

Felix chuckled. "I almost respect that trader of yours. He's just about as clever as you."

Kayla smiled and gave Felix's midsection a tighter squeeze. He had no idea. That was one of the things she adored about Carl. The thought of his unknown whereabouts caused her smile to fade. They needed to get to the cavern and try to see if Brant could locate him. If that didn't work, she was nearly out of options. She'd either have to hope Alec would find him or offer herself up to Lars. Neither option was very appealing.

"We're almost there," Kayla spoke into her headset as she noted the familiar landmarks.

For the most part, they were driving blind. They'd deactivated the normal guidance system to evade OmniLab and the Coalition for as long as possible. Between Felix managing to scramble the detection systems and Mack offering a distraction, she hoped they had enough time to find Carl's location.

"Head east about ten klicks and you'll see the marker for Sector Twelve. There's an old building still standing nearby where we can hide the speeders from view."

Felix turned the speeder and headed in the direction Kayla indicated. He slowed as they approached the building and pulled into the partially collapsed structure. They didn't bother to set up the UV guard; it would just be another indicator advertising their location. Their best bet was to get below ground and out of the range of any aerial detection.

Brant parked beside them, and Kayla motioned for the two men to follow her. Since Carl had begun some preliminary excavations, equipment had been left in place for them to drop down without having to set up their own. Even so, she bent down and ran a quick check to make sure it was sound. On the surface, the smallest mistakes could sometimes be the deadliest.

Satisfied that everything was in order, she climbed into a

harness. At Brant's perplexed look, she chuckled and showed him how to use the unfamiliar equipment. Sometimes it was hard to remember he'd spent his life in the towers and all of this was new to him.

Kayla slapped her gloved hand against the button to begin lowering the cable. It wasn't as safe to drop down without a spotter, but it was far more dangerous to stay above ground where Lars or the Coalition might find them.

As they descended into the ruins, Felix said, "I don't have a good feeling about this, crazy girl. Your Omni boy here doesn't have a clue what he's doing. There's no way to know if this energy thing is going to help you find your lost trader."

Kayla gripped the cable and glanced down, trying to judge the distance to the bottom. "Me neither, but I don't have any other ideas. I'm not going back to the towers yet, and I won't endanger any other ruin rat camps."

"This Lars guy really seems to want OmniLab's council leader," Felix mused. "Why not just give him up? Regardless of the outcome, you'll be out of danger and so will your trader."

Brant shifted in the harness awkwardly and glared at the ruin rat. "You seem to forget Master Tal'Vayr is the one currently holding your trading contract. Endangering him could jeopardize the entire infrastructure of the towers."

Felix snorted as they reached the bottom. "You seem to forget I don't give a fuck about your towers, your trading contract, *or* your leader. I'm only interested in getting Kayla out of this situation alive."

Once her feet touched the floor, Kayla unhooked her harness and dropped it to the ground. She leaned over and yanked off Brant's harness, tossing it aside.

"I'm going to do my best to make sure Alec *and* Carl get out of this safely. I don't want anything to happen to *either* of them." She put her hands on her hips and looked at Brant.

"All I want is one more shot at trying to find Carl my way. If you can't locate him using my energy, I'll agree to contact Alec. Deal?"

Brant hesitated and then nodded.

Kayla turned back to the dark-haired ruin rat. "I get it, Felix. I hated the towers for a long time too, but I've started to get to know some people there." She sighed and adjusted the light on her helmet, sweeping her gaze around the dilapidated room. "The people in the towers aren't that different from us. In some ways, they're more trapped than we are on the surface. Their trap is just a gilded cage. If anything, I pity most of them. They've never known what true freedom feels like."

Felix frowned. Kayla took a step forward, pushing some debris aside with the toe of her boot. "Once all this is said and done, I'm going to do everything in my power to build that damn tower for the ruin rats. We need to stop living apart and start working together. The Omnis don't know how to navigate the surface, and they need us to help find more resources. In return, they have access to things we don't."

She motioned for them to follow and tentatively led the way through the ruined rooms of what once was an upscale apartment house. "I think it's time to get rid of these trading posts and the old ways of doing things. If we're all going to survive what's to come, we need to work with the Omnis to accomplish our goals. We need each other, whether we like it or not. So please, Felix, can you put aside your contempt for OmniLab for a little while?"

Felix swore under his breath and stepped over a partially collapsed wall. "You're killing me here, Kayla." She halted and looked back at him. At her insistent glare, he shrugged. "Yeah, fine. I told you'd I'd help, so let's do it."

"Good," she agreed and headed deeper into the ruins with the two men following behind her.

The familiar pathway had been cleared more than she'd anticipated. New stability supports had been installed, and more than a few crates of supplies had been brought down. Carl had definitely been busy.

A rush of energy swirled around her as she approached the natural cavern. She now recognized it as the same energy that had prompted her to look in that direction in the first place. It was familiar, like an old friend. It was almost as though that particular thread of energy had been waiting years for her to call upon it.

They reached the natural cavern, and she had to bend slightly to enter the area. The two larger men had a bit more trouble. Although Carl and his crew had widened the passage, it was still narrow. They'd also installed some lighting to help offset the dark interior. They'd still need to do a great deal more excavation to move in the rest of the equipment and bring in a crew to run a full analysis though. It would probably take one or two fully manned teams to utilize the river to its fullest potential. That was even without knowing its origins or where it led.

Kayla pressed her gloved hand against the rocky wall. "We're almost there. The ground is slippery once we drop down, so be careful."

Both men murmured their acknowledgement. Kayla gripped the edge of the opening and dropped down, recalling the last time she'd been in the cavern. Hopefully, Brant could keep her from causing any more earthquakes this time.

As she moved toward the center of the cavern and the underground river, she pulled off her helmet and gloves. Brushing her hair away from her face, she inhaled deeply. The air was heavy and thick with moisture. Glancing back at the two men, she saw equal signs of astonishment. Until now, they had only seen images of the cavern and river. The reality was something completely different.

"This is incredible," Felix whispered almost reverently. "Fuck me, Kayla. How the hell did you find this?"

She bit her lip. If the ruin rats and Omnis were going to work together, they needed to start revealing some of these secrets that kept them segregated. Besides, she owed Felix nothing less than the truth. "Well, you know all the energy stuff we've been mentioning?"

At Felix's nod, she explained, "I don't really understand what all of it means, but I have the ability to sense missing or lost objects. When I was down here before, I caused an earthquake and a passage opened. I followed the trail of energy and it led me here." She turned toward the rushing water, feeling a sense of rightness about being in this space. Everything had been leading her here for so long. She just didn't know why. "I guess the river was lost and waiting for me to find it."

Felix frowned. "That's what all that energy talk was about?" He jerked his thumb at Brant. "And why you insisted on bringing this guy along? How long have you known about this?"

Kayla sighed. "Not long. It wasn't until Alec brought me to the towers and showed me I had these abilities. I must have blocked it out when I was a kid. Maybe it was self-preservation or something." Leo would have probably left her in the ruins if he'd had even a small inkling about her secret talents. She shrugged. "I don't know. I still don't know how to use the energy very well, but I'm hoping Brant can help me with that. If we can get an idea where Carl's being held, we can tell Alec where to focus his search. I was hoping Mack could help narrow down the location of the Coalition camp, but that's out of the question now. I'm not sure how close I need to be to find Carl."

Felix nodded and knelt next to a stalagmite, investigating the surface upward until it united with a stalactite. She watched him for a moment and turned to Brant. "What do you think? Are you ready to try this?"

Brant frowned. "In all honesty, Kayla, I don't like this plan. You channeled an enormous amount of energy to me just to escape from Lars. You're still shaky." He paused for a moment, as though unwilling to admit his next words. "If things don't go well, I'm unsure whether I can negate your abilities. I'm having some difficulties containing the energy you sent to me."

Kayla bit her lip and sent out a small thread toward him. It snapped and sparked against her borrowed energy. He was carrying too much and felt unbalanced. "I think you need to get rid of some of it."

He looked around the cavern. "I'm not sure how to do that safely here."

"I have an idea," she offered and motioned for Brant to sit on the cavern floor across from her. Once he was on the ground, she held out her hands to him. He hesitated and then took her hands in his. A spark of power between them flashed briefly.

Felix's eyes grew wide. "Whoa. What the hell was that?"

"Residual energy transference," Brant replied dryly and arched an eyebrow at Kayla. "If the connection between us is strong enough that even a non-sensitive could detect it, this could prove dangerous."

"I want to try to shift and rebalance the energy between us," Kayla explained. "Try sending some of the excess back to me."

Brant's brow furrowed, but he seemed to find her reasoning sound. He nodded and then concentrated. It seemed to take very little effort for the excess energy to shift. Like a magnet attracting its counterpoint, it flooded back to her with a sharp slap. She jerked at the contact and then relaxed as it settled back around her. Reaching out with her senses, she explored the energy around Brant. He was no longer crackling or sparking. She could sense the power within him, but it appeared to have equalized.

"Better?"

Brant blinked as he adjusted to the new energy level. When he nodded, she said, "Good. Alec showed me a little about how to find lost or missing objects. I can tell you what he told me, but I can't seem to make it work on my own. I think he guided my ability." She bit her lip, trying to remember exactly how she'd located the small glass globe Alec had hidden in his quarters. "I think what we need to do is have you act as the focus and visualize Carl's location. I'll be the battery backup to provide you with the power as you need it."

"Very well," Brant agreed. "What do we need to do?"

"You need to concentrate on the item you want to locate. In this case, close your eyes and visualize Carl's boots. You seem to notice everything, so that shouldn't be too hard. I'm sure you remember what they look like."

Brant snorted. "I only notice things in the sense that I'm searching for weapons or potential dangers. Foul-smelling footwear isn't high on that list."

Kayla glared at him and barely resisted the urge to smack him. "Dammit, just try." With a huff, she muttered, "There's no doubt you're related to Alec. No one else could be this much of a pain in the ass otherwise."

Brant chuckled and closed his eyes. After a long moment, he said, "Very well. I'm imagining his boots."

"Good," she said, barely suppressing her excitement. Maybe this wild idea would actually work. "Thread your— er, my energy through the image."

As he did so, she felt the balance between them shift. Kayla concentrated and began to send a steady stream of energy directly into Brant. His hands tightened around hers as she began to fill his depleting well.

"Now picture the boots in more detail. Focus on filling in the gaps in the image. Do you see Carl? How does he look? What do you see in the background? Can you get a sense of the direction?"

A crease marred Brant's forehead. "Hold on. Just wait. I'm trying to... I think I see something."

She leaned forward anxiously. "What? What do you see?"

Even Felix at this point was watching them with interest. He moved over to them and crouched down.

"I see a floor, like in one of those temporary camps."

"Focus on Carl," she instructed. "Is he okay?"

Brant swallowed. A bead of perspiration formed at his temple and began to travel downward. Whatever Brant was doing was taking a toll on him. Hoping it would solidify the vision, Kayla strengthened the energy flowing to him.

"I don't... I don't think he's wearing them. There's a... It looks like there's a pile of clothing on the floor next to the boots. I see a man standing nearby though. I don't recognize him, but he's wearing a Coalition uniform."

Confusion and worry filled her. Who was the mystery man? Why would Carl have taken off his boots? Where was he?

Her heart pounded as she took a steadying breath. She needed to focus. It was getting harder to feed Brant energy. The vision was demanding more and more, but she was still feeling weak from the earlier transference. They needed to hurry.

"Okay. I want you to focus on the room. Then try to see beyond the room. Can you get an idea of the direction of their camp?"

"I see..." Brant's voice trailed off, and she could feel him searching. There was no other way to explain it. There wasn't a bond between them, but she could almost visualize him wielding and manipulating her energy. It wasn't as effortless as Alec's ability, but it was better than her own skills. "It's a room of some sort. There's some equipment. I can't... I don't know what else..."

Kayla swallowed, desperation urging her to continue giving Brant what he needed. Her fingers trembled in Brant's hands as she channeled more into him. "Pull back from the vision a little, Brant. Try to see outside the room."

She felt him draw on the last vestiges of her strength, draining her even further. Her entire body trembled, and the world began to waver as the edges of her vision started to dim.

Felix looked back and forth between them worriedly. "Dammit, man. Stop whatever you're doing. She's going to pass out."

At his words, Brant's eyes flew open and he jerked his hands away. Kayla fell forward into his lap. Unharnessed power sparked through them at the contact.

"Fuck, that hurt," Kayla winced, rubbing her arms and willing the energy to stabilize.

Brant looked down at her, his forehead creased with concern. "Why didn't you stop me?"

She squeezed her eyes shut. "I need to find him, Brant. I don't know what else to do."

"You're going to get both of us killed," he muttered, pulling her closer and wrapping his arms around her. He began slowly trying to send her energy back toward her, equalizing his own stolen energy.

A sound from the nearby tunnel caused all of them to turn. Brant jumped up and scrambled to draw his weapon. Men dropped in from the cavern entrance wearing full UV protective gear and weapons. Kayla winced at the sight of the OmniLab symbol.

Dammit. How do they keep finding me?

When she felt Alec's cool air energy brush against hers and then envelope her, she swore. Her hopes of trying to keep him safe in the towers had failed. It was only a matter of time before the Coalition saw the gathering of forces and Lars arrived. She needed to get Alec out of here.

Kayla struggled to stand, hating the fact she was so weak, and finally allowed Brant to help her up. She leaned against him, unsure if her legs would support her weight.

Alec pulled off his helmet and narrowed his eyes on Brant. A sharp crack of wind energy whipped through the cavern, throwing Brant backward into a stalagmite. Kayla staggered from the sudden loss of support as Brant was ripped away from her.

Felix managed to catch her arm, holding her upright so she didn't collapse completely. Brant coughed and choked, grabbing at his throat as he struggled to breathe against Alec's energy onslaught. Kayla's eyes widened at the fury in Alec's expression as he advanced on his security officer.

"You dare betray me? Stealing energy from my bondmate?"

With a wave of Alec's hand, Brant was thrown to the side and crashed into the cavern wall. He collapsed onto the ground, coughing and sputtering as he gasped for air.

"Alec, no!" Kayla shouted, trying to get Alec's attention. "Brant didn't do anything wrong. He saved me. I shared my power with him so we could escape from Lars."

Alec hesitated for a moment, and she felt his energy pulse along their bond, sensing her emotions. He looked back and forth between her and Brant before waving for the other security officers to help Brant.

Ignoring Felix standing beside her, Alec pulled Kayla into his arms. He looked her up and down as though trying to assess her wellbeing. Despite her irritation at his arrival, she was glad to see him. He was one of the few people she trusted, but it was still too dangerous for him to be here.

"Are you all right? Gods, Kayla, you could have been killed. Why did you leave the towers? I told you I'd do everything in my power to find Carl. None of this was necessary."

She dropped her head against his chest, feeling his cool air energy surround and caress her. The weakness was starting to fade, and she felt a little more like herself.

"I had to get the supplies to Leo's camp. They were in trouble and couldn't wait. Then I thought about trying to find Carl by using his boots as a focus object. You said proximity was important. I knew my chances would be better on the surface. Brant agreed to help."

When he didn't reply, Kayla looked up into his eyes. "Don't blame Brant for what happened. He argued against it the whole time, but I kinda bullied him into it." She gripped his jacket tightly, afraid of what his presence could mean. She couldn't lose both Alec and Carl. "Lars is going to know you're on the surface, Alec. You have to get back to the towers."

Alec sighed and brushed a strand of hair away from her cheek. He bent down and pressed a kiss against her forehead. "No, Kayla. If Lars wants a challenge, I'm going to give it to him. That's the only way this is going to end."

Horror filled her, and she pushed him away. "What the hell are you thinking? This isn't a fucking game, Alec. Lars wants you dead."

A soft voice sounded from the cavern entrance. "Kayla, this is his right. If Alec has chosen to accept Lars's challenge, you cannot interfere."

She turned to see her mother walking toward her, looking out of place in her OmniLab protective gear. Kayla's heart lurched in fear. Of all the people from the towers, she wanted these two as far away from the dangers on the surface as possible.

"Seara? Why are you here?" Kayla jerked her head back to meet Alec's gaze. "Have you *completely* lost your mind? Lars is a couple sandwiches short of a picnic and you brought her *here*?"

Alec rubbed the bridge of his nose and didn't answer. Seara gave her a sad smile and maneuvered along the rocky ground, guided by an OmniLab guard. "I needed to be here, Kayla. I didn't fully realize it until we were a few miles away." She looked around the cavern and added, "We're less than a mile from where the original ruin collapse happened. This is where I lost you and your father. I didn't expect to find so much beauty so close to such painful memories."

A feeling of panic began to grow in the pit of her stomach. Kayla tried to swallow, but her mouth had suddenly gone dry. She looked back at Alec, silently pleading for him to deny Seara's words.

Alec frowned. "I'm sorry, Kayla. I didn't want to upset you by saying anything. After you caused the earthquake that opened this cavern, I had a suspicion and checked the coordinates. We believe your spirit energy has always been drawn to this location for some reason. Perhaps it was the river that called to you the entire time. Perhaps there's something else down here that we need to discover."

Kayla shook her head, not liking what she was hearing. Dozens of lives had been lost or ruined because of that damned ruin collapse. A sudden fear struck her, and she gripped Alec's hand. "The ruin collapse when I was a kid, I didn't..."

"No," Alec assured her, "it wasn't your fault. Even if Edwin hadn't confessed, you didn't have those abilities as a child."

Even so, the similarities were too disturbing to discount. Looking around at Alec, Seara, Brant, Felix, and all the guards, Kayla couldn't shake the sense of foreboding that was gripping her.

"Alec," Brant moved toward them, rubbing at his side where he had hit the wall, "I want to apologize to you. I never meant to—"

Kayla pulled away from Alec and kicked Brant in the shin. Seara gasped and the security officer swore loudly, rubbing his leg and scowling at Kayla. "What the hell was that for?"

"Shut up, Brant."

Alec frowned, looking back and forth between them. All she needed was for Brant to start saying what had transpired and Alec would toss him back into the wall. What had happened was her fault. She'd pushed Brant into agreeing with her demands.

"He's loyal to you, Alec. You can trust him."

Alec glanced down at her briefly before turning back to his half-brother. Emotions warred through Alec along their bond. With another silent urging from her, Alec finally extended his hand toward his brother. Brant hesitated for a long moment and then shook Alec's hand. Kayla let out a sigh of relief.

"I apologize," Alec said. "I shouldn't have jumped to conclusions."

Brant bowed his head. "No, you were correct. I overstepped myself. I never should have—"

"You both are idiots," Kayla declared, cutting Brant off again and ignoring his glare. "Now that we've all made nice, can we please focus on the Lars situation? We need to get the hell out of here."

Alec nodded, scanning the rocky terrain and jagged stalactites. "I agree. We only left a handful of men stationed topside. We didn't know what to expect down here or if you were alone."

"Excuse me, Master Tal'Vayr," a guard interrupted with a

grim expression. "We just got word that Lars Cerulis is outside the tunnel with two full squads of Coalition forces. He's demanding entrance and wishes to issue challenge."

Kayla stiffened.

Dammit. We're out of time.

CHAPTER THIRTEEN

"LOCK DOWN THE CAVERN," Alec ordered. "No one is allowed in or out until the challenge is resolved."

Kayla listened while Alec began issuing last-minute instructions to Brant and a few of the nearby guards. Apparently, they were going to allow Lars to enter with four guards. Even so, that was four too many. It was made even worse by the number of Coalition forces gathered on the surface. She'd bet her last credit that even if Lars lost the challenge, she and her people weren't walking out of here unscathed.

"Are you insane?" Kayla hissed at Alec.

"Those are my men on the surface," Alec replied in an even tone, the stiff rigidity of his posture belying his otherwise calm façade. "Until the challenge is resolved, Lars won't harm them. If he believes I intend to avoid his challenge, they'll be executed in retaliation. I won't have their deaths on my hands."

"What about leaving through the secondary exit and meeting him topside? You can't be serious about doing this challenge thing down here. You'll bring the whole cavern down on top of us."

Brant stepped forward and nodded. "I agree, Master Tal'-Vayr. You'll be at a disadvantage down here."

"No more than Lars. We're both air channelers." Alec paused for a moment, considering the terrain. "Although being down here is less than ideal, the surface holds dangers too. I can negotiate to have most of our men taken to the surface until this is resolved."

Seara stepped forward, clasping her hands together. "You can dismiss some of the guards, but Kayla and Brant will both need to remain here. I don't intend to leave either."

Kayla scowled. "I think I'd rather drag Lars's ass down here and cut off body parts until he tells us where he stashed Carl."

"Patience, love," Alec advised. Reaching for her hand, he brought it to his lips in a gesture of affection. "In accordance with our traditions, no harm may come to anyone here, on their side or ours, until the terms of the duel are satisfied. We'll make every effort to find Carl, but we need to resolve the challenge first."

Kayla narrowed her eyes at him. She refused to make any promises. "Great. There's a bunch of people pointing weapons at each other on the surface waiting to shoot each other, and we're stuck underground."

Seara gave her a sympathetic smile. "It will be over soon enough."

That didn't make her feel any better. As Alec began discussing with Brant what weapons Lars and his escort would be allowed, she scanned the cavern and the placement of the remaining guards. Underground, they were all easy targets. Kayla might not be able to protect everyone, but she could do something.

"I'll be right back," Kayla murmured and headed away from them.

As she passed the guard standing closest to Felix, Kayla

feigned stumbling on the wet, rocky ground. Using the momentum to bump into the guard, she quickly palmed the commlink fastened to his belt. With an apology and disarming smile, she continued toward Felix.

"Nice lift," the ruin rat observed in a low voice.

She grinned. "Caught that, did you?"

Felix snorted and leaned against the stalagmite. "Tell me you swiped that so we could get the hell out of here. I don't want to be anywhere near this place when the fighting starts. Things don't look good for your Omni lover over there."

"He's not my lover," she retorted.

Felix didn't reply but merely raised an eyebrow and gave her that cocky smirk. She huffed at him. "Don't be an ass. Regardless of whether or not I'm sleeping with him, I don't want him to die. You shouldn't either. That Omni is the ticket to freedom for the ruin rats."

"Not from where I'm standing, crazy girl. You've been up in that tower too long if you think differently."

Kayla leaned in closer to Felix. "I get it. You have no reason to trust any of them, but you know me."

"Do I?" The mirth faded from his expression as his gaze took on an uncharacteristic hardness.

A hollow feeling formed in the pit of her stomach. Had she finally burned her last bridge with the ruin rats? Showing Felix the energy stuff had been risky, but she hadn't had much of a choice. Either way, she wouldn't back down. Not from him.

Kayla tilted her head back and met his fierce glare with her own. "Fuck you, Felix."

A slow smile crept over his face, and his eyes crinkled at the corners. "Tempting, but you have enough company in your bed. Although, these Omnis seem a little uptight for your usual tastes."

She punched him in the arm. He grinned lazily, but there was still that hint of hardness under the surface.

"What's your plan, crazy girl?"

Kayla darted a quick look at Alec and Brant. It looked like their conversation was winding down. "I'm still working on that. If you want to bail, go ahead. Alec says no one will be harmed until the challenge is finished. He's sending some of the guards back to the surface."

"What are you going to do?"

"I need to stay down here." Kayla paused for a moment and glanced over at her mother. "If you stay, I need a favor."

"No promises. If shit goes bad, I'm out of here."

That was probably the best she could hope for. Kayla angled her body away from the guards and handed Felix the stolen commlink. "I need you to make sure Seara gets out. Trace the pathing out of here from the secondary exit. Do whatever you have to and get her out of here."

Felix glanced over at her mother and pocketed the commlink. "The cavern map is on this?"

Alec called over to her. "Kayla? Can you come over here?"

She held up her finger and turned back to Felix. "It should be. If we get split up, I'll meet you back at the towers. Just focus on Seara." She paused, considering the man in front of her. Most ruin rats didn't do something for nothing. They were always focused on the bottom line. Even though she had a history with Felix, it wasn't fair to ask him to endanger himself. Getting involved with an Omni was always hazardous to a ruin rat's health. Regardless of whatever promises he'd made to his brother, Felix didn't owe her that. "You do this, I'll owe you a debt. You can name your price."

Felix arched a brow, surprise etched on his face. "You've changed, crazy girl," he murmured. "There was a time I didn't think you'd make that sort of offer for anyone other than my brother and Veridian."

"I loved him, Felix," she whispered, lowering her gaze. "I'm sorry I couldn't save him. I've replayed that day a thousand times in my head. When Pretz died, something in me died too."

Felix reached out to touch her arm. She lifted her head and found his eyes filled with pain that mirrored hers. "He loved you too, Kayla. Anyone with eyes could see you two were crazy about each other. I read through OmniLab's files back at Rand's camp. What happened to him wasn't your fault."

She managed to swallow, emotion making her throat dry. Even though Carl and Veridian had told her the same thing, part of her had never fully believed it. Hearing it from Felix, though, eased something within her.

"He looked up to you, Felix. Pretz wanted you to be proud of him. He used to talk all the time about buying his way into the towers. He wanted to take care of you, the same way you'd always taken care of him."

"Fuck," he muttered, blinking and looking away toward the river. "If you make me cry, I'm going to kick your ass."

She laughed, grateful for the moment of levity.

Felix turned back to her and jerked his head in Seara's direction. "This woman means that much to you?"

Kayla smiled and nodded. "She's my mother. I don't know her very well yet, but I want to get the chance."

Felix swallowed. "Then I'll make sure you get that chance."

Overwhelming gratitude and affection rushed through her at his words. She threw her arms around his neck and hugged him tightly. "Thank you, Felix."

He held her close and said in a gruff voice, "Promise me you won't disappear on me again, Kayla. You're all I have left of my brother. I can't lose you too."

She pulled back and nodded. "I promise. I'm not going anywhere."

"Good," he replied, glancing over at Alec. "Maybe if you actually make this tower happen for the ruin rats, we can make Pretz's dream become a reality. He wanted us both in the towers."

"He did," she agreed, realizing he was right. "It's strange how things work out."

"Yeah," he murmured and motioned toward where Alec was waiting. "I think your Omni is getting impatient. I'll keep an eye on your mother for you."

Kayla smiled up at him. He gave her a roguish grin and swatted her butt when she turned away. She turned around and made an obscene gesture, but he just laughed. She shook her head in mock exasperation but couldn't wipe the grin off her face. At least something was going right in the world. Ruin rat humor was a very welcome diversion at the moment.

Brant was speaking in a low voice when she approached Alec, and she only managed to catch the last part of his conversation.

"—won't be able to block her. That could be construed as interfering with the challenge."

She looked back and forth between Alec, Seara, and Brant. "What are you talking about?"

Seara turned to her. "Brant won't be able to negate your energy channeling once the challenge begins. Strong emotions can cause your energy to flare, but you'll need to try to keep it tempered as much as possible. We need to make sure you don't cause another earthquake."

"This just keeps getting better," Kayla muttered under her breath.

Alec took her hand once again, lacing his fingers with hers. The sudden contact caused their bond to flare to life. She relished in the closeness, reading a myriad of conflicting emotions from Alec. They rushed by too quickly for her to be able to tell each of them apart. "Lars is on his way down now. I need you to stay close until he issues his challenge."

"Does he have Carl with him?"

Alec shook his head. "No. Our security forces reported that only Coalition military were on the surface. It's most likely Brant's vision was accurate and Carl's being held in one of their camps."

Kayla nodded. She'd been hopeful, but Brant's description of the floor in the camp had left little doubt. She just didn't understand why Carl wouldn't be wearing his boots. If something had happened to him, she'd kill Lars herself. The whole challenge thing could be damned for all she cared.

She leaned against Alec. "So how are you planning on handling this whole thing with Lars?"

"Yes, I'm curious how Alec is going to handle this situation as well."

Kayla froze at the sound of Lars's voice as he entered through the cavern entrance with Miranda and three men wearing the signature gray of the Coalition uniforms. She'd half-expected to see Sergei, but he wasn't in sight. The OmniLab guards moved to allow Lars and Miranda to pass, but each side kept their hands on their weapons and eyed the other with wariness.

"Lars," Alec greeted his cousin with a nod and pulled Kayla closer to him, "I don't suppose there's any chance of resolving this peacefully?"

Lars's eyes that had once reminded her so much of Alec turned cold. "Not unless you have a way of bringing Anne back. Your actions killed my sister, just like your father killed my mother."

"Lars," Seara took a step forward, her hands outstretched in a peaceable gesture, "Alec had nothing to do with Edwin's actions. He was little more than a child."

"He had the opportunity to warn us," Lars snarled and clenched his fists in anger. "He may have been young, but so was I. Anne was even younger than both of us. She was the same age as your daughter. If Alec had given us warning, we could have done something. Instead, he kept silent and simply watched as we were exiled from the towers."

Seara shook her head. "No, Lars, Edwin was a tyrant. Alec was just as much a captive as we all were. What happened rests solely on Edwin's shoulders."

"You're wrong, Seara," Lars retorted, his shoulders rigid as though he were trying to rein in his temper. "The entire council is at fault, including you. United, the council could have stood against Edwin. Instead, they allowed him to turn OmniLab into a dictatorship. Anyone who stood against him was banished. You're *all* at fault."

"You're right," Seara agreed. "We all share some blame. But this..." She gestured between Alec, Kayla and Lars. "None of this is necessary. Miranda, where is your father? Where is Trenon? Does he know what you intend?"

A trace of uncertainty flickered in Lars's eyes. In that moment, Kayla wondered if Lars was acting without the support of the rest of the exiles. When she was in the Coalition's camp, Trenon had appeared to support a challenge between Lars and Alec. Maybe that had changed though. If Trenon didn't support it, was there a chance this could be resolved peacefully?

Seara must have suspected the same thing because she took another step forward. "You don't have to do this, Lars. I knew both your mothers. Neither one would want this for you. You and Alec were raised almost as brothers. You've already lost your sister. Don't risk losing the rest of your family."

Unfortunately, her words had the opposite effect. It seemed any mention of Lars's sister was a catalyst. Seara realized her error a moment too late. The doubt in Lars's eyes had now been replaced by cold fury. His entire body stiffened, and he turned his focus back on Alec.

"I issue a challenge, Alec Tal'Vayr, for the bond of Kayla Rath'Varein."

"What the hell? This is bullshit!" Kayla threw her hands up in exasperation. "You don't even like me. For fuck's sake, you *stabbed* me!"

"That's enough, Kayla," Miranda snapped. "The challenge has been issued. You may be new to our ways, but this is one of our oldest laws."

"Really? You want to start something with me? We can go a round or two without the boys. I owe you payback for your cheap shot." Kayla arched an eyebrow and took a step forward. She still harbored a grudge from when Miranda had shot her while she was in the Coalition's camp. Alec wrapped his arm around her and pulled her against him. She glared at Miranda but didn't fight his hold.

"I accept your challenge, Lars Cerulis."

Kayla jerked her head up to scowl at Alec. She was surrounded by idiots. It was tempting to blast them all with a giant energy ball in the hopes of knocking some sense into them. With her luck, though, she'd probably hit a stalactite and cause it to crash to the ground. Sensing her thoughts, Alec gave her a reassuring squeeze. She closed her eyes tightly, took a deep breath, and tried to count to ten.

She only made it to three before Alec's energy surrounded her, filling her from within, and caused her irritation to fade away. She turned into him and looked up to meet his gaze. The adoration in his eyes was staggering. He cupped her face, caressing her skin with his touch and energy. "I love you, Kayla Rath'Varein."

She swallowed, trying to suppress the raw emotion threatening to overwhelm her. "Don't do this, Alec," she whispered, wrapping her hands around his wrists. "I don't want to lose you."

"You won't," he promised, but his words lacked conviction. Although he tried to hide it, their bond revealed his concern. He and Lars were closely matched in power. However, while Alec truly didn't want to harm his cousin, Lars was focused on vengeance.

Kayla bit her lip. Life was far too fragile, and she'd spent too much time resisting her feelings for Alec. He deserved to know the truth.

Moving even closer to him, she said silently, *"I've never thanked you for finding me and reuniting me with my mother. You showed me a different world, one with thousands of possibilities, and protected me each time I stumbled. As a ruin rat, I never gave much thought to the future. But you changed all that. You changed me, Alec. Thank you."*

His energy wrapped around her, cascading gently over her skin. Trailing his fingers across her cheek as though memorizing her features, he said, *"You changed me too, Kayla. You've inspired me and so many others to stand up for what we believe in. You've shown me a new way to see the world and made me look outside of myself. I hope you understand what a precious gift you are to all of us. No matter what happens, I hope you don't ever lose that spirit within you."*

Her heart clenched at the myriad of emotions his words evoked. There had to be a way to stop this duel from happening.

Alec dipped his head and pressed his lips against hers. Kayla melted against him, letting her body mold to his. Wrapping her arms around his neck, she gave into the emotions she'd been holding back. She loved him, and no matter what happened, she always would. It might not be the same type of love she felt for Carl, but it wasn't any less either. It was just... different.

He pulled her even closer against him, the warmth of his skin heating hers. With desperation in his embrace, he deepened their kiss. It was almost as though he knew it would be the last time they would hold each other.

"I'm sorry, Kayla," he whispered and stroked her cheek. Silently, he added, "*I won't be able to shield you from my emotions during the challenge. No matter what happens or what you sense through our bond, I want you to promise me you'll stay back. You cannot get involved in this.*"

She started to object, but he gripped her arms tightly. "*I need your promise, Kayla. I can't concentrate on doing what needs to be done if I'm worrying about you.*"

Sitting on the sidelines went against her nature, but she wasn't willing to risk distracting him. She jerked her head in a nod. A sudden rush of relief flowed through him and into their bond.

"You'd better kick his ass, Alec."

His mouth curved upward in a small smile.

"Touching," Lars mused, annoyance coloring his tone. "I can't help but wonder how it feels to love someone and know their heart belongs to a trader. Tell me, Alec, what is it like knowing Kayla prefers an ordinary human over yourself?"

Alec's jaw clenched, but he didn't respond to Lars's attempts to bait him. Instead, he pressed a kiss against Kayla's forehead and took a step away from her. Seara moved forward to stand beside her as Kayla curled her hands into fists to keep herself from strangling Lars. All things considered, strangling him might not be a bad thing.

Alec took a few steps toward Lars. "Before we begin, I want to know where you're holding Carl. Regardless of the outcome, he needs to be released."

Kayla's throat tightened at the sudden rush of emotion.

Lars glanced over at her, obviously surprised by Alec's request. "He's being held at a Coalition camp." He gestured to Miranda and added, "After the challenge, Miranda will make sure he's released unharmed."

Kayla looked over at the blonde and saw her nod. "I'll be sure he's returned to Kayla."

Alec inclined his head. "My men have been instructed not to interfere in the challenge. We can begin when you're ready."

Lars stepped forward and held his hands up, palms outward. "Then let's do this, cousin. It's been a long time coming."

Without another word, Alec pressed his hands against Lars's palms. There was a flash of blue light where their hands touched. Kayla doubled over and gasped at the sudden rush of energy that filled the cavern. It welled along her bond with Alec and seemed to magnify in its intensity. She felt something shift inside her as though her bond with Alec had moved ever so slightly. It hovered, suspended and unanchored, giving her the almost surreal sensation of disconnection. She could also sense Lars through their bond. Kayla shivered at the discomfort and sheer malice emanating from him.

Seara leaned over her and urged, "Just breathe, Kayla. It's temporary. The bond has to be shifted so both of them have equal footing. It wouldn't be fair if Alec could draw upon your energy during the challenge and Lars couldn't. Your bond with Alec should still be stronger than what Lars has taken. Your feelings for each other are too powerful."

Kayla gaped at her mother. "Are you telling me they're both going to be pulling energy through me? Are you kidding me? Who makes up these screwed-up rules?"

Seara shushed her and whispered, "Alec will try to avoid pulling energy through you. I don't think Lars will be able to pull much, even if he wanted to. You can try to block some of the effects. If necessary, form a shield around yourself. You can protect yourself, but you can't interfere."

Before Seara could explain further, Kayla's attention was drawn back to Lars and Alec. The surrounding air became charged with electricity. Several of the guards slowly backed away from the two men as though sensing something was about to happen. Suddenly, Alec and Lars dropped their hands away from each other. Lars gave a sharp wave of his hand, and a whirlwind of energy erupted around Alec.

Kayla recognized it as the same type of energy Lars had used when he cut off her air. Alec gasped and quickly yanked the energy threads away from Lars. He then lifted his palms, sending a surge of air outward, throwing Lars into the air. Lars flew upward, weaving the air energy around him, and floated back toward the ground. Before his feet had even touched down, he was launching another assault toward Alec.

The sharp crack of air was nearly deafening, and the smell of ozone filled the cavern. The two men hurled energy back and forth, weaving it in complex patterns Kayla couldn't even begin to decipher. She gathered her energy around her and, despite her earlier words to Seara, found herself hoping Alec would tap into her power and kick Lars's ass into next week.

But he didn't. Kayla could see the strain on both men as perspiration dripped down their faces, dampening their exposed skin. The air in the cavern already felt heavy with moisture, but the electrified energy made it almost suffocating. Both men's breathing became labored as each one struck out at the other again and again. They began using their energy as a whip. Kayla winced as a sharp crack of air slashed across Alec's cheek. Blood trickled from the wound, and Kayla's heart thudded in her chest. She clenched her hands even tighter, trying to suppress the feeling of panic growing inside her.

Loose dirt, rocks, and gravel were kicked up and became

weaponized projectiles. Seara wove a protective field around herself and Kayla to keep them from harm. The cavern walls began to tremble ever so slightly, and Kayla wondered how much more they could withstand. If they kept this up much longer, they could possibly bring the entire ruins down upon them.

Alec landed a sharp blow on Lars, knocking him into a nearby stalagmite. The force was enough to loosen the connecting stalactite, and it came crashing down. Miranda cried out as Lars tried to move out the way, the falling rocks barely missing him. A *crunch* was heard as the bones in his wrist were crushed. He pushed upward, ignoring the pain, flinging out his good hand and throwing the stalactite back toward Alec. A large piece of rock met its mark and hit him in the shoulder, spinning him around before he could block it.

He dropped to his knees, and Kayla felt him draw upon her power as he ripped the energy away from Lars once again. Lars coughed and choked, retaliating by trying to dislodge more of the rocks from the walls. Kayla felt an opposite pull as Lars also tried to pull upon her energy.

A wave of nausea crashed over her. It was like being torn in two. Alec must have sensed it because he abruptly released his hold upon her energy. Lars took the opportunity to pull more energy through her, using it to strike out again at Alec. Rocks pummeled him, ripping into his jacket and slicing into his chest.

Alec struggled against the onslaught, slipping on the wet ground. The stupid ass wouldn't tap into her energy to fight back. Icy-cold water hit her boots, and she looked down to see the river water rising behind her.

"Alec! The river! Lars is tapping into the river. He's also a water channeler," she shouted at him.

Brant grabbed her, dragging her away from the water. A huge wave crashed over the ground, and she stumbled out of his grip. Seara slid backward with a cry. Kayla reached out, grabbing her mother's hand and trying to hold on.

"Felix!" Kayla cried out. "Get Seara! I'm losing her."

She barely heard Felix's response over the sound of her pulse pounding in her head. As soon as the water receded, her mother's hand was yanked from hers as Felix pulled her away. Energy roared through her as Lars increased his attack. Another wave struck, and Kayla clawed the ground, trying to find purchase. Freezing river water pummeled over them, brutal in its intensity. She coughed and gasped, trying to catch her breath.

Kayla grabbed a stalagmite and lifted her head, catching a glimpse of Alec. He was still fighting, but she could sense he was weakening. She managed to brace herself as another wave crashed overhead. There was nothing for Alec to grab on to, and he slid toward the river.

"Alec!" she screamed, hurling energy through their bond to strengthen him. She didn't care about the challenge or any of it. He couldn't die.

Drawing upon more energy than she'd ever channeled, she flooded him with her power. The rush of energy sliced through her like a thousand daggers. Blood dripped from her nose, but she didn't dare stop. A red, hazy mist coated her vision. She blinked, trying to focus on Alec. Lars yanked more energy through the bond and she staggered, nearly losing her grip on the stalagmite. It was too much.

Fury ripped through her at the thought she was being used to hurt Alec. The two idiots might be trying to kill each other, but she'd be damned if she was going to let Lars use her like this. Kayla blinked, trying to look around the cavern and find a way to stop Lars. A few of the guards had fallen into the rapidly moving river and others were pulling them back to shore. More were grabbing whatever they could to brace themselves against the onslaught. The guard nearest her was bleeding from his head and looked on the verge of passing out.

Couldn't Lars see what he was doing? There was more at stake than just the stupid bond. They were all going to die. Her eyes fell on Brant, who had managed to help Felix pull Seara to relative safety.

Brant met her gaze and rushed back toward her. He slid along the ground, grabbing at the stalagmite, and shouted over the whipping wind, "Get away from the river. Take my hand."

Kayla reached for him, energy sparking through them at the contact. She jerked back, gripping the stalagmite even tighter as another wave crashed over them. An idea began to take shape in her mind. It was crazy enough that it just might work.

"I need you to trust me!" Kayla yelled, reaching for him but not releasing the stalagmite. She had no idea if this would even work, but she was desperate. If touching him and channeling energy could give Brant the ability to act as an Inner Circle member, she might be able to temporarily form a bond with him—or rather, transfer a permanent bond.

Taking a deep breath, she reached out along the unanchored bond she shared with Alec and Lars. Gripping it with her energy threads, Kayla yanked it toward her, pulling away from both men and pushing it into Brant. If Alec wouldn't take her energy, she'd make damn sure Lars couldn't take it either.

It wasn't a natural merging. By design, Brant was unable to naturally form any sort of bond. Lars had called her a conduit, but she hadn't fully understood what that meant until now. Brant could never hold a bond, but she could act as one for him. To the Shadows, she was the mystical connection linking them to the surrounding energy.

Because she'd given Brant so much of her energy earlier,

he was technically the equivalent of an Inner Circle member. If her theory was correct, this would allow Brant to temporarily hold a bond until her energy left him. Once it was gone, that would be the real test.

"Don't let go of the bond!" she shouted, digging her fingers into Brant's arm to strengthen their connection.

He nodded, grasping the bond holding them together, and pulled it to him. With a searing blast of heat, he burned through her energy, embedding the unanchored bond deeper into his psyche. Through a combination of force of will and energy, she sensed him struggling to hold on to it while the battle raged around them. As the energy within Brant began to dwindle, the bond began to waver, unable to anchor itself to an energy user. She dropped her hand quickly so the bond couldn't revert to her.

With a sharp *crack*, pain ripped through her as the bond was destroyed. Kayla cried out, dropping to her knees. She gasped and tried to take a breath as tears streamed down her cheeks. Faintly, she heard people shouting but couldn't make out the words.

What happened? Did I kill Alec?

She just wanted to negate the bond, not destroy it. Wrapping her arms around her midsection, Kayla tried to keep herself from falling apart. This pain was worse than when she'd destroyed the bracelets.

"Kayla, what have you done?"

She lifted her head to find Seara kneeling beside her. Her mother brushed her hair back away from her face, searching her expression. Kayla turned her head, the sudden movement making her nauseous, and she retched on the ground. When the ground stopped spinning, she lifted her head.

Lars and Alec were kneeling on the ground, suffering equally. She didn't know how it was possible, but they were all still alive. Hell, it hurt like a bitch, but it was worth it if they were all still breathing. Brant was a little green around the gills, but not nearly as bad as the rest of them.

The absence of the bond was like a raw, festering wound. She ached inside as though part of her soul had been ripped away. Alec lifted his head to meet her gaze, and the look of agony on his face was nearly her undoing. She reached out to him through their energy connection, but there was nothing. Their bond was well and truly destroyed. Alec dropped his chin to his chest, his body quaking silently as though struggling to overcome the pain.

Lars, however, seemed to be recovering faster. Perhaps it was because he only had a trace of the bond during the battle. Kayla watched as the renegade Omni tried to stand, cradling his shattered wrist.

Seara looked over at him. "Stop, Lars. I don't know how, but the bond is destroyed. The challenge is over."

Lars shook his head, using the rock wall to pull himself upright. "No. It was... never about the damn bond." He paused, pushing away from the wall, and tried to catch his breath. That simple act of exertion had cost him. "Alec killed Anne. It won't be over until he pays for what happened."

Lifting his uninjured hand, another wave of energy ripped through the cavern. Alec, still trying to recover from the loss of the bond, was unable to block the attack and went flying along the rocky ground toward the river.

"Alec!" Seara screamed, reaching outward and using her own earth energy to stop him from falling into the rushing water. The ground trembled, and a steep ridge rose to prevent Alec from plummeting into the icy depths. Brant dove toward him and grabbed Alec's hand, pulling his half-brother back to safety.

Undeterred, Lars pulled on more energy threads. Wind whipped through the cavern as dirt and debris began to fall from the ceiling. Seara gasped and looked upward, shouting at

Lars to stop. Kayla pushed up from the ground, struggling to stand despite the pain.

Was Lars really that intent on revenge that he'd kill them all?

Kayla swallowed as memories from another ruin collapse came rushing back to her. She'd be damned if she let him bury them alive. Not again. She lifted her hand, gripping the emerald necklace she still wore around her neck. It had belonged to Alec's mother who had saved her life in the ruin collapse as a child. Lars's mother had owned the matching stone to this one, but it had been lost in the ruins when she'd died.

There was only one thing left to try. If Lars wouldn't listen to any of them, perhaps he'd listen to someone else. Kayla gripped the necklace tightly and yanked it from her neck. Holding it up, she gathered as much energy as possible and channeled it directly into the stone. If they claimed she was a spirit channeler, she'd better damn well be a spirit channeler. The green pendant began to glow, filling the cavern with an almost unearthly green light.

Some of the guards gasped as a shadowy visage appeared before them. As Kayla channeled more energy into the stone, the image began to solidify, and features became identifiable. A ghostly woman stood on the rocky ground and gave Kayla a sad smile before turning toward Alec. The love and longing on her face was heart-wrenching.

Alec lifted his head, shock and disbelief on his face as he stared at the image. With her long, blond hair and blue eyes the same shade as theirs, it was clear of her familial connection to both Lars and Alec.

Lars staggered forward, leaning against the wall for support. "How—how is this possible? What sort of trick is this?"

"Kayla," Alec whispered. "What are you doing?"

She didn't answer. Instead, she focused on channeling more energy into the necklace. The woman moved forward, almost floating, and knelt beside Alec on the ground. She looked over his injuries as though each one pained her. Lifting her hand, she held it over him, and Kayla watched in amazement as his injuries began to heal.

"Mother," he whispered and reached up, his hand passing through the ghostly image's figure.

She shook her head and moved away, turning to look at Lars. The ghost slowly approached him, and he stumbled backward, bumping into the wall behind him. She motioned for him to hold out his shattered wrist.

Lars's gaze darted to Alec and back to the ghost.

"Aunt Catherine?"

The woman nodded and gestured to his wrist again, seeming to grow impatient at the delay. Lars held out his arm, and she covered it with her transparent hand, sending healing energy threads through him. He winced as the bones began to knit back together and the rest of his injuries began to heal.

Catherine studied Lars with a sad smile and pointed to Alec. Her mouth moved, but no sound emerged. She said it again, appearing frustrated by her inability to speak. Pointing to Alec again, she mouthed the word a third time. "Family."

Lars's shoulders drooped, and he lowered his head. Catherine shook her head and knelt in front of him, her eyes pleading. She interlaced her fingers over her chest and then pulled them apart, showing him they were both breaking her heart.

Kayla swallowed, beginning to feel fatigued from the effects of channeling so much energy into the pendant, but she needed just a little more time. As though sensing her need, Seara laid her hand on her arm, boosting Kayla's failing energy supply. Kayla gave her mother a thankful nod before turning back to watch Alec's mother.

Lars had slumped to the ground, defeat reflected in his entire demeanor. Alec stood, slowly made his way over to his cousin, and dropped to the ground beside him.

"Lars," he managed, emotion choking his words as he looked at the kneeling image of his mother. "She's right. We're family. I swear by the blood of our ancestors that I'll spend the rest of my life trying to make up for the pain and hurt you went through. I'm so sorry for my part in what happened to you and to your family."

Lars stared at his mother's twin sister and the tears that trailed down her cheeks. "She looks so much like her. Like Anne too."

Alec nodded, looking up. "They were all beautiful. None of them deserved to die. My father got what he deserved for taking their lives."

Lars ran his hands through his hair in dejection. "Then it's true," he murmured. "You *were* the one who killed him."

"Yes," Alec admitted, gazing at the sorrow-filled eyes of the ghostly illusion. "It needed to be done. He'd caused too much pain for so many of our people, all because he was power-hungry and greedy. He wanted to remove Andrei Rath'Varein as council leader and his other efforts had failed, so he arranged for the ruin collapse. Then he imprisoned most of the Inner Circle, using their energy for his own purposes."

"A single death would never be enough," Lars muttered.

Alec's mother gestured between the two men once more, her eyes pleading.

Lars swallowed and nodded. "Be at rest, Aunt Catherine. Alec will not come to harm from me."

Relief filled her gaze, and she extended her hands toward both men, brushing her cool energy over them one last time. She then turned to Kayla and nodded at her, as though telling her to release the energy.

Kayla did as Catherine wanted, and the pendant dimmed. She staggered slightly, and Brant grabbed her, supporting her weight so she wouldn't fall. She couldn't remember the last time she was this tired.

Pushing up from the ground, Alec approached her and Brant. With a slight nod, Brant released her, and Alec took his place. "Why did you do it, Kayla?"

She leaned against him, pressing her cheek against his chest. Although she could feel Alec's energy surround her in a warm embrace, their disconnection was complete. She could no longer feel him within her or sense his thoughts.

"I couldn't just let him use my energy to kill you, Alec. You weren't willing to use my energy to fight because it might hurt me, so I did the only thing that might work. If there was no bond, there was no reason for a challenge."

He lifted her chin to search her expression. "You're more vulnerable now, Kayla. The bond between us was meant to protect you."

Brant stepped forward and shook his head. "No, she won't be vulnerable. Kayla will never be forced into anything. I don't believe she can destroy the bonds of others, but she can destroy her own or prevent it from happening. Even if she didn't have this ability, she wouldn't need to worry. I swear here and now to protect her to my last breath."

Alec frowned and studied his half-brother. "Why are you making this offer?"

Lars chuckled and stood with the help of Miranda. "Haven't you figured it out, Alec? Shadows can use Kayla's energy to become the equivalent of Inner Circle members. It's only temporary, but their abilities could completely change the tower hierarchy. You were so closed-off to her energy during the fight, you didn't feel what they did."

Kayla shook her head. Lars was right about Shadows being able to use her, but he was wrong about Brant. She couldn't sense Brant in the same way she had with Alec, but there was now an instinctual knowing between them. His offer of protection didn't stem from some misguided attempt to attain power. Instead, she had the sense his offer of protection was to prevent anyone from misusing her. Brant also wanted to reassure Alec she would be protected. Alec deserved to have a chance to find someone who would love him the way she loved Carl. She suspected Brant felt far more loyalty to Alec than the High Council leader realized.

Kayla looked up at him. "It's not about power, is it Brant?"

Brant gave her a slow smile. "It would make more sense to everyone if I said yes. But no, it's not." He looked back at Alec. "You have an opportunity very few Drac'Kin receive. Your permanent bond has been broken. You two now have a choice. You can decide to renew your permanent bond, or you can take this opportunity to decide what you both truly want."

Alec's brow furrowed, and he turned to look at Kayla. As he reached up to cup her cheek, she felt a light trail of energy float over her. Indecision warred across his face.

She smiled up at him. "You were the one who told me a bond doesn't negate your feelings, Alec. I'll always love you, but do you really think we're right for each other?"

Alec sighed and ran his thumb along her jawline. "If I had never seen you with Carl and the way you two complement each other, I might say something different. I do love you, Kayla. But I have the suspicion we'd probably end up strangling each other in a month's timespan."

She laughed and hugged him, knowing he was probably right. In the short amount of time they'd spent together, they'd both driven each other equally crazy.

Brant snorted and muttered under his breath, "I'd give it two weeks tops."

Kayla pulled back and wrinkled her nose at Brant. When

the security officer chuckled, she grinned. Brant was finally starting to act more human.

She turned back to Lars, who had been watching the entire exchange. "Will you tell me where you've taken Carl?"

Lars frowned and then motioned to Miranda. "Contact the camp and arrange to have him released." He turned to Alec and clasped his hands behind his back. "What does this mean for my people?"

Before Alec could reply, Seara stepped forward. "It means you will all return home. You were wrongly expelled from the towers. We may not be able to fully make it up to you for the injustices you were dealt, but Alec and I will do everything within our power to restore your heritage and family's position."

Kayla looked down at the emerald pendant she still held in her hand and offered it to Lars. "Until we recover your mother's pendant, you should keep this one. It should stay in the family—yours *and* Alec's."

Lars hesitated, eyeing the necklace with longing. His fingers curled into fists as though he were resisting the urge to snatch it from Kayla's outstretched hand. He swallowed and looked toward Alec, who nodded at him.

"Take it, cousin. Kayla's right. It's only fitting it should remain in your care. This is only one of the first things we'll give back to you."

Lars took the pendant from Kayla's outstretched hand, cradling it reverently. A sense of rightness filled her. Alec squeezed her midsection as though he, too, sensed it. She looked up at him and smiled, feeling the beginning of hope settle over them.

One of the guards pressed his hand against his earpiece. "Excuse me, Master Tal'Vayr. Trader Carl Grayson is on the surface with an urgent message from the Coalition. The towers are under attack."

CHAPTER FOURTEEN

KAYLA COULDN'T MAKE it to the surface fast enough. The moment she was clear of the lift, she started searching the group of OmniLab personnel for Carl. The sight of him wearing the stolen Coalition protective gear sent a rush of giddy relief through her.

"Kayla!" he shouted, reaching toward her.

She tossed her helmet aside and threw herself into his arms, burying her face against his chest. He wrapped his arms around her, holding her as tightly as she held him. The whole engagement thing between her and Alec was just going to have to be canceled. They'd find another way to keep Alec safe. She loved this man and wasn't willing to spend another minute denying it.

"You're okay," Carl murmured, pulling back and looking over her as though inspecting her for damage.

She looked up at him, memorizing the details of his face, and ran her hands up his chest and down his arms. Now that she knew he was safe, the fear that had been sitting like a weight in the pit of her stomach finally began to ebb. His shoulders relaxed, and his eyes softened as he continued to gaze down at her.

She smiled up at him, cupped his face, and pressed a kiss against his lips. "So are you. I guess neither one of us can die that easily."

He tightened his grip, yanking her closer and holding her in his embrace. "Don't even mention dying. When I found out you'd come to the surface to find me, I almost lost my mind. I was terrified something would happen to you."

Kayla squeezed her eyes shut and listened to the sound of his heartbeat. Each beat was one more reminder of how much she needed him. "I had to try to find you, Carl." She lifted her gaze to look up at him. "You came for me when I needed you. I had to do the same."

"Sweetheart, I'll always be there for you," he murmured, reaching up to tuck her hair behind her ear. She leaned into his touch, relishing the contact.

Alec pulled his helmet off as he approached from the lift. "I hate to break up your reunion, but I need to know about the attack."

Carl lifted his head to focus on Alec but didn't release Kayla. "Sergei gave me the coordinates to track Miranda and Lars. He only gave us a one-hour window to negotiate before they were scheduled to attack. It wasn't enough time. As soon as I arrived here, we tried to contact the towers to verify whether the attack has commenced. All communication with the towers has been shut down."

Alec walked over to the guard manning the communication center. "Report."

"We're still trying to get through, sir, but there's nothing but static. The communication center for the towers is offline."

Brant stepped forward and added, "The Coalition troops

that escorted Lars to this location withdrew about thirty minutes ago."

Alec frowned. "Where are they now?"

The OmniLab technician shook his head and adjusted the screen in front of him. "With the communication feeds down, we were unable to track their retreat. Our surveillance systems are offline until we can reconnect to the towers. They headed in a northwest direction, but that's all we know."

"Keep working on it," Alec snapped.

Carl tightened his arms around her. Kayla lifted her head to see him glaring at Lars and Miranda as they emerged from the lift. Carl pulled her behind him and started to move toward them, but Kayla plastered her body against him. "Stop, Carl, don't! The challenge is over. I'll explain everything later, but we need them."

He hesitated, but the fury in his eyes didn't diminish. "I doubt that."

Alec raised his hand in a warning gesture and moved in front of his cousin, blocking Carl's visual. "Your grievances will need to wait, Trader Carl."

"Carl," Kayla urged, tugging on his jacket to draw his gaze back to hers, "it's over. Brant helped me break the bond with Alec."

He blinked, his gaze darting back and forth between her and Alec. "What? The bond is gone?"

At Alec's nod, Kayla laughed and wrapped her arms around Carl's neck. "I'll tell you everything later, but Alec and Lars have worked most of it out."

Carl pulled her closer, burying his face in her hair. "I didn't think it was possible."

"Me neither," she murmured, not wanting to release him. If the towers weren't being threatened at this very moment, she'd say to hell with everything and show him how much she loved him. Instead, she lifted her head and looked into his eyes. "I love you, Carl Grayson."

"Kayla," he whispered, pressing a soft kiss against her lips, "I fell in love with you after the first time you made me chase you across half the district. I'll always love you. I don't care how many bonds need to be broken. I'm not letting you go."

Kayla swallowed and looked away, trying to get hold of the emotions that threatened to overwhelm her. She wouldn't cry, dammit. He chuckled and lifted his hand to tuck a lock of hair behind her ear. Curling her fingers into his jacket, she said, "If anyone else had said that to me, I'd kick their ass."

"Trust me, I know all too well," Carl agreed, darting a glance at Alec before turning back to her. He shifted her slightly to withdraw a small tablet from his pocket and held it out to her. "Sergei gave me this to track Miranda and Lars. He wanted you to contact him with it. The deadline's expired though. I don't know if it'll still work."

Grateful for the change of subject so she wouldn't turn into a blubbering mess, Kayla accepted the device. It appeared innocuous, but appearances could be deceiving.

"We need to run a scan before I try it," she said, lifting her head to look at Alec and Brant. "Do you guys have the equipment here to check it?"

Brant motioned for one of the technicians to test the device. Kayla handed it over, keeping an eye on the screen while they started analyzing the tablet.

"What do you know of the Coalition's plan to attack the towers, Lars?" Alec's accusatory tone cut through the air, distracting her from the on-screen analysis.

Lars began pacing, moving away from Alec and spouting off a string of profanity Kayla had only heard from the most creative ruin rats.

Miranda glanced worriedly at Lars. "There must be a mistake, Alec. The Coalition was only supposed to get into position. Lars instructed them to wait until we returned with Kayla."

Lars paused, turning around to face his cousin. "If they released Carl, the Coalition must have gotten impatient. Sergei wasn't pleased with my attempts to capture Kayla. He was under pressure to launch the attack but agreed to wait as long as possible." Lars glanced at Kayla, his expression worried. The dark shadows under his eyes were even more noticeable in the stark light on the surface. "Sergei thought Kayla might be able to prevent any unnecessary bloodshed. She'd made an impression on him."

Alec frowned. "What are the chances they held off?"

Lars shook his head. "None. If Sergei gave Carl a deadline, he would have honored that. The Coalition is nothing if not efficient. They don't make baseless threats."

"Dammit," Alec swore. "Do you know the details of their plan?"

Lars clasped his hands behind his back in a familiar gesture Kayla recognized as belonging to Alec. Now that the two men were standing side by side, it was impossible not to see the similarities between them. "Before I share any additional information, I need assurances no retribution will be made against anyone exiled from the towers."

Kayla gaped at him. "For fuck's sake, Lars. You're going to sit here and make demands when the towers are under attack? Can't we figure this shit out later?"

"I'm afraid not," Lars replied, not taking his eyes off Alec.

"You have it," Seara declared, the finality in her tone making it clear she wouldn't tolerate any arguments. A small trail of energy threaded through her voice, sealing her next words in an irrefutable oath.

"On my honor as a Rath'Varein and a Drac'Kin, and as the appointed co-leader of OmniLab's High Council and member of the Inner Circle by right of birth, I hereby and forevermore affirm that no repercussions or retribution shall be made against any of those wrongfully exiled by Edwin Tal'-Vayr. Furthermore, all familial and individual titles, accounts, and holdings shall be reinstated immediately. From now until the last of the energy in this world is destroyed, I will honor this vow."

If she hadn't been watching so closely, Kayla would have missed the slight tremor of relief that went through Lars. He kept his head held high, though, focused entirely on the petite, dark-haired woman who led the towers. Miranda, on the other hand, lowered her gaze, but not before Kayla caught the brief shimmer of tears on her cheeks.

Seara stepped forward, offering her outstretched hands to both of them. "Lars, Miranda, we share the same origins. Tell us what we need to know so we can all return home together."

Lars bowed deeply, taking Seara's proffered hand, and pressed his forehead against the back of her palm in a gesture of respect. When he straightened, it was as though a tremendous weight had been lifted from his shoulders.

"We've spent the past several years infiltrating the towers and making alliances with the Inner Circle Shadows. The Shadows were drafted to override security at our signal and allow the Coalition forces to enter. From there, key areas of the towers were to be targeted and secured."

Brant had a look of disgust on his face. "Those traitors. I've heard rumblings of discontent, but I had no idea this was going on. How many of the Shadows have been compromised?"

"At least two dozen, possibly more. The Shadows would make recommendations about others who might be inclined to join us. From there, Trenon assessed each target to determine who we approached. We believed you were loyal to Alec, so our agents did not contact you."

Seara reached for Lars's arm. "Where is Trenon? I can't imagine he would condone an attack on the towers. There are thousands of innocents living there. This plan is endangering all of their lives."

"Trenon Noltreck is not the same man you knew," Lars admitted and glanced at Miranda. The woman lowered her head in shame. "None of us are the same, Seara. We might have planted the seeds of mutiny, but it was OmniLab who fostered their growth. The Shadows made the deal for a place among the Coalition, provided they assisted in bringing OmniLab under Coalition control."

"The Shadows can't suppress the Inner Circle indefinitely. The Coalition will have to move quickly for their plan to work," Brant observed.

"You're correct. There may be a way to salvage this," Seara agreed and turned back to Miranda. "Our trials have changed all of us, not just those who left the towers. Your father has always been a charismatic man and orator. Edwin viewed him as a threat because he had the ability to incite people to rally behind him. We need him now if we're going to convince the Shadows to stand down."

Miranda shook her head. "I'm not sure he'll agree. He was at one of the Coalition's outlying camps waiting to hear word about the attack. If they've already begun, I don't know if he's still there or if he's traveled to the towers with the rest of our people. I can try to get word to him and tell him about your oath. He doesn't know Lars and I came here to find Kayla."

Alec motioned toward one of the guards. "Ready one of the transports."

"I should accompany the transport," Miranda suggested. "My father might believe it's an attack unless he sees me with them."

Alec inclined his head and turned back to the technician scanning the tablet. "What's the status of the tablet scan?"

"As far as I can tell, it's a simple tracking and communication device. Without running more extensive diagnostics, I'm not able to isolate whether there are other more covert features."

Kayla leaned over the technician to study his findings. It was what she'd expected, but part of her wished they had more time so she could take apart the device to better study it. "No time like the present. Let's try to reach Sergei. Maybe he can shed some light about what's happening or stop it entirely."

"Go ahead," Alec agreed, placing his hand over hers. "Be careful with what you say. Without knowing exactly what's happening back at the towers, I'm afraid we're at a disadvantage."

Kayla nodded and accepted the tablet from the technician. She pressed a button on the device and waited. Nothing happened. She pressed the button again. No response.

Lars stepped forward. "If the attack has commenced, Sergei won't be able to negotiate. Most likely, all transmission frequencies have been locked down to provide support to Coalition forces."

Felix took the device from Kayla, studying the foreign technology. "It's not all hopeless. If this was used as a tracker, we can reverse the code to find its origination point."

Carl shook his head. "I'm not sure if that will do any good. The signal most likely originated from the camp where they were holding me. By the time Sergei released me, most of their forces had already left, and the remainder were getting ready to deploy."

Lars inclined his head. "Carl is correct. There are many Coalition base camps scattered around the various districts. The camp where Carl was being held would have been abandoned as soon as they initiated the attack. I have knowledge of two other camps. The locations of the others were not shared with us. "

Carl frowned. "I don't know how that's possible. I know my district fairly well and we've never seen them in my area."

"They're very good at staying hidden," Lars explained. "The Coalition's cloaking technology is more advanced than anything I've ever seen, so it would be almost impossible to detect them unless you're practically right on top of them. The size of each camp is smaller, with maybe under a hundred people, which is designed to minimize the impact if one of them was discovered. They all operate independently, with each camp leader in the area reporting to a commander. In this case, Sergei."

Kayla didn't bother to hide her surprise. She hadn't realized Sergei's position was quite so high up. Shaking her head, she said, "If there's no point in tracing the tablet back, we might be able to use their communication signatures to tap into their feeds. If so, we'll have inside information about what they're planning."

"It could work," Felix mused, turning over the device and prying it apart.

Lars frowned. "I've seen some of their security. Even if you *could* get past it, you'll be too late to use it. Our best hope is to return to the towers as quickly as possible. Sergei will be manning the command center nearby. His second, Pavel, will be overseeing the initial sweep of the towers. Once it's secured, Sergei will move to the towers, along with most of their reserve forces. I wasn't privy to all their plans, but I can tell you what little I know. Do you have a map of the towers?"

Alec motioned for one of the technicians to pull it up. Lars leaned forward, studying the map, and said, "Once the Shadows give them access, the Coalition will move in. Residents will be urged to return to their quarters where many of them will be locked in. Those who resist will be executed."

He paused and then began pointing at certain areas on the screen. "The Coalition, in conjunction with the Shadows, will then focus on locking down the main control room, generators, security, databanks, and food distribution centers. Once they gain control of these key areas, they'll create a stranglehold on the towers."

Seara shook her head. "Our people will be massacred. The Inner Circle won't stand down. With the Shadows negating their abilities, they won't be able to fight back. We depend too heavily on our powers."

Alec leaned over to study the map. "With the communication systems offline, we need to assume the Shadows have either already allowed them into the towers or they are about to open the doors. It's imperative we stop them before they take control of any of those key areas."

Kayla glanced over at Brant. "How many of the Shadows know how to manipulate energy? If I flooded them with my energy, would they know how to use it?"

"Not likely," Brant admitted. "I've received much more extensive training than many of my counterparts. It wasn't easy to handle your energy, even with my background. You might be able to offset their abilities, at least temporarily. It'll be dangerous though."

Carl placed his hand on her back, and Kayla glanced up into his worried eyes. She leaned against him and said, "If they've already moved into the towers, I don't think we have much of a choice. If we can throw them off their plan a little bit, we might have a chance."

Alec frowned. "As much as I hate to say it, I'm afraid you might be right. The last thing I want to do is put you in more danger, Kayla. We need to return to the towers immediately to get a better idea about the situation."

At Alec's order, the remaining OmniLab guards began packing up and loading the convoys. Felix shook his head, still working on the Coalition tablet. He glanced over at Kayla. "There's a problem your new friends haven't addressed."

Kayla sighed. "Yeah. The communication with the towers is offline. Since they've already shut that down, it's likely that getting inside the towers is going to require some creativity."

Felix leaned over and tweaked her nose. "This is why I like working with you. Life is always more entertaining."

She grinned at him. "Always."

———

KAYLA WATCHED the last of the OmniLab transports pull out. Time was ticking down. With Felix trailing behind her, she flung a bag of supplies over her shoulder and headed in the direction of the hidden bikes.

Alec and Seara both had reservations about her plan. They'd wanted her to bring Brant with her, but Kayla had refused. Brant wasn't comfortable on the bike, and she needed people who knew how to ride. Speed was going to be a deciding factor here.

"Are you sure we can catch them?" Carl asked over the headset. Alec had given him a speeder to ride after insisting the Coalition vehicle he'd borrowed needed to be left behind. There was most likely a tracking device installed. They couldn't afford to relinquish any advantage, no matter how slight.

"No clue, but I'm going to try," Kayla replied, ducking into the dilapidated building where they'd stored the ruin rat bikes.

Felix threw his leg over the speeder and started up the engine. "Leo won't agree to help. He's more stubborn than you."

Kayla laughed and pulled her bike out of the building. "I'm counting on that stubbornness to convince him."

She programmed the coordinates Felix had given her to the new ruin rat camp location. Hopefully, she could cut them off before they got too far out of range. Their bikes would be loaded down with supplies, so they'd be moving much slower.

Kayla sped off in the direction they'd most likely be traveling, pushing the speeder into overdrive. They'd had almost forty minutes of hard driving before they caught a glimpse of a large dust cloud in front of them.

"That's them," Kayla called out into the headset, crouching forward as she thrust the bike into higher speed. Pulling up alongside the lead bikes, she motioned for them to pull over. Leo's dark helmet obscured his face, but he glanced over at her and held up his middle finger. She returned his gesture and deftly cut him off.

Leo angled the bike, kicking up more dust and gravel as he skidded sideways into an abrupt stop. He jumped off his bike, fists clenched, and Kayla could hear him swearing and shouting at her from underneath his helmet. Mack got off his bike and engaged the portable UV shield.

Leo yanked off his helmet. "What the fuck? You're trying to kill me now by running me off my bike? I figured you'd try for something a little simpler. Maybe stabbing me in my sleep. At least then I'd get a few moments of peace before the end."

Kayla tapped her foot, impatiently waiting for a lull in Leo's rant. "Are you finished, old man? I didn't chase you down because I missed you."

"Well, boo-fucking-hoo. I could have gone a million more lifetimes before I missed you too." Leo's eyes narrowed on Felix. "And you. I didn't give you those coordinates so you could bring Kayla here to kill me."

Felix gave a half-hearted shrug. "You didn't specify one way or the other."

"Worthless," Leo muttered, raising his hands in surrender. "Can't find decent help nowadays. The whole fucking world is going to shit."

Mack tucked his helmet under his arm. "Why are you here, darlin'?"

Kayla gave him a warm smile. "I'm going to need your help. All of your help."

"No," Leo said with a scowl. "Not gonna happen. I don't care how much you flutter your eyes at Mack. It's a hell no."

Carl climbed off his bike and approached them. "The Coalition is attacking the towers. With the loss of life and destruction of resources, how much is anyone going to be willing to share with the ruin rats? It could be years before the trading camps are reestablished, if ever. How long can you all survive without regular supplies?"

Leo didn't reply, but the lines on his face deepened.

"Leo," Kayla began, knowing this conversation could go either way, "I know this isn't your fight, but you know the ruin rat camps will be the first to suffer. Now that the districts have been mapped, how useful will you be to the Coalition? They aren't interested in trinkets from the ruins."

Leo narrowed his eyes on her. "More useful alive than dead if we get involved in OmniLab bullshit."

Mack frowned and gestured back at the group of people on speeders. "We're not fighters, darlin'. Not on the scale you're talking about."

"That's bullshit," Kayla declared. "We're *all* fighters. Every day, all of us fight for our survival. Every minute of every hour is spent trying to figure out how to survive the next. You know better than anyone in those towers what it means to fight and live for your freedom."

When they didn't respond, Kayla pushed ahead, raising

her voice so the others could hear. "If we succeed, OmniLab will be in your debt. With your help, they've agreed to build another tower specifically designed for the ruin rats. You'll have access to medical care, food, and other supplies. In exchange, you can continue scavenging on the surface for artifacts and resources."

One of the ruin rats called out, "Is this for real?"

"OmniLab hasn't done shit for us!" someone else yelled. "Why would they bother now?"

When others began voicing their agreement about Omni-Lab's self-interest, Kayla resisted the urge to swear. She would have been on their side of the argument less than a month ago. They had no reason to trust OmniLab. A gloved hand pressed against her back, and she looked up to see Carl standing beside her. His gesture was more than just affectionate reassurance. He was letting her know they were in this together.

"It's true," Carl shouted, drawing the attention of the ruin rats. His presence was a powerful statement to the rabble-rousing group. Carl had more than earned his reputation as being a fair trader, and as a known representative of Omni-Lab, his words carried far more weight than hers.

"For those of you who don't know me, I'm Trader Carl Grayson. I've been a trader in one of the eastern districts for the past several years. At the request of Alec Tal'Vayr, co-leader of OmniLab, I've taken Kayla to the towers to meet with a designer. They've already developed some preliminary designs to build a tower for your people."

Several shocked exclamations of disbelief and skepticism echoed around them, but underneath it all was a cautious hope. Carl must have sensed it because his next words reinforced this. "The only chance your people have to make this new tower a reality is to stand with OmniLab now. If you walk away, I can promise you the Coalition won't make this same offer to you. You may be able to live on your own without supplies for months, or even years, but your best chance for survival is to work with us. We need your help as much as you need ours. Stand with OmniLab now, and show the Coalition we're united."

The ruin rats started talking back and forth, but the tone had shifted. There was now an undercurrent of excitement among the skepticism. Kayla smiled up at Carl and slipped her hand in his. She knew some of them would still balk at the offer of living in a tower, but this was a beginning.

Leo rubbed his chin, glanced over at his camp, and turned back to Kayla. He eyed their clasped hands with a thoughtful expression. "What exactly are you proposing?"

A wave of relief rushed over her. He wasn't outright refusing anymore. If they got Leo on board, most of the ruin rats would follow him. Leo hadn't managed to stay camp leader for this long because of his winning personality.

"Come with us," Kayla urged. "The two leaders of OmniLab are here on the surface. We have a plan to stop the Coalition, but we're going to need your expertise. The Coalition has inside information about the towers and their infrastructure, but they don't know how we operate. We're the wildcard they won't be expecting."

Mack and Leo glanced at each other. Finally, after a long moment, Leo nodded.

"We're in."

CHAPTER FIFTEEN

"We're about ten minutes away," Kayla advised over her headset.

It had taken her far longer to mobilize the ruin rats than she'd hoped. After arguing with Leo about whether all the ruin rats should travel with them, they'd finally come to an agreement. Some of the supplies had been offloaded and redistributed to other bikes to expedite travel to the towers, but that meant the remaining ruin rats would be traveling even slower behind them. There was always a risk that an overzealous camp could overtake them and steal the supplies, but it would be far more dangerous if the towers were overthrown. All their lives could be in jeopardy.

Alec's voice came over her earpiece a moment later. The anger and frustration in his tone was unmistakable. "We're positioned a few miles from the towers. The coordinates are being sent to you."

Kayla tightened her grip on the steering mechanism. If Alec was still outside the towers, then their suspicions had been correct—the towers were completely locked down. The Coalition must be further along in their plan than they thought. She lifted her hand, waving toward Carl to let him know the direction they were headed.

If she hadn't been given the coordinates, she never would have spotted the temporary OmniLab shelter. They'd adopted similar cloaking technology the Coalition had used to mask their presence on the surface. She made a mental note to get her hands on the schematics once all this was done.

Kayla pulled her speeder under the shelter and shut off the engine. Swinging her leg over the side, she pulled off her helmet and hung it on the handlebar. Brant nodded a greeting, watching as the rest of the ruin rats pulled up behind her.

"Where's Alec?"

Brant pointed toward the center of the compound. "He's with the communications technician. We're still trying to contact the towers."

Carl motioned for her to go ahead without him. "Find out what's going on. I'll get Leo and everyone sorted."

She glanced at Brant, who was eyeing the ruin rats with suspicion. Apparently, he still held a grudge for Leo's perceived betrayal earlier. She leaned over to Carl and added, "You might want to make sure Brant doesn't kill anyone."

Felix jogged up behind her and took her arm. "I'd be more worried about your Omni pal. If he keeps walking around with that stick up his ass, he'll end up tripping and falling on his face. Although, that might be an improvement." At Brant's scowl, Felix chuckled. "Come on, crazy girl. Let's go see what trouble we can get into."

Kayla grinned at him, but it didn't last. The deeper they moved inside the temporary shelter, the more grim expressions she saw. A thick tension emanated from every Omni they passed. The reality of the situation struck her. These people had never known anything except the towers, which, to them, represented safety and security. They were now locked out, their prosperous existence threatened. Fear and desperation were beginning to set in. The combination could prove even more dangerous.

Felix leaned in close and whispered, "You feel it too?"

She nodded and hastened her pace. The sooner they resolved this, the better.

At that moment, she spotted Alec and Lars standing together. They were looking down at a console screen where a technician was working. As though sensing her presence, Alec looked up and met her gaze.

She peered over the technician's shoulder. "What do we know?"

Alec rubbed the back of his neck. "All the secure frequencies, including the priority ones, appear to be locked down. The signals from the towers are completely offline. They're not registering our equipment on the network. We've sent a few people to try to access the bay doors for the towers, but they weren't successful."

Kayla frowned, looking over the communication data. "What about the trader camp channels? Have you tried contacting them through there?"

The technician shook his head. "They're offline as well."

Felix studied the screen. "Do you mind if I try something?"

The technician glanced up at Alec, who nodded his assent. When the technician stood, Felix slid into the vacant seat. He began pulling up the communication relay and studying the channel maps. "Veridian and Xantham know we're on the surface. They would have set up a way for Kayla to contact them if things got bad."

"You're right," Kayla agreed, leaning forward and pointing at the screen over Felix's shoulder. "There. Try that frequency. Veridian and I used that as a distress frequency when the traders were moving in or if we didn't want our camp leader to monitor us. It's not secure, but we just need a way to communicate."

Felix entered a few commands and switched to the indicated frequency. At Felix's nod, she began speaking. "V, this is Kayla. Are you there?"

There was a lengthy pause filled with static. Felix pressed the button, and Kayla repeated the same phrase again. A moment later, Veridian's voice came over the speaker. "Kayla? You're okay?"

She let out a small laugh, relief flooding through her at the sound of his voice. "Oh, just getting into the usual amount of trouble."

There was another pause before Veridian replied. "I'm all too familiar with your brand of trouble. It seems to be catching."

Felix frowned, adjusting some of the settings. "We've got listeners on this frequency, Kayla. You need to hurry. They're tracing the transmission origin."

With a nod, she leaned forward and rested her hands on Felix's shoulders. "Make sure Cruncher keeps you out of trouble. We don't need another Aurelia Data Cube incident. I'll see you soon."

"You too," Veridian replied. "V out."

Kayla motioned for Felix to cut the transmission.

Alec frowned at her. "Why do I get the feeling far more was communicated than what we heard?"

Felix chuckled. "Because there was. Kayla told him we're outside. They've got big trouble inside the towers. My guess is the Coalition has already secured most of the key areas."

Kayla nodded. "That's my take too. Before I left Carl's camp, I showed Cruncher a program I wrote that circumvented OmniLab security protocols by manipulating the base support systems. I used the program to access Ramiro's camp when I stole the Aurelia Data Cube. If Cruncher can tweak that program, he can hack the bay doors to get us access."

Alec raised an eyebrow. "How long will it take him?"

"Less than an hour," Carl spoke from behind them. "Cruncher knows her program well enough that he's already developed a patch to be used within the towers. I sent it over to our scientists for review, but it was still being tested. OmniLab should still be vulnerable to her program."

Kayla scowled, crossing her arms over her chest. "He patched it? You didn't think to mention this?"

The corner of Carl's lips curved in a smile. He wrapped his arm around her and pressed a kiss against her temple. "We've been a little busy. When all this is over, I'll make sure you're all caught up."

Kayla harrumphed but melted into his side. "Where's Leo? When they get the doors open, we're going to need them."

"They're making some modifications to their speeders, and Brant's outfitting them with weapons. We're limited with supplies, but your friends are being surprisingly resourceful with what we have on hand."

Alec frowned. "I'm not sure how much assistance they can provide. They don't know the layout of the towers or the security measures in place."

Lars held up his hand. "On this, I agree with Kayla. Don't discount their ingenuity."

The show of support from Lars caught her off guard. She tilted her head, studying him. It was going to take some time before she adjusted to not having to worry about getting another knife in the ribs. "Great. Now that we have that settled, what's the plan? We need to hurry before Cruncher gets the door opened."

———

KAYLA CROUCHED DOWN and reviewed the map of OmniLab. She and a small group had separated from the temporary camp so they could enter the tower. Seara had reluctantly agreed to stay behind with the remainder of their forces until the entrance was secure. If things didn't go well, it wouldn't do the towers any good for both council leaders to be captured.

Kayla rubbed her nose as she tried to figure out the best route to take once they got inside. "The security area is closest. We could hit that first to test my energy against the Shadows."

Alec shook his head. "No. We'll just have to hope it does. We need to head to the main control center right away. They'll use biometric scanners to track our movements until we regain control of that area. Until then, we'll have targets on our backs."

"Won't these scanners flag us as not being part of the towers?" Leo asked with a scowl. She'd tried to explain about the energy stuff, but he'd made it clear he didn't believe any of it. Kayla just hoped he didn't jump ship when he found out the truth.

"No," Carl said, lowering his binoculars and offering them to Leo. "If the Coalition members are already in the towers, they would have had to lift the biometric restrictions so they could access priority areas. Your people aren't in the database either, and they won't be expecting you. "

A grunt was Leo's only response as he lifted the binoculars to watch the sealed bay doors. Kayla passed the map tablet over to Mack. Waiting was making her antsy. "On the plus side, even if Cruncher can't get the doors open, we could walk up and knock. I bet they'd let us back in," she said with a smirk.

"I'd rather avoid capture," Alec replied dryly.

She shrugged and shifted her weight. Maybe they could

blast the door open. Between Alec and Lars, they had some pretty heavy-duty fire power over here. "What kind of reinforcement do those doors have? Maybe we could just..." She wiggled her fingers in the direction of the door.

"There's enough reinforcement on the doors that by the time we got through them, we'd have alerted every security force within the towers. We don't know how many of our people have been compromised." Alec paused, and Kayla studied him, wondering about the direction of his thoughts. Even if it was liberating being alone in her head, she'd come to depend on using their bond to read his emotions. It was going to be an adjustment.

Alec turned back toward the sealed doors. "However, I'm not discounting the idea. If your friend doesn't come through, we may have no other option. At least we'd have the element of surprise on our side. I'm just not sure how much damage we'd cause to the towers."

Felix lifted his head from the tablet he'd been studying. "Shit. We've got a major problem. They were able to trace the signal transmission location from your conversation with Veridian. Seara's ordering the temporary camp to move out of range."

"Dammit," Alec swore, his hands clenching into fists. "We're going to have to go in hard."

"Wait," Kayla urged, grabbing his arm to stop him. She turned back to Felix. "How do you know? Did they see anyone?"

"Not yet," he admitted. "The trace just completed. We don't have more than a few minutes."

She studied the doors. "Can you tell where the trace originated?"

Felix's eyes lit up in understanding and he grinned. "From inside the towers."

"Perfect," Kayla replied and pointed at his tablet. "We

need to open up the communication again and make sure they use the right door."

Carl arched an eyebrow, a small smile playing on his lips. "If we can't get the doors open, you want the Coalition to open them for us?"

Kayla nodded. "Something must have gone wrong. Cruncher should have gotten the doors open by now, unless something happened."

"If they traced our location, it's safe to assume they traced the other end too," Felix said with a frown. "I hope your friends cleared their system or abandoned their hardware."

"Do it," Alec ordered. "We're running out of time."

With a nod, Felix pulled up the channel map. He held out the device, and Kayla spoke into the microphone. "V, this is Kayla. Are you there?"

He didn't respond, but Kayla didn't expect him to either. Even so, she tried to bury her worry over the lack of a response. She waited several heartbeats and repeated the transmission. If they hurt Veridian or anyone else, she'd kill them.

"They're tracing it," Felix informed her.

Carl reached over and squeezed her hand. "I'm sure they're fine."

With a nod, she repeated the transmission a third time before abandoning the ruse. "That should be enough to get them to open the door. Anything more will have them suspicious."

Alec glanced over at Felix's screen. "How long until they lock on our location?"

Felix entered a few commands. "No more than a few minutes. They've already narrowed down the area based on the previous transmission. At the very least, it's unlikely the other camp will be a target."

As soon as he finished speaking, the bay doors began to

open. A wave of armed guards wearing the dark-gray of the Coalition emerged on speeders. The harsh sun glinted off the metal on their speeders, nearly blinding in its brilliance.

Kayla wiggled her fingers at Alec. "How about that finger wiggle now?"

He gave her a wry smile and looked over at Lars. "How about it, cousin? A game of bowling with Coalition soldiers? See which of us can knock over more?"

Lars's eyes widened a fraction and then narrowed. "Kayla's rubbed off on you."

Both men stood, and the air became infused with electricity. Kayla breathed in the sharp and slightly sweet smell of ozone as they both raised their hands. A thunderous *crack* pierced the air as they expelled the built-up energy in a crashing wave. Coalition soldiers were thrown from their speeders like a handful of pebbles tossed carelessly in the dirt.

Leo swore and stumbled backward from where he'd been perched in a crouch. Kayla held out her hand, helping to pull him upright. "*Now* will you believe me?"

"What the fuck is this?" the older ruin rat demanded. He jerked away from her, his eyes narrowing in suspicion. "You can do this shit too?"

She shifted her weight, avoiding his gaze. "Not exactly. I'm still learning. I keep causing earthquakes for some reason."

When Leo started swearing, Mack intervened. "Kayla's still the same person. She just has a bit more kick now. Let's do this and be thankful they're on our side."

Tossing Mack a grateful look, she hurried after the advancing group. Alec and Lars were doing something with their energy, preventing the soldiers from rising. Kayla ran and caught up to them just in time to see Brant shoot one of the prone guards.

She skidded to a halt, jerking her gaze to Brant. He

grabbed her arm, propelling her forward. "He was a Shadow. We need to move. I don't know how long Alec and Lars can keep this up."

Kayla lifted her head. She could see the perspiration on both men. The waves of energy threaded through the air in complex patterns she couldn't begin to decipher. They were also doing something to hold the bay doors open, but the strain was taking its toll.

She waved the rest of the group forward. "Run! Head for the doors!"

Dropping her head to her chest, Kayla tucked in her shoulders and ran for all she was worth. Her feet hit the floor of the bay, and she slid forward on the slick surface, trying to stop her momentum.

Alec and Lars were both faltering but moving forward slowly, the strands of energy in the air becoming weaker. The Coalition soldiers were starting to rouse, the ones further away managing to regain their footing. The rest of her group was rushing toward the towers, but it wasn't fast enough. Leo stumbled, and Carl stopped to help the older man up. Her heart was beating wildly in her chest. They were too far away. Kayla stepped forward, determined to provide Alec and Lars with additional energy to give everyone more time.

Brant grabbed her, yanking her backward. "No, Kayla. You need to conserve your energy."

She struggled against his ironclad grip. "They can't keep it up. The soldiers are getting up."

Brant cursed when a particularly painful jab landed in his side. "Dammit, woman. Stop fighting me."

Kayla elbowed him in the gut, trying to make him release her. She didn't want to hurt him, but she needed to get to Alec and Lars. "Let go of me, Brant. They need my help."

"Stop struggling and look at the damn energy threads," he snapped.

She squinted her eyes, trying to see what he was talking about. Alec and Lars had woven a bubble of suppressing protective energy around their group. As they moved closer to the entrance, the energy moved with them. They were struggling, but it was clear they were conserving their energy to protect everyone.

"Oh," she murmured.

"Uh huh," Brant agreed and released her. "Sometimes I think you're more fire channeler than anything else. Come on. We need to get control of the doors."

She turned, spotting Felix at a nearby control panel. "Can you hack it?"

Felix frowned but didn't look away from the screen. "Working on it."

Kayla moved over next to him and pulled up the security overlay on the monitor beside him. Their fingers flew over the controls in an intricate dance as they anticipated one another's moves and countermoves.

Footsteps pounded on the concrete, and she lifted her head just as the remainder of the group rushed inside. The doors slammed shut behind them, sealing the Coalition soldiers outside.

"Got it!" Felix announced. "I've temporarily overridden the doors. The soldiers are locked out, but we can't keep it like this for long."

Alec leaned against the wall, trying to catch his breath. "It'll have to be enough. They already know we're inside. We need to move out now."

———

STEALTH WAS a necessary sacrifice for speed. Their footsteps echoed on the floor as the group rushed down an abandoned corridor. The fluorescent glow of the overhead lights flickered, casting a sickly light on the eggshell walls. Every few yards, an emergency light would flash a warning. A computerized voice spoke over the loudspeaker announcing a mandatory lockdown. All residents were urged to return to their family quarters immediately and await further instructions.

They turned a corner, and Alec held up his hand, halting their progress. In a low voice, he said, "There's no way to know how many are in the control center. I'll go in first and draw them away from the door. Brant, stay with Kayla and point out the Shadows. There may be more than one."

"No," Lars objected. "Let me go in first with Kayla. They know we're here, but they may not know which side I'm on. The confusion may be enough to buy some time. Brant can follow behind us. The Shadows can pick up our energy signatures, but they won't be expecting him as out of place."

Alec shook his head. "It's too risky. We might have a chance to subdue them if we all go in."

Lars put his hand on Alec's arm, and a ripple of energy charged the air. Kayla straightened, looking back and forth between them, understanding they were communicating silently but not able to listen in.

After a long moment, Lars released Alec. "You need to trust me, cousin. The Coalition knew Kayla was my target, and it won't be surprising that she's with me."

Alec pinched the bridge of his nose and nodded. "Very well."

Lars glanced down at Kayla. "Follow my lead and stay close. They need to know you're under my control. With any luck, they'll think you're bonded to me."

"Shit," Kayla muttered with a scowl. "I hate playing a fucking damsel in distress."

Carl's hand on her back was a warm and comforting weight. That simple gesture was a reminder of everything at stake.

She sighed. "Fine. Whatever. Let's just do this."

Lars took her arm, motioning for the rest of the group to stay back. Kayla glanced back at Carl, the worry in his eyes landing like a heavy weight in the pit of her stomach. She looked away and took a deep breath, curling her fingers into fists. The pressure of her nails cut into her palms, the pain bringing her back to the present.

With renewed determination, they approached a large double door. A palm print reader was embedded in the wall adjacent to it. A small, almost unnoticeable red light shone over the doors, indicating the presence of a security camera. Lars ignored the palm print reader, staring fixedly at the light, and waited. His head was thrown back as though silently demanding the door to open.

After a long moment, the door beeped and slid open.

Huh. Go figure. She'd never tried just staring down a camera before. She'd have to try that sometime.

The control room was larger than Kayla had expected, with security monitors affixed to every wall. Individual stations were set up for dozens of people, and the images on the screens flickered to show countless places around the towers.

A group of armed men wearing Coalition uniforms pointed their weapons at them. One of the soldiers approached, quickly searching them and removing their weapons. Kayla took the opportunity to study the room while she was patted down.

At least twenty more Coalition forces occupied the surveillance stations, while a group of bound OmniLab personnel sat on the floor against one wall. Two more armed men watched over them. It was promising that they hadn't been killed outright. At least the Coalition was making an effort to preserve life.

Another soldier stepped forward, and his eyes narrowed

on them. This one appeared to be in some sort of position of power. He spoke a few words in a foreign language to Lars, gesturing to Kayla with his free hand as he spoke. Lars replied, pulling Kayla tighter against him. While they argued back and forth, Kayla's eyes fell on another man standing on the far side of the room. The naked hatred and menace in his eyes left her with a cold chill.

He wore the OmniLab security uniform with the gold ouroboros symbol fastened to his arm. The weapon at his side was holstered, but his hand grazed the weapon as he walked toward them. It was a subtle taunt, reminding her he viewed her as an enemy and wouldn't blink an eye if he used his weapon on them. There was no doubt in her mind he was a Shadow.

"Well, if it isn't the Cerulis bastard and Alec Tal'Vayr's little bitch," the man said with a sneer.

Lars straightened, his body ramrod straight as he focused on the Shadow. "Watch your tongue. If you want a place with the Coalition, you need to learn some respect."

"Respect?" the man scoffed, stepping forward and slapping his hand to the butt of his weapon. With that one gesture, the threat definitively moved out of the subtle zone. "You want to talk to me about respect?"

The Coalition man watched this exchange and held up his hand. In a thick accent, he said, "Enough. We have mission. Lars, until status is confirmed, you stay here under guard."

The Shadow glared at them. "He's working with Alec Tal'-Vayr. There's no other explanation for them being here together. None of the Inner Circle can be trusted."

Kayla had been quiet up until this point, but she needed to distract the Shadow and bring him within touching distance. The trick would be to engage him without encouraging him to use his weapon.

"That's bullshit," she argued, focusing directly on the irate man. Lars tightened his grip on her arm in a warning, but she ignored it. "Lars was exiled from the towers, and I've lived my whole life on the surface. We're both about as far from your Inner Circle as you can get."

"The Princess of the Towers doesn't think she's part of the Inner Circle?" the Shadow mocked. "I've seen you cozying up to the council leader, batting your eyes at him. He even assigned you your very own pet Shadow. Where *is* Brant, by the way?"

Kayla pulled away from Lars, intent on provoking the Shadow even more. Lars hissed her name in warning, but they were running out of time. If they caught Brant or anyone else on the security feed outside the door, they were screwed. She tilted her head, taunting the Shadow. "What's the matter? Jealous? Did *you* want to be assigned to protect me?"

She tossed her hair back and took another step forward, putting an exaggerated swagger in her step. "Or maybe you were just jealous of all the pretty Inner Circle people and their energy? Is that it? How does it feel to be on the outside looking in?"

"Bitch," the Shadow hissed.

"Kayla," Lars barked her name, reaching for her arm. "Not him. Stop."

She jerked out of Lars's grasp, taking another step toward the Shadow. "I can feel your lack of ability from here. No wonder Brant was chosen over you. You're not even a decent Shadow, are you? I'm surprised the Coalition even pretended they wanted you in their ranks."

She'd pushed too far. The Shadow reached for his weapon, and Kayla leapt toward him, intent on stopping him. Shouts sounded throughout the room, but she scrambled, focusing only on trying to touch any part of his bare skin. Her fingers made contact, and she flooded him with energy.

He gasped, and she clamped her fingers around his forearm, forcing the energy into him. He tried to push her away, but his body spasmed uncontrollably. Concentrating on forcing more energy into him, she missed his hand coming up. With a sharp *crack*, pain in her cheek erupted and her head whipped back. A sharp burst of energy slammed into her, and she was flung backward, striking the wall.

"You don't think I know what you can do?" he shouted, lifting his hand and flinging more energy at her. Pain, like thousands of tiny daggers, pierced her skin and she screamed. They dug in deeper and twisted, the agony unlike anything she'd ever known.

Another sharp gust of air swept through the room, and the assault stopped almost as quickly as it had begun. Kayla barely recognized Lars's cooler air energy lowering her to the floor. She slumped down, tears stinging her eyes as she tried to remember how to breathe.

"Try it again and I'll kill her here and now," the Shadow threatened.

"Shield yourself!" Lars yelled, struggling in the grip of the Coalition guards. She had to get up.

Focus, dammit. Pain is a tool that can be used.

Kayla pushed herself off the floor, unsteady but determined. She grasped the energy threads, fumbling with them, and tried to form a shield.

The Shadow laughed. "She can't shield against her own energy." He reached down, wrapping his fingers around her neck, and slammed her into the wall as though she weighed nothing. Stars danced across her vision. "Lars didn't tell you who helped Miranda test the bond, did he?"

Kayla dug her nails into the Shadow's arm, scratching and clawing, trying to get him to release her. She kicked out, struggling against his grip. He squeezed her neck even tighter and leaned in close. "That's right. I'm the one who figured out you can fuel Shadows with your energy. You're going to be very useful to us once you've been brought to heel."

"Ruin rats will never be brought to heel!" a voice shouted, plowing into the Shadow. Kayla fell to the ground, coughing and choking. She pushed to her hands and knees, lifting her head to find Leo wrestling with the Shadow and swinging a knife at him. Carl gripped her arm and helped her to her feet.

Chaos filled the room as the small group of ruin rats and OmniLab forces fought the Coalition soldiers. Shots were fired, and shouts filled the air. A nearby console exploded, showering glass and debris over them. She ducked, flinging her arms over her head.

"Where's the Shadow?" Alec shouted over the commotion.

Kayla coughed, her throat still painful, and pointed to the man rolling around on the floor with Leo. The ruin rat camp leader was spouting curses. His knife had disappeared, and he was now swinging his fists, while yelling something about how he'd be the one to bring the OmniLab bastards to heel. The Shadow's weapon was also missing. She glanced around but couldn't tell where it had gone in the chaos.

Alec rushed over to the Shadow, but before he could intervene, a powerful burst of energy sent Leo into the air. His body crashed into the ceiling and fell to the floor in a heap.

"Leo!" Kayla screamed, racing over to him. He was lying on his side, his body twisted in an unnatural angle.

"Don't move him," Carl urged, kneeling beside her. "We don't know what's broken."

"Leo," she whispered, moving closer to assess the damage. There was too much. Between the obvious broken bones and the deep gash across the side of his face, it didn't look good. Blood dripped onto the floor, forming a dark puddle on the ground. Carl pulled off his shirt and handed it to her.

Leo coughed, struggling to breathe. "Don't look at me like that. I'm fine. Just need to catch my breath."

Kayla nodded, her heart clenching as she pressed Carl's shirt against Leo's face to stop the bleeding. It wouldn't do much good unless they got him medical attention right away. Even so, she wasn't sure the towers had the capability to heal injuries this serious. She didn't think her injuries from being stabbed were this severe.

Around her, the guards and ruin rats were still fighting. The Coalition soldiers were quickly getting the upper hand, leaving a trail of crumpled bodies on the floor. Carl turned, firing his weapon at an approaching Coalition soldier. Kayla scanned the room, trying to find the Shadow. He was the biggest threat.

The Coalition soldiers had grabbed Alec, thrusting a weapon against his neck. The Shadow wiped away a thin stream of blood from his mouth and glared at the council leader. Alec's capture had charged the room with an almost unnatural energy. Seeing their leader threatened, the remaining OmniLab guards immediately dropped their weapons to the ground and held up their hands in surrender.

The Shadow advanced on Alec, no longer bothering to mask the raw fury and hate on his face. "Not so tough now, are you?"

Alec held his head high, refusing to respond to the man's baiting. Kayla grabbed a shard of broken glass from the ground and stood. There was a distinct heaviness coating the energy threads in the room, making them slippery and almost impossible to grasp. The Shadow must have expelled her energy on Leo and was now suppressing the room. She took a step forward, tightening her grip on the jagged glass. Blood dripped down her hand as it cut into her, but the pain was inconsequential. This asshole would learn that not all Inner Circle members fought with energy.

Concentrating on her target, she barely heard Carl's voice calling out to her. She couldn't stop. These men had hurt Leo, her family, and threatened everything she held dear. Her vision narrowed, a red haze coating the world. Her only focus was on the Shadow's neck and the pulsing artery beneath the skin.

Time slowed.

The Shadow lifted his weapon toward Alec. Kayla leapt toward him, raising her makeshift blade to plunge it into his throat. The Shadow staggered, and the glass shard missed its mark, barely scratching the surface of his skin. Kayla crashed into him as he crumpled to the floor.

The room became electrified as the energy came alive again. Kayla rolled to her side, still gripping the glass shard. Something had changed, but she wasn't sure what. Undeterred, she focused on the Shadow on the ground beside her. Only a thin trail of red marked his neck where she'd made contact.

She lifted the glass shard, ready to plunge it into his neck, but a strong arm gripped her around the waist and lifted her off the floor. They ripped the glass shard from her hand, dropping it on the ground. She struggled against them, almost feral in her desire to escape. Screaming obscenities and shouting, she fought against her captor.

"Kayla, stop! He's down," Carl's voice sounded in her ear.

She blinked away the red haze and stopped fighting, realizing who held her. Horror struck her when she saw the angry scratches on Carl's arms.

"Ah, *Milaya*," another voice interrupted. "I knew if I found trouble, I would find you."

Kayla jerked her head up, meeting the gray eyes of the Coalition commander. Her stomach plummeted. His arrival was either very good, or very bad. She wiped the blood from her palms on her pants. "Sergei, it's about time you got here. You suck at answering your calls."

"Apologies," he said with a grin and holstered his weapon. "I was otherwise engaged."

She glanced down at the Shadow on the floor, not feeling an ounce of remorse. With a bravado she didn't quite feel, she said, "You know, this is the second time you've stolen a kill from me."

Sergei raised an eyebrow, cocking his head to study her. "Indeed."

Kayla tensed, watching him navigate the room and approach her. The casual way he stepped over bodies sent a chill through her. No matter what illusions of camaraderie she had with Sergei, there was no mistaking the cold ruthlessness of the man in front of her.

The Coalition guards were still holding Alec, a weapon against his neck. He straightened, his bearing proud and uncowed. His blue eyes flashed with barely suppressed anger as he glared at the Coalition leader. "You will not be able to hold the towers. Whatever deal you made with the Shadows is only temporary. They cannot hold our Inner Circle indefinitely."

Sergei didn't appear fazed by Alec's announcement. Instead, he looked almost bored. "Perhaps."

Alec's eyes narrowed. "If you execute us or keep suppressing our abilities, you'll find there will be very little resources to harvest. Our economy is dependent upon the Inner Circle."

Sergei inclined his head. "You are correct. That is why we are speaking."

Alec stiffened. "You have a proposal?"

Sergei didn't answer right away. Instead, he turned to Kayla. "Tell me, Kayla. What do you think of living in these towers?"

Kayla frowned, trying to gauge Sergei's intent. His expression was unreadable. Even so, she decided to go with the truth. "It's a pretty enough cage."

Sergei arched a brow. "A cage?"

She glanced down at Leo's unconscious form, trying to ignore the sharp pang of worry that flashed through her. Mack was now beside him, pressing Carl's discarded shirt against his face to staunch the bleeding. The head injury was secondary. The possibility of a broken neck and internal injuries was the most troubling. They needed to hurry this along before more lives were lost. There was still a chance Leo could be saved.

"Yeah, a cage," she repeated, making an effort to tear her gaze away from her former camp leader. "I prefer the freedom of living on the surface, but there's an element of safety here in the towers. I understand why it appeals to some, but there's got to be a happy medium somewhere."

Sergei's eyes twinkled as though she'd give him the answer he wanted. "We searched OmniLab's archives. You intend to build a tower for your friends?"

Her eyes widened a fraction, guessing the direction of his questions. "Yeah. We're talking about changing the design so it offers a safe haven but allows easy access to the surface." She paused for a second and cocked her head. "How many people are in the Coalition?"

His lips curved into a smile, and he leaned against a desk console. "Thousands. We have almost one thousand looking for new home."

Kayla swallowed, quickly doing the calculations in her head. That many people would require a complete redesign of the initial schematics or else it would never support such a population. The problem was acquiring additional resources to fund the construction. They were already depending on the ruin rats to forage for building materials, but Sergei's proposition would make the task even more daunting.

Alec had been quiet, simply listening to their exchange. At Sergei's announcement, he shook his head. "Impossible. That many people would put too large of a drain on our supplies. We may be able to offer a home to a few dozen of your people, but we cannot support a thousand. We've already had to begin supplementing additional resources to make up for our existing deficit."

Kayla scowled at Alec, willing him to shut up. If there was one thing she'd learned about dealing with OmniLab traders, it was that they were powerful negotiators. Alec might know how to run the towers, but there was only one man here who could possibly turn the tides. She glanced over at Carl and nodded toward Sergei.

Carl caught her meaning and addressed the Coalition leader. "He's right, Sergei. OmniLab has already started running tests on an underground river to increase the tower water supply. Unfortunately, the towers don't have many people trained to navigate the ruins on the surface. Kayla has proposed allowing the ruin rats to help forage for supplies and resources in exchange for housing. What can the Coalition offer OmniLab?"

Sergei regarded Carl for a long time, as though weighing his words. He gave Carl an approving nod. "You make valid point. Any agreement must be beneficial to both sides." He turned back to Alec. "Your offer is not acceptable. You will take two hundred into towers immediately. Three hundred more will stay on surface outside. In return, they will all help harvest resources and build new tower. You have one year to finish construction. Another five hundred will move into tower when complete."

Kayla swallowed. She wasn't sure what the towers could support, but Sergei's demands seemed a little extreme. They'd be hard-pressed to finish the construction in that timeframe, especially since the ruin rats were still so disorganized.

Apparently, Alec agreed. He didn't reply immediately, but the tension in his shoulders belied his concern. He looked to be on the verge of refusing, but Lars pulled away from the guards and stepped forward.

"Alec, it can be done. There are roughly two dozen Inner Circle members still on the surface and living with the Coalition. If we all return to the towers, you'll have us to help supplement the power needed for construction and acquiring resources. That doesn't even take into account the aid Kayla can provide."

Alec regarded his cousin for a long moment and then nodded. "Very well. I agree to the Coalition's terms."

"Good," Sergei replied, pushing away from the wall. "Now you have another problem. Your High Council has been taken hostage."

Alec froze, his eyes narrowing on Sergei. "I demand you release them at once."

Sergei didn't appear impressed by Alec's mounting anger. "You misunderstand. *We* do not hold your people. Your Shadows have taken your High Council hostage."

Lars frowned. "How many Shadows are holding the room?"

Sergei shrugged. "Perhaps a dozen. This was not done on our orders. Some Shadows still hold other areas with my men."

Alec studied Sergei. "In the interest of our agreement, will you aid in the rescue of our people?"

Sergei shook his head. "No. Your High Council is held by *your* people. We will not interfere with internal matters. If you do not resolve conflict, we will negotiate with them."

Anger, quick and volatile, colored Alec's expression. Before he could express his fury, Lars held up his hand to stop him. "We understand. Our struggles are not yours. We will require safe passage to the council chambers. Will your men stand down?"

"Of course," Sergei replied. "We will escort you there. You may bring any allies you need."

Lars nodded, turning back to his cousin. "Alec, we need to get in touch with Seara. Miranda should be back with Trenon by now. Are there any Inner Circle members who are not part of the High Council that you trust completely?"

"A few," Alec replied, stepping over to a console. "I can get a message to some of them and have them meet us here."

Kayla glanced down at Leo and the other injured. "We need to get some medical personnel in here too. We're going to need as many allies as possible if we're going to take on the Shadows."

CHAPTER SIXTEEN

KAYLA PACED BACK AND FORTH. The medical team was on their way to assess Leo's condition, and the Coalition soldiers had stabilized him as much as possible before preparing him for transfer to the medical ward. The surly ruin rat was still unconscious, and Kayla couldn't help but worry. With the extent of his injuries, he had a long road to recovery.

"He's going to hate sitting out of this fight," Mack observed, checking the charge on his weapon.

Kayla nodded, not pausing in her movements. She'd counted the steps from one end of the room to the other at least a hundred times. Restless energy threatened to bubble over. She needed a task instead of just pacing and worrying over Leo's condition.

"Do we have access to the security feeds in the council room?"

Felix didn't bother glancing up from where he was hunched over a console. "Nope. They're offline. The Shadows must have manually disabled or destroyed them. We've got eyes outside, but that's it."

She only managed a handful of steps before stopping in her tracks. "What about audio?"

Carl turned away from his console and studied her. He'd been using the equipment to reach out to Cruncher, Veridian, and the rest of Carl's camp. The group was detained after the Coalition had traced their transmission, but they were otherwise unharmed. Sergei had ordered them to be released, and they were now heading to the control center to reconvene with them.

Carl pulled out his earpiece. "What are you thinking, Kayla?"

She made a sweeping gesture of the entire room. "All this. We have access to virtually everything from here. Don't we also have access to everyone's commlinks? Even if the Shadows have taken away the High Council's commlinks, we should be able to hack into them. We can use their devices to force-enable audio and maybe even video."

Felix's eyes lit up, and he started entering commands. "That could work. We might be able to extract some usable information."

Brant sat down at the console next to him. "I'm sending you the list of High Council members. Lars also compiled a partial list of Shadow recruits targeted by the Coalition. We won't have complete information until Miranda and Trenon arrive, but we may be able to isolate the traitors' identities by cross-referencing their locations. We can try accessing each of their commlinks."

Felix nodded and hunched his shoulders, his fingers flying over the controls. Beside him, Brant pulled up a map of the towers and began using the biometric scanners and facial recognition to mark the locations of each Shadow.

Kayla watched over their shoulders until Carl wrapped his arm around her. He pulled her against him and pressed a kiss against her temple. "You okay?"

She nodded, leaning into his embrace and soaking up his reassurance. "Yeah. When all this is done, we're going to disappear for a few weeks and go play in the ruins."

He chuckled and squeezed her midsection. "It's a promise."

The door pinged and slid open. Ariana and Jason Alivette entered with an escort of Coalition soldiers. Jason's expression was marked with fury as his gaze swept the room. It hesitated on Lars before targeting Alec. He strode over to the council leader. "What the hell is going on? We got your message, but you're working with the Coalition? This doesn't make sense."

Ariana placed her hand on her brother's arm. "Jason, calm down. Alec asked us here for a reason."

Alec's face was grim, and he clasped his hands behind his back. "Thank you both for coming. The short answer is, the Shadows have taken the High Council hostage, including your father. We need your help to extricate the council members. There are very few people I can trust with something of this sensitive nature."

Ariana paled. "My father wasn't answering his commlink earlier. Do you know if he's all right?"

Alec shook his head. "I'm sorry, Ariana. We don't know much. We're working on trying to get information about what's happening inside the room." He reached out to gently touch her arm. "I swear to you, we'll do everything possible to make sure he's returned unharmed."

Ariana lowered her gaze. "I know you will, Alec."

Alec turned back to Jason. "Can I trust that you'll both be willing to offer your aid?"

"Of course," Jason nodded impatiently. "What needs to be done?"

Alec gestured to Lars. "You remember my cousin, don't you? He's been instrumental in coordinating this effort. Seara is on her way here with Trenon and Miranda Noltreck. We're hoping that, with everyone's help, we can subdue the Shadows."

Ariana gave Lars a warm smile. Holding out her hands, she walked over to the former exile. "Lars, it's wonderful to see you again. I wish the circumstances were better, but I'm so glad you've returned to us."

Lars took her hands in his and leaned forward, pressing a kiss against her cheek. "Ariana, you're even more beautiful than I remembered. I appreciate your kindness." He nodded toward Jason. "It's good to see you again as well, old friend."

Jason hesitated for a minute and then clasped Lars's hands. "Alec says you're still a bastard."

Lars grinned, the expression softening his features, making him appear even more like Alec. "He's correct."

Ariana's eyes fell on Leo, who was still being worked on by the Coalition soldier, and she frowned. She approached him and knelt on the floor, her delicate hands fluttering over his prone form. "This man's injuries were caused by an energy attack." She frowned, lifting her head to meet Kayla's gaze. "This is *your* energy? Did this man harm you?"

Kayla's eyes widened, and she pointed to the corner where the dead Shadow's body remained. "Fuck no. The Shadow used my energy to toss him on the ceiling." She took a tentative step forward. "Can you help him?"

Ariana nodded, focusing again on Leo's injuries. "Yes, to a degree. My abilities don't work as well on non-sensitives. Since it was an energy attack, I may be able to do more for him. At the very least, I can accelerate his healing and pull him out of danger."

Kayla watched as the young woman spread her hands over Leo's body. A strong energy, unlike anything she'd ever experienced, poured out of Ariana's palms and into Leo. The deep wound on his head began to knit back together. A gasp went through some of the Coalition soldiers and even the ruin rats.

Jason moved forward to stand protectively over his sister, arms crossed, and glared threateningly at everyone as though daring them to approach. Ariana lifted her head to meet the stunned expression of the Coalition guard. "His neck is broken. I need you to remove the transport brace so I can reset the bones."

Lars stepped forward, repeating the request in their language. The man nodded and quickly removed the brace, almost falling backward in his haste to get away. Ariana didn't react, her attention once more completely focused on Leo. She reached down, her fingertips lightly caressing his neck.

Leo's eyelids fluttered open, and he muttered something unintelligible before closing them again. The visual result wasn't as dramatic this time, but it was astounding on an energy level. Complex energy threads spun out from Ariana's fingers and encircled Leo's neck. Finally, Ariana sat back on her heels and folded her hands in her lap.

"I cannot do more without harming him. More than anything, the human body needs time to heal."

Jason helped his sister to her feet. Kayla approached them, unable to tear her eyes away from Leo. The older ruin rat now appeared to be resting more comfortably. "He'll be okay?"

Ariana nodded. "Yes. He'll be much as he was before."

Hope welled up inside Kayla as she looked down at the man who had raised her. Leo was stubborn, pig-headed, and infuriating, but she loved him. If it weren't for him, she would have died in the ruins along with everyone else. The thought of losing him now was crippling. He'd probably tell her to toughen up and remind her that everyone has their time, but that was a lesson she was willing to wait to learn. She swallowed, trying to suppress her emotions, and lifted her head to look at Ariana.

The young woman's eyes were filled with understanding. She stepped forward and embraced Kayla. In a soft voice, too low for anyone to hear, she murmured, "He loves you too, Kayla. You've always been the child of his heart."

Kayla blinked back the tears threatening to fall. She didn't know how Ariana knew how Leo felt, but her words had the ring of truth. In an uncharacteristic move, she hugged Ariana tightly. "Thank you for helping him."

A moment later, the door opened and Seara walked inside with Trenon and Miranda, the former exiles. Veridian, Cruncher, Rand, and several others from the trading camps also entered. Relief flooded through Kayla, and she rushed over to Veridian. She threw her arms around him and hugged him tightly. Even though Carl had told her they were fine, seeing them whole and unharmed eased her lingering worries. They were safe. They were all safe. Veridian laughed and returned her hug.

Alec stepped forward and welcomed them. "I'm glad you're all here. We've got a dangerous situation going on, and we're going to need everyone's help to make sure we can get everyone out safely."

––––––––

KAYLA LISTENED to Alec detail the plan. Carl would be overseeing the members of the trading camps. Since they couldn't be sure which security forces had been compromised, the trading camps would be acting as technical support.

Alec would take a small force of Inner Circle members and ruin rats to the security wing. Since the Shadows were part of the security forces, it was critical they were removed from the equation. The plan was to use the Inner Circle to draw the Shadows out from the security offices and then rely on the ruin rats to disable them. After seeing Leo's miraculous healing, the ruin rats were both awestruck and a little envious.

Every one of them had seen friends or family members die on the surface from ailments that weren't nearly as severe as Leo's injuries. If there was a chance they could prevent these needless deaths from happening in the future, they were willing to throw a few punches and create a little havoc. A few of them high-fived, and Mack cracked his knuckles, not bothering to hide his glee.

The only part of the plan Kayla didn't like was that Seara and Trenon would be going into the council room to confront the renegade Shadows face to face. Seara insisted Alec remain behind because both co-leaders couldn't risk themselves. Alec wasn't happy about this, but Seara had put her foot down. There was no changing her mind.

Kayla disagreed with the whole thing. No one had ever died from negotiating via commlink, but Seara was convinced this needed a more personal touch. This plan was a disaster waiting to happen.

"This is a mistake," Kayla insisted for the second time. "If you give Felix a bit more time, he can hack into the audio. Once we get more information, you can make a decision. If you guys go walking in there, there's no guarantee you'll come back out. They've already taken the rest of the High Council hostage, why would they stop with you?"

Seara reached out and touched her arm. "Kayla, I understand your concerns, but we're running out of time. The Shadows have been holding the High Council for hours. We don't know if they need medical attention or even why they're being held. If I show up as co-leader of the towers, it will let the Shadows know we're willing to listen to their complaints and take them seriously. Besides, Trenon is a skilled orator. I'm sure he can help us convince the Shadows to release the councilors."

Trenon puffed out his chest at the praise. Kayla scowled, crossing her arms over her chest. For such an amazing negotiator, Trenon hadn't done that great of a job at convincing her to switch sides. She fell silent and listened as Alec continued detailing the plan.

Brant was frowning too, but he hadn't raised any objections. Kayla carefully moved away from the group, heading toward where he was standing. She bumped his arm and whispered, "You don't like this plan either?"

He hesitated and then shook his head. She sighed, considering the alternatives. Brant knew better than anyone whether his brethren would stand down. If he thought the plan was crap, it probably was. She couldn't let Seara walk into that room. There was too much at stake.

Kayla nodded toward the door and said in a low voice, "Come with me."

Brant raised an eyebrow but followed her toward the exit. As she passed Sergei, Kayla touched his arm and motioned toward the door.

The moment she was outside, she addressed both men. "We need eyes in that room. I intend to buy Felix some time until he finishes hacking the comms. If Seara goes into that room, she'll end up as another hostage."

Brant frowned. "What's your plan, Kayla?"

She looked over at Sergei, remembering the first time they'd met. "That day you brought me the vodka, you attached a tracker to my shirt. It had audio capabilities too, didn't it?"

Sergei paused, considering her question for a long moment. "Yes."

Kayla nodded. She'd guessed as much when they'd raided the camp the next morning, but it was nice to have it confirmed. Lisia had confessed to letting the Coalition know she had returned, but only a select few had known Brant's position as a security officer or that OmniLab was increasing camp security the following afternoon.

"I tried to bug Carl's camp back when he was trying to recruit me. Afterward, he installed detectors at the entrance to prevent that from ever happening again. Your bug never set off any alarms though. You have technology that OmniLab can't trace, don't you?"

The corner of Sergei's mouth curved up into the hint of a smile. "You are correct."

She grinned at him. "I seem to have lost the last one you gave me. Any chance I can get a replacement? After all, I am a friend to the Coalition and all that."

He chuckled. "That can be arranged."

Brant looked skeptical, and Kayla knew he'd be much harder to convince. "Look, I know it's not a great plan, but it's better than the one they're hatching in there. If you have another suggestion, I'm open to it. I know you don't want anything to happen to Alec or Seara either. If we can open communication lines with the Shadows, they can negotiate from a distance. This will protect them. You know that."

"I'm not disagreeing," Brant admitted. "Your presence will intrigue them enough to get them to listen, but I don't think it's wise to put yourself at risk either. I can go without you."

Kayla cocked her head. "Do you really think they'll listen to you?"

When he hesitated, she sighed. "You already heard what Lars said about why they didn't approach you. If you show up, there's no incentive to keep you alive. You don't have anything to offer them on your own. They know about my connection to Alec and Seara though. Plus, I have an advantage with my abilities that Alec and Seara can't duplicate."

Brant frowned. "There's no guarantee they'll listen to either of us."

"There's a better chance of them listening to us rather than more Inner Circle members," Kayla pointed out. "You hated the Inner Circle when we met. You probably still do, and quite frankly, I don't blame you. Most of them are pompous assholes."

When he didn't disagree, she plowed ahead. "You know the Shadows. You've worked with them most of your life. You can appeal to that side of them. As for me, no one knows better what it's like to live between worlds. I can act as Alec and Seara's representative while keeping them safe from harm. At the very least, it'll get comms in that room so they can figure out what the hell is going on."

"I had a feeling you'd figure out another way to try to get me killed," Brant muttered, pinching the bridge of his nose. "All right. Let's do it."

Pleased she'd gotten him to agree, she turned back to Sergei. "Will you escort us to the council chambers? If your men see you, they'll stand down. I don't want anyone to know what we're doing until it's too late to stop us."

Sergei arched an eyebrow. "And if you are killed by these Shadows?"

Kayla shrugged. "I'd rather not die, but at least your agreement with Alec still stands. If he and Seara are killed, who's going to enforce your treaty?"

"Very well. One of my men will bring transponder," Sergei agreed and then paused, considering her for a long moment. "I will be disappointed if you die. I have come to admire you more than most." Without waiting for a response, he turned away and began speaking into his commlink.

A voice sounded behind her. "Kayla, I'm not letting you do this without me."

She spun around. Carl's dark eyes glittered with anger as

he strode toward her. Kayla took a half-step backward, surprised by the intensity in his expression. Carl grabbed her arms, holding her in place.

"Carl, I have to—"

"No," he argued. "I know better than to try to stop you, but I'll be damned if you do this without me. I almost lost you the last time you went into that room. It's not happening again."

She shook her head. "You can't. We need you here to coordinate with the ruin rats and the trading camps. They won't trust anyone else."

"Bullshit," Carl declared, his eyes narrowing. "Rand can handle the trading camps. Your friends know and trust Felix. Both he and Rand already have a working relationship. They can handle it." His gaze softened slightly, and his grip loosened. "Don't ask me to walk away from you, Kayla. If you were in my shoes, you wouldn't do it either."

Kayla swallowed, pressing her hands against his chest. His heart beat a steady rhythm beneath her fingertips. He was right. If their situations were reversed, she'd move hell and earth to get to him. She already had and would do it again in a second.

"Your shoes not being on your feet is part of the reason we're in this mess in the first place," she muttered.

At Carl's questioning look, she shook her head. "Never mind. It's not important." She lifted her hands to cup his face, not caring that Brant was witnessing this intimate moment. Hopefully, they'd have many more moments together, but just in case things went bad, she wouldn't waste another second.

"Carl, I wanted you to stay behind because I can't stand the thought of something happening to you. I still can't, but you're right. I won't ask you to let me do this without you." She brushed her fingers along the edge of his unshaven jaw, feeling the rough texture under her fingertips. "You've shown me in a thousand different ways that I can always count on you. I hope you know I'll always do the same for you."

"Sweetheart..." Carl began, his voice deepening.

Kayla shook her head, pressing her fingertips against his lips to silence him. She needed to get this out or she'd lose her nerve. "I'll probably keep screwing up and making mistakes. I've had a long time to be on my own, thinking I was better off not needing anyone. Leo warned me about protecting my heart and not getting too attached, but Ariana made me realize something. Leo didn't really believe that either. It might make things easier in the short term, but our ability to love makes us stronger. I've always been stronger with you by my side. You give me something to fight for and something to believe in. I can't lose that. I can't risk losing you."

Carl wrapped his arm around her and pulled her against him. "Are you finished?"

When she nodded, he lowered his head and kissed her as though she was the very breath he needed to survive. She melted against him, her body molding perfectly against his. They both fit together—two people no longer belonging to either world but straddling the chasm merging both. It didn't matter that there wasn't an energy connection between them. The depth of love she felt for this man was stronger than any metaphysical bond. They needed each other, and together, they made each other stronger.

Brant cleared his throat.

Carl broke the kiss but didn't release her. "I'm not willing to risk losing you either, sweetheart. No matter what happens, we're in this together."

"Together," she agreed, smiling up at him. "Now, let's go kick some Shadow ass."

———

KAYLA STOOD outside the council chamber and hesitated before the imposing doors. The last time she'd been in this room was when Edwin had held her on trial. Alec had saved her then, in more ways than one. It was now her turn to do the same for him.

Brant glanced down at her. "If you're not sure about this..." His voice trailed off, but his meaning was clear.

She shook her head, determination filling her, and pounded on the door with her fist. "Try again, Fluffy. You're not getting out of this."

Brant grimaced at the nickname but didn't reply. Brant and Carl stood on opposite sides of her, like sentry guards guarding a treasure. She didn't feel like much of a treasure though. If anything, she felt decidedly short sandwiched between the two giants overshadowing her.

Sergei had disappeared down an adjacent hall, out of sight from the doors. After attaching the transponder to Carl's stolen uniform to better blend in, he'd warned them it would take at least ten minutes for them to finish configuring the device. The device was an upgraded design and had both audio and video capabilities, but there would be no way to communicate with them once they were inside.

He'd also reminded them that the Coalition needed to remain a neutral third party. Once they walked through the doors and into the council room, they were on their own. Although the Coalition wouldn't offer any aid to the Shadows, they wouldn't help her or OmniLab either. The pin, he explained, was simply a replacement for the one she'd already been given. Nothing more.

She suspected if Sergei really had a say in things, he would have helped them. But from what Lars had indicated earlier, Sergei was operating under someone else's authority. The only way Sergei or the Coalition could intervene was if the new treaty with OmniLab were threatened or if Kayla could assure them of victory. It wasn't the first time she'd managed the impossible.

Kayla blew out a breath, feeling naked without any weapons. At Brant's insistence, all three of them had disarmed. He claimed the Shadows would search them before allowing entry and they'd just be providing them with more weapons. She'd argued about keeping her knife, but apparently, the tower security forces knew about the hidden blade in her belt. Fortunately, improvisation was her way of life.

If they managed to get out of this, though, she was going to wipe her OmniLab file clean. The thought of everyone knowing her business or where she hid her weapons was becoming rather inconvenient.

When the occupants didn't respond, Brant banged on the door. The door rattled from the reverberations of his fist. "It's Brant. Open the damn door. I'm out here with Kayla Rath'Varein and Trader Carl Grayson. We need to talk to you."

Kayla could barely make out some muffled noises within the room. She shifted her weight and glanced behind her, worried that Alec would come charging in any second. They needed to hurry. The council room wasn't showing up on the security feeds, but the antechamber they were in was still being monitored. Felix probably already knew what she was doing.

"Any suggestions?" Brant remarked dryly. "They don't seem receptive to talking."

Kayla scowled, wishing they could just blast open the door. Wait. Could she? She cocked her head, studying the door and its design.

Carl frowned. "Kayla? What are you thinking?"

"It's time to try my own brand of finger wiggling," she

explained and shoved her energy toward the door. It was inelegant, more raw power than anything else, but something happened. The movement was slight, but the door didn't seem quite as secure.

"I can keep flinging energy at this door until it blows apart," she shouted. "Or you can open the door. Come on, don't you want three more hostages?"

"Are you insane?" Brant hissed, grabbing her arm.

She pulled away from him, wiggling her fingers in Brant's direction. "We've already played the energy game today. Let your friends have a turn."

"Kayla, maybe you should listen to him," Carl suggested. "We don't know what's going on inside that room. The council members could be in danger."

"Yeah, and I'm not going to let anyone else join them. If they don't open the door for us, they won't open it for anyone." She flung more energy at the door. There was a loud *crack* as something splintered, but the door still didn't open. Raising her voice again, she shouted, "Do you hear that? A couple more good energy pulls and we'll have some firewood."

"Enough," a muffled voice sounded from the other side of the door.

Kayla could sense small tendrils of shadow energy wrap around her, shackling the energy threads coating the air. It wasn't as potent as Brant's shadow energy, but it was noticeable. She wasn't sure if this other Shadow simply wasn't as strong as Brant or if it was because they were also suppressing other people.

There were more noises, as though barricades were being moved away from the door, and it finally opened a fraction. A weapon poked out, pointed directly at her. She stared into the barrel, hoping the person on the other end didn't have an itchy trigger finger. She slowly raised her hands and lifted her head to meet the owner's gaze. A tall, dark-haired man with flinty eyes stared down at Kayla.

"Josten," Brant said, identifying the man in front of them, and held up his hands to show he didn't have any weapons either. "We're unarmed. We simply wish to speak with you."

The man's gaze swept over them and assessed the room behind them. He grabbed Kayla's arm, jerking her inside. She stumbled, only staying upright because of the man's iron grip. Two other men stood nearby and grabbed Brant and Carl.

Rough hands pushed her up against the wall for the second time that day. With brisk movements, she was patted down and searched. She would have objected to the invasiveness, but the guard's thoroughness was rather impressive. They didn't bother searching her belt. Instead, the guard yanked it off and tossed it to someone else. They'd also made her remove her shoes, taking the time to search them as well. Apparently, Brant had been right about the weapons. *Damn.* She owed him an apology.

When they finished, she was led over to the side of the room where a small group of people wearing formal robes were being held. Brant and Carl were still being searched. The brief reprieve gave her an opportunity to assess the situation.

The former council chambers were in complete disarray. Furniture was toppled on its side, some pieces destroyed beyond any recognition. Either an intense battle had raged in the room or a bomb had gone off. The council members had been split into two separate groups and were being held on opposite sides of the room. At least twenty armed guards wearing the distinct OmniLab security uniforms were scattered throughout the room watching over their captives.

The room was thick with the slippery shadow energy. Kayla could sense the council members trying to grasp energy threads under the thick blanket, but the threads kept moving out of their reach.

A loud scraping noise caught her attention. She turned, discovering she'd been right about the sound of a barricade being moved. They'd finished searching Carl and Brant and were now moving the barricade back into place, effectively sealing them in the room—like a tomb.

Kayla turned back to the guard who had pulled her into the room. "You're Josten?"

The man inclined his head but didn't speak. A weapon was still loosely held in his hand, but the casual way he carried it implied he wasn't a stranger to using it. If he had half the training of Brant, he'd make a formidable foe. For all her teasing, she knew Brant had treated her with kid gloves. The man standing in front of her had no such inclination. Kayla just hoped she wasn't wrong about her assessment of the Shadows.

"Is this really necessary?" Brant demanded after one of the guards led him and Carl over to her.

"Your presence is somewhat suspect, Brant," Josten replied, his voice deeper and holding much more grit than she'd expected. "Especially since you've brought Tal'Vayr's bondmate and a trader with you."

Kayla scowled. Seriously? Was that her identity now? Why wasn't Alec referred to as *her* bondmate instead? "How about you just call me Kayla?"

Josten glanced over at her but didn't seem overly interested in her request. He turned back to Brant. "Why are you here?"

"To try to reason with you," Brant began and gestured to the room. "This situation does not further our cause. What are you thinking taking the councilors as hostages? What do you hope to accomplish?"

One of the men who had moved the barricade back into

place took a threatening step toward them. He was at least a head shorter than Josten, with a small scar at the corner of his lip. It made his lip turn slightly downward, giving him the appearance of a permanent scowl. "We won't be treated as second-class citizens any longer. The High Council needs to know what's it like to be pushed around and deprived of everything."

Brant regarded the other man. "Are you even listening to yourself, Rob? You think the High Council will suddenly see our side of things if you terrorize them?"

"It's better than letting them push us around like chess pieces," he retorted, the vein at his temple throbbing.

Kayla studied the Shadows in front of her and the others within the room, trying to decide on the best approach. Josten appeared more even-tempered, while Rob was a loose cannon. The other guy standing near them hadn't said anything yet, leaving her to believe he was more of a follower than a decision maker. Some others were listening to their conversation, while the remainder focused on the council members they guarded.

She needed to stall until the transponder activated. "I get it."

Rob sneered at her. "You don't get anything, but you will. You're just like all the rest of them."

Kayla blew out a breath, resisting the urge to give in to her impulses. It was tempting to slam her fist into the asshole's nose, but it wouldn't help anything. She needed to appeal to Josten and maybe some of the others.

"Yeah, I do get it. I get it far more than almost anyone here in the towers." She lifted her head, silently daring Rob to challenge her words. "I know what it's like to live between two worlds and not fit into either one of them."

Josten didn't reply, but he didn't dispute her words either. She took that as encouragement and squared her shoulders, determined to make her point. "I grew up on the surface and spent my whole life believing I was a ruin rat. Shit didn't change for me just because Alec found me one day and brought me to the towers. I didn't grow up learning their ways or even knowing I had weird woo-woo abilities. I don't fit in here. I probably won't ever fit in, but I've changed too much to ever go back to my old way of life. So here I am, stuck between two worlds but not fitting neatly in either one."

Rob scoffed. "Are we supposed to feel sorry for you?"

Kayla wrinkled her nose. "For fuck's sake, no. I wasn't asking for your pity. I don't feel pity for you either. It's a useless emotion. I'm just telling you I understand where you're coming from."

Josten watched her thoughtfully. "What's your point then?"

Good. She had his attention. Now she just needed to keep it. The transponder should have activated by now. "My point, Josten, is that we're not so different. In fact, I'd argue that we have more similarities than you probably realize."

Josten's eyes narrowed. "I find that hard to believe."

Kayla gestured at Brant. "When I left the towers, I asked Brant to come with me. I needed him. I respect the hell out of him and trust him implicitly. There are only a handful of people in this world I can say that about."

Brant glanced over at her, his eyes widening in surprise. Rob didn't seem to be buying what she was selling, but Josten was still listening. A few of the other Shadows were also paying them a great deal of attention.

"Even though he's a Shadow? Even though he suppresses your abilities?"

Kayla nodded. "*Because* he's a Shadow and can suppress my abilities. I don't know what the hell I'm doing most of the time, and Brant has looked out for me. Trust me, none of us want to see if I can collapse the towers simply because I got a little overzealous with the energy shit. I know Brant won't let that happen. I trust him."

Brant straightened. "You should listen to Kayla. She's treated me the same as everyone else, no better and no less. She's a pain in the ass, but for entirely different reasons than we're used to. There's no pretense. Even when she was told about my relationship with the Tal'Vayr line, it didn't change anything in her eyes."

A fourth man had wandered over while they spoke. "You openly acknowledged your ties in front of her?"

When Brant nodded, Kayla harrumphed. "I think this whole bloodline thing is bullshit. Who cares? We all share common origins. At least one of our parents could do the woo-woo finger wiggle. Big fucking deal."

Another Shadow shook his head in disbelief. "We're not the same. The Inner Circle won't accept us."

Rob pointed his weapon in her direction. "This is some sort of trick. She was probably sent here to say whatever they think we want to hear. They'll do anything to have us release the High Council. We should just end her now."

Carl jumped in front of her, holding up his hands and trying to draw the weapon toward him. "Kayla was not sent here by anyone. In fact, she came here against orders. She wanted the chance to talk to you."

Kayla put her hand on Carl's back and nudged him, trying to get him to move. He refused to budge. The infuriating man was determined to put himself in harm's way to try to protect her. She poked her head around him, but he moved in front of her again, blocking her from sight. He continued speaking as though she weren't there.

"All of you know her history. Kayla stands up for people who need a voice. She's stood up for the ruin rats and demanded they have a tower built for them. She's stood up for the Inner Circle against the tyranny of Edwin Tal'Vayr. She's stood up for the people of the towers and agreed to an engagement with Alec to promote stability. And now she's willing to stand up for you. If you kill her, you'll be destroying one of the staunchest supporters you could ever have."

Brant nodded, also stepping in front of her. Now both men were acting like a blockade. "Carl speaks the truth. Kayla asked me to bring her here because she believed you might be willing to listen. We all want this situation to end peaceably."

"Rob, holster your weapon," Josten ordered.

Only when the volatile Shadow had lowered his weapon did Carl step aside. Kayla sighed, recognizing the need to tread carefully. Emotions were running way too high. There had to be a way to keep stalling without getting in the line of fire. "You have no reason to trust me, but I might be able to prove to you why I believe the way I do."

"Explain," Josten demanded.

"I don't know how or when this whole segregation thing started, but you're just as much a part of the Inner Circle as me. No, you can't manipulate energy on your own, but you can negate it. Haven't you ever wondered why you have that ability?"

"Lies!" a woman shouted. "The Shadows are abominations. They are *nothing* like Inner Circle members."

Kayla's head whipped around to find a furious blonde being held in place by an armed guard. Her makeup was smeared, her hair disheveled, and the arm of her fancy robe was torn. The naked hatred in her expression left no doubt this woman wanted to see each of the Shadows terminated.

Kayla blinked, trying to remember whether she'd met this woman before. "Really? I seem to recall another Inner Circle member holding all of you hostage once before. What's the difference this time, except you don't have a snazzy bracelet to go with your outfit?"

The woman huffed, jerking away from the Shadow holding her as though his touch burned her. She gathered her robes around her, pulling herself ramrod straight.

"I'm Lenora Ballentor, member of the High Council. You're a foolish girl for walking in here and spreading these lies. The Shadows are nothing like us. If you knew anything about your heritage, you'd know this." She turned toward Josten and the other Shadows. "If you don't release us immediately, I promise you'll pay for this transgression. I'll see each of you exiled from the towers. You can*not* continue to hold us."

Kayla crossed her arms, staring hard at the woman. "You're sitting here spewing threats at a bunch of people holding weapons on you? I'd say you're the stupid one, lady."

The woman's face turned an angry, mottled red. "How dare you speak to me that way. I've been on this council for more years than you've been alive. Your father would be shocked to hear about your behavior."

"Lenora, shut up," another man barked. "You're making things worse. Let Kayla speak. I want to know where she's going with this."

Kayla frowned at the silver-haired man sitting on the floor and leaning against the wall. He looked somewhat familiar, but she didn't remember meeting him. "Have we met?"

"Devan Alivette, dear," he replied. "We haven't been formally introduced."

"Alivette?" Kayla frowned, trying to remember where she knew that name. She snapped her fingers. "Aha. You're Ariana and Jason's father. Nice to meet you. Well, sort of. Bad situation, but you know what I mean."

He gave her a tired smile and gestured for her to continue speaking with their captors. She turned back to

Josten and the other Shadows. They were growing impatient.

Time to step things up a notch.

"When Alec was teaching me, he showed me there were four basic elements aligned with our abilities. Each element had a contrasting element, a counterbalance."

Rob crossed his arms over his chest. "You don't think we know all this already?"

She nodded. "Yeah, but that's not exactly true. He realized I'm a Spirit channeler, with the ability to channel all four elements."

An eerie stillness fell over the room with her announcement. Alec probably wouldn't be happy with her sharing this information, but it couldn't be helped. She needed to stall, and there were limited options.

"Impossible!" one of the council members shook their head.

Kayla shrugged. "Impossible or not, it's true. Alec thought my ability to channel all four elements meant my energy could shift to strengthen my partner's counter energy. While that's true, it has more implications than any of us realized, especially when it comes to Shadows."

Josten took a step forward, his attention solely focused on her. "How so?"

"You all negate energy, while I can channel all of it. I'd say there are two other elements that weren't included in these lessons: Spirit and Shadow. To put it simply, I can channel my energy into a Shadow, turning them into an Inner Circle member."

A few of the council members gasped.

Brant nodded. "We tested it, and it's true. The energy doesn't last, but Kayla was able to share her energy with me. Using basic energy theory, I was able to use her energy just like any Inner Circle member."

"Show me," Josten demanded.

Kayla nodded, not surprised by the request. She'd demand a demonstration too. It was tempting to throw one of the Shadows off their game by channeling energy into them, but there were too many of them. "I can do that, but you won't have your abilities until you expel my energy."

Brant cleared his throat. "Kayla, why don't you link with me? We can move to the center of the room since there's no furniture. If we're away from the other council members along the wall, they'll be better able to sense my change of energy."

Her eyes flew to meet Brant's gaze. With a nod, she let him know she understood he was trying to communicate the layout of the room to the transponder. "Sure."

Josten frowned, suspicion etched on his face. He strode over to Carl, pressing his weapon against his neck. "Go ahead, but remember, if this is some sort of trick, the trader will be the first to die."

Kayla swallowed, her mouth going dry and a hard lump forming in the pit of her stomach. "There's no trick and no reason to hurt Carl. I'm simply going to show you how similar we are."

Carl gave her a nod of encouragement, and it took everything she had to walk away from him. As though sensing her reluctance, Brant took her arm and led her to the center of the room.

"Relax," Brant whispered and held out his hand. "Just channel a small amount of energy into me. They just want to see the change in energy fluctuations."

Kayla nodded, acknowledging the instructions, and took his hand. They didn't need to know how much energy she could channel. She reached for the energy threads within the room, but they were still oily and slick, proving difficult to grasp. It might be possible for her to force her way through the Shadow barrier, but they didn't need to know that. If Alec didn't come through in time, it might be helpful to keep this information in reserve.

Pretending to be affronted, she scowled and jerked her head up to meet Josten's watchful gaze. "Mind dropping the shadow energy? I'm still learning my way around all this energy stuff."

Josten inclined his head, and the shadow energy retreated from the area around her. Kayla took a deep breath for the first time since she'd entered the room. Until now, she hadn't fully realized the effect of having her abilities suppressed. It was a little like have one of your senses suddenly severed—you didn't really notice it until it was gone. When it returned, the world became more vivid and full of color.

Brant cleared his throat, pulling her attention back to the situation. It might be interesting to explore the phenomenon later, but first she had a demonstration to perform. Kayla reached for the nearest energy threads, weaving them together, and channeled some energy into Brant.

There was a collective gasp from the people in the room. She cut off the energy transference, but even she could detect the difference in Brant. The energy threads that had once avoided him were now moving around and through him. If she hadn't known who he was, she'd never have known him as anything other than a traditional energy channeler.

Keeping his movements slow and deliberate, Brant lifted his hand and used air energy to slowly move a chair across the room.

"I have access to all the different elements, but the quantity is limited. Once the energy is spent, I revert to the Shadows. Through contact, Kayla can maintain a connection and share her energy with me."

Josten stepped forward, his hand brushing through the

energy stream and negating it. It didn't recognize him. At least, not yet. He frowned. "She can do this with any of us?"

Kayla nodded. "I believe so. I've only tried it with Brant, but I don't see why it wouldn't work with all of you."

"How could Alec have allowed you to sully yourself by creating a connection with them?" Lenora demanded, shock and horror on her face.

"Enough, woman!" Josten spun around and targeted her with his weapon. "One more word and I will end you. You have no power here, not anymore."

Kayla frowned, looking back and forth between Lenora and Josten. At least the weapon was no longer aimed at Carl, but this situation wasn't much better. Kayla was the one usually riling people up. Her skills weren't as sharp when it came to defusing tense situations. There had to be a way to distract them.

"I can try it with you, Josten," she offered.

Josten's head whipped back to her. A mixture of hope, apprehension, and then suspicion flew over his face in rapid succession. She held both hands outward, trying to show him she meant no harm.

"It's up to you. We can try it and see if it works. If you think I'm going to try anything, you can kill me."

"Kayla!" Carl barked, the word a sharp criticism to her suggestion.

She glanced at him and shook her head, begging him with her eyes to trust her. Josten wouldn't risk killing her, not if there was a chance she could change their future. She may not have grown up with the Shadows, but she recognized desperate hope from her time with the ruin rats. It was all the same, whether here or on the surface.

Before Josten could respond, one of the other Shadows stepped forward and offered him a commlink unit. "We've got a problem, Jos. There was an explosion in the security offices. Henri and Nick aren't responding anymore."

Josten grabbed the commlink and studied the screen for a long moment. He tossed it back to its owner and pointed his weapon at Kayla. "Why did Alec allow you to come here? What's his plan?"

Fuck. Things just went from bad to worse.

Sending a silent plea to Alec to hurry the hell up, she focused on the irate Shadow in front of her. Keeping her voice even, she replied, "The original plan was for Seara to talk to you. I didn't agree with that, so I grabbed Brant and came here. Carl saw us leave and followed."

Josten narrowed his eyes at her. "You expect me to believe Alec Tal'Vayr allowed his bondmate and the only known spirit channeler to walk in here unarmed?"

Kayla crossed her arms and lifted her head in defiance. "I didn't wait around to ask his permission."

"Kayla's telling the truth," Brant insisted. "She was worried about her mother putting herself in danger. The plan was for Alec to target the security offices while Seara negotiated with you."

"Then why hasn't Seara come to try to rescue her daughter?"

Shit. Good question. Kayla squeezed her eyes shut and tried to think of a believable reason.

"She probably wanted to," Carl suggested. "More than likely, Alec convinced her that a rescue could jeopardize Kayla's safety. They probably decided to take back the security offices so they could find out what's going on in here. They won't risk putting Kayla or the High Council in danger until they know what's going on."

Carl's explanation seemed feasible because many of the Shadows relaxed a fraction. Kayla took a steadying breath.

Marcus Staghorn, one of the council members, spoke up.

"As we told you before, we're willing to negotiate with you for our release. If you tell us what you want, we're in a position to listen to your complaints and discuss a resolution."

Rob scowled at the man. "Why should we believe you'll honor anything you say right now? You'd swear to just about anything. Your word doesn't mean anything. Not anymore."

Kayla was really starting to wish she'd punched Rob when she had the chance. "I know you guys want things to change. The High Council can make that happen. This situation isn't really that bad. You have options. You haven't hurt anyone."

Lenora sniffed. "You can't reason with animals."

Kayla lost her patience and glared at the woman. "Shut the hell up, lady. Be thankful you're still breathing. The Shadows have shown remarkable restraint. If it were me, I'd have already shot you."

Lenora's eyes widened, and her mouth gaped. "You can't speak to me like that. How dare you!" She gestured to Josten. "You're no better than that... that abomination. Only someone who has corrupted their energy threads could link with one of them."

Josten's jaw clenched in anger.

Brant held up his hand to get the Shadow's attention. "She's baiting you, Josten. You know she's always hated you. Just ignore her. Not all the council members have the same prejudices. Marcus Staghorn has been honorable in his dealings with us. If he's willing to negotiate, you should consider it."

In a low voice, Kayla asked Brant, "Why does she hate Josten?"

"Josten's father is Lenora's husband."

"Oh," Kayla murmured. "I can't say I blame him for preferring another woman's company. She's kind of a bitch."

Brant made a small noise of agreement.

Josten glanced at them but didn't make any other indication he'd overheard their exchange. Instead, he turned to the Shadow who had given him the commlink and spoke quietly to him.

Kayla took the opportunity to study each of the Shadows. They didn't seem to have much of a focused agenda, but maybe she could help them along. "Do you think Josten's father could reason with him? Or any of the Shadows' parents? Maybe we can still salvage this."

"It's not likely," Brant replied. "There's too much of a divide between us. I don't know if a peaceful resolution is possible."

Someone pounded on the entrance door, and a booming voice called from the opposite side. "This is Trenon Noltreck. I'm here with Seara Rath'Varein. We'd like to speak with you."

Astonishment filled most of the faces in the room. Many of the council members looked at each other, unsure what this development meant. The Shadows didn't look pleased at the news either.

"Trenon Noltreck? Isn't he one of the exiles?" one of the Shadows asked.

Josten frowned. "Yes. He's supposedly working with the Coalition."

"Not anymore," Rob observed. "The bastards must have double-crossed us."

"You're right," Josten agreed, stepping forward and grabbing Kayla's arm. The sudden move surprised her, and she didn't have a chance to react. Josten spun her around, yanking her against him in a chokehold.

Carl reached out to make a grab for her, but Rob shoved him against the wall. He pressed his weapon against Carl's chest. "Move and you die."

Kayla grabbed the arm around her neck, preparing to blast Josten with energy. A slight shake of Brant's head made her pause. Brant took a small step forward, holding up both hands to show he had no ill intent.

"You don't need to hurt them. Kayla and Carl are innocent in all of this."

Josten's arm tightened around Kayla's neck. "No lies, Brant. Did Trenon Noltreck make a deal with OmniLab?"

Someone pounded on the door again. Seara's muffled voice called out, "This is Seara Rath'Varein. Is everyone okay inside?"

Kayla made a small noise and tugged at Josten's arm. If he kept applying this amount of pressure, she'd lose consciousness. He relaxed his arm a fraction but didn't release her. At least she could breathe again.

"Trenon wants back in the towers," she managed on a gasp.

Josten looked down at her, loosening his hold on her a little more. "He made a deal?"

She nodded, or rather, tried to nod. "Yeah. Amnesty in exchange for fighting the Coalition."

Rob glanced back at them but didn't lower his weapon from where he held it against Carl. "Something isn't right. The Coalition had all the key areas locked down. They wouldn't have allowed Trenon into the antechamber if he switched sides. It would have been a fucking bloodbath out there, but we haven't heard a word from our contacts."

Before Josten could respond, a loud explosion rocked the room. Debris and plaster fell from the ceiling in a large dust cloud. Metal canisters made a distinct *clang* as they hit the floor. Shouts filled the air and smoke filled the room, obscuring Kayla's vision.

"Now, Kayla!" Brant yelled.

Kayla pressed her hands tightly against Josten's arm, forcing energy into him. He jerked away, releasing her, and she dropped to the floor. The air was a little clearer closer to the ground, and she caught a glimpse of Carl and Brant wrestling with Rob and another Shadow. A hand grabbed her ankle. She rolled, using her other leg to swipe at her would-be captor. There was a grunt, and the hand fell away.

She scrambled across the floor, determined to get to Brant and Carl. The shadow energy in the room was lessening, and the air became electrified as the council members began tapping into their energy. A crash and a scream sounded from somewhere behind her, but Kayla didn't look back.

An arm wrapped around her midsection, pulling her upright. She jabbed her elbow into the person, twisting her body to escape their grip. They swore, dropping her on her butt.

Kayla yelped at the jolt that radiated from her tailbone all the way up her spine. She started to push off the ground, ready to launch an attack on the figure standing over her. The distorted face within the helmet was more than a little familiar. Pausing, she leaned forward and squinted to see through the smoke. "Mack? Is that you?"

"Glad to see you remember some of those moves, darlin'," he shouted over the commotion and offered her his hand.

Relief flooded through her. She took his hand and stood, trying to look around the smoky room. There were a lot more people now, all of them fighting—some with weapons, some with energy. With the limited visibility, it was nearly impossible to identify anyone. She glanced up at Mack, noting the heads-up display embedded in his borrowed OmniLab helmet. At least he had a way to identify who was on their side. She leaned close to him and shouted, "Go back. I need to find Carl."

"Felix wanted us to get you out of here," he yelled, gesturing toward the thickest part of the smoke where they'd made their entrance.

Kayla dodged as a piece of furniture flew over her head. The Inner Circle members who had been released from the shadow energy were fighting back with a vengeance. With the limited visibility, it would be almost impossible for the council members to tell who was on their side. They were as likely to attack the ruin rats as they were to attack the Shadows.

Mack scanned the room and pointed to their left. "Your trader's over there. I'll grab him while you head out."

"No!" she shouted, grabbing his arm.

The ruin rats were great at distractions, minor skirmishes, and misdirection. But they didn't have the extensive training of the elite Shadow security officers or the energy-wielding capabilities of the High Council. Even she had more fire-power at her disposal than her former campmates. She'd asked for their help, but that was when they were up against the Coalition. She'd never intended for them to face these odds. Leo's injuries were proof enough they were out of their element. She needed to put a stop to this. Now.

"This isn't your fight, Mack. Get our people out of here."

Mack hesitated, but he finally nodded and turned away. Kayla hunched down and moved forward, trying to stay close to the ground where visibility was a little better. She'd only taken a handful of steps when someone flew into her, knocking her off her feet, and collapsed on top of her. The force of the blow stole her breath.

Kayla shoved at the unconscious man, trying to ignore the building panic of not being able to breathe. He was too heavy to move. She pushed, trying to roll away, but he had her pinned. Unable to get a breath, she couldn't even call out. Desperate now, she ignored the oily grip of the shadow energy still encompassing the room and threw her energy outward, reaching for Alec. But... there was nothing. Alec wasn't there. The bond they'd shared and relied upon was gone, dissolved by her own hand.

Her vision started to dim, the sounds of battle sounding further away. If she lost consciousness, she'd die. In a last-ditch effort, she reached into the deepest part of her and tried to channel as much energy as possible. If she couldn't move the man off of her, Brant would sense her energy. Even if no one else did, he would pick up on her energy signature. He had to.

There was no answer, and the battle continued without her. As the world grew dark, her last thought was of Carl. He'd given her a glimpse of a world with love, hope, and possibilities. Kayla had wanted that with him more than anything.

Ruin rats weren't supposed to feel regret, but that was a lie too.

CHAPTER SEVENTEEN

KAYLA BLINKED OPEN HER EYES, trying to focus on the face staring down at her. Carl's worried eyes met hers. She looked him over, wondering if he was real or her imagination. A small cut at the corner of his mouth drew her attention. It was bleeding. He must be real; otherwise, she'd never imagine him hurt.

She started to sit up, but agony ripped through her. It felt like a speeder had parked on top of her chest. She managed a cough, but it only made the pain worse. At least she could breathe though. Sort of. But yeah, this was definitely reality, and it was a bitch.

"The fucker fell on me."

Carl's expression changed to one of stark relief. "Sweetheart, I thought I was too late..." He shook his head and managed a weak smile. "Try not to move yet. The medics are on their way here. We don't know how badly you're injured."

"You're hurt," she whispered, reaching toward his cut.

He shook his head. Capturing her hand in his, he pressed a kiss against it. "No. It's just a few scrapes. Don't worry about me."

She frowned, catching sight of Brant out of the corner of her eye. Several of the Shadows were standing around her with their hands raised. The heavy coat of shadow energy blanketed her, adding weight to the heaviness already on her chest. Some of the council members and ruin rats were standing just beyond them.

"Can you..." she stopped to cough again, the pain sharp and stabbing in her chest, "...make them stop. It's hard enough to breathe."

"Yes," Alec said, glancing over at Brant and the rest of the Shadows. He gave them a nod, and they lowered their hands. The lingering shadow energy slowly receded from the room. It still hurt, but breathing was a bit easier. Alec knelt beside her, taking the hand Carl wasn't holding. "Is that better?"

She managed a nod. "Where's Seara? Is she okay?"

Her mother's voice sounded from somewhere behind Alec. A moment later, Seara was also beside her, gently brushing away the hair from Kayla's face. Her mother's eyes were filled with tears, but a relieved smile was on her face. "I'm right here. I'm not going anywhere."

Kayla relaxed a fraction at seeing her mother unharmed. "What happened?"

"You almost brought down the towers. Your earth energy seems to flare up when you're threatened," Alec explained.

Dammit.

She'd done it again. Kayla tried to sit up to assess the damage, but pain lanced through her again, followed by a swift wave of nausea.

Carl shook his head, gently pressing her back to the floor. "Please, sweetheart, try to remain still."

Kayla squeezed her eyes shut, willing the room to stop spinning. The thought of trying to move again wasn't something she was willing to tackle at the moment. She never thought she'd be anxious to see those stupid medics so soon. "Shit. I was trying to get Brant's attention. How bad is the damage?"

"We don't know yet," Alec admitted. "Fortunately, most of the residents had already been on lockdown in their quarters. This tower was built to withstand energy attacks, so we're hoping the damage is minimal. We're checking on the residents now and having our engineers run some assessments."

She opened her eyes once more, feeling uncomfortable at all the people hovering over her. "The Shadows stopped me, didn't they?"

"Yes," Alec said, glancing over at Brant and the rest of the Shadows. "You managed to somehow break through the shadow energy and send out more power than most of us have seen. They all had to step in to stop you."

Kayla frowned. That shouldn't have happened. She'd sent out a lot of energy, but it wasn't any more than what she'd done before. "It's getting stronger, isn't it?"

Alec nodded, squeezing her hand in reassurance. "Yes, but we think it's because your energy reacts differently around shadow energy. That's why you were able to break through their normal barrier."

Seara gave her a small smile. "We heard what you said to the Shadows. Your energy is connected to theirs. You've never been in close proximity to so much shadow energy. We believe it somehow magnified your abilities."

Kayla looked back and forth between Seara and Alec, a hundred questions forming in her mind. "What do you mean? Isn't their energy supposed to suppress mine?"

"It is," Alec agreed. "You've never conformed to our normal rules though. It took the combined strength of the Shadows to stop your energy. Without their help, all of this could have ended badly."

"No kidding," she muttered, not wanting to think about what could have happened. Although training wasn't her idea of fun, it looked like she needed to make it a priority. There was no way she could risk anything like this happening again. "So I guess just having Brant follow me around isn't going to be enough?"

Alec lifted his gaze again, looking over the Shadows still within the room. "No, I don't believe so. I suspect this is why Spirit channelers are so rare."

"What do you mean?" Carl asked, still holding her hand.

"Our numbers have always been fairly evenly distributed between the different elements," Alec explained. "Counterbalances are extremely important to us, and this is no exception. The Shadows greatly outnumber Kayla, but I think that's by design. If we had more Spirit channelers, the result could be disastrous."

Brant nodded, taking a step forward. "I agree. One Shadow could easily subdue several energy channelers, but Kayla blasted through their shield without much effort. I never dreamed she could break through like that."

Seara looked up at the Shadows with gratitude. "All of this has made it clear that we need you, and you're an important part of the towers. You should not be treated as second-class citizens or any differently from the other Inner Circle members. It's been proven today that you're one of us, no better and no worse."

Seara stood, her gaze sweeping each of them. "I want to apologize to all of you. On behalf of myself and the rest of the Inner Circle, we were wrong. As you've reminded us today, your gifts are a blessing and should be treated as such. It is you who have kept us in check, preventing our own destruction and keeping us safe from harm."

Seara paused to gaze down at Kayla. Her mother's eyes

were filled with a love so pure and staggering that, for a moment, Kayla wasn't sure if it was the pain in her chest making it difficult to breathe. This was what Veridian had wanted her to have, she realized. This was her second chance. This was a second chance for all of them. Her family wasn't confined to the boundaries of the surface. It extended beyond the ruin rats, to Carl's camp, and into the towers where she was born.

Seara smiled at her and turned back to the Shadows. "My daughter was correct. You are part of us as much as we're part of you. I hope you can one day forgive us for all of our past mistakes."

Josten took a step forward. A bruise darkened the side of his face, and his uniform had been torn sometime during the fighting. "Will the Inner Circle acknowledge our familial ties?"

Seara clasped her hands together, her gaze lowering as though trying to find the right words. When she raised her head again, her eyes were filled with regret. "I wish I had the power to give you what you want. I may not be able to repair the rifts between you and your families, but I can make sure you're given the same rights as every other Inner Circle member. The rest, hopefully, will heal in its own time."

Josten nodded, accepting the truth in her words. "What punishment will be given for our crimes here?"

Alec released Kayla's hand and stood. She tried to sit up to stop him, but pain shot through her. Crying out, she reached for him with a small energy thread, brushing against him and trying to draw his attention.

"Dammit, Alec, don't punish them. Haven't they already been punished enough?"

Alec knelt back down beside her, taking her hand once again and accepting the energy. *"You're the most stubborn woman*

I've ever met. If you'll remain still until the medics get here, you can have a say in their punishment."

Despite her pain, she couldn't help but smile. It wasn't their permanent bond, but the small contact was still reassuring. It felt right. No matter what happened in the future, Alec was a part of her life and always would be. This time, though, they both could dictate the terms of their friendship.

"Deal," she agreed. *"I want the Shadows to help build the tower for the Coalition and the ruin rats. Working with Leo will be more than enough punishment. Just watch."*

"Very well." Alec let out an exasperated sigh. He lifted his head to address the Shadows once more and said, "In recompense for your crimes here today, you'll be assigned as laborers to assist in the construction of the new tower. Once the construction is complete, you can take your place as Inner Circle members."

Lenora pushed her way forward. "This is outrageous! I *refuse* to acknowledge them as Inner Circle members. They attacked us, imprisoned us, and have proven to be untrustworthy."

"This is not your decision, Lenora," Seara declared, staring down the woman with a cold glare. "Alec and I are in agreement on this matter. OmniLab, from this day forward, recognizes shadow energy as one of the powers of the Drac'Kin. All rights, benefits, and titles shall be bestowed upon them as members of the Inner Circle."

"Witnessed," a voice called out from behind the Shadows. Another voice echoed the same sentiment.

Marcus Staghorn moved to stand beside Lenora. "Put aside your personal issues, Lenora. With the way we've treated them, I'm surprised they didn't rebel before now. When push came to shove, they saved us. We'd be buried under a pile of rubble if they hadn't stepped in when they did."

"I will *never* acknowledge them as one of us," she hissed.

"You will," Seara said, her tone firm and unyielding. "If you refuse to enforce the will of the High Council, you will be confined to your quarters. We will not allow you to jeopardize the stability of the towers based on a personal slight."

Lenora jerked back as though slapped. She glared at Seara but didn't offer any more objections.

The sounds of voices and hurried footsteps interrupted the conversation. Carl brought Kayla's hand up and kissed her knuckles. "It's Sergei. He agreed to escort the medics here."

She caught a glimpse of the tall, blond foreigner entering the room, followed by several others. Sergei grinned at her and winked.

"Ah, good," he said in lieu of a greeting. "You managed to live. I had some concerns."

Kayla wrinkled her nose at Sergei. "I seem to get hurt whenever you show up. Maybe one of these days we can stop meeting like this."

Sergei threw his head back and laughed. "I can have my men bring up another bottle of vodka, if you like. We never did finish getting to know one another."

Carl glowered at him. "I don't think so. Where's the medic?"

Ariana stepped out from behind Sergei and knelt beside Kayla. "If she'll allow it, I can heal her. The other medics can treat some of the others."

Alec started to move out of the way, but Ariana stopped him. "No, stay. Your bond strengthens her."

Alec hesitated and then shook his head. "There is no bond, Ari. It's been dissolved."

Ariana froze, looking at Alec with something akin to shock. She opened her mouth to ask, but then lowered her gaze to focus on Kayla. "May I touch you? I'll try to be gentle."

"Yeah," Kayla agreed, more than a little curious after watching her heal Leo. Ariana placed her hands gently on Kayla's head, and a gentle warmth emitted from her palms. Although Kayla wasn't exactly sure what Ariana was doing, she was definitely using energy. Different types of energy threads were being woven together in complex patterns, their frequencies aligning to resonate with hers. Ariana moved downward, pausing now and then to focus on a certain area. It tingled, but the sensation wasn't unpleasant.

Kayla glanced over at Alec to find him watching Ariana. That same look of regret and longing was in his eyes again. Through the small connection she'd forged with Alec, she could pick up some traces of his emotion. There was a definite attraction there but also sadness. Something had happened between them, but she wasn't sure what. She glanced over at Carl, a question in her eyes. He gave her a nod, indicating he'd noticed something between Ariana and Alec too.

Interesting.

As though sensing Kayla's gaze and her perusal along their connection, Alec turned back to her. The connection between them fell silent, as though he were suppressing his emotions. His features once again became schooled into an unreadable mask. "How are you feeling?"

"Much better," Kayla admitted, sitting up once Ariana finished. She was able to take a deep breath without any pain. "You're an incredible healer."

Ariana sat back on her heels and smiled, the expression making her radiant. "Thank you for helping rescue my father."

Kayla glanced over to where Ariana's father was standing. The older man was talking to another council member. "I'm glad he's okay."

Carl reached down to help her to stand and then pulled her into his arms. Kayla went willingly, the strength of his body surrounding hers in a protective cocoon. She rested her head against his chest, inhaling his familiar scent and listening to the steady beat of his heart.

Alec stood and helped Ariana up, but he didn't release her hand right away. They stared at each other for several heartbeats and then someone called out for Alec. He released her hand quickly, as though recalling himself, and turned away to speak with one of the council members. Jason came over a second later and ushered Ariana over to their father.

Kayla glanced over at Brant, asking him with her eyes what was going on. The security officer gave her a knowing smile and nodded. Yep. He'd caught the exchange between Alec and Ariana too. There was definitely something between them. Kayla darted another glance at Alec and couldn't help but smile. She wondered if Ariana might have something to do with the choice Brant mentioned when they'd broken their bond.

Kayla rested her head against Carl's chest again, not willing to release him just yet. She loved him beyond all reason. Love should be a choice, she realized. Even when circumstances seemed to dictate your path in life, you always had a choice. It might be more difficult to take the more challenging path, but the most valuable things in life never came easily. That was part of the reason she'd always thrown herself into dangerous situations, chose the most hazardous ruins to scavenge, or tackled every obstacle with almost single-minded determination. If life and love were easy, it wouldn't be nearly as rewarding.

She lifted her head to look up at Carl. In him, she'd found her second chance. Maybe Ariana was Alec's second chance at something too. At least, she could hope.

Kayla reached up to touch Carl's face, and his eyes softened as he gazed down at her. She remembered what she'd told Brant when she cornered him outside the restaurant: Life isn't always forgiving enough to give you second chances. And if you're fortunate enough to get a second chance, you better learn your lesson quick because you can be damn sure there won't be a third.

She looked around the room, studying the faces surrounding them. There was an eclectic mix of ruin rats, trading camp people, and Inner Circle members. Medics moved from person to person, treating their injuries. It was strange to see some of the people she valued the most all within the same room. With what they'd accomplished today, they were all going to be okay.

"Kayla," Veridian's voice called out from behind her.

She whirled around toward the double doors. Veridian, Felix, Cruncher, Xantham, Jinx, and several others had entered the room. Her eyes filled with tears at the sight of them. Veridian ran over to her and enveloped her in a hug.

"You're okay," he whispered, his face pressed against her hair. "I heard the audio feed when they found you. I thought you were gone."

She shook her head, clutching him tightly. Now her family really was complete. "You should know better, V. I'm a ruin rat. We don't die that easily."

Veridian pulled back, frowning at her. "What the hell were you thinking pulling a stunt like that? First, you decide to steal an artifact. Then, you climb into bed with a trader. Then, you get kidnapped and stabbed. If that wasn't enough, you take on the Coalition and try to single-handedly rescue the towers. I swear, you're going to give me an ulcer. I probably have ulcers on top of my ulcers. Leo had no idea what he was signing me up for when he charged me with keeping you out of trouble."

He hugged her again, and in a voice choking with emotion, he said, "But I wouldn't change you for anything. You're my family, Kayla."

She tried to blink away the tears that threatened. "You've always been mine too, V."

"Quit hogging her," Felix joked, stepping forward to give her a hug. "See, this is what I've been missing. Life's always more exciting with you around, crazy girl."

Kayla laughed, wiping away the tears that had manage to escape. Dammit. This wasn't helping her carefully cultivated badass image. "I'm glad you're here, Felix. I really have missed you and all the trouble we used to get into. I'm sorry about everything that happened, with Pretz, bailing on you, all of it—"

Felix shook his head, pressing his fingers against her lips. "I get it. I made my brother a promise to look after you though. When I heard he'd been killed, I was worried you were in over your head." He lifted his head to look over at Carl. "You were, but you also had good people at your back. You were right; for a trader, he's not a bad guy. It takes someone with the balls of a ruin rat to storm the towers with you. I think Pretz would have liked him."

She looked up at him, hope and sorrow welling within her. "You really think that?"

"Yeah, I do," Felix said and hugged her again. In a low voice, he whispered, "But anytime you want to kick things up a notch and get into more trouble, I'll be here for you."

"Deal," she agreed with a laugh.

Carl pulled her back into his arms, eyeing Felix with trepidation. "Do I want to know what he whispered to you?"

She grinned. "Probably not."

He sighed and shook his head, muttering something about troublemaking ruin rats under his breath. Kayla laughed. He was so right.

She leaned against him again, a small smile on her face as she watched the occupants of the room. Rand was going to each of the trading camp members and ruin rats who had stormed the room, checking on each of them and introducing himself to the ones he didn't know. Yep. Both he and Carl shared a lot of similarities. If Rand's behavior was any indication of the future relationships between the trading camps and ruin rats, she had a lot of hope that this new tower would heal the rifts between their people.

Alec and Seara, on the other hand, were both busy talking with Sergei, the Shadows, the former exiles, and some council members. The merging of all these different groups and their goals warmed something within her. They were all getting second chances at a new beginning.

Brant was standing next to Alec listening intently, but he must have felt her gaze on him. He turned to her and winked before focusing again on his half-brother. Oh, yeah. The upright Shadow was definitely mellowing.

Carl turned her in his arms. Tilting her head back, he tucked her hair behind her ear. "You won, sweetheart. It's over."

Kayla smiled up at him, letting her love for this once hated trader reflect in her eyes. The greatest victory was having him here by her side. "No, it's not over. Not even close. It's a new beginning for all of us, and there isn't anyone I'd rather share it with than you."

His gaze softened. "You're right. It *is* a new beginning. But, I'm still going to hold you to an old promise."

Kayla blinked, trying to recall what she'd promised. So much had happened, the past few days seemed like a blur. "What promise?"

He grinned, pulling her even closer. "If I remember correctly, you said that when all this is done, we'd disappear together for a few weeks and go play in the ruins. I hope you know I'm going to hold you to that."

She laughed and threw her arms around his neck. The future was suddenly looking even brighter. "I did, didn't I? Well, Trader Carl Grayson, that's a promise I have every intention of keeping."

AFTERWORD

Thank you so much for reading Tremors of the Past!

If you want more of The Omni Towers series (and to find out what trouble Kayla and your other favorite characters have been getting into), keep reading for a sneak peek of Ariana Alivette's story in Drop of Hope.

If you enjoyed Tremors of the Past and want more books in The Omni Towers series, please consider posting a review on Goodreads and/or your preferred retailer's website. I use your reviews to determine which books to work on next.

I absolutely love hearing from my readers! You can visit me on Facebook or sign up to be notified about new releases by visiting www.jamieawaters.com.

Happy Reading!

SNEAK PEEK

Dangerous secrets can lurk under the water's surface...

THE OMNI TOWERS SERIES BOOK 4

Ariana Alivette has lived a life of perceived luxury in the elusive Omni Towers. While most of the remaining survivors around the world are struggling to survive, Ariana has been locked away to protect a dangerous secret. But, even the walls of a gilded cage can't last forever.

When Ariana makes the decision to reveal her secret to save a life, she suddenly finds herself targeted by those determined to use her for their own ambitions. Ariana must quickly learn the rules of this new world and do whatever is necessary to master her own fate, because one wrong decision means losing her life—and her heart.

DROP OF HOPE

Ariana ran toward the priority elevators and plugged in her earpiece. She could hear the child's screams in the background. "Paul, talk to me. How bad is her condition?"

"It's worse than we expected. We're trying to stabilize her now," Paul explained over her headset, the worry in his voice indicative of the precariousness of the situation. "The transport team is working on her, but we've got burns covering about thirty percent of her body. Are you in your quarters?"

"I just left. I can meet you in the training room."

"No. It'll take too long," Paul argued, pausing for a moment to issue some instructions to someone. "Can you head directly to the medical ward? We'll have to meet you there. I've sent instructions there to have a clean room ready."

Ariana swallowed, praying to whatever gods might be listening they wouldn't take an innocent life far too soon.

"I'll be there in a few minutes," she informed him and disconnected from the commlink call.

"Ari?"

Ariana glanced down the corridor to find Alec hastening

toward her, but she couldn't stop while a child's life was in jeopardy. Pressing a button on the priority elevator, she said, "I'm sorry, Alec. I can't talk right now. I have to hurry."

His blue eyes were marked with concern. "What is it? What's wrong?"

"It's Mira," Ariana managed, pressing the button again and willing the elevator to arrive faster. She needed a blasted override code for these situations. Realizing who stood beside her, she grabbed his arm. Alec wasn't just a friend, he was also one of the High Council leaders.

"Alec, I need you to override the elevators. Mira's being transported to the medical ward right now. She was in an accident in the training room, and there are burns covering most of her body. I need to meet the medical team right away."

Alec paled and quickly entered in his override code. "I'll go with you. She's the promising young fire channeler from the Gavron family, right?"

Ariana nodded as the elevator doors opened. While Alec entered his code again to bypass all other floors, she said, "Yes. She's only eleven. I'm not sure what happened or why there wasn't a water channeler monitoring the situation, but I could hear her screaming over my commlink."

Ariana squeezed her eyes shut at the rush of emotion that went through her. She'd met Mira only a handful of times and was reminded of a bright, pixie-like child with an insatiable curiosity and passion for life. The thought of not being able to prevent that precious light from extinguishing was more than she could bear.

The elevator shot downward and she gripped the handrail tightly, worry for the young girl nearly overwhelming her. Desperate for a distraction, she opened her eyes to find Alec's alluring blue eyes watching her. The depth of unspoken emotion and concern spoke volumes about how much he cared for a little girl he barely knew. It made her respect and admire him even more. He'd always cared so much, but rarely let anyone see his true feelings.

He had always fascinated her own curious nature and made her want to learn more about him. She'd had a hard time keeping her distance from the moment she'd met him. But everything had changed since then, and she needed to remember some things happened for a reason.

"I'm sorry for brushing you off," she murmured, casting her gaze downward and not wanting to reveal too much of her own feelings. "Did you need me for something?"

"Don't ever apologize for something like that, Ari," he said gently, reaching over to touch her hand. A gentle caress of comforting air energy washed over her, stirring her own energy to the surface. "You're trying to save a life. What I wanted to talk to you about can wait."

She bit her lip, lifting her gaze to stare at the descending numbers on the panel. It was moving rapidly, but not fast enough. "Please distract me, Alec. Otherwise I'm just going to worry about things I can't control. Once I'm in the medical ward, everything will change and I can focus on what needs to be done."

Alec searched her expression for a long moment, indecision clearly warring on his face. He rubbed the back of his neck and said, "I... I was hoping you might consider talking to Kayla again about training."

Ariana blinked up at him, surprised by the request. She had the feeling that wasn't what he intended to ask, but she wouldn't intrude by prying. Besides, her energy needed to be reserved for the little girl who desperately needed her help. "I thought Kayla *had* been training over the past few months. She hasn't?"

Alec hesitated. "Somewhat, but she's been distracted with the construction and river excavation. I know she respects you, especially after you healed her former camp leader. She's been working with me and her mother on her air and earth talents, but she needs to make training more of a priority. If you mention it to her again, I'm sure she'll listen to you."

The elevator doors opened, and they stepped out into the medical ward. It was too quiet on the floor and the surrounding energy threads were moderately stabilized, so Mira must not have arrived yet. Turning back to Alec, she nodded. "Of course, I'll be happy to speak with her."

"I'd appreciate it." Alec paused, studying her for a long moment. As his eyes roamed over her face, her stomach did a neat little somersault at the intensity in his gaze. He took a step toward her and said, "Ari, I know this isn't the best time, but I was wondering if you'd be willing to have dinn—"

Voices and commotion exploded from the far side of the corridor as the medical team emerged from the service elevator with a stretcher. Even over the din of noise, she could hear the soft whimpers of a child in pain.

"I'm sorry, Alec, I have to go," Ariana called over her shoulder, running down the hall and toward the little girl who desperately needed her. She only hoped her healing gifts would be enough this time.

ABOUT THE AUTHOR

Jamie A. Waters is an award-winning science fiction and paranormal romance author. Her first novel, Beneath the Fallen City (previously titled as The Two Towers), was a winner of the Readers' Favorite Award in Science-Fiction Romance and the CIPA EVVY Award in Science-Fiction.

Jamie currently resides in Florida with her two neurotic dogs who enjoy stealing socks and chasing lizards. When she's not pursuing her passion of writing, she's usually trying to learn new and interesting random things (like how to pick locks or use the self-cleaning feature of the oven without setting off the fire alarm). In her downtime, she enjoys reading, playing computer games, painting, or acting as a referee between the dragons and fairies currently at war inside her closet.

You can learn more by visiting: www.jamieawaters.com